THE MEMORY KEEPER
OF KYIV

ERIN LITTEKEN

Boldwood

First published in Great Britain in 2022 by Boldwood Books Ltd.

1

Copyright © Erin Litteken, 2022

Cover Design by Head Design Ltd

Cover Photography: Shutterstock

A CIP catalogue record for this book is available from the British Library.

Paperback ISBN: 978-1-80426-959-6

Ebook ISBN: 978-1-80415-757-2

Kindle ISBN: 978-1-80415-758-9

Audio CD ISBN: 978-1-80415-765-7

Digital audio download ISBN: 978-1-80415-756-5

Large Print ISBN: 978-1-80415-760-2

Boldwood Books Ltd.

23 Bowerdean Street, London, SW6 3TN

www.boldwoodbooks.com

To the Ukrainian people. Your strength and resilience are an inspiration, then and now.

If only one man dies of hunger, that is a tragedy. If millions die, that's only statistics.

— JOSEPH STALIN

Dear Readers,

The seeds of this story took root in my mind even before Russia invaded Crimea in 2014, and now I sit drafting this letter while the news of Russia's brutal attack on Ukraine—its cities, its civilians, its future—plays on the television in the background. I never imagined the release of my novel on a past assault of the Ukrainian people would coincide with such a parallel tragedy.

Ukrainians today are fighting for their country with a strength and tenacity that has captivated the world, but it is impossible to deny that history is repeating itself. It's horrifying, and we must do better.

As the granddaughter of a Ukrainian refugee from WW2, the poignancy of this war devastates me. While we can't change history, we can all learn from it and do something to help the Ukrainian people today. I'm so pleased that my publisher, Boldwood Books, will be donating a portion of each sale to DEC's Ukraine Humanitarian Appeal.

My heart goes out to the brave Ukrainians defending their country, their culture, and their lives, both then and now. *Slava Ukrayini!*

Erin Litteken

1

CASSIE

Wisconsin, May 2004

Cassie's facial muscles twitched in rebellion, but she forced her mouth into a big, fake smile as her daughter entered the kitchen. She hoped if she smiled long enough, hard enough, Birdie would respond, but the little girl stared back, expressionless.

Cassie fought the urge to bang her head into the wall.

Birdie's wide blue eyes contrasted sharply with her dark, tangled hair. The pink princess pajamas she'd wanted so badly for her fourth birthday now rode halfway up her calves and forearms. They'd shrunk. Or she'd grown. Maybe both. Cassie didn't seem to be good at noticing these things lately.

Harvey plopped down at Birdie's feet, his tail thumping the floor as his shaggy brown fur warmed her bare ankles.

"The dog keeps a better eye on Birdie than I do." Cassie rubbed her hands over her face and resumed her typical routine of forcing out meaningless banter. She couldn't bear the quiet. It gave her too much time to remember.

"Good morning! Did you sleep well? What would you like for breakfast? I have overnight oats, eggs, or I can make some quinoa, fruit, and honey if you want."

Cassie was failing on many levels of parenting, but no one could say she didn't feed Birdie well. The pantry overflowed with organic snacks bought in bulk, and the fruit bowl on the counter always contained several different options. Cassie didn't care if she skipped dinner or ate saltines for breakfast, but she was determined to make sure Birdie received all of the nutrition she needed, even if her clothes didn't fit or she never spoke again.

Birdie pointed to the carton of eggs Cassie had taken out of the fridge and the frying pan on the drying rack in the sink. Cassie picked them both up and brought them to the stove while Birdie got out a spatula and the butter dish.

"One egg or two today?" Cassie asked. She did this all the time, trying to trick Birdie into answering without thinking. It never worked. Birdie hadn't talked in fourteen months, one week, and three days. No reason why today should be any different.

Birdie opened the carton, took an egg in each hand, and held them out to Cassie.

"All right. Two eggs it is. Why don't you make the toast?"

Birdie padded toward the toaster and popped a piece of sprouted grain bread into it.

Cassie glanced around the messy house as the two eggs spattered and snapped in the pan. Mail stacked in a pile so high it threatened to topple over, dog hair balls growing at an alarming rate in the corners on the floor, and a garbage can that seriously needed to be emptied didn't exactly paint a picture of a happy home. A year and a half ago, she would rather have been caught dead than live in a house this messy.

Her laptop peeked out from beneath a stack of newspapers. Cassie winced to see it so forlorn, but she hadn't been able to bring herself to write anything since that night. She threw a dishtowel over it so she wouldn't have to keep staring at another example of her failure, then slipped the eggs onto a pink plastic plate and placed them in front of Birdie at the table. As her little girl dug in, Cassie watched the dark yellow yolks run into the toast Birdie had made and sighed. Another day, just like yesterday and the day before. Never moving forward, never healing, never getting on with life. She had to fix it, for Birdie's sake, but she had no idea where to start.

The doorbell rang and Cassie froze. Even now, after all this time, the sound of the doorbell still terrified her. She pulled her ratty robe closed and tied it tight as she walked to the door. Her psychiatrist would say she was using the robe as a defense mechanism, attempting to block out whatever was at her door trying to get in. Cassie would say she didn't want company to see her tattered old pajamas. Maybe that's why she'd quit making appointments with that shrink.

She pulled open the door, and her mom, disheveled and wan, managed a half-smile before she hiccuped a sob back and barreled her way in to wrap her arms around Cassie.

"Oh, Cass. I had to come tell you in person; I didn't want you driving yourself after you heard."

Cassie stiffened and pulled away from her mother's arms. "Tell me what?"

"Nobody has died," she said. "It's nothing that bad."

"Mom, what are you talking about?"

"It's about Bobby."

"Bobby?" Cassie pictured her wrinkled ninety-two-year-old grand-mother, long ago christened Bobby when a young Cassie had butchered the Ukrainian word for grandma, *babusya*, and refused to use the traditional nickname, *baba*.

"There's been an accident."

Cassie's heart skipped a beat. Maybe two. She drew in a ragged breath and tried not to let panic overtake her, but the words were the same ones she'd heard last year, right before her world fell apart.

Cassie let her mother guide her into a chair at the table. Anna leaned over and kissed Birdie on the top of the head. "Hello, my darling."

Birdie smiled silently up at her grandmother while sopping the yolk off her plate with her toast.

"It happened Friday, but I didn't want to worry you until I knew more." Anna sat next to Birdie.

Cassie counted the days back in her head. "Mom, that was two days ago! Bobby's been hurt for two days and you couldn't call?"

"Like I said, I needed to speak to you in person. When I found out she wasn't in danger of dying, I decided it would be best for me to drive here and tell you. I couldn't leave her side until today."

"Tell me everything now," Cassie ordered, her voice quaking.

Anna glanced at Birdie and rested a hand on her shoulder. "Birdie, Grammy and Mommy are going to talk. Do you want to go watch TV?"

Birdie picked up her plate and put it in the sink, then walked past the piles of mail and newspapers toward the living room. When the sound of cartoon music filled the air, Cassie turned back toward her mom expectantly.

"Last week, she went for one of her walks." Anna said. "She went further than she normally does, and I don't know if she got turned around or what, but a car struck her as she crossed a busy street."

Cassie jolted upright. "She got hit by a car? Are you kidding me?"

Anna held up her hand. "She's fine. She had a mild concussion and a few stitches. No broken bones. It's amazing she walked away so unscathed."

"Where is she now? Is she home yet?"

"No, and that's why I'm here. She should be able to go home this afternoon, but she needs company. Just someone to be there and to help her with things."

Cassie nodded. "Do you want her to come here? Stay with me?"

Anna looked around the kitchen with a skeptical expression. "I don't think this would be the best place for her. Her doctors aren't nearby; she's not familiar with anything here. Look, what I'm thinking is that this is an opportunity for you to make a change. Leave this town, this house, these memories behind, and come back home."

Cassie laughed, and the bitterness that echoed through the room surprised even her. "You think I can just leave my memories behind? You think I can close the doors here and it will be like Henry never existed?"

"No, honey, of course that's not what I meant." Anna cradled Cassie's cheek. "You'll never forget him. I thought maybe it was time for a fresh start, in a new place, where the memories aren't so overwhelming. And since Bobby shouldn't be on her own, it seemed like the perfect opportunity for you to go stay with her for a while. Just lock this place up and walk away."

"Just walk away? From my life? My home?' Cassie shrugged off her mother's touch as the dull ache that always preceded a crying jag throbbed in her throat.

"Cassie, let's be real." Anna gripped Cassie's hand and stared her down. Apparently, the niceties were over. "I want you to tell me truthfully that you're happy here, right now. Tell me that you are making this a welcoming, safe home for Birdie. Tell me that you even have a life outside this mess!"

Cassie's mouth dropped open in surprise. Her mom usually kept this beast-mode side of her personality wrapped under a layer of not-so-subtle suggestions and passive-aggressive jabs. This attack was definitely not her typical mode of action.

"I'm at my wits' end with both of you, if you want to know the truth," she continued. "Bobby is stubborn. She's refusing to consider even looking at any type of assisted living homes. And you? Well, I spend so many sleepless hours worrying myself to death over how you are coping with everything down here. When a woman loses her husband, no matter what the circumstances, she needs to be around family to heal. I want to help you, but you never let me. Now, here is the perfect opportunity to get you and Bobby together to help each other, and I want to make it work."

"Basically, you want both of your problems tucked away together so you don't have to worry about them as much. That's why you really came here, isn't it?" Cassie stood up so fast her chair clattered to the floor behind her. She was being unfair to her mother, but she couldn't help it. Her emotions these days vacillated between apathy and anger and left no room for anything else. "I need to get some air, and Harvey needs a walk. I'm sure Birdie would love to spend some time with you while I'm gone."

She stomped over to the back door and, even though the spring weather was balmy, she put on the long winter coat that covered up the fact that she was still wearing her robe. She shoved her feet into boots, grabbed Harvey's leash, and slammed the back door behind her.

Harvey, oblivious to Cassie's anger, jumped and barked excitedly as she clipped his leash onto his collar and left the yard. She tried to clear her thoughts as he sniffed around the trees in front of the house.

Her mom wasn't wrong. Memories surrounded her here. Initially, after the accident, the house enveloped her—safe and comforting. But lately, a stifling, trapped feeling had overshadowed that comfort. After all, this wasn't her real home; they'd only lived here six months before the accident. Henry's company had transferred him to Madison, Wisconsin temporarily, and it was only supposed to be for a year, so they'd rented the first place they could find with a fenced yard for Harvey. The transfer came with a huge bonus, and after the year was up, they'd planned on moving back to Illinois and buying their own place.

They'd spent hours dreaming about that home. She wanted an old farmhouse on acreage with a barn and fruit trees. Henry wanted a cabin with a pole barn and woods. But the accident changed all that.

Luckily, the sympathetic landlord had let her extend the lease month–to–month after the original year–long contract expired.

She rounded the corner in front of her home and stared at the brick bungalow. Unimpressive, it sat too close to the street and lacked the charm of the other houses on the block. She didn't stay because she liked this house or felt closer to Henry here. She stayed because it was easier to maintain the status quo and keep going through the motions of a bare–bones existence. Wake up, eat, take care of Birdie, sleep, repeat.

Harvey pulled on the leash, excited to go back inside. Cassie saw Birdie peeking out through her bedroom window. She waved excitedly, then spun away; it was the most expression Cassie had seen out of her in months.

How much had she thought of Birdie as she struggled from day to day? How many of her decisions were based on what Birdie needed to thrive versus what she, Cassie, needed to survive? Cassie didn't like the answers to those questions, so she usually avoided asking them. Her mom had ruined that for her.

She trudged into the house; her mom still sat in the same place at the kitchen table. She turned to Cassie as she entered and raised her hands in the air. "I swear, honey, I didn't say a word to Birdie, but as soon as you walked out the door, she ran to her room."

Cassie unclipped Harvey and hung up her coat. "That's fine. She likes to play in there."

"She's not playing, Cass. She's packing. She must have overheard us talking."

"Did she..." Cassie trailed off, not wanting to ask the question.

Anna gave her a pitying look. "No, she didn't talk to me."

Of course she didn't. Birdie's silence was just one more shining example of Cassie's failure as a parent to help her cope with the accident and loss of her father. She sank into the chair across from Anna, defeated. "What's your plan?"

Anna grabbed both of Cassie's hands in hers. "I want to help you pack up and leave. Make a clean break of it, no time to think or change your mind. I'll help you with everything. I promise I wouldn't be doing this if I didn't think it was best for you. You know I've been on you to move back for months."

"Now you have the perfect excuse," Cassie finished for her.

"Now your Bobby needs you," Anna said. "And I think you need her, too. Why don't we pack up the basics? Your clothes, toiletries, and any food that would spoil. I'll come back with you when you're ready to get Henry's things."

"I've already done that," Cassie said. "Last month, Henry's mom came down and helped me go through his clothes."

"Oh, well, that's one thing done then." Anna's voice rose an octave.

The all too familiar guilt crept up on Cassie. "I'm sorry, Mom. I know you'd offered to help before. I wasn't ready then. But it got to a point where I couldn't breathe with all of that hanging over me. I had to get it out, and Dottie happened to be visiting when that moment came."

Anna's lips pressed together, and she wrapped Cassie in a hug. "Oh, my sweet girl."

Cassie hugged her mom back and melted into her, just like she had when she was a kid. Unexpected pinpricks of relief tickled her scalp, and she sighed. "Okay, Mom. I'll come home."

Anna pulled back and gave a tremulous smile. "This will be best for everyone. You'll see." She hesitated, then went on. "Honestly, I'm worried about Bobby. Even before the accident, she's been... different. You know how she is. Always moving, always working. But now, I'll catch her sitting at the table, staring off in a daze like she's in another place, talking to herself in Ukrainian."

"What's she saying?"

"I don't know," Anna replied. "Usually she won't talk to me when she's like that. It's like she's so deep in her memories that she's not aware of what's going on around her. The other day, I asked what she was thinking about, and when she finally responded, all she said was 'sunflowers'."

"Maybe she's thinking about what she wants to plant in her flowerbeds."

"No." Anna drummed her fingers on the table. "She's never planted sunflowers. She always told me they made her too sad."

2

KATYA

Ukraine, September 1929

"Do you girls want a turn?" Uncle Marko asked. He held up his pride and joy, the only camera in their small village of Sonyashnyky. Sunlight glistened off the lens and Uncle Marko pulled out a handkerchief to polish it for the twentieth time that day. He nodded towards the house, which everyone else had used as a backdrop, but Katya's gaze danced over to the bobbing heads of the sunflowers behind him. The brilliance of the cloudless blue sky complemented the golden orbs of the sunflowers in a color combination so rich and beautiful it made Katya's heart ache.

"Well?" He shoved the handkerchief back in his pocket.

"Yes! But over here, please." Katya grabbed her older sister's hand. "Come on, Alina. Mama wanted us to get a photograph together today."

Alina reached up and smoothed the dark wisps escaping Katya's braid. "Let me just fix your hair."

"I'm sure it's fine." Katya dragged Alina across the yard. She wanted to get this picture out of the way now so she didn't forget and earn her mother's ire, and they would find no better backdrop than the sunflower field.

"All right, but you must smile," Alina said. "I don't want you looking sour-faced."

Katya scowled and dropped Alina's hand. "I'm never sour-faced."

Alina's mouth twisted into a quirk as she straightened Katya's shirt. "Of course you're not."

"Scoot closer," Uncle Marko instructed as he turned the camera to face them.

Alina wove her arm into Katya's. "Come here." She tilted her head toward Katya's. "No matter how much I annoy you, you're stuck with me. Sisters forever."

Katya's irritation vanished at hearing the phrase, which their mother had reminded them of whenever they'd fought growing up. *You may as well get along. You'll be sisters forever.* It had become a joke between them, uttered whenever one irritated the other, and never failed to reduce the tension.

The camera clicked, and Uncle Marko grinned. "Perfect!"

The first soft strains of accordion and fiddle music trickled down the road, indicating the groom and his party were approaching, and inciting a frenzied, last-minute burst of energy. Katya pulled away from her sister as women shrieked, ribbons flew, and dishes of food appeared on every flat surface. She scooped up a basket of sunflowers and ducked low to avoid her aunt's flailing arms. Escaping the chaos, she took her place with Alina and their cousin Sasha behind the fragrant, flower-laden table that blocked the door to Sasha's house. Katya set her basket next to the others and clasped her hands together to still their trembling. Through squinted eyes, she strained to identify the men marching down the dirt road toward them.

"Stop doing that." Alina elbowed her. "You're scrunching up your nose, and it's so unbecoming."

"I'm trying to see." Katya elbowed her sister back, then nervously plucked at a flower woven into one of her thick, dark braids. When her gaze landed on Pavlo, the tall, wide-shouldered man walking next to the groom, her heart quickened. She touched a tentative finger to the cheek he'd kissed the week before. That one impulsive move had changed everything between them. She needed to talk to him, but unsure of what to say, she'd avoided him earlier at the church ceremony.

"I see Kolya," Alina said, interrupting Katya's thoughts.

Alina had been in love with Pavlo's older brother Mykola, or Kolya, as everyone called him, for as long as Katya could remember. Luckily for her, the feeling was quite mutual.

Aunts, uncles, cousins, and friends spilled out of the house and gathered around the table as the rollicking music intensified. Sasha's sister Olha, the bride, remained inside, waiting for the groom to pay his ransom to her family.

After a few minutes, Boryslav, puffed up with pride, strode into the yard, carrying a basket and a bottle of vodka. Surrounded by his closest friends and family bearing more of the same, he approached, and Sasha called out, "Why have you come here?"

Boryslav broke into a wide smile. "To receive my beautiful bride, Olha!"

"And what have you brought to show your appreciation for Olha?" Alina asked.

Boryslav set his basket filled with sweets and money down on the table, and Katya's mouth watered at the sight of the fine chocolates. Nobody from their village made anything like that; Boryslav must have traveled a great distance for them.

"Is that all you think our lovely Olha is worth?" Katya asked the question she'd been instructed to issue, trying hard not to meet Pavlo's probing eyes.

"Of course not!" He waved his arms, and two of his groomsmen came forward bearing baskets with loaves of bread. "Olha is priceless, but I have brought these gifts in my appreciation of her."

Pavlo, on his right, bowed low as he set Boryslav's offering down on the table. He threw a grin and an easy wink Katya's way, and she stumbled over her next question.

"Tell us of Olha's beauty, Boryslav."

"Ah. That's easy. Her eyes sparkle like the bluest sky on a summer day. Her long golden hair ripples like the wheat shining in the sun. Her smile brightens the room and brings men to their knees."

Katya almost laughed at the idea of Pavlo speaking such words of love to her, but the burning intensity of his gaze on her face stopped her short, and she dropped her eyes.

Sasha took up the questioning, then Boryslav's party sang his praises to balance the negotiating and ensure that Boryslav wouldn't "pay" too much for Olha's hand. Of course, all of this was fun and games. Olha couldn't be bought any more than Boryslav could march to her house and claim her. Playing out this old tradition was only a fun part of the wedding festivities, and the crowd laughed and cheered along with the entertainment.

After Boryslav was finally granted permission to enter the house, the party could finally begin. In no time, the tables set up outside were laden with delicious foods—meat, potato, and sour cherry *varenyky*, *holubtsi*, potatoes, slabs of ham, loaves of bread, cheese, fruit, and, of course, the intricately decorated wedding bread: *korovai*. People took seats around them, chatting, as liquor flowed from the bottles Boryslav had presented earlier in the day. The musicians began to play next to the open area set aside for dancing.

Katya found Mama and Tato talking to Mama's cousin, Lena, and her husband, Ruslan. Concern creased their faces as they spoke in hushed tones.

"When they arrived in my brother's village last month, the process started right away. They formed brigades, set up headquarters, and arrested some of the villagers and deported them." Ruslan leaned closer to everyone, his voice low. "Those with the nicest houses were the first to go, of course."

Questions hovered on Katya's lips, but she didn't dare speak them. The minute she started, her parents would shift the conversation to something they considered more appropriate for her ears.

"Deported where?" Tato uncorked a wine bottle.

"I heard they are sending them to Siberia." Yosyp, Pavlo's father, joined the group as Tato began filling glasses.

Fedir, Pavlo's older cousin, lowered his voice. "I've heard the same. My uncle told me they forced the whole village to join the collective farm."

"This all sounds a bit exaggerated." Mama waved a hand dismissively. "They can't take our animals and land without our permission."

Ruslan held out his glass. "My brother's village is closer to the city and much bigger than ours. Perhaps they won't bother coming all the way out here."

"We're close enough to the city. Do you really think the Soviets are going to make a distinction between the villages? We're all part of the Kyiv Okruha," Uncle Marko said.

Katya thought of the hours Uncle Marko had spent walking and taking trains to the beautiful city on the Dnieper River to buy his camera. Though they were officially part of the Kyiv region, the actual city was nearly 150 kilometers away.

"It doesn't matter. They will go wherever they want. Ukraine is fertile and plentiful, and Stalin thinks we should be the breadbasket of the Soviet Union," Tato said. He swirled the liquid in his cup but didn't drink. "To achieve that, he wants us to give up our land and join collective farms. This has been going on in villages all across Ukraine for months, and they could arrive here at any time."

"But Stalin said collectivization must be voluntary for it to work," Uncle Marko insisted.

"I've heard he's changed his stance again. It makes me nervous." Tato sipped his wine.

Uncle Marko set his glass on the table. "I still say they won't force us to collectivize. The choice will be ours."

Tato's mouth curled in disgust. "When has the choice ever been ours when it comes to Moscow, Marko?"

A small gasp slipped past Katya's lips, and Tato glanced at her. "That's enough talk for now. Today is for celebrating Olha and Boryslav."

Katya's father took her arm and led her away from the crowd.

"Tato, what were you talking about?"

"Nothing you need to worry about." His voice wavered so slightly Katya wasn't sure she heard it. "It's all rumors."

"What are you doing?" Alina grabbed Katya by the shoulders and swung her around, her joy infectious. "Stop listening to old men gossip. It's time to dance!"

Nothing could dissuade Alina when she had an idea in her head, so Katya swallowed down her concerns and allowed herself to be dragged through the crowd. She snuck a glance back at her father, who frowned and threw back his drink.

"Your brow is furrowed." Alina pressed her finger into the space between Katya's eyebrows. "Relax, Katya. We can worry about everything tomorrow. Tonight, we have fun!" She grabbed a glass of fruit sweetened *kvass*, a fermented drink made with rye bread, took a swig, then passed it to Katya.

Despite, and perhaps because of, the feelings of unease that plagued her, Katya followed her sister's lead. She raised the glass and forced down her apprehension along with the beverage that tickled as it rolled into her belly. Music filled the air. Stomping feet and laughter punctuated the lilting sounds of the fiddle as it tangled with the accordion, bandura, and *sopilka* flute to create the rhythm pulsing through the night.

Her gaze drifted to where the men had begun to dance and landed on Pavlo. The vigorous dance moves highlighted his muscled physique, and a surprising surge of longing shot through her as she admired him.

He saw her watching and grinned, and she snapped her head away, her emotions tangled into a blurry mess. What if the kiss and these feelings caused them to lose the close friendship they'd enjoyed all sixteen years of her life? He was her best friend.

Alina nudged her and giggled. "You look awfully guilty. Did something happen? Has he finally told you how he feels?"

Katya let out a shaky breath. Alina didn't know that Pavlo had kissed her. But suddenly her sister's words resonated, and Katya turned to stare at Alina. "Wait, what do you mean? How does he feel about me?"

"Oh, please! Everyone knows about you two." Alina laughed over her shoulder as she flitted away toward Kolya's arms.

"Knows what?" Katya's question trailed off. Was Alina speculating or had Pavlo talked to her? With a guilty glance around, she made her escape from the stifling crowd. Away from the throngs of people, she gulped deep breaths of the sweet night air.

How had she gotten to this point? A year ago, she'd have collapsed in laughter at the idea of her and Pavlo together in this way. Yet here she was, thinking again about the moment last week that had changed everything.

She'd run across the field to Pavlo's farm to see if they had a few extra eggs for Mama, who was baking a dessert for the wedding. Pavlo's parents had walked down to the village, and Kolya was over at Katya's house with Alina, so it was Pavlo who opened the door, shirtless and toweling off his hair.

Katya rolled her eyes at his appearance. "Don't you put on clothes before you answer the door?"

His movements, long and languid like a confident tomcat, complemented his typical, relaxed manner, and he grinned. "I was washing up. I had a mishap with a runaway piglet. He bested me in a mud pile, and I ripped my shirt."

She snorted back a laugh. "Oh, I wish I'd seen that."

His eyes narrowed, and he tossed down the towel. "I bet you do. Well, what brings you here?"

Katya tamped down her smile. "Oh, don't be so sensitive, Pavlo. Mama needs two eggs and we're out."

"We'll have to check the henhouse. I ate all of the eggs this morning."

"Fine. I'll check it on my way home."

"I'll come along." He moved toward her.

She took a step back. "Don't you want to put on your shirt?"

"I'll do it later," he said with a shrug.

She arched an eyebrow at him, then turned on her heel and marched off toward the coop. He shortened his pace to match hers but remained silent.

She glanced at him as they stepped inside. "Something wrong?" She reached under a hen sitting in a nest box. The hen gave a startled cluck, and Katya shushed it.

"No," he said, his voice tight.

Even as a small boy, he'd never been able to keep anything from her, and curious at his odd mood, she watched him out of the corner of her eye as she placed two eggs into her pocket. She handed him two more, which he set on top of the nest box before turning back to stare at her.

"What? Do I have hay in my hair?" She smoothed her unruly braid. "I was helping my father put it up earlier."

"Your hair looks perfect." His words were husky and low.

Katya's heart gave an unexpected lurch. Her tongue, suddenly fat and useless in her mouth, couldn't function. "Thanks for the eggs," she finally managed to say and stepped past him toward the path to her house.

Her grand exit failed when her foot sank into a hole, and she stumbled. Pavlo dove forward and caught her against his bare chest. She looked up, her face inches from his, and he stilled, holding her there, pressed against him. She could see every thick, honey-colored eyelash framing his bright hazel eyes and the splash of freckles scattered on his nose. Everything around her faded away as, for the first time, she really saw him, and her stomach somersaulted. Heat from his body scorched her hands and, now very aware of their close proximity, she scrambled to push him away. His arms tightened around her waist for one brief moment, as if he was reluctant to let her go. He leaned forward and put his lips against her ear, and the soft touch made the hair on the back of her neck snap to attention.

"You're going to need more eggs," he whispered.

Her breath, which she'd been inexplicably holding, came in a sudden gasp. What was he talking about? And what had she expected him to whisper in her ear? Then, as her upper leg registered the damp of the wet yolks from the broken eggs in her pocket, he moved his lips to her cheek and kissed her.

If he hadn't still been holding her close, she would have fallen over again, though she'd never admit that to him.

He pulled back with a confident smile, and she did the only thing she could think to do. She slapped him.

"What are you playing at, Pavlo?" Confusion clouded her mind, but anger simmered at the surface. Who did he think he was to kiss her without asking?

Still smiling, he touched the bright red handprint on his cheek. "I'd expect nothing less from you, Katya. Think on it. Sort out your feelings. I've decided what I want. You let me know when you know what you want." He leaned over, picked up the two extra eggs, and placed them in her shaking hands.

She took them, her body tingling from its contact with him, and ran home.

Since that day, she'd replayed the scene in her mind over and over. Had he planned it? What did he mean he'd decided what he wanted? What did she really want, now that he'd ruined their easy friendship?

Whatever happened moving forward, that kiss couldn't be forgotten.

"Katya! I couldn't find you."

The sound of Pavlo's deep voice made goosebumps pop up on her arms. Striding across the distance between them, his smile glowing in the dim light.

"I didn't know you were looking for me." Katya's pulse pounded in her ears as she fought to control her physical reaction to him. "I needed some fresh air to help me think."

"Are you still thinking?" He reached out and twirled an errant lock of her hair on his finger.

She froze, unsure what to do. Her thoughts tangled, and an onslaught of irrelevant words burst out of her.

"Oh, not about that. Mostly the harvest, really. I was thinking we should—"

Pavlo cupped her face in his large, calloused hands and pressed his thumbs to her mouth, silencing her rambling. "I can think of nothing but you."

Everything else faded away as he pressed his lips to hers, and she melted into him, rising up on tiptoe to slide into his embrace.

When he drew back to look into her eyes, she stood motionless, gaping at him with her jaw hanging open. The kiss on the cheek last week might have confused her, but this kiss made the decision for her. She could never deny the feelings surging between them.

"Is that all it takes, Katya? One kiss renders you, the loudest girl I know, speechless?" He laughed as his sandy brown hair ruffled in the breeze. "Perhaps I should have tried that long ago. It would have given me a lot more peace in my life."

His teasing cost him a hard punch in the arm, and he chuckled as he rubbed the sore spot. "Some things change, and some stay the same. Will you hit me every time I kiss you?"

"Maybe." She shrugged and smirked. "I haven't decided yet. And just because I let you kiss me doesn't mean you should forget that I can still best you in many ways."

"How could I forget? It's part of your charm."

A stream of laughter trickled toward them from a group of men standing outside the party, and Katya bristled at the intrusion into this special moment. "Let's take a walk and get away from the crowd," she suggested.

"A walk under the stars with a pretty girl? I can think of nothing I'd rather do." With a bow, Pavlo held out his elbow, and she rested her hand in the crook of his arm. They strolled along into the peaceful night, and in that moment, Katya was the happiest girl in the world.

3

CASSIE

Wisconsin, May 2004

Two days later, the small house Cassie had called home for the last year and a half was completely packed up, cleaned, and ready to be locked down. It helped that she and Henry had put all the extras—golf clubs, fancy china, and wedding gifts they'd never used—in storage before they'd moved in.

"I called your landlord, Cass. I told him we'd leave the keys on the kitchen counter," Anna called out as she hauled the last of the kitchen wares out to her car.

"You did? And he was okay with me leaving like this?"

"Oh, yes, he sounds like a very nice man. He said he understood. He can't refund you for the rest of the month's rent, of course, but he'll send you the security deposit once he checks everything over."

"Thanks." Cassie shoved a box into the back of the SUV and slammed the trunk.

"Here, give me the keys. I'll go lock up. You make sure Birdie is buckled in and ready to go." Anna held out her hand.

Cassie took a deep breath, forced a smile, and complied, because that's what one did when Anna was running the show. She didn't want to walk through the house again, anyway. Nothing remained inside but sadness.

Cassie leaned into the back seat. "Hey, little bird, are you ready?"

Birdie nodded once, her eyes wide and shining with excitement.

"Are you glad to be moving back home?" Cassie asked.

Birdie nodded again.

"I think I may be, too. This will be a fresh start for us." Cassie tugged the seatbelt over Birdie and her booster seat. "Don't tell Grandma, okay? I don't want her getting a big head over this."

Birdie smiled, her chubby cheeks rosy and soft, and Cassie melted. When was the last time she'd seen that sweet smile? How much of Birdie had been lost this past year while Cassie wallowed in her own grief?

"Let's go!" Anna jogged down the porch steps. "I'll lead the way and you can follow."

"Sounds like normal," Cassie said, as she slid behind the wheel.

Driving had changed for Cassie after Henry's car accident. Even though he'd done everything right and followed all the rules of the road, someone else hadn't, and their mistake had cost Henry his life. How can someone left behind get over that fear of the road? Her shrink had a lot of answers, but she didn't agree with any of them. While driving, her coping mechanism of choice was loud, happy music paired with a white-knuckled death grip on the steering wheel and hyper-vigilance. Her upper back never reclined. She literally sat on the edge of her seat, alert for any possible danger.

This type of driving left her exhausted, so she avoided cars when-ever possible. She and Birdie walked to the library and grocery store and didn't feel the need to go many other places. So, three hours later when they pulled up in front of Bobby's brick ranch, Cassie's back ached, her head throbbed, and her arms flopped off the steering wheel like cooked spaghetti noodles.

"We're here!" she called to Birdie cheerfully, despite her stiff muscles and trepidation at the sudden move. Birdie looked at her with raised eyebrows and Cassie grimaced. Even her five-year-old could tell when she was faking it.

She pushed open the car door and let the cold air wash over her face. The pounding in her head lessened, so she stepped out and stretched her arms behind her and bent forward, letting her body unwind.

Birdie unbuckled herself and flew out of the car and up to the front door. A warm feeling swelled up in Cassie's chest; the house looked just as it did when she was a kid. Long flower beds ran along the front wall. In the summer, they overflowed with peonies, hollyhocks, zinnias, and cosmos. Now, the small perennial sprouts were hard to tell apart, and the bare spots cried out for their annual planting. The empty beds called to Cassie, and for the first time in a long time, she had the urge to do something more than merely exist.

"I thought we could get you settled, then go pick up Bobby." Anna sidled up next to Cassie and put her arm around her daughter.

"Sounds good," Cassie replied. "Let's get the first load, then."

In no time, they had the personal belongings they'd need stacked up in one of the guest bedrooms and the extra household items stored in the basement. On the way out, Cassie paused at the holy corner on the west wall of the living room. *The icons must face east*, she remembered Bobby telling her. Two old, ornate pictures— one of Jesus and another of Mary holding the baby Jesus—hung on the wall with a beautiful embroidered *rushnyk* draped over them. Each end of the cloth hung down the sides of the frames and bore a mirror image of a red tree adorned with flowers, vines, and birds. On the bookshelf below, a few smaller prints of saints, a prayer book, blessed candles, a jar of holy water, and incense completed the space where Bobby prayed daily.

Cassie didn't consider herself to be religious, but the importance of this holy corner to Bobby made it special to Cassie. Her anxiety over the sudden move melted away as fond memories of Bobby filled her thoughts. She wanted to be here to help her and to give Birdie a chance to really get to know her great–grandmother.

"Will you run this to Bobby's room for me?" Anna stepped inside the front door and held out a laundry basket filled with folded clothes. "I meant to drop it off earlier, and I forgot."

"Sure." Cassie took the basket and walked it back to the bedroom at the end of the hall. The room smelled like Bobby's perfume, and another wave of nostalgia washed over her. She set the basket on the neatly made bed, then paused at the sight of a book splayed open on the nightstand, as if someone had set it down, intending to come right back. A burned nub of a candle rose up from a mound of melted wax crusted over a tarnished candleholder, in sharp contrast to the large modern lamp towering over the scene.

Cassie leaned closer at the sight of the tiny Ukrainian words filling every square inch of space on the yellowed page. It wasn't a book. It was a journal.

Carefully, she lifted the worn tome and closed it, running her fingertips down the scuffed brown leather cover. Grooves and scratches punctuated the surface and spoke of its long, well-used life.

As a history and journalism major in college, she'd tried for years to interview Bobby for different research papers. Bobby had refused every time. *The past is done, Cassie. We must look to the future.*

It wasn't very useful advice for a budding historian. Bobby's evasiveness had only furthered Cassie's desire to find out more about her grandmother's life, and each time she had an opportunity, she tried again. Eventually, she'd given up. Bobby's stubborn streak was the stuff of family lore for a reason. But, if Bobby was slipping into the past like her mom said, Cassie needed to understand it if she wanted to help her.

Cassie closed her eyes and spread her hand over the cover. Warmth pulsed through her, as if she could feel the words coming to life, painting the picture of the stories and history inside. The hair on her arms stood up, and she shivered.

"Cassie? Are you ready?" Anna's voice broke the spell.

Her eyes opened. "Yeah, I'll be right there."

Cassie pressed the book to her chest, and she gave a sigh of regret. If only it were that easy. She thought about slipping the journal into her room so she could investigate it further, but taking such a personal item probably wouldn't be the best way to start off this new living arrangement with Bobby, especially if Bobby came looking for it. Plus, having never learned Ukrainian, she couldn't even read it. She set the book on the nightstand and gave it one last longing look, wondering what answers it held, then headed out to the car.

4

KATYA

Ukraine, January 1930

"Who is that?" Mama halted in front of Katya as they left the church one cold winter evening.

Katya stepped around her to get a better view of the village square. Lined with shops, several houses, and the church, it formed a small clearing where vendors set up on market days. Today, it stood empty as a group of people and two wagons approached from the east. The dark colors and sharp lines of their caravan stood out like a harsh stain against the soft grays and white of the snowy landscape.

"Tato?" Katya looked at her father, who had placed a hand on her shoulder as people spilled out of the church behind them.

"I told you, Viktor," Ruslan said, before Tato could reply. "It's Stalin's men ."

A low murmur rose through the crowd as Katya counted roughly two dozen people trudging along in front of the wagons. The air sparked with apprehension, and she pulled her coat tighter, as if she could cocoon herself away from the unknown threat walking toward them.

Pavlo, Fedir, and Kolya came to stand by them as the newcomers parked their wagons. Pavlo gave her arm a quick, reassuring squeeze. A man who introduced himself as Comrade Ivanov, their Communist Party Leader, stepped up on the wagon to address everyone with his thin, reedy voice.

"Comrades! It seems we have caught you at the perfect time. Everyone is to stay for a mandatory meeting so we can tell you about Comrade Stalin's wonderful plans for you."

Comrade Ivanov introduced the small group of Twenty-Five Thousanders, a contingent of the approximately 25,000 Russian-speaking Soviet volunteer activists deployed across Ukraine, who would be collectivizing their village.

"Throw off the shackles of capitalism and choose a better life. Our farms will prosper when we pool our resources and work together!"

With his shiny shoes, city clothes, and pale face, Katya doubted he knew much about farming, but that didn't stop him from continuing.

As he laid out the plan of signing over livestock and land to the collective, Katya watched an activist nail up a colorful poster to the church door depicting a smiling man and woman with a tractor. The caption read:

Work happily and the harvest will be good spring, summer, fall, and winter.

Prokyp Gura bumped into Katya, the smell of alcohol potent as he pushed through the crowd to introduce himself to Comrade Ivanov.

"Some people seem excited about this," Katya said, as Prokyp gestured toward a poster and tapped his chest proudly.

"Some people are idiots," Pavlo replied.

Fedir leaned close to her and Pavlo and nodded toward a group of activists. "Look at them taking notes."

Their pencils scribbled furiously as they walked down the roads branching off the village square and inspected nearby homes. One man knocked on a wall of the Krevchuk's house. He spoke to another man, then wrote something down.

"Notes on what?" Katya asked.

"Probably on who has the biggest house." Fedir shook his head in disgust. "They need to live somewhere, don't they?"

Katya's eyes widened. She longed to reach out and cling to Pavlo's steady hand, but his fists were clenched tight at his side.

* * *

As they walked home that night, Katya couldn't hold back her questions. "It makes no sense. Why would anyone give up their independence?"

"Stalin has been pushing collectivization all over," Tato said. "It was only a matter of time before communists arrived in our village. He believes that if the land and labor are organized, the yield will be greater. His Soviet Union will reap the benefits of what we sow." He shook his head in disgust. "It's the same story every time, for centuries. Everyone wants Ukraine's fertile soil for their own, and nobody wants to let Ukrainians rule it."

"You said it was just rumors!" Katya felt something fundamental break inside her at her father's betrayal. "Now you say it was only a matter of time?"

"I didn't want to worry you." Tato slowed his pace to walk alongside her. "And I'd hoped they wouldn't come here. I prayed."

"A lot of good that did." Katya kicked at a rock on the road, wishing she could aim it toward Comrade Ivanov.

"Kateryna Viktorivna Shevchenko!" Mama barked. "Don't mock prayer or your father."

The only time Katya heard her full name from her mother was when she was getting scolded. Color bloomed on her cheeks as she gave a muffled apology.

"The whole idea is ridiculous!" Fedir shook his head in disgust.

"Maybe so, but these activists truly believe in this plan." The worry in Tato's tone made Katya shiver in the cold night air.

"Conviction doesn't make them right," Pavlo said. He let his hand brush against Katya's and held it there, pressed against her skin. She shivered again, but this time, not from the cold or worry.

"No, it doesn't," Tato agreed. "They've never owned their own land or worked their own farm. They don't know the satisfaction in harvesting the crop you sowed and nurtured, feeding your family, and planting the seed you saved from your fall harvest to start the process again in the spring." He spread his arms and gestured toward the fields surrounding them. "That's what makes us farmers."

"Exactly." Mama gave a tight nod and placed her hand on Tato's shoulder. "Why would we surrender that?"

"We won't!" Katya said firmly.

* * *

The next morning, as Katya leaned against the warm flank of the cow, the sound of a child wailing broke through the hypnotic rhythm of milk squirting into the pail. She grabbed the bucket so the cow wouldn't kick it over and peered outside. Her father stood near the road, talking to Polina Krevchuk. Behind her rested a handcart with some clothes and her two young children.

Katya walked over in time to hear Polina say, "They came in the middle of the night and arrested my husband. They said he was a *kulak* and they were taking the house for Party headquarters." She set her jaw and tried to hold back tears.

Katya blinked as she recalled Fedir's comment about the activists looking for big houses, and the way that activist had checked the soundness of the Krevchuk's walls. They were one of the wealthier families in the village and had a larger and nicer home than most.

"Where are you supposed to go?" Tato asked.

"They said we had to leave the village immediately if we hoped to avoid being arrested as well. I'm going to see if my brother will take us in."

"What about your animals? Your possessions? Could you take nothing?"

Polina sniffled. "We were able to take only some clothes."

"How long will they keep your husband?" Katya asked.

The woman choked back a sob. "I don't know."

Katya struggled to find something to say, but all she could do was wrap her arms around Polina as she wept into her hands.

Mama appeared with a small loaf of bread wrapped in a cloth. "Here, Polina. It's not much, but it will fill your stomachs on your travels."

"Thank you." Polina straightened and wiped her nose. "We need to get moving. I have to get my children to safety before nightfall."

As they walked away, the youngest child started crying again. "Where is my Tato? I want my Tato!"

Katya clenched her fists. "It's not right. How can the activists kick them out of their own home?"

"No questions right now, Katya." Fatigue etched dark circles under Tato's eyes. "Come, we must finish our chores."

* * *

That evening, at the next mandatory meeting, Katya learned that four other men had been arrested in the night and their wives and children put out of their homes. All, like the Krevchuks, were wealthier families in positions of respect and power in the village.

Katya perused the crowd gathered in the church. As the activists droned on, people laughed and talked, but a few went over to the long table and added their names to the Party roster.

"Some are actually signing up," Katya said.

Pavlo waved his hand. "Only the weak. They've failed on their own and think the collective will take care of them."

Fedir scoffed. "Not likely." He nodded toward the speakers. "I doubt these fools have ever even been outside the city, let alone stepped foot on a farm. Just yesterday, I saw one mistake a goat for a sheep."

"Did you see that Prokyp is now part of an activist group?" Pavlo asked. "The village drunk trying to tell us how to work our land. Unbelievable!"

An activist woman walked by and thrust a paper into Katya's hands. "Come, join the *Komsomol*. Leave these old ways behind and usher in the new age!"

Pavlo peered over Katya's shoulder at the picture of two exuberant young adults raising their hands in salute to Joseph Stalin.

"The Communist Youth Organization Needs You! Stalin Needs You!" Katya read aloud. She met Pavlo's gaze. "We're not doing this."

"Of course not." Pavlo's eyes narrowed as he took the paper and crumpled it.

Anti-kulak posters and banners for the Young Pioneers—the younger counterpart of the Komsomol—went up everywhere.

Young Pioneer! Learn to Fight for the Working Class Cause!
Let Us Destroy the Kulaks as a Class!
Throw Kulaks Out of Your Way! The Sworn Enemies of Collectivization!

Tired of listening to the redundant speeches, Katya stared at the posters during the meetings, but they made no sense to her. What was wrong with this life? She loved working with her father in the fields and taking care of their animals. She enjoyed her days spent cultivating the family garden with her mother, then putting up the harvest so they had good food all winter. Why should any of that change?

As the days passed and meetings continued, the church, which had been requisitioned for all Party meetings, became unrecognizable. All of the holy icons were removed, replaced with red fabric and banners espousing the benefits of collectivization and communism. Many villagers still privately scoffed at the idea of the collective farms, but the communists' ranks were slowly beginning to fill with poorer, disillusioned farmers who believed the anti-*kulak* propaganda.

Talk of rising up against the *kulaks* became the activists' battle cry, and Comrade Ivanov stoked the fire. "For years you have slaved for *kulaks* while they take all of the profits! They live in their fancy homes and mock you! No more! Now is your chance to take what is rightfully yours!"

"Now a *kulak* is anyone who isn't failing?" Fedir said under his breath. "Anyone who has the money to hire help at harvest or own a second cow? That's all it takes for Stalin to consider them wealthy farmers?"

However, even Fedir had reined in his outbursts since members of the OGPU, Stalin's secret police force, had slipped into the village in the middle of the night. With their olive tunics and steely gazes, they monitored the crowds for any sign of disrespect or dissension, and their intimidation worked. Nobody wanted to draw their attention and risk being arrested.

"Stalin has decided that Ukraine must be class-free in order for these collective farms to succeed." Tato spoke in a low voice.

"But how can he make that happen?" Katya chewed on her nails as the stony glare of an OGPU officer passed over her.

Nobody answered her, and Comrade Ivanov's voice boomed. "Down with the *kulaks*! Down with the *kulaks*!"

"We need to stand up to them now," Fedir said. He bounced on the balls of his feet, thrumming with nervous energy.

Katya felt Pavlo tense next to her as he grabbed Fedir's shoulder. "Be smart. Now is not the time, Fedir. The OGPU is watching."

Fedir shrugged off Pavlo's grip. "There will never be a good time! I can't listen to this anymore. And neither should you!" He cupped his hands around his mouth. "Take your communist ideas and leave! We don't want you here!"

A few gasps fizzled through the crowd. Comrade Ivanov stopped mid-sentence, his mouth hanging open, as he slowly turned and glowered at Fedir. He stepped back and spoke to the woman at his side. The crowd, unsure of how to react, waited on Fedir to do more, but Kolya and Pavlo dragged him outside before he could speak again.

Tato sucked in a worried breath. "That was foolish."

* * *

Even though Katya and Pavlo were both on errands for their mothers, the time spent together walking home from the market was welcome. A few tenacious leaves clung to the naked branches of the trees lining the road and rattled in the winter winds. Katya shivered and turned her face up to the sun, wishing its warmth could reach her.

"Where are all of these fancy *kulak* houses the activists speak of?" she said. "Very few people I know have anything like that."

Pavlo pursed his lips. "In their eyes, a tin roof is fancy, or an extra room built on your house. By their standards, if you aren't wretchedly poor, you're a *kulak*." As they came to a fork in the road, Pavlo took her hand. "Come, let's not talk of such things. I want to enjoy this morning with you. Have I mentioned that you look particularly lovely today?"

"You have not," Katya said as she twirled the loose hair at the end of her braid. "Feel free to elaborate."

Pavlo's deep, rich laughter echoed around them. "I could go on and on about it, but first I must stop by my cousin's." Pavlo nodded toward Fedir's house down the road. "He asked me to look at a harness that needs to be repaired. Then, I'll list all the evidence of your beauty."

Katya laughed. "Fine, but we mustn't be long. My parents will wonder where we are."

Pavlo grinned as they turned down the narrow road leading to

Fedir's. "Of course. We wouldn't want them to get the wrong idea about me."

"You're lucky that my father thinks so highly of you, or he'd be a lot stricter with me."

"That may change when I tell him of my intentions," Pavlo said.

"Oh? And what would those be?"

"If I told you, then it wouldn't be a surprise." He raised her hand to his lips, and Katya shivered.

Despite everything, she couldn't remember a time as perfect as this exact moment. Pavlo not only thought her beautiful, he had intentions for her. That knowledge made it hard to worry about anything else.

They walked along for a few more minutes of blissful happiness before Pavlo dropped her hand, and Katya snapped back to reality.

"Fedir's front door is open." All of the playfulness in Pavlo's voice disappeared, and dread splashed over her like a cold bucket of water.

He raced through the yard, his feet crunching on broken glass as he went inside. On the front door, Katya touched a dark, wet streak, and the coppery smell of blood filled her nose. She stared, dumbfounded, at the red liquid on her fingers.

"Pavlo." She stepped past the doorway and held up her quaking hand.

Before her, a scene of utter chaos filled the small space: chairs overturned, the table on its side, broken dishes and clothing scattered all over the floor.

"He's gone!" Pavlo's voice cracked.

Fear swelled in her chest. "Do you think it was the OGPU?"

Pavlo clenched his jaw, and a narrow muscle on his temple flexed. "Who else could it be?"

She looked around the tiny house. "But he's not a *kulak*!"

"He mocked the Soviets at the meeting last night, remember?" Pavlo's words vibrated with anger. "Now it seems anyone who speaks out against them is a *kulak*, too."

5

CASSIE

Illinois, May 2004

As they entered the hospital, Bobby's accented English echoed down the hallway. Cassie gave a short laugh as she glanced at Anna. "She can't be too bad off. She sounds like she always did."

They followed her voice and found her, red-faced and irritated, scolding a young nurse.

"I am done! They said I could go home! I do not need more tests."

"What's going on?" Anna rushed into the room as Cassie watched the scene unfold.

"I'm sorry, ma'am," the nurse said. "I had to check her bandages one more time before discharge. I didn't mean to agitate her, but everything looks good. I'll get the doctor to sign off on her paperwork, and you guys will be ready to go home."

"Thank you." Anna turned to Bobby. "I've brought you some visitors!"

Cassie took her daughter's hand and entered the room.

Bobby's wrinkled, sunken face bore the brunt of her recent accident. Purple bruises flowered out around her left eye and the papery skin on her cheeks had torn in several spots. Her flattened brownish gray curls stuck out from under the bandage on her temple, and light abrasions peppered her arms. Her eyes still snapped with fire, though, like the Bobby Cassie remembered, who ran her household with an iron fist and had a mind like a steel trap.

Bobby smiled as they approached her bed, and Cassie hugged her. Bobby's slight form surprised Cassie; bones poked through her hospital gown. She'd lost weight.

"Cassie! You're home! This is wonderful."

Her face softened as she saw Birdie.

"Ah, and my little bird has come to me." She opened her arms and Birdie climbed onto the bed and sank into her embrace.

Bobby rubbed a gnarled hand down the girl's hair. "There now, you are safe here."

Cassie glanced at her mother. Anna beamed at the reunion and mouthed, "I told you so."

Cassie rolled her eyes and sat next to Bobby. "How would you like some visitors for a while?"

"I do not need a babysitter! Is that what your mother told you?" Bobby glared at Anna. "I am fine to live at home by myself."

"I know that," Cassie said. "I thought you could use—"

Bobby's eyes narrowed, and Anna kicked Cassie's leg.

Cassie grimaced and tried again. "I thought maybe it would be okay if Birdie and I stayed with you for a bit. I want to come home, and Mom doesn't have much room over at her house. So, I was hoping you wouldn't mind us staying with you. Until we found our own place, I mean."

"Oh, of course." Bobby broke into a wide smile. "I'd love for you to stay with me. I can show Birdie how to plant flowers. She can be my helper, like you were when you were a little girl, Cassie." She squeezed Birdie's hand, and the girl nodded enthusiastically.

"Great!" Cassie replied, standing. "So, let's get you out of here."

"Nick!" Bobby's face creased into a smile framed by a thousand feathery wrinkles, as she looked past Cassie.

In the doorway stood a tall, broad-shouldered man dressed in navy-colored pants and a shirt with a fire department logo on it. His tanned skin nearly matched his sandy brown hair, and the monochromatic coloring made his bright blue eyes stand out in stark contrast.

"Sorry to interrupt. We were here for a call, and I heard you were going home, so I wanted to stop by. You're feeling better?" His low, melodic voice filled the room. Bobby's smile widened as Birdie buried her head in her great–grandmother's shoulder.

"Yes, I'm much better. Nick, this is my daughter, Anna, my granddaughter, Cassie, and my great-granddaughter, Birdie." Bobby shone with pride as she introduced her progeny.

Nick stepped forward and extended a hand toward Anna. "Nice to meet you all."

Birdie peeked up at him from the protective shelter of Bobby's arms, then ducked back down again.

The tiny room exceeded capacity with all the people squished around Bobby. Cassie stepped around her mother and shook his hand, ignoring the warmth and strength pulsing through him, and appraised the stranger. Yes, he was good looking, she decided, but he seemed familiar with Bobby. Too familiar.

"How do you two know each other?" she asked, her voice sharp.

He held her hand a beat longer than a typical handshake, then let go as he answered. "I was one of the medics who brought her in."

"Do you normally do that?" Cassie asked, not bothering to hide the suspicion in her voice. "Come see past patients in the hospital, I mean? Isn't there a rule against that? Some privacy laws or something?"

He laughed, revealing two deep dimples on either side of even, white teeth. "No, it's okay. As long as I don't disclose her medical information, I think it's fine if I say hi."

"Cassie, don't be rude," Bobby scolded her. "Nick is also the grandson of my friend, Mina."

"Mrs. Koval?" Anna asked. "I was so sorry to hear about her passing a few months back."

Nick dropped his gaze. "Thank you. I miss her a lot."

Bobby shot Nick a sympathetic look. "Mina left Nick her house. He moved in last month, so he stops by sometimes to check on me. He brings me my newspaper when the weather is bad. Sometimes, he takes home extra food I make so it doesn't go to waste."

"She's really taken me under her wing," Nick said. "It's been a pleasure getting to know her."

"It's nothing. I'm happy to do this for Mina. Nick is a good Ukrainian boy." She gave a nod of satisfaction, as if this fact alone trumped all others and pushed Nick to another level of glory.

"Well, I wasn't born there, but I was very much raised with all of the Ukrainian traditions. First generation here," Nick said.

"Me, too," Anna said. "We're grateful for your help, Nick, but we don't want to put you out." She turned to Bobby. "Mama, when you said a neighbor boy was helping you, I thought you meant a young kid earning extra spending money."

"You never asked." Bobby shrugged.

Nick raised his hands in surrender. "Really, it's no trouble. Plus, it's nice to practice speaking Ukrainian. I'd hate to lose it after all those Saturdays my Baba made me go to Ukrainian school. But I need to get going. I just wanted to say hello." He strode forward and planted a kiss on Bobby's weathered cheek. "Take care now."

"Thank you, dear," Bobby replied, patting his hand.

"Nice to meet you all." Nick gave a wave as he backed out the door.

As soon as he was out of earshot, Cassie said, "I still think that's kind of weird. Haven't you ever seen those crime shows about handsome strangers getting the elderly to sign over their bank accounts and estates?"

"You are terrible." Bobby glared at her. "So suspicious."

"Or are you so naïve?" Cassie folded her arms.

Bobby's voice hardened as she looked at Cassie. "That is one thing I am not." After several moments, her voice and shoulders relaxed. "Maybe he's just a good boy who misses having family around? Did you ever think about that?"

"No. It's much more likely he's a serial killer."

Anna gave a half-smile. "Well, that seems a bit extreme. He seems nice enough." Then, when Bobby turned away, she leaned close to Cassie and whispered, "Keep an eye on him, though."

* * *

Bobby remained silent on the ride home, and it wasn't until Anna went ahead to open the front door, while Cassie helped her from the car, that she spoke.

"Does she still not talk?" Bobby shot a glance toward Birdie, who'd skipped ahead after Anna.

Cassie's face tensed. "Not since the accident."

Bobby nodded. "Everyone grieves differently."

They walked slowly up the sidewalk together. "I know," Cassie said. "But it's so hard. I feel like I'm failing her."

"Bah," Bobby scoffed. "Takes time. You will see."

They watched as the little girl leaned over and inspected one of the hollyhocks newly sprouted next to the front stoop. A smile lit up her face.

"See, she's a happy girl," Bobby said. "When she is ready, she will talk."

"How can you be so sure?" Cassie asked as they made their way through the front door.

"I am familiar with loss," Bobby said.

"I know, but Grandpa was almost eighty when he died. You guys at least had a long marriage together."

Bobby closed her eyes and took a deep breath. "I'm not talking about him."

Cassie stared at her, but before she could ask any questions, Bobby said, "It's late. I'll go to bed now. Can you help me to my room, Cassie?"

That night, while Anna read to Birdie, Cassie wandered into the kitchen. She pulled open the refrigerator door and chuckled at the sight of a small ham and a jar of mayonnaise. The loaf of bread on the counter rounded off Bobby's favorite quick meal: a ham and mayonnaise sandwich. They would need to grocery shop soon.

A scrap of paper sticking out from under the flour canister on the counter—atypical in Bobby's tidy kitchen—caught her eye. Curious, she tugged, and the corner of another piece followed. Cassie lifted the whole container and found a pile of small squares of paper covered in spidery script. She held one up to the light and peered closely at the unfamiliar Cyrillic letters.

"What's that?" Anna asked as she came into the kitchen.

"I can't read it." Cassie held one out to her mother.

Anna took the paper and squinted at it. "It's Bobby's handwriting."

"Right, but what does it say? And why are there a dozen of them?" Cassie pointed at the pile on the counter.

Anna frowned. "I don't know. I never learned to read Ukrainian."

Cassie sorted the slips of paper. "How strange."

"It's probably just lists for groceries," Anna said. "Put it back where you found it so she doesn't get upset."

"What if it's something else?" Cassie asked. "Notes about people she once knew or stories about her life."

Anna snorted. "Wishful thinking. You know she never talks about her past."

"Maybe it's different now that she's getting older," Cassie said. The journal she'd found flashed through her mind. "Maybe she's ready to share her memories."

Anna let out an exasperated sigh. "Doubtful. I've tried my whole life to get information about Bobby's past, but she'd never talk. All I'd get is," Anna adopted a terrible imitation of Bobby's accented English: *"the past is done. All you can do is look to the future."*

"What did your father say?" Cassie asked. Her grandfather had died when she was six, and her memories of him were few and fuzzy.

"Sometimes he'd talk about farming when we'd plant the garden, but if I asked him anything specific about his childhood or Ukraine, he'd change the subject." She laughed as she remembered. "He used to eat all of the leftovers. If I couldn't finish my food, he would, then he'd wipe the plate clean with a piece of bread. And if there was something questionable in the fridge, he'd eat it, even if he had to scrape some mold off to do it."

Cassie blanched. "Bobby isn't much different in that regard. I'm always afraid to eat leftovers from her fridge. You never know how old they really are. Even if it's from two weeks ago, she'll tell you it's still good."

"I know," Anna agreed. She closed her eyes, lost in thought. "God, I haven't thought about this in years, but one time, I found my dad sitting in the middle of the garden, crying."

She opened her eyes and met Cassie's. "I was young, and it scared me. I tried to give him a hug and ask him what was wrong, but he wouldn't talk. He kept running his hand over all of the vegetables and sobbing. It's like I wasn't even there." Anna shook her head. "I tried asking him about it later, and he pretended he didn't know what I was talking about. Like I'd made it all up."

"Did you tell Bobby?" Cassie asked.

"I told her I thought my father was sad," Anna said. "She told me everyone has things in their past that makes them sad, but you have to push through it."

Cassie twirled the note absently as she thought. "Remember when I had that family history project in college? She'd refused every other request to use her past for research papers. I thought she wouldn't be able to say no to a genealogy paper. But she wouldn't do it, and she told me the same thing, about looking to the future and not worrying about the past. I finally had to go interview Dad's Aunt Maude, and nothing remotely interesting ever happened in her life."

Anna laughed. "She's a sweet lady, but unless you're super into couponing, she's not too exciting."

Cassie traced the Ukrainian words. "Have you ever seen Bobby journal?"

"Like, write in a diary? Never. Why?"

"I saw one in her room the other day. I couldn't read that either," Cassie said.

"Do you think it's hers?"

"Maybe. It looked really old," Cassie said. "I'm thinking about asking her about it and these notes." She held them up.

"Good luck with that." Anna stood and paced across the kitchen. "Cass, I need to tell you something."

"Nothing good ever comes after that line."

Anna gave a weak smile. "Bobby's doctor thinks she might be in the early stages of Alzheimer's. She's got some tests scheduled, but this isn't the first time she's wandered off and gotten lost."

Cassie's stomach lurched. "Why didn't you tell me that before?"

Anna shrugged. "I don't know. I guess I didn't want to admit that Alzheimer's was a possibility, but her doctor thinks it's time we got her evaluated."

"Do you think it's connected to her speaking Ukrainian and zoning out?"

Anna rubbed her face. "Yeah, maybe. She gets confused sometimes, too."

Cassie twirled one of the notes on the table. "Or maybe she's just getting old and finally wants to think about all of her repressed memories. Maybe she needs us to help her process it."

"I hope so, but don't count on it." Anna stifled a yawn. "Sorry, I'm exhausted. Do you need me to stay or are you good if I go home?"

"I'm fine. Go get some rest."

Anna gave her a quick hug and a promise to return tomorrow. As her mother walked out the back door, Cassie tucked a few of the notes in her pocket before putting the rest back.

6

KATYA

Ukraine, February 1930

As the weeks passed, the villagers settled into the routine of twice-weekly Party meetings. When the activists weren't organizing the collective farm or the communist groups, they marched about the countryside and tried to convince individual households to join.

"I heard Fedir was sent to the train station," Tato said one evening.

"To be deported? Where?" Katya asked.

"I don't know. Siberia, maybe?"

"Kolya and his family tried to say goodbye, but they wouldn't let anyone see him," Alina said.

Katya shuddered at the memory of finding Fedir's house in such disarray. "I hate to think of what they did to him."

"We must do our best to keep our heads down and not draw attention to ourselves," Tato said. "Things will settle down soon, I'm sure."

For the first time in her life, Katya didn't trust Tato's words. She didn't see how any of this could settle down or where it was all headed.

Yet she was going on with her life. Every day she got up and did her chores, helped her mother, and broke away to see Pavlo as often as she could. Amid the collapse of their village life, she was dreaming of her future, and it felt wrong.

Mama cleared her throat. She hated talk about what was going on in the village and preferred to ignore the situation altogether. "I need someone to take this to Oksana's house." Mama held out the basket filled with a jar of borscht and a loaf of bread. "She's been ill, and a good meal will be a big help to them."

Katya threw aside her mending and jumped out of her chair. "I'll go!"

A chuckle escaped Tato's weary face. "Even after a day spent helping me clean out the barn, you can't sit still, can you, Katya?"

"I feel like taking a walk." She shrugged and grinned when Tato winked at her. She'd do anything to get out of patching clothes, and he knew it.

"She shouldn't go alone. Go along with her, Alina," Mama said. "You've been working on your embroidering all day. It will be good for you to take a break."

Alina stretched her arms over her head and sighed. "You're right. My eyes are starting to ache. A walk will be nice."

"It's late, so don't linger," Tato said, all traces of amusement gone from his voice. "Drop the food off and come right home."

"Yes, Tato." Katya buttoned her coat and wrapped a thick shawl over her head. Continued tensions with the activists kept everyone on edge, including her normally placid father.

Outside, the snow sparkled under the stars and the still, cold air made Katya's lungs sting when she inhaled. She stared up at the sky, then her gaze fell on Pavlo and Kolya's family farm across the field.

"Missing Pavlo?" Alina teased.

"No." Katya glared at her sister, then smiled. "Well, maybe."

Alina laughed as she set off down the road. "Let's hurry. Maybe he and Kolya will stop by this evening."

"Did they say that?" Katya ran after her, giddiness at the possibility of seeing Pavlo tonight making her steps light.

They giggled and chatted as they walked and were nearly there when a gunshot cracked through the night air. The food basket slipped from Katya's fingers and spilled onto the frozen ground. She raced down the moonlit path toward her aunt and uncle's house, the bread and soup forgotten. Alina yelled for her to stop, but Sasha's screams rang louder and kept Katya's feet moving.

Alina's long legs reached her easily and she tackled Katya to the ground. They landed in a snowdrift next to the barn, hidden from view. Katya's pulse pounded in her ears, and terror made her body shake.

"Stop, Katya!" Alina hissed into her ear. "We have to get out of here!"

Limbs tangled, and their heavy coats twisted around them like a vice, but it didn't keep Katya from trying to wrestle away from Alina. Her arm throbbed where Alina's hand dug into it.

"No!" Katya wrenched her left leg from under Alina and rolled onto her stomach. Snow made its way into her boots and under the thick skirt she wore, the icy crystals numbing her legs. "We have to help them!" The restrained whisper made her throat ache.

Katya ripped off her coat, popping the buttons, and scrambled away from Alina. Sasha's screams quieted to a whimper but still hung heavy in the air over their uncle's quiet pleading.

"Please!" Alina begged as she grabbed Katya's leg. "You know it's too late for them! What do you think will happen if you run out there?"

Katya hesitated. Her sister was right, but how could she live with herself if she did nothing, just like everyone else?

"You will be killed," Alina said, answering her own question when Katya didn't. "And then what? What will become of Mama and Tato if they lose you, too? We need to go home, now!"

Her reference to their parents stopped Katya in her tracks. "I can't. You can go if you want. I need to at least see what happens. We can peek around the corner of the barn and not be seen."

Alina wrung her hands and looked in the direction of their home. "Fine. But we stay together. Don't try to leave me again."

The full moon reflecting on the snowy ground illuminated the scene in front of the girls. Two burly OGPU men in tall black boots and dark overcoats dragged their sobbing aunt out of the house. Already in her bed clothes and without a coat, Aunt Oksana flinched as the snow touched her bare skin.

Two other men stood in the yard with their pistols pointed at Uncle Marko. One, a small and skinny activist, looked to be Katya's age. His pale face showed the shadows of a faint mustache, and he glanced at the older grizzled man next to him for direction.

Sasha, with her baby brother Denys in her arms, stood in the same spot Katya had sat with Sasha on her sister Olha's wedding day only a few months before. Sasha's older brother, Serhiy, nearly a grown man, stood behind them, closer to the house. When his mother struggled in the snow, he moved to help her.

"Stay right there!" The younger activist pointed his gun at Serhiy. It wobbled in his grip. "Or this time we shoot to kill!"

"She's sick. That's why she didn't come out with us." Serhiy held his hands up in the air while he took slow steps toward his mother. "I'm just going to help her."

The younger activist lowered his arm slightly, as if he accepted Serhiy's response. The other activist did not. He pointed his weapon and shot Serhiy.

When the gun went off, Katya lunged forward, her lips parting to yell for Serhiy to run, even though it was too late. Before she could get a sound out, Alina's hand clamped over her mouth. She pulled Katya against her chest, her heart pounding in Katya's ear, as they watched Serhiy fall. He landed on a bed of fresh, untouched snow. His blood spilled fast, spreading into a circle of scarlet around his motionless body.

"Never accept insolence from these people. It makes you look weak," barked the man who had pulled the trigger. The young man nodded, his mouth hanging open and his eyes glued to the pool of blood seeping out around Katya's cousin.

Aunt Oksana's guttural wail pierced Katya like a knife. Her aunt struggled to get to her firstborn son, but Uncle Marko, agony carved on his face, pulled her away from their home and their dead child.

Sasha whimpered and turned away from Serhiy's body. Her eyes, wide with shock, blinked rapidly as she stared out into the night. Katya ached to call out to her, to save her, but she didn't. She couldn't.

Katya's bravado faltered, and her lower lip wavered as three of the men ushered the family away. The young one stayed back to drag Serhiy's body to the woods. Katya and Alina sat in the cold, clinging to each other, until they marched out of sight.

Katya's voice, hoarse from holding back screams, shattered the silence. "We must go tell Mama and Tato what happened."

Alina nodded, and they made their way down the path back home, picking up the bread and broken jar of soup along the way and stepping over the streak of spilled red borscht that stained the snow, just like Serhiy's blood had.

Katya squeezed her eyes shut as the possibilities of what Sasha and her family would endure flashed through her mind. The tears she had done so well to contain now dripped down her face and froze into frosty crystals on her cheeks. The sharp report of the gun had finally stopped ringing in her ears, but the image of Serhiy and the red snow still burned in her eyes as they entered their yard.

Small but pleasant, their home was typical for the village. Wattle constructed walls hugged the ground under a thatched roof. An entry area served as a storage space and led into an open main room that housed a large, whitewashed *pich* stove. Decorated with painted flowers, the *pich* served as the heart of their home. The thick brick walls kept the whole house warm in the winter and jutted out into the room with ledges and alcoves.

Katya stepped into her home and looked at it with new eyes. The kitchen sat on the far side of the room where the oven opened up and a shelf held spots for kettles and pots. On the other side of the *pich*, tucked on a long bench, was Katya and Alina's bed. The rest of the open space held a bed for her parents and a table and chairs. Fragrant dried flowers and herbs hung in bunches from the ceiling, and brightly colored embroidered pictures decorated the walls. Before today, she'd felt safe here.

Mama sank into a chair as they relayed their story, then buried her face in a handkerchief. "My sweet sister. And those poor children."

"Did the activists think they were *kulaks*?" Katya fought to keep her voice steady.

"Probably." Tato rubbed his jaw. "The bar is low these days."

"But they did nothing wrong!" Katya cried. "Where does this end? People are disappearing in the middle of the night. Families deported. Where do they go? Are they even still alive?"

"Katya, lower your voice," Tato said. "Stalin wants *kulaks* to be eliminated by any means necessary. It doesn't matter how. He just wants them gone."

Mama gave a strangled cry as Katya paced angrily.

"What can we do now? We can't sit here while they're taken away." Katya clapped a hand over her mouth as the words spewed from it. Her faced flamed with her own hypocrisy. She had done just that, only a few minutes ago.

Tato put his arm around Mama's heaving shoulders. "It's not that simple. What do you expect? I march down to the state headquarters and demand their freedom? I would be arrested with them. I have seen it happen several times over. Nothing we do can bring them back."

The activists had made it very clear that helping a *kulak* was a crime. People brave enough to try to fight back or help family and friends hide had been caught and deported right alongside the ones they'd tried to save.

Katya clenched her fists. "But what can they do to all of us? If we all stand up for our friends, for our family, together, then what can they do to our whole village?"

Tato grimaced. "Don't you see? They are already doing it to our whole village. How many empty houses are there? How many families deported? Would you chance me being arrested or shot to appease your need to do something? Or do you ask that I let my wife or daughters go and risk being arrested? I'm left with no choice here, Katya. You must see that!"

His words deflated her, and she drooped into the chair in front of the warm *pich*. She tried to imagine Tato powerless to protect his family. The thought terrified her, yet when she looked at the stoop in his shoulders and the dullness of his eyes, it seemed he already felt that way. Stalin's plan to terrify the remaining Ukrainians into subservience so they would join his regime was working just as he'd hoped.

Mama dabbed at her eyes with her damp handkerchief. She went over to the eastern facing wall where she kept her holy icons and dropped to her knees in front of the images of Jesus Christ and the Virgin Mother holding the Holy Child. A white *rushnyk* cloth with two intricately embroidered red trees of life—one on each end—hung down either side of the pictures and framed the area where the family prayed. She lit the blessed candle, closed her eyes, and folded her hands.

Katya bit back an exasperated sigh. Praying wouldn't do Sasha or the rest of her family any good now. She turned to her father. "We're not going to sign up for the collective, are we?"

"We will do everything we can to avoid it," Tato said, but his voice lacked its usual vigor.

* * *

As Katya lay with her back pressed against Alina's in their tiny bed later that night, sleep eluded her. She couldn't stop replaying the day's events in her mind. Serhiy's blood, Sasha's screams, Aunt Oksana's anguished cry. They were gone now, probably forever, and Katya had done nothing. She squeezed her eyes shut and willed the images to leave her brain, but it was useless. She reached under the pillow and pulled out the bundle of scrap papers she kept wrapped around the stub of an old pencil and, with only the moonlight that crept in through the window illuminating the page, began to write what she'd seen until her eyes grew heavy and sleep finally came.

The next day, she hurried through her morning chores of milking the cow, feeding the livestock, and gathering the eggs, then made her way across the snowy field separating her farm from Pavlo's.

She found Pavlo outside, heading toward the barn, and fell into step with him. "Can we talk?"

Her cold hand twisted into his warm one, and he gave it a squeeze. "Of course."

He led her inside and toward the horse stalls. They each grabbed a brush and, together, worked on grooming an old mare. Katya told him everything that had happened the day before, and he listened, his face growing darker with each word she spoke.

7

CASSIE

Illinois, May 2004

Silence engulfed the house. Bobby had been sleeping for an hour, and Birdie lay tucked in the bed Cassie had once snuggled into as a child.

"This is my new normal," Cassie murmured to herself.

She opened the duffel bag with her clothes and toiletries and took a few minutes to hang up her shirts and put her other clothes in the dresser. Henry's face grinned up at her from the family portrait she'd tucked in the bottom of the bag.

She set it on her nightstand and smiled, remembering how they'd laughed that day as the photographer had tried to put them in such awkward poses. The one in the frame had turned out to be the best shot, and Birdie's little face wasn't even looking at the camera. She stared adoringly up at her father.

How could she have imagined that two weeks later, their whole world would change when Henry took Birdie out for ice cream? She closed her eyes, remembering every word, every movement, like they were tattooed on her brain.

"I don't know, it's nearly bedtime," Cassie had said, winking at Henry over Birdie's head.

The little girl hopped off the bicycle and popped the kickstand out like she'd been doing it for years.

"Please, Mom? Pretty please!" she begged.

"Oh, come on, just this once, Cass! It's not every day a girl learns how to ride a bike without training wheels!" Henry gave his daughter a high five.

"How can I argue with that logic?" she laughed.

Henry took her hand. "Come on, you should join us!"

"I can't," she said. "I have to get this article sent off to the editor tonight. You guys go. Bring me home something good."

"All right, we'll get you some to go. Come on, Birdie! Race you to the car!" Henry circled around Birdie and then took off toward their sedan.

Birdie squealed in delight. "Bye, Mom!"

Cassie watched as Henry tucked Birdie into her seat and fastened the buckles. Always safety conscious, he'd insisted on the very best car seat on the market when Birdie came along.

They backed out of the driveway and headed down the street to their favorite ice cream place two miles away. If Cassie hurried, she could get the article proofed and sent off before they got home.

But they never came home. Instead, a police officer knocked on her door, and her whole world changed.

Cassie tried to choke back the tears, but a sob escaped her. Henry had died on impact when the semi-truck blew through a red light. Birdie, buckled in on the other side of the car, had survived. Doctors put her into a medically induced coma so her brain swelling would go down and hopefully prevent brain damage. For five days, Cassie put mourning the loss of her husband off while holding her unconscious daughter's hand in the hospital and funneling all her thoughts and energy into willing Birdie to wake up.

Birdie woke up on day six and impressed doctors with her recovery, but she wouldn't talk. After a battery of tests, they all agreed it was a psychological issue and she would talk when she was ready.

Fourteen months later, she still wasn't ready.

"Cassie?" Bobby's voice and a knock broke through Cassie's grief.

She blew her nose and put on her fake happy voice. "Come in."

Bobby pushed open the bedroom door and made her way to the bed. Cassie slid over as Bobby sat next to her and pulled her close. "Come here, my sweet girl."

Cassie pressed her cheek into the soft flannel of Bobby's nightgown as Bobby rubbed her back. A wave of nostalgia washed over her and suddenly, she was nine years old again and Bobby could fix anything for her. A fresh flood of tears poured down her face as she wished that were really true, but nobody could make this better.

"There, now. It's good to cry. Let the pain out."

She clung to her grandmother, and Bobby smoothed her hair. As her tears slowed, she sat up and wiped her face with a tissue. "I miss him so much."

"Of course you do," Bobby said. "And you always will. But you have to find a way to go on without him."

Cassie nodded. It was the same sentiment her mother had expressed, but for some reason, it felt less abrasive coming from Bobby. "I don't know how."

"It takes time. Do you ever talk to him?"

"What do you mean?"

Bobby gave a nonchalant shrug. "In the old world, we asked loved ones to come to us. Give us advice. Watch over us. You could ask Henry. Maybe a message from him will give you closure."

Cassie's eyes widened in surprise. "Did that ever work for you?"

Bobby stiffened as she pulled away from Cassie. "Maybe long ago. Not anymore." She stood, her shoulders drooping with weariness. "We should get some rest. Good night, Cassie." She shuffled out of the room, mumbling in Ukrainian.

"What are you saying?" Cassie called after her.

Bobby paused in the doorway and gripped the frame. "It's something my father used to say to me when I was young."

"What is it?"

Bobby turned to face Cassie and closed her eyes, as if retreating into herself. Her voice broke as she translated the words into English. "Just make it through today, and hope tomorrow will be better."

8

KATYA

Ukraine, May 1930

"Here, Katya. You're old enough now, and we may as well enjoy it while we can. Who knows when the activists will come take it?" Lavro poured a generous amount of *horilka* into a small cup for the next toast and handed it to her. Lavro made the best *horilka* around, and his brew never went out of demand.

For the first time during a gathering of neighbors like this, she was being treated as an adult. She glanced over at her parents and noted her father's slight nod. Her mother, however, frowned, so Katya pretended not to see her.

Pavlo's teasing voice spoke close, his breath tickling her ear. "Be careful. Lavro's *horilka* isn't for little girls."

She drove an elbow into his side and raised her cup with the other hand.

"Slava Ukrayini!" Lavro boomed as he stood, raising his glass.

Katya followed his lead, and echoed, "Glory to Ukraine!"

She shot back the drink, and the air in her lungs pushed out in a sharp rush. Lavro guffawed and stared at her with an expectant look on his face.

"Very good!" she choked, forcing a smile as the fiery liquid seared a path down her throat and warmed her stomach.

Satisfied with this praise, Lavro nodded as he continued to chuckle at her discomfort.

"I told you!" Pavlo grinned.

"I can handle it fine," Katya rasped.

Pavlo laughed and took her hand as Tomas began to speak. She tightened her grip on his rough, calloused hand and gave a contented sigh.

"Stalin has sent his activists here to take what is ours!" Lavro's cousin Tomas roared, catching everyone's attention. Lavro had invited several neighboring families to his house to enjoy a big meal and, as Katya had suspected it would, the discussion turned to the collective.

"We won't give it to them!" Lavro yelled as he began pouring another round of drinks for another toast. Katya abandoned her cup on the table so someone else could use it and took several steps back, ignoring Pavlo's snicker next to her.

"But that is not all he wants!" Tomas slapped the sturdy table with his hand for emphasis after he barked out each word.

Katya leaned forward, like everyone else, to better hear what he had to say.

"He seeks to crush us, to take away our spirit and everything that is Ukrainian. He sends in his activists, his Party, and his OGPU hanchmen. These Twenty-Five Thousanders! Fools from cities who don't know a wheat kernel from an ear of corn, brought here to make us join their collective farms. They try to tell us how to farm. Bah! Then, they take our priests, teachers, and our leaders. Our brothers, sisters, and neighbors! Stalin's men arrest them without a trial and deport or shoot them." Tomas slammed back the shot and banged down his cup as he looked at each person in turn.

Katya shuddered at the mention of people being deported. They hadn't heard any word from Fedir, Sasha, or her aunt and uncle, and she missed them. Still, Tomas's words mesmerized her. All around the room, everyone stared at him, riveted by his narrative. His voice surged through Katya and made her want to fight Stalin with her bare hands.

"But he isn't stopping at our people. No, now he wants our live-stock, our land, even the very tools we use to work it. Everything! We are to even give up our vegetable gardens! They want us to do the work and then depend solely on the Soviet government to pay us back with the fruits of our own labor! No!" he finished, slapping the table again. Slowly, his eyes scanned the room.

"I take care of my family, not some collective farm," Lavro said.

"But those who do not give in are branded *kulaks*," Tomas said. "What is a *kulak*, anyway? Anyone who disagrees with Stalin. Anyone who gets in the way of his big plan. They don't like you, then you are a *kulak*, and they can do whatever they want with you!" His voice rose with every word, until he was yelling.

A rustle of unease rippled through the crowd, and Pavlo shifted closer to Katya. The warm solidity of his body pressed close calmed her as people began to shoot worried glances around the room. Everyone agreed with Tomas, but the simple truth was that speaking such blasphemy aloud could get you killed. Anyone could be a spy. Anyone could turn you in.

"Still, some of our very own people welcome them with bread and salt! What are they thinking? These traitors to Ukraine will come to regret their choice, mark my words!" He waved a frustrated hand toward the remnants of the loaf of bread Lavro's wife had made for tonight.

Katya, along with each person attending, had ripped off a piece and dipped it in salt while entering the house. She tried to imagine her neighbors performing the same treasured tradition of hospitality for the man who had shot her cousin Serhiy, and anger made her see red.

"There are more of us here in our village than them. Their forces are far away; we must strike now and take down the activists they send to our villages before more come. Show them that we will not bow down to their will!" Tomas raised his fist in the air and shook it.

Katya sat, breathless, as people began to respond to his rousing talk. It was as if Tomas had looked inside her mind and vocalized all the things she couldn't. They should be fighting back! They should be standing up for themselves!

Always a strong presence in the village, Tomas somehow had managed to avoid arrest thus far. Now, here he was doing the very thing the state officials hoped to prevent—uniting them.

"And if that doesn't work?" A voice spoke out from across the room.

"We will fight for what is ours, and we will hold out as long as we are able. But if they force us to join their farm, then they will get nothing. They will not have our livestock."

"Nothing? How?" Katya asked without thinking. Mama reached over and pinched her arm in warning, but she had to know. "What can we do to stop them?"

"Maybe we can't stop them," Tomas said. "But we can ruin what they want before they take it."

"But they want the horses, the cows, and the chickens. How will you ruin them?" Tato asked.

"Kill them. Salt the meat and store it or sell it. They can't run their collective farms without any livestock. They want our farm tools, too. So, break the tools, ruin the plows, burn your implements. If they don't have what they need, the collective farms will fail, and then maybe they will give up this ridiculous plan."

Her mother gripped her arm. "Come, Katya, it's getting late, and we must get you home."

"I'm fine, Mama," Katya protested, but the daggers shooting from her mother's eyes left no room for discussion.

Pavlo squeezed her hand. "I'll meet you later, all right?"

Katya barely had time to nod a reply to him as Mama dragged her out of the house. Tato followed, offering apologies.

Mama crackled with anger. "We should have never gone there. I didn't know that he was going to talk about a revolt."

Tato scanned the area. "I never met that young man who sat near the door."

"Lavro said it was his cousin, but still, how do we know we can trust him? How can we trust anyone these days? Everyone in the village is turning against each other." Mama shook her head. "And with Katya there! I thought it was a simple gathering of friends, not a call for resistance."

Katya kept her voice even. "I'm not a child anymore, Mama, and I think Tomas was right. We should have stayed longer to see if they plan anything."

"No!" Mama clutched a hand to her chest. "It's far too dangerous!"

"What's dangerous is sitting back and doing nothing while they take everything from us," Katya said, careful to speak clearly and make her point. Lavro's *horilka* left fuzzy thoughts competing for attention in her head.

"Hush, Katya. Your mother is right. We should have left even earlier. I'm only glad Alina stayed home with Kolya and his parents." Tato frowned. "I should have made Pavlo come home, but he's old enough now to make his own decisions."

Katya's shoulders tensed. "And I'm not?"

"No, you're not," Mama snapped.

"I agree with a lot of what Tomas said, but to say it in front of everyone like that is foolish. Nothing good will come of what happened tonight," Tato said. He put an arm around Mama's shoulders, and Katya could see that her mother was struggling not to cry.

* * *

The next morning, Lavro's knocks woke them. Katya strained to hear what he said to Tato, but she couldn't make anything out.

"What is it?" Mama asked as Tato closed the door, the creases between her eyes deepening inside her furrowed brows.

Tato rubbed his chin. "They came and took Tomas away in the middle of the night."

Mama's sharp intake of breath was the only sound in the room for a minute. Katya's bravado faltered as she watched awareness transform her mother's face from sleepy to terrified. They were at the meeting with him, so they would also be on the list of traitors.

Mama wrung her hands. "At least Alina wasn't there, so she should be safe."

Alina sat on the edge of their bed, hugging a shawl to her chest with wide eyes.

Tato snorted. "You think that matters? She's part of this family, and if they label us as enemies of the people because of last night, they will label her as one too."

"We must prepare, just in case." Mama got to her feet. "Katya, Alina, gather your warmest clothes and whatever food we have into bundles. If we're to be deported to the cold of Siberia, we'll be ready.'

Nausea rolled over Katya, and her legs dragged like lead weights as she hurried to do her mother's bidding. She made small bundles of extra clothes, blankets, and some dried fruit and bread, and, with shaking hands, stuffed them into old flour sacks. Last night, she'd wanted to fight back, and now, she only wanted to disappear.

When she'd finished, she paced the room. "Do you think they'll really deport us?"

"I don't know. Sit down, Katya," Mama said. "You're making me nervous."

"Sorry, Mama." Katya dropped into a chair next to Alina, who'd taken up some mending. "How can you sew in a time like this? I can't even think straight."

"I sew because I have a hole in my good skirt, and it needs to be repaired." The forced calmness in Alina's voice only made Katya more anxious.

"I want to see Pavlo," she said. She craved his calming presence like the town drunk craved *horilka*.

"We can't go anywhere," Alina said. "You know that."

Katya jumped up as an idea occurred to her. "Maybe we can! Maybe we should take the wagon and leave the village."

Tato set his jaw. "I will not be chased off my land."

"Where would we go?" Mama asked. "Nowhere is safe. They're checking travelers, and we could be stopped and arrested on the road just as easily as here. No, we should wait here. Maybe they won't realize we were there, and it will all blow over."

So, all that day they waited for the OGPU to come. At every noise, they jumped, certain that it was death knocking on the door. After lunch, Kolya, Pavlo, and Yosyp came and talked to Tato for a few minutes, but they didn't stay to visit, and Katya didn't get to speak to Pavlo alone. They shared a look, he squeezed her arm, and then his father ushered him out the door. He didn't want to leave his wife home alone for long.

Katya stared after him as he walked away, worried it would be the last time she ever saw him, and an awful feeling of helplessness rushed through her. Was this her life now? Constant fear and worry?

When they made it through the daylight hours, Mama became convinced that the OGPU men were waiting for the darkness of the night like they typically did. Nobody slept, expecting state officials to come barreling through the door at any moment to take them, but they didn't come that night either. Over the next few days, Katya allowed herself to be lulled into a sense of complacency and, with Tomas gone, talk of resistance abated in the village.

* * *

Spring and summer blurred together into their typical flurry of labor. Katya's family worked hard in their fields—sowing their spring crops, tending their kitchen garden, and today they'd finished taking in the winter wheat harvest they'd planted last fall. Her back and legs ached, but it was the satisfying ache born of a good day's work. Katya relished it, though she couldn't help the sigh of relief that escaped her as she sat on the stool next to the cow for the evening milking.

"Katya?"

Pavlo's voice made her jump, and she spun around.

"What are you doing here?"

Pavlo's smile didn't reach his eyes as he pushed the door closed. "Can't I come see my girl?"

"Of course, but I can tell something is bothering you." She stood and hugged him, ignoring her stiff muscles and inhaling the smell of woodsmoke and leather oil that was uniquely him.

Pavlo's hand absently stroked her hair. "There's a group of activists going around taking surpluses of grain and food from homes to fill government quotas. They say it belongs to the state, and if you aren't in the collective, you owe twice as much as someone who is."

"How did you find this out?" Dread soured her stomach as she thought of the beautiful golden wheat stacked in their barn, waiting to be threshed.

"They came to my uncle's house. They took everything he had, even the seed he'd put away for his fall planting of winter wheat." Pavlo pulled away and paced. "It's a ploy to get them into the collective. Take their grain so they can't plant or make bread—then they have nothing unless they join and get their own goods doled back out to them for a price."

"My father mentioned hiding some grain." The cow lowed impatiently, so Katya sat back on the stool and began to milk as she talked. "I know the taxes he'll have to pay will be high, but maybe we should separate what we have left. Keep small stores of it—and other things we may need—in different areas."

Pavlo grinned, and this time, his whole face lit up. "Ah, Katya, you're so smart. I came here to tell you the same thing. It's not much, but it's something to do at least."

* * *

The next week—with their parents' blessing—Katya and Pavlo each took a small tin of wheat, as well as some food, and met in the woods behind their homes. Walking under the clear, cold starlight with Pavlo almost felt like a treat, until Katya snapped a twig underfoot, and they both froze in fear. When a few minutes passed with no one stepping out to arrest them, her pulse slowed.

"I'm sorry," she whispered. "I'll be more careful."

Pavlo squeezed her hand, his voice low. "I'm just glad to be alone with you."

Despite the relative newness of their romance, the ease born of a lifetime of close friendship made it feel natural to pull him closer. This evolution of their camaraderie into love rang true in every part of her being.

As they moved deep into the woods, Katya pointed to a large, gnarly oak that would be easy to find again. "There's a hole in the base of that tree. We can hide everything there."

Pavlo nodded. "We'll fill it in with leaves, too, so no one will notice it."

They worked as fast as they could, digging into the rotting leaves and dirt with a small spade Pavlo had brought before tucking the tins into the hole. As Katya brushed her hands off on her skirt, Pavlo leaned over and kissed her.

Her body stilled as his lips met hers. Even amid the fear and worry, his touch still made her tremble. When he pulled away, reality rushed back in like a cold splash of water, and she moved toward him again, desperate to erase the frightening truth of their lives. Pavlo gave a low groan and kissed her, his lips moving fast and hot across hers. His hands tangled in her hair and ran down her back before he pulled away again.

"We should get back before we do things we shouldn't yet," he said, his voice low and husky.

A surge of frustration flashed through her. "Yet? What are you waiting for? You love me, don't you?"

Pavlo's eyebrows shot up, and he began to laugh. He covered his mouth to muffle the sound, but his shoulders still shook with mirth.

"It's not funny!" Katya stood and glowered at him.

"You're right," he sputtered out between throes of silent laughter. Finally, he took a few deep breaths and sighed. "Such spirit you have. This is why I love you. And this is why I want to marry you. Soon. Before we go any further down this path. But, with all of the uncertainty in our lives, I have not been able to earn the money I need to court you properly. Please, let me fix that." He took her hands in his. "Katya, you have been my best friend forever. I love you more than life itself. Marry me. Say you'll be my wife, and we can weather what comes together."

"Yes! Yes!" She threw her arms around him with such gusto that they toppled backward, laughing out loud, and for a moment, forgetting they should be quiet. He kissed her then, silencing them both.

"Maybe we can marry alongside Kolya and Alina," she said. "Their wedding isn't far off."

"The sooner the better," Pavlo agreed, before giving a short chuckle. "Do you remember when you scattered the chickens after my mother asked me to fetch one for supper?"

Katya laughed, then slapped her hand over her mouth. "How could I forget? You were so mad you dangled me over the pigpen, threatening to drop me in. My mother would have killed me for ruining my good clothes!"

Pavlo stroked her cheek with his work–roughened hands. "You fought like a rabid dog. You've become a fierce and beautiful woman, but that was the first time I saw you as anything more than a bossy, trouble-making girl, and I knew, someday, I would marry you."

"That was two years ago! You waited long enough to tell me of the plans you'd made with my life."

"We were young yet. I didn't want to scare you off."

"Yes, very wise to avoid scaring me off by trying to throw me in with the pigs," Katya giggled. "Well, since you're sharing this with me, I'll tell you what I noticed that day."

"What did you notice, other than how bad the pigs smell?"

"Well, you were always a small boy. Skinny. No muscles."

"I thought you were going to tell me something flattering." Pavlo frowned.

"I am!" Katya said. "That day, when you were holding me, I noticed that you were no longer a skinny boy."

"Oh." Pavlo grinned. "Then what was I?"

"A man. A man with thick arms, strong from working in the fields. A man with a broad chest and an easy smile. I even noticed that you had some whiskers finally growing in." She tickled his chin and shrugged. "Eh, I wouldn't say I loved you, but I thought you were at least starting to improve."

Pavlo threw his head back and shook with silent laughter, then wrapped his arms around her and nuzzled her neck. "I lied. I have loved you since the first time we toddled around the fields together while our parents harvested. You have always been the one for me."

They made their way home, holding hands. Katya thought she might burst from both the adrenaline rush of sneaking around hiding food and the overwhelming love she felt for the man next to her.

"You are my calm in this storm." She raised his hand up and kissed his knuckles.

They met again the next night, and the next, until they'd secreted away a lot of the extra stores of food from their households, hauling rye, millet, flour, and buckwheat to the forest and fields, hiding them in areas they had played in as children. They detailed the locations in sparsely worded notes tucked under a loose board in Katya's barn loft so they wouldn't forget where anything was, and then they waited.

* * *

A few weeks later, a sharp banging on the door woke her.

Tato stumbled to the door, still in his nightshirt and struggling to put his pants on as he went. Her eyes fell to the bundles of clothes and blankets that still rested next to the door—her mother refused to put them away in case they were arrested—and she shivered.

"Who's there?" Tato called out. His tall, strong frame filled the doorway, but his white-knuckled grip gave away his fear that he could not protect his family from what lay on the other side of the door.

Katya's heart banged so hard against her ribs she thought everyone must hear it thumping. She wrapped a shawl around her shoulders as she pulled them back and stuck her chin in the air. Alina touched her hand and Katya gripped it, trying to quell her sister's trembling.

A voice with a Russian accent bellowed, "We've come to collect your grain for your taxes. Open up!"

It had taken some convincing to get Mama to agree to sending things out to be buried in the fields and woods, but now, her eyes met Katya's across the room, and gratitude shone in them. Despite the tension in the room, a small sense of victory surged through Katya.

Tato looked over at Mama. She stood up, pulled herself to her full height, and nodded her head. He opened the door and they barreled into the small home so fast that Tato barely had time to get out of the way. The door slammed into the wall, and two large men in dark over-coats began scanning the room with narrowed gazes.

Katya's smile faded. She'd never seen the first man with the accent, a Russian with dark hair, and mustache. One of the Soviet officials brought in for collectivization, he exuded power, but he was not the muscle of the group. That role fell to the local drunkard, Prokyp. He bullied, stole, and begged when he needed to and had never done a productive thing in his life. All of the wrongs Prokyp imagined done to him were used to fuel his fire against his fellow villagers, making him the perfect pawn for the activists to employ. Everyone despised him.

The hulking frames of the men overshadowed the slight woman with them. Even bundled heavily in wraps, Katya recognized her: Irina, the wife of the village teacher. They probably made her come to lend a sense of security, as she was a local, but the look on her pinched face erased any smidgen of reassurance Katya might have felt. Irina's pale cheeks led to nervous eyes that darted around, afraid to land on their faces and connect with them.

"Where is your grain?" Prokyp growled. "Our collective is not filling its goal."

"We aren't members of the collective." Tato drew himself up and glared at Prokyp. "My grain is my own."

Katya swelled with pride at her father's strong words.

Prokyp chuckled, and Irina flinched as if someone had struck her. "Even better. You say you're not members. Well, then, your tax is even higher."

"We have nothing left." Tato stood firm but paled. "We've given everything for taxes. I filled my quota."

"The quotas have been raised," the Russian man said. The high, nasally voice didn't match his tall frame, and his face wore a look of disgust as he perused their home. "Search the place." He nodded toward Prokyp.

"You can't do this!" Katya said.

"Silence your child." The Russian glared at Tato. "Or I will do it for you."

Her father shot her a murderous look, and she bit her lip. Sweat popped out on her forehead as Prokyp lumbered around their home, overturning beds and blankets and pulling open cupboards. He found some butter and a small sack of flour meant for bread making the next day and passed it to Irina, who placed it in her bag without looking up.

Mama winced as they took the food, but her face remained an

emotionless mask until he reached the corner of the house that held the religious icons. With undisguised glee, Prokyp swung his hand across the shelf, pushing holy water, candles, and the psalm book to the ground. He tore down the *rushnyk* Mama had lovingly stitched to adorn the religious icons and knocked down the pictures. They crunched under Prokyp's feet as he reached over to take the cross off the wall and slip it into his bag.

With a low moan, Mama slapped a hand to her mouth and leaned onto the table. Irina's eyes skittered toward them, then fell to the ground in sympathy. She turned her back to the men and hastily crossed herself.

"Is that necessary?" Tato spoke through gritted teeth.

Prokyp ignored him and made his way to Alina and Katya. They stood together, hands still clasped. "And you girls?" he said in a disgusting, sweet voice. "You pretty girls. Do you have any grain hidden in your clothes? We've found quite a bit sewn into the skirts of the fair ladies of our village."

Katya's stomach threatened to heave as his dirty hands reached toward Alina. She whimpered as he placed his paws on her shoulders. Slower than necessary, he ran his hands down along the sides of her breasts to her hips. His lips curled into a repulsive sneer as he made his way down her legs.

"Take your hands off her!" Fury surged through Katya, and she yanked Alina back at the same time her father stepped closer and shouted, "Don't touch my daughters!"

A sharp click echoed in the room, and everyone froze. The Russian's cocked pistol pointed at Tato. "Are you resisting orders? If you are, we will have to label you an enemy of the people. We all know what happens to enemies of the people. I could shoot you right now, and nobody would care."

Katya's head buzzed. All the anger she'd felt morphed into sheer terror as she stared at her Tato. His beet-red face glistened with sweat and his hands curled slowly into fists, the anger crackling off him like a hungry fire seeking fuel. If someone didn't intercede, he would be shot for attempting to murder Prokyp with his bare hands.

Mama, too, saw his inner struggle, for she stepped in front of Tato and spoke calmly. "I apologize for my husband's behavior. He's over-protective of his daughters. He didn't mean what he said. We'll cooperate, I swear it."

The Russian smirked and lowered his gun. Dropping Alina's hand, Katya pulled her father into a hug and spoke in his ear. "Please, Tato, there is no harm done, but we can't lose you. Please." She felt the tension lessen from his body, but vibrations of anger still throbbed like the veins on his neck.

Prokyp watched the scene with amusement, then sauntered back over to his cohorts, smiling. The Russian turned to him and asked with complete sincerity, "Have you been offended by this man? What would you like to do, Comrade?"

Prokyp glanced at Tato and then at Alina, who was white as a sheet, but holding her head high as Mama had taught them to. Katya's legs wobbled, so she locked her knees and held her breath as they waited for this fool to decide the fate of their family.

"I suppose I can overlook it this once, as long as he and his family promise to cooperate fully in the future." His gaze lingered on Alina. "But we shall have to check back here often to make sure they are behaving."

Another activist pushed into the house with a large sack of wheat balanced on his shoulder. "I found this, and another just like it, hidden in the barn loft."

Katya's heart sank. She'd worried the wheat in the barn wasn't hidden well enough, but Tato thought it safe out of sight beneath the hay.

"You can't take that!" Tato shouted. "It's my seed for planting this fall!"

"This will pay your quota. For now." The Russian waved a hand dismissively, as if suddenly bored by them. "Come, we must move to the next house."

The woman cast an apologetic look toward Mama and hurried behind the men as they left. The door swung wildly in their wake, and none of them moved until Tato strode forward and slammed it shut, though not before Katya saw the activists' cart stacked high with sacks of grain, just like the ones they'd taken from the barn.

9

CASSIE

Illinois, May 2004

The next afternoon, Anna bustled into the kitchen, arms full of bags. "I've brought sustenance!"

Cassie set down the book she'd been reading, stood, and took a bag from her mom. "Thanks. This is a big help."

"Well, I didn't want you worrying about leaving Bobby. Where is she?"

"She's taking a nap. Birdie was about to do the same, weren't you?" Cassie gave her daughter a weary glance. The little girl looked up from the picture she'd been drawing with the new box of crayons Anna had brought the other day.

"Oh, I was thinking Birdie and I could go for a walk." Anna looked hopefully at Cassie. "Just around the block. The fresh air will help her go down for a nap, don't you think?"

Birdie jumped up and down, her hands clasped under her chin.

Cassie threw her arms up in resignation. "It's worth a try. Nothing else has worked today."

Birdie clapped, then held up her picture to show them.

"Very pretty," Anna said. "Those look like sunflowers."

Birdie nodded vigorously as Cassie peered down at the drawing. "This is really nice, Birdie." Cassie traced her finger around one of the dozens of sunflowers that filled the page. In the center, two long haired stick figures held hands. Birdie added a few small flowers to their hair, then threw down her crayon and ran to put on her shoes.

"Seems like she's ready," Cassie said. "Why don't you go now, and I'll put the groceries away?"

"Great!" Anna said. She grabbed Harvey's leash. "Come on, Birdie."

Birdie pulled on her shoes as Cassie began unpacking the bags.

"Pretty random assortment, Mom," Cassie said as she pulled out a second container of baby spinach leaves and a package of beef bones. "I hope you're coming over to cook all this stuff."

"It's what Bobby wanted," Anna called out before stepping outside.

Cassie stored most of the food in the fridge and dug around the cabinets until she found the best places to put the macaroni and cheese and granola bars. She thought Bobby would at least have had some sardines or instant rice tucked away for a quick meal, but the cabinets were surprisingly bare.

She had everything put away and a kettle of water on for tea when Birdie and Anna returned.

"You'll never guess who we ran into down the street," Anna said. "Nick!"

"Who's Nick?" Cassie kissed Birdie on the cheek. "Go lay in your bed. I'll come check on you in a little bit, okay?"

"You know, Nick. Mrs. Koval's grandson. From the hospital?"

Cassie set the box of teabags on the table. "Oh. Him. I'm having tea. Want some?"

"Sure," Anna said as she sat down. "Well, remember we thought it was a bit weird how eager he was to help with Bobby?"

"Yeah. I haven't seen him." Cassie poured hot water into two mugs and set them on the table. "Though the newspaper was on the front porch mat this morning. Perfectly centered."

"Probably him," Anna said with a nod as she selected a teabag and dunked it. "Anyway, I really like him."

"That's quite a turnaround from, 'keep an eye on him.'" Cassie made air quotes with her fingers.

"I know," Anna said. "But Birdie and I saw him working in his front yard at the end of the block, and get this: he was planting hollyhock bulbs."

"So?" Cassie shrugged as she took a seat.

"For his grandma." Anna sat back smugly, as if this explained everything.

"His dead grandma?"

Anna nodded, grinning.

"You are inordinately happy about this. What's the big deal? Are you sure you feel all right?" She rested the back of her hand against her mother's forehead. "You're not warm."

Anna laughed and pushed her away. "I'm fine. My point is, not many men often think about their grandmothers, let alone plant flower bulbs in their yards to commemorate them. He's a good guy."

"So, you're basing your entire assessment on the fact that he's planting flowers?" Cassie raised an eyebrow at her mother as she dropped a teabag into her mug.

"For his dead grandmother!" Anna leaned forward. "That's the crucial factor. Anyway, we stopped and chatted for a few minutes, Birdie hiding behind my legs, of course, and he really is a nice guy. He said he'll keep an eye out for you guys around the neighborhood."

"Now he's keeping an eye on me?" Cassie shook her head. "You really know how to do a total one-eighty, Mom."

Anna smiled. "Someday, you'll see what I mean. It's the little things you look for in a man, Cassie. They can tell you so much. And this is one of those little things."

"I'm not looking for anything in a man." Cassie glared at her mother.

"I know that." Anna blew on her tea. "He asked about you."

"What? Why?" Cassie's face flushed, and she dropped her head to hide it from her mom.

"He must have noticed your wedding ring." Anna tapped the plain gold band on Cassie's finger. "He asked when your husband would be joining you."

Cassie pulled her hand back, her voice flat. "Did you tell him my husband is dead?"

Anna's expression softened. "In nicer terms, yes. He said he was really sorry to hear that, and if there was anything he could do to help as you settle in, to let him know."

"Well, isn't he the perfect neighbor," Cassie grumbled.

"You don't have to get snippy." Anna put her hands up in surrender. "I just wanted to let you know that we don't have to worry about him like we were."

Cassie frowned. "I'm not so easily convinced."

"About what?" Bobby asked as she came into the kitchen. Her hair was rumpled, and her eyes sleepy. She lowered herself into the chair and scooted toward the table.

"Nothing," Cassie said. "Do you want something to eat?"

Bobby didn't respond. Her gaze had locked on Birdie's drawing, still sitting on the table. Her face paled, and she put her knobby left hand to her chest. "What's this?"

"Birdie drew it earlier," Anna said. "Isn't it pretty?"

Birdie, who had ignored Cassie's request to lay down and snuck back into the kitchen, clutched at Bobby's arm. She pointed at one of the girls in the drawing, then pointed at Bobby. Bobby's head snapped around to stare at Birdie, then jerked back toward the picture.

Birdie's smile wavered as Bobby's eyes filled with tears, and she looked at Cassie.

Cassie swallowed the reprimand for Birdie about not staying in bed and rushed over and took the drawing. "It's lovely, Birdie. I think Bobby's just not feeling well right now."

Bobby patted Birdie's hand, then pushed herself up out of the chair. "Yes, it's very good. I think I'm going to sit on the patio for a bit. Get some fresh air." She shuffled to the back door.

Cassie exchanged a worried glance with her mother as she waited for Bobby to get out of earshot. "We should go after her."

Anna waved a hand. "Go ahead."

"Me?" Cassie raised her eyebrows.

"We always end up fighting. Maybe she'll open up to you more."

"Doubt it," Cassie said, but she pulled open the glass door and poked her head out into the warm spring air. The scent of dirt and new life filled Cassie's nose as she inhaled. "It's nice out here today," she commented, trying to break the ice. "I love the smell of spring."

Bobby pulled an old leatherbound book out of her housecoat pocket, ignoring Cassie.

"What's that?" Cassie tried to control her excitement at seeing the journal from Bobby's nightstand again. She slid into the chair next to her grandmother.

Bobby stroked the scuffed cover and spoke slowly, as if the words pained her. "This is me. Or who I once was."

It's hers! Goosebumps rose on Cassie's arms, and she stilled, afraid to break the trance Bobby seemed to be under.

"I thought if I waited long enough, it would be easier to go back." Bobby opened the book, and an anguished sigh escaped her lips.

Cassie leaned closer and peered down at the crowded writing. She couldn't read the Ukrainian words, but her hands itched to grab the book so she could finally touch a tangible part of Bobby's elusive past.

Bobby's fingers trembled as they made contact with the page, and she closed her eyes. "I told him I would."

"Would what?" Cassie said. "Told who?"

"But I can't. I can't do it." She closed the book and shoved it back into her housecoat pocket. Cassie cringed at the lost opportunity, but as the book slipped away, a picture slid out and floated to the floor.

Cassie let it fall without comment, afraid that if Bobby noticed it, she'd tuck it away with the book and she'd never see it again. She promised herself she'd return it to Bobby after she had the chance to look at it.

Bobby glanced up toward the big mulberry tree in her backyard. "Do you see that owl?"

Cassie followed Bobby's gaze to where a large brown owl perched on the branches of the tree.

"Isn't it strange to see one out during the day?" Cassie asked, trying to keep up with the odd turn in the conversation.

Bobby tightened her lips. "It's a sign. It's waiting for me to die."

Cassie gaped at her. "Don't say things like that!"

The owl hooted and flew away, as if admitting its complicity in Bobby's death.

Bobby waved away Cassie's words. "Young people today don't remember the stories. Last week, a sparrow flew into my bedroom window."

"So? That means you have really clean windows."

"Now this owl. And Birdie's drawing." Bobby bowed her head. "All of these things mean something, Cassie. She's waiting for me."

"Who is waiting for you?" Cassie turned to face her grandmother. "Bobby, are you sure you're feeling okay? You're acting really strange today."

"I must answer for what I've done." Bobby stood on shaky legs and hobbled back into the house, the journal in her pocket thumping against her leg as she went. "I need a little time alone. I'll be in my room."

As the door shut behind Bobby, Cassie leaned over and picked up the picture. The faded black and white photo bore the creases and wrinkles of age. Two teenage girls with identical smiles looked out at her. They each wore a wreath of flowers in their braided hair and white shirts with finely detailed flowers and vines on the sleeves. Arm in arm, they bowed their heads toward each other in an obvious display of affection. In the background, a field of sunflowers stretched to the sky.

10

KATYA

Ukraine, October 1930

Nobody expected the early snow that fell and covered the beauty of fall's golden colors, but Katya loved it. Large pretty flakes floated down from the sky, slowly blanketing the brown earth, and pieces of it snuck into the house when she opened the door to admire the white landscape.

"I can't believe it's snowing already." Alina leaned over Katya's shoulder and stared outside.

"I think it's beautiful," Katya said.

Alina frowned. "Yes, but it's not what I'd imagined for today."

"None of it is, though, is it?" Katya put her arm around Alina and squeezed. "But we'll still be happy. We're getting married today!"

Despite all of their plans for the big day, they'd had to make concessions. It couldn't be a grand affair like Olha and Boryslav had enjoyed. The push to join the collective farm remained strong. Arrests and deportations kept everyone on edge as activists patrolled and made house visits in search of grain, gold, jewels, and anything else they claimed they needed. A large wedding would only draw attention, so it had to be small, secretive, and soon.

"Let's be thankful that my cousin Vasyl is now a priest and hasn't been deported yet. We're lucky he's in the area now so he can marry you quietly," Mama said. "Now close the door. You're letting all the heat out."

"That's right. Remember, girls, always look to the future." Tato pulled on his coat as he bestowed one of his most often-used fatherly pieces of advice on them. "Now, I'll leave you ladies to get ready. I'm going to see what the men are up to."

"I don't mind that we can't have a big wedding," Alina said a few minutes after Tato left. "This will be more intimate."

"Yes, it will." Katya twisted Alina's thick raven locks into two braids. "And a big wedding doesn't change your love for each other. Any fool can see you two are meant to be."

"I've loved him as long as I can remember. And I could say the same for you and Pavlo. You, who used to tease me about how lovesick I was, are now worse than me!"

"Maybe so," Katya admitted. "I know it's too soon for this, but I want to see how it looks." Katya set the myrtle wreath *vinok* on Alina's head and stepped back to admire her sister. "You look stunning, Alina."

"Oh, you do." Mama sat down at the table with a bundle of their clothing.

"How lucky we are to have such wonderful men nearby," Alina said as she swapped places with Katya so she could braid Katya's long, dark hair. "To think, the two little boys who came to play in our yard would be your future sons-in-law! Now, our families will be doubly connected."

Alina's face glowed with joy, and Katya hoped she looked half as lovely today as her sister.

"These turned out so beautiful." Mama unfolded the skirts and shirts they had been working on for the ceremony and ran her hand down the embroidered sleeves. "You know, when I decided to marry your father, my mother and I—"

Mama froze as the door burst open and Kolya stumbled in. His normally sunny face was clouded over with terror as he scanned the room.

"Kolya!" Mama gasped. "What's wrong?"

Along with the wood smoke and clean, cold winter air, Katya smelled fear on him, and it leeched its way over to her and crept into her bones. In an instant, she was out of her seat and striding toward him without any conscience thought of doing so. "Where is your brother? Where is my father?"

He ignored her, and his wild eyes locked onto Alina's.

Katya repeated herself, louder, and his lips trembled with what he wanted to say, but no words came out.

She couldn't bear his silence. Though small next to his large frame, Katya reached up with a quick hand and slapped his cheek. He didn't flinch, but he finally looked down at her with a dazed expression.

"Speak!" Her voice, now frantic with worry, cracked. "Tell us what happened!"

Kolya gulped. Sweat beaded on his forehead, despite the chill in the room. His breaths came short and fast.

"They... the activists and OGPU came..." He spoke haltingly, as if he had forgotten how to do it, but when he finally started talking, the words flowed as if he were purging himself of the violence he'd witnessed. "I was in the barn. I saw them coming down the road, but I stayed back." He shook his head, as if disgusted with himself and repeated, "I stayed back."

"Go on, then!" Katya ordered.

"My father and yours met them outside. They said someone turned my father in as an enemy of the people. When they tried to arrest him, he protested, and they shot him." Kolya's voice broke. "Another man threw your father to the ground and kept a rifle pressed to his back. I heard Pavlo yelling, so I ran around to the back of the house. I thought

I could come in the kitchen window and help him, but it all happened so fast."

"Did they shoot my father?" Katya fought to keep her voice steady. "What happened to Pavlo?"

Kolya stared at the ground as he went on, his face a pale, emotionless mask. "A man hit Pavlo in the back of his head with the butt of his rifle, then shot him. My mother screamed, and threw herself on him, and they shot her, too. They said it would be easier to just kill them all."

The cold knot of fear that had formed when Katya first saw Kolya twisted in her belly. Slowly, it spread throughout her, turning her veins to ice, numbing everything. Her body went limp and her knees wobbled, but the ice kept her frozen, and standing.

"No!" Katya shook her head. "You're wrong!"

Kolya gave a strangled sob. "I wish I was."

"And what of my husband?" Mama was on her feet now, hands clasped in front of her chest.

"They arrested him." He grabbed a chair and collapsed into it. "My family is dead," he said. "My whole family is dead, and I hid like a coward while they were murdered."

Mama choked back a sob and sat back in her chair, her fist in her mouth. Alina rushed toward Kolya and took him in her arms.

"I have to see him." Katya went to the door and put on her coat. She could picture his smiling face clearly, laughing and telling her this was all a sick joke. Katya shook her head to clear it. She needed to stay focused. She needed to keep the ice running through her veins until this was done. "And we have to go to Tato. Right, Mama?"

Her words finally prompted Mama to action, but she moved slowly, as if uncertain of what to do. She pulled on her shawl and stood, her eyes glassy. "Yes. That's right."

Katya stared at her mother in surprise, waiting for the strong woman who always knew what to do to issue instructions, but her mother remained motionless at the door.

"Kolya and I will go to his farm, and you and Alina must go see about Tato," Katya finally said. "He was only visiting. He shouldn't be charged with anything."

Mama nodded stiffly. "Yes, that's a good plan."

Katya followed Kolya to the door, the image of Mama dazed and speechless stuck in her head. While Mama froze, immobile with fear, Katya had stepped up and taken charge. The change of roles disconcerted her.

As they stepped into the snowy day, those thoughts faded away. Pavlo needed to be taken care of; Tato had to be saved. She had to focus on what must be done rather than to think of what had happened. Later, she would let herself sort through the confusion of the day.

I am ice. I feel nothing. Katya chanted this over and over to herself as she walked behind Kolya, stepping carefully into each snowy footprint he made. Her refrain and concentrating on where she stepped kept her feet dry and her mind occupied enough so that she could almost not think about what had happened. Almost.

Five minutes later, she followed Kolya through the front gate. Sorrow pervaded the atmosphere and the warm, welcoming mood she'd known her whole life was now tainted with fear and the metallic smell of blood.

Yosyp lay across the doorway, half inside, half outside, his body sprawled awkwardly with one leg tucked under the other and his torso twisted to the side. Fat snowflakes fell on him, dusting his dark hair and slowly covering his body. Congealed blood glared out from his chest. Her hand flew to her mouth as her stomach lurched. She closed her eyes and prayed it had been a quick death.

"I'll bring him inside." Kolya spoke at her shoulder, his voice hoarse. "You go in to Pavlo and my mother."

The front door hung open, swaying gently in the wind. She stepped over Yosyp's body and into the house. It took her eyes a second to adjust to the dim room from the glaring white snow, but as the scene came into focus, she wished the snow had left her blind forever.

Blood splattered the walls. Chairs lay turned on their sides; linens were strewn all over the floor. Despite the chaos, two tin mugs still rested on the table where Tato had probably sat with Yosyp, discussing the situation in the village or the upcoming marriage of their children.

Her gaze dropped to Pavlo, stretched out on the floor right inside the door, his face turned away from her and his shoulder soaked in blood. Pavlo's mother lay face down over his chest, her arms splayed out around him.

A strangled sob lodged in Katya's throat. Tears rolled out of her eyes and their heat on her cold cheeks surprised her. The ice she'd imagined running through her couldn't keep her safe from this pain. She was melting.

She dropped to her knees at their sides. A trickle of sweat ran down between Katya's shoulder blades, and her hands shook as she pulled the older woman onto her back next to her son. Her eyes, the same color as Pavlo's, stared up, wide with surprise. Streaks of Pavlo's blood smeared her face and hair. With soft fingers, Katya closed her eyes. Her hand came away wet with blood, and a small cry of anguish slipped past her quivering lips. She wiped it off on her skirt, but the skin on her fingers throbbed where it had touched.

A jagged pain tore through her gut as she dragged her eyes to Pavlo. Although she could see his body lying there in a pool of blood, the idea that she would never talk to him again was so foreign that it felt impossible. How could they not stare up into the clouds together and pick out pictures? How could they not fight over the names of the ten children they wanted to have together? How could she have a future without him in it?

She took a deep, shuddering breath and willed herself to go on. *I can do this. I must do this.* She gripped his good shoulder with a tremulous hand. Despite the cold day, his skin still felt warm through his shirt. She paused, closing her eyes and gathering what strength she had left, then, resolutely, pulled him toward her. His head rolled, landing next to her lap.

Katya stared down into the face of the man she loved and gasped as his eyelids fluttered. A tiny glimmer of hope rushed through her, and she jumped to her feet in disbelief.

"Kolya, come quick! Pavlo's alive!" Katya fell back to her knees and ripped open Pavlo's shirt to reveal the bullet hole: a clean shot into his upper back with an exit wound out of his shoulder.

"He's alive?" Kolya dropped down next to her and peered at the wound. "The bullet went right through him. Maybe it didn't hit anything vital."

"Let's get him on the bed," she instructed, her voice shrill.

With Katya at his feet and Kolya gripping under his arms, they moved Pavlo's limp body to the bed on the *pich*.

"Go fetch hot water!" Katya grabbed a sheet and began ripping long bandages. Together, she and Kolya carefully cleaned the wound, then splashed it with some *horilka* that had been set aside for the wedding celebration. Pavlo thrashed as the liquor burned his wound, but he didn't wake up.

"He's lost a lot of blood," Kolya said as Katya dried the skin around the gash.

"He'll be fine." Katya glared at Kolya, daring him to disagree. "Now prop him up so I can wrap this bandage around him."

"His head is bleeding, too. Where they hit him." Kolya tilted Pavlo's head so Katya could view the large knot behind his ear, seeping blood. "That's probably why he's unconscious."

"Maybe he passed out from the pain," she said.

Kolya snorted. "Not Pavlo. He is as tough as old leather."

"That's why he'll be fine now," Katya said with a firm nod. Nothing could make her think otherwise. She'd thought she'd lost him forever, but this mercy, this reprieve, had given her another chance with him, and she'd be damned if she let him slip away again.

Mama and Alina burst into the house, but before they had a chance to speak, Katya shouted, "He's alive! Pavlo's alive!"

Mama rushed over and examined him. "You've cleaned it well, Katya? We cannot risk infection."

"Yes, like you showed me when Tato cut his hand. Where is he?"

Mama straightened. "He's being held."

Katya's heart sank. Mama pressed her lips tight, the look on her face warning Katya not to ask any more questions.

"We can't prepare them for burial like normal, so we'll have to make do." Mama bustled around the room, directing Alina and Kolya. She told Katya to stay with Pavlo, which she would have done regardless of her mother's orders, but Katya had never been more grateful to have her bossy mother take charge again.

Kolya hovered at Katya's shoulder, touching and checking Pavlo every few minutes. "I need to be the one to tell him. About our parents."

Katya nodded. She had no desire to be the bearer of that bad news.

The rest of the day passed in a blur. Nobody spoke of it, but fear worried them all. On top of everything that had happened, the knowledge that the OGPU could come back after any one of them in this house for being relatives of the deceased and arrest them as enemies of the people hung over their heads.

Pavlo woke as they finished the last of the cleaning up.

"Katya," he moaned. "Is that you, or am I dreaming?"

She dropped the rag she'd been using to wipe blood off his arms and leaned over him.

"It's me, my love. I'm here." She cupped his face in her hands and kissed him, full on the mouth in front of everyone. He groaned as their lips met, whether from pain, pleasure or both, she didn't know. "I thought I'd lost you!"

"You'll not be so easily rid of me." He gave a weak smile and winced as Katya pulled away.

"It's good to see you awake, brother," Kolya said. His eyes glistened.

Pavlo struggled to sit up, his face pale and drawn. "Where are our parents?"

Kolya gripped Pavlo's good shoulder and dropped his gaze. "They're gone."

Pavlo stretched his head up and looked toward his parents, laid out on the table, then squeezed his eyes shut and dropped back into the bed.

"There was nothing more you could have done," Kolya said.

"Maybe. Maybe not," Pavlo said.

Katya took his cold hand and brought it to her lips, her heart aching for his loss.

"Pavlo," Mama said. "If you can walk, I think it would be best to bring you to our house. I know we should sit up praying through the night over the bodies, but it's not safe here."

"Yes, we can't stay here." Kolya wiped the back of his hand over his eyes as he stared at his parents. "They wouldn't want us to risk our lives. We can come back for them tomorrow after we talk to the priest."

Pavlo took a deep breath and nodded. "We should go, then. Can you help me?"

Kolya and Katya braced Pavlo up between them as they trudged back across the snowy field. He gritted his teeth and only stumbled once, but never cried out.

They situated him in the bed Alina and Katya normally shared on the side of the *pich* stove and Kolya made up a pallet on the floor. Tonight, the girls would sleep with their mother. Mama threw another log into the *pich* and they fell into chairs around it. Katya pulled hers up to Pavlo's bed so she could hold his hand.

"Talk to me, Katya. Tell me a story." He spoke through white lips. "I need a distraction until I fall asleep."

Katya read the pain in his eyes and moved from her chair to perch next to him on the bed. They played this game often, telling each other tales of what was to come and what had passed. She racked her brain for a safe story to tell that didn't involve his parents or her father.

"Do you remember the time I snuck out of my house with one of my mother's honey cakes? She'd made it for a party we were supposed to go to, but I took it and found you. We climbed into the hayloft and ate every last crumb."

A trace of a smile played on Pavlo's lips. "You told me you'd made the cake for my birthday. But then you cleaned the plate, put it right back where you'd found it, and told your mother a dog must have eaten it."

"Hush." Katya didn't feel like laughing, but she forced a chuckle out for him. "My mother never found out about that."

The conversation waned and, in the silence, the enormity of the day suddenly overwhelmed Katya. Her mind buzzed with fatigue and her body sagged into the bed. She laid her head next to Pavlo's and cupped his cheek. Despite her weariness, her voice came out strong. "I can't lose you. Ever! Do you hear me? We have our whole lives planned out, and you have to be here for it."

Pavlo squeezed her hand in reply. "I'm here, Katya. You saved me."

When someone knocked on the door, Alina whimpered and Kolya jumped to his feet, but Mama's calm voice quieted everyone.

"It's probably cousin Vasyl, the priest. For the wedding, remember?"

Kolya dropped his head into his hands, and Katya sat up as Mama let Vasyl in and told him what had happened.

He closed his eyes, his lips moving in a silent prayer, then took Mama's hands. "No one is safe. What's become of our world?"

Nobody had an answer for him. Mama ushered him to a chair, and he glanced around the room as he went, pausing as he took in Pavlo's bandages.

"Well, we have a funeral to work out, but I could still marry you today, if you wish." He stroked his beard and considered each of them in turn.

"No!" Kolya jerked his head up. "Not today."

Katya nodded in agreement. She didn't want to marry today anymore either. She'd hadn't even thought about the wedding until

Vasyl arrived. How could she, after all that had happened? And with Tato gone?

"Don't you think they should wait? It's too soon after this tragedy," Mama said. "And my husband would want to be here."

"Normally, yes. Of course, nobody wants to rejoice so soon after such loss, but during these terrible times, I encourage young people to hold onto whatever happiness they can find, anytime they find it." He glanced at Pavlo and Katya. "We can never know what tomorrow will bring."

Alina stifled a cry, and Kolya took her hand. "I'm sorry. I can't mix what should be the happiest day of my life with the most devastating. I need time. Maybe next week we can revisit it."

"Of course," Alina said. "We'll wait."

"Well, for the same reason we cannot have a large wedding, we cannot have a typical funeral," Vasyl said. "Especially because of the way they were killed. They would be labeled enemies of the people, and anyone attending the funeral would be considered the same. It must be quiet and quick. We can have a short service in their home. At night would be best, and no one but immediate family should be included."

* * *

Mama set out the traditional towels and glasses of water for Pavlo and Kolya's parents to drink and wipe their tears away with in the time their souls lingered before the funeral. This was one of the few post-death rituals they would be able to do for them. When Mama had done it for Serhiy, it had brought Katya some comfort. Now, the seemingly paltry gesture made her angry.

"I'll need help unloading the coffins and lowering them into the ground. They're too long for me to handle myself." Kolya picked at the fried *salo* and onions Mama had prepared for the wedding that now served as their funeral meal.

The fatty meat stuck in Katya's throat, along with the tears she refused to let out.

"Maybe you could ask a neighbor to help?" Mama said.

"It's best if we don't involve anyone else in this," Kolya said. "I couldn't bear any more blood on my hands."

"Your hands?" Katya stared at him in disbelief. "This is not your fault, Kolya. You must know that!"

"Maybe it's not my fault, but I didn't stop it. And nothing you can say will change that. I have to live with it." He pushed back from the table and their meager dinner.

Pavlo grabbed his arm. "Kolya, you couldn't have stopped this from happening. Don't you know how happy it makes me that you stayed safe?"

Kolya pulled away from Pavlo and put on his coat. "I need to finish this."

"Alina and I helped you make the coffins." Katya stood and rested a hand on Pavlo's shoulder to calm him. "We can help you dig the graves, too."

"No. I'd like to do that myself." Kolya kept his eyes trained on the ground. "I need to do this part alone."

"Not alone," Pavlo said. "I'll come with you."

"No!" Katya fought down the panic rising in her chest at the idea of Pavlo leaving her sight. "You're not well enough to dig!"

"Maybe not, but I'll not let my brother bear this burden alone. I won't dig much, if you'll forgive me that, Kolya, but I'll be there with you."

Kolya gave Pavlo a quick nod and left, slamming the door behind him.

Katya started to protest again, but Mama touched her arm. "Leave them, Katya. They mourn."

Katya threw her hands in the air and sat back down. "Fine, I'll do the chores here, and I'll go take care of your animals, too. If I just sit here, I'll go crazy."

"Thank you." Pavlo pressed his cool lips against her cheek and she forced herself not to hold him there with her, where she could keep him safe. He winced when his heavy coat fell on his wound, and Katya cringed with him as if his pain were her own.

Mucking stalls, scooping feed, milking the cow, then trudging back across the field to do the same at Pavlo's farm kept Katya busy, though her mind kept wandering to her gentle father, locked up in a cold cell. She shivered as she tried to remember how warmly he'd dressed yesterday. Surely they would let him go soon, she told herself. He'd done nothing wrong. Then again, neither had anyone else. Nothing made sense anymore.

Vasyl was the only other person besides them who came to say goodbye to their loved ones. Of course, everyone in their small village had heard what had happened, but nobody asked about the funeral or offered to help. The risk was too great.

Vasyl read prayers over their bodies, then helped them carry out the coffins. They stopped and tapped the end of each coffin on the doorjamb three times to allow the deceased to part with their home, then made their way to the cemetery. Mama walked at the head of the procession, holding in a *rushnyk* the remnants of a holy icon picture Prokyp had smashed. Kolya, with Pavlo beside him, drove the wagon with the bodies, and Vasyl, Alina, and Katya followed behind on foot. Despite the cloak of darkness, fear of discovery amplified every creak of the wagon and kept everyone silent and on their guard.

Vasyl said a few words, then they lowered the coffins into the ground. Pavlo used his good arm, but still leaned heavily on Katya afterward, so she braced her strong legs, wrapped her arms around Pavlo's waist, and held him up while silent sobs for his parents racked his body. The short service ended moments after it began; even the ability to truly mourn their loved ones had been taken from them.

* * *

A cold gust of air followed Mama into the house as she dropped into the chair by the *pich*. Her blank face gave Katya no clues as to what she'd learned on her trip to the village that morning to coerce the guards to let Tato go. She'd insisted on going alone in case they got angry and arrested her, too.

"What did you find out?" Katya asked, trying to ignore Mama's puffy, tear-stained face and the sinking feeling in her belly. "A few more days and then they'll let him go? Right?"

"He's not there." Mama tried to control her emotions, but it was a futile effort. A low sob slipped past her lips and she fell to the floor. "They deported him last night. I didn't even get to say goodbye."

"No, Mama." Katya shook her head. "Not Tato. That can't be right. Maybe they are lying to you."

Alina dropped to her knees and embraced their wailing mother. Katya knew she should go to them, to mourn together the absence of their father, but she couldn't make her feet move. Instead, she squeezed her hands into fists so tight her fingernails cut into her skin as she contemplated a life without Tato's gentle smiles and wise guidance.

"We will go tell Vasyl to wait," Alina said, after Mama's wails had subsided. "We cannot marry on the heels of Tato's deportation."

Mama's head snapped up. "Do you want to marry this man?" She wiped her eyes with one hand and jerked the other toward Kolya.

"Of course," Alina said. She glanced over at Kolya, and her eyes softened.

"And you, Katya?" Mama turned her steely, tear-filled gaze on her younger daughter. "You want to marry Pavlo, right?"

Mama's voice shook Katya out of her daze, and she looked up at Pavlo. Her pulse quickened. She did want to marry him, with all of her heart. But to marry without Tato here? To celebrate her love for Pavlo while her father moved further away from them by the minute? This wasn't the plan. "Yes, Mama, but—"

"Then you have to marry today." Mama held up a hand to silence

Katya. "I pray you can have a small piece of the happiness I shared with your father, and if you want that, then you must take it now. You saw what happened to the church. It's nothing but a building for Party meetings. No, you must marry now while we still have a priest in the village to do it, because God knows how long it will be before they take him from us, too." She crossed herself and said a prayer under her breath.

So, only a few days after the funeral, and the day after Tato had been deported, Kolya and Alina and Pavlo and Katya married in their house. For those brief few minutes, as the priest bound their hands together with the *rushnyk* Mama had made for them, Katya stared into Pavlo's face and felt whole. Love welled up in her for the man she was now connected to for life, but when her eyes fell on her mother, standing alone, wringing her hands and biting back tears, reality came crashing back down and tainted any joy she'd felt.

"Your father would want you to be happy today," Mama said afterward as she hugged them. "What does he always say? 'Look to the future.'" Her voice cracked, and she buried her face in her handkerchief.

The smile trembling on Katya's lips fell away.

11

CASSIE

Illinois, May 2004

Cassie rubbed her eyes and yawned as the delicious smell of pan-fried dough and fruit wafted into her room. Anywhere else, that smell would mean coffee cake or pancakes, but here, it only meant one thing. Blintzes. Her mouth already watering, Cassie jumped out of bed and headed toward the kitchen.

Bobby and Birdie sat at the table, elbow to elbow, working. In front of them rested a platter of thin crepes Bobby must have already fried up. Next to it lay a bowl of a sweet farmer's cheese mixture to stuff them with.

"Now you fold this part over, see?" Bobby demonstrated. Birdie, squinting in concentration, carefully folded the last bit of the crepe over the filling and then smiled widely at the finished product. Her eyes glowed with pride, and she held it up for her mother to inspect.

"Beautiful!" Cassie smiled, relieved to see both Bobby and Birdie in such good spirits again. Birdie's presence seemed to cheer up Bobby, and in the last couple of days, she hadn't spoken about any more harbingers of her death.

"When I was a girl, we called them *nalysnyky*," Bobby told Birdie. "My favorite kind are with cherries, but we will have to make do with putting strawberries on top today."

"I'd love to hear more about when you were a girl," Cassie said, sitting at the table. Maybe if she could get Bobby to talk openly about her past, she wouldn't drift away into it so often. Her gaze dipped toward the canister where she'd found the cache of hidden notes. She still hadn't figured out a way to translate them.

Bobby pursed her lips, and Cassie readied herself for the expected refusal, but instead, Bobby said, "Maybe. I'll think about it. After all, I don't have much time left here."

Cassie inhaled sharply. The idea of losing Bobby, of losing another person she loved, made her stomach roll.

"I wish you wouldn't talk like that, Bobby. I hate it."

"I'm sorry." Bobby patted Cassie's hand. "But I'm not a young woman. I won't be around forever."

Cassie swallowed hard. "I know that, but there's no need to dwell on it."

"I'm not dwelling. I'm stating facts."

"What if we talk about when you were young, while Birdie naps?"

Bobby didn't reply, and Cassie knew she should stop there, but she didn't. "Maybe you could even show me your journal?"

Bobby froze for a few moments. Then, as if she hadn't heard Cassie, she started to rise from her chair. "We need more strawberries."

"I'll get them." Cassie jumped up as she cursed herself. She'd pushed too hard. "You should be resting."

"I'm fine!" Bobby said, but she sat back in her chair. "Like I told your mother and those doctors."

"I know, but I'm here, so I may as well help." Cassie set the strawberries down on the table and tried to smooth over her gaffe. "You know, I can't remember the last time I had blintzes."

"You don't make them?" Bobby narrowed her eyes at Cassie.

"Not really." Cassie gave a weak smile and shrugged. "It's not the same, doing it without you."

Bobby snorted her disapproval. Cassie hadn't fooled her.

"Honestly," she said, sitting in the chair next to Bobby and lowering her voice, "I don't want to do much lately. Ever since Henry…"

Bobby's eyes softened. "That, I understand. But life goes on, and so we must look to the future, yes? And little girls must eat, so we make blintzes! Here, see if you remember how."

She handed Cassie a crepe and demonstrated again how to spread the filling and fold the crepe around it so nothing would leak out. Her old, arthritic fingers flew, despite her swollen joints, and the end product was perfection.

Cassie tried to follow suit, but when she made her last fold, sweet cheese dribbled out of one corner.

Bobby made a clucking noise and shook her head. She glanced over at Birdie's work. "Try again. See, like Birdie. She is making beautiful blintzes!"

Birdie beamed at the praise, then pointed at the empty plate.

"No more to make," Bobby agreed. "Now, we put strawberries on top and eat them. Go wash your hands."

Birdie ran to do as she was told, and Bobby leaned closer to Cassie. "She's a good girl." Bobby's eyes angled toward where Birdie stood at the sink. Her slender legs poked out from another pair of too-small pajamas.

"I wish she could go back to the way she was before the accident."

"She'll come back to you," Bobby said. "Give her time."

"It's been over a year."

"There is no time limit on grief. You should know that." She gave Cassie a shrewd look. "What about you? Are you back to normal? You used to carry a journal with you everywhere and write constantly. I don't see you doing that anymore."

Cassie swallowed the lump in her throat. Bobby had always been so perceptive. "I don't have anything to write now."

Bobby patted her hand. "When Birdie is ready, she will talk, and you will have her back. When you are ready, you will write. Now, eat some blintzes."

* * *

Later that afternoon, after tucking Birdie in for a nap, Cassie walked down the hall to Bobby's room. She clutched the old picture of the two girls that had fallen from the journal and the odd notes from under the flour canister and hoped that, despite the sudden end to their earlier conversation, her grandmother would be ready to talk. The way she'd been going on about all of her portents of death made Cassie worry.

"Bobby?" Cassie knocked and the door opened a few inches. Through the crack, she saw Bobby perched on the bed, oblivious to Cassie's presence. The small candle on the nightstand flickered in the dim room. Anguish twisted Bobby's face. She gripped a pencil tight in her good hand and pressed it into an open notebook, writing slowly and deliberately.

Cassie froze, unsure of how to proceed. Should she let Bobby know she was there? Or wait and see what she did next?

Before she could decide, Bobby ripped the sheet out of the notebook and shuffled over to her closet. She dug back behind some clothes on a shelf and shoved the note into a box. Then, she blew out the candle and climbed into bed. Her eyes closed immediately, as if the whole process had exhausted her.

Cassie looked down at the picture in her hand, and with a sudden burst of courage, took a step into the room.

Bobby shifted in her bed. "Alina? Is that you?"

"No, it's Cassie. I wanted to check on you." She walked over to her grandmother and straightened the blankets. "Who's Alina?"

"Oh. Cassie." The disappointment in Bobby's voice punched Cassie in the gut. Bobby forced a wobbly smile and ignored the question. "I left something for you in your room."

"Thank you. You didn't have to do that."

Bobby turned away from Cassie. "I'm very tired now, and I'd like to be alone."

"Okay." Cassie turned, tiptoed out of the room, and closed the door, but not before she heard a muffled sob. She hesitated, her hand still on the doorknob, then went to her room. If she pushed any harder, Bobby might shut down completely.

On her nightstand, she found that Bobby had left her a notebook like the one she'd been using. Cassie smiled. She'd moved home to take care of Bobby, but so far, Bobby seemed to be far more in tune with what Cassie needed.

Cassie flipped through the blank pages, then ran her fingers over the wobbly English words Bobby had painstakingly penciled for her on the inside cover.

Just make it through today. Tomorrow will be better.

Bobby's father's advice. It was kind of bleak, but how many times had Cassie told herself to just make it through today? She'd have to work on believing the part about "Tomorrow will be better."

She set the notebook down. Not yet. She wasn't ready now, but maybe soon, she'd give journaling a try.

She took a deep breath and headed for the bathroom, eager to squeeze in the shower she'd missed that morning.

The bathroom, like everything else in the house, looked exactly the same as it had when Cassie was a kid. The matching avocado green bathtub, sink, and toilet still screamed out 1970, and the orange shag bath rug supported the theme.

Cassie turned on the faucet and opened the linen closet to grab a towel.

Instead of towels, toilet paper, and the other bathroom essentials, the narrow cabinet was filled with canned goods. Peas, green beans, corn, tuna, and spam, all stacked in tidy rows.

Cassie closed the door and checked under the bathroom sink. There, she found the towels and four canisters of oatmeal. A prickle of worry crept down her spine. Why were the kitchen cabinets bare and the bathroom cabinets full of food? This was definitely not the behavior of a person in their right mind.

As she rinsed shampoo out of her hair and tried to think of ways to broach the topic with Bobby, someone banged on the door.

Startled, she shut the water off. "I'll be right there."

When more banging was the only reply, Cassie grabbed a towel and wrapped herself in it. "Birdie? Hold on, I'm coming!"

The banging grew more frantic. "Okay, okay!" Cassie glanced at her clothes lying in a pile on the sink, wrapped the towel closer, and threw open the door.

"What's wrong?"

Birdie jumped up and down, pointing toward the living room. Cassie looked down the hall and saw the front door swinging open. Birdie grabbed her hand and dragged her toward it. As she stepped out of the bathroom, she reached back and grabbed Bobby's old pink housecoat off the bathroom hook.

"Where's Bobby?" Cassie asked as she pulled the baggy garment around herself. "Did she go out there?"

She nodded, her little face twisted into a frown, and Cassie realized Birdie must have overheard her and Anna talking about Bobby wandering off.

"You did the right thing by telling me. Now, you stay here. Do not leave the house!" Cassie grabbed Birdie by the shoulders and gave her a shake before she ran out the front door and scanned the street. After her behavior this afternoon, Cassie didn't want Bobby out by herself.

Bobby had almost made it to the street corner, and now stood looking around.

"Bobby!" Cassie called. "Wait there for me! I'm coming!"

She turned to go back inside to grab her shoes when she saw Bobby start to move again out of the corner of her eye.

"No! Wait!" Cassie yelled, but Bobby didn't hear her. She shuffled toward the busy intersection. Clothes forgotten, Cassie sprinted barefoot down the sidewalk. "Bobby! Stop!"

A gray truck pulled up next to Bobby, and a man jumped out of it. He ran around to Bobby and took her by the elbow.

Panic coursed through Cassie. Not even a week here and she'd already let her grandmother escape, and now she was being abducted.

"Hey! Leave her alone!" Fear propelled her as she ran, oblivious to the hard pavement bruising her feet or the housecoat flapping against her legs.

The man glanced up and smiled as Cassie reached them.

"Hey, Cassie. I was just helping her across the street," the man said at the same time as Cassie breathlessly demanded, "What do you think you're doing with her?"

"You don't remember me, do you?" he asked. His eyes twinkled, as if he was amused by her thoughtlessness.

"Um..." Cassie stared at him through narrowed eyes, her chest still heaving from the exertion of her sprint. "Oh, right. From the hospital. Mick."

"Nick, actually," he chuckled. "Glad to see I made an impression."

"Sorry. Nick. Of course." Cassie pushed wet hair off her cheeks. "You look different without the uniform."

Nick glanced down at her housecoat. "I could say the same about you."

Cassie's face flamed. "Look, I'm sorry about this. I'm not sure if she's sleepwalking or what, but she was napping when I jumped in the shower. She wandered outside, and I didn't have time to get dressed."

"I'm not sleepwalking, and I'm not deaf," Bobby snapped, but confusion clouded her eyes. "I am a grown woman, and I wanted to go for my walk. I always walk in the afternoon. I went a little early today because I couldn't sleep. What's the fuss?"

"The fuss is you're not supposed to go for a walk without telling me, and you almost walked out in traffic again," Cassie said.

"I did not!" Bobby stamped her foot. "I was waiting for the cars to pass. Don't overreact, Cassie." Her whole demeanor changed as she smiled at Nick and patted his hand. "It's so good to see you again. You must come over to eat with us soon, yes?"

Cassie scowled at the rebuke and Nick grinned. "Sure, that would be great. How about we get you home now?"

Cassie took one of Bobby's arms and Nick took the other and they guided Bobby back into the house where Birdie stood at the door, clutching her stuffed puppy dog and watching.

"Do you want to try to lie down again, Bobby?" Cassie asked. "Maybe you'll be able to sleep now that you've had some fresh air."

Bobby nodded, so Cassie walked her back to her bedroom and got her settled in. Not wanting to face Nick in a housecoat again, she stopped by her bedroom and threw on a T-shirt and shorts.

At the entrance to the living room, she paused and listened, surprised to hear Nick reading aloud. Birdie sat in the far corner of the room, her back to Nick as he used silly voices to differentiate the characters. Birdie wouldn't look at him, but her shoulders shook with silent laughter at the comedic delivery.

Cassie softened at the sight of his big hands holding the small board book, a hopeful look on his face as he directed his voice toward Birdie. She walked into the room as he finished a page and sat in the chair across from him.

"This isn't your first time reading Dr. Seuss, is it?" Cassie asked as Birdie crept closer to Nick.

He blushed. "Of course not. Me and the Doc go way back. Sorry, I saw the book sitting here, so I thought I'd read it. For nostalgia's sake."

"Right," Cassie said, a small smile playing on her lips. "Out loud. With voices and everything."

"Well, if you're going to do something, you should do it right." He set the book down. "But now that your grandmother is safe here, I should probably get going."

Birdie, still facing away from them, but now almost next to the couch, spun around and grabbed the book, then pushed it back into his hands.

Shocked, Cassie held her breath. Since the accident, Birdie had become a shy, frail shell of her formerly vivacious self. She never attempted to communicate with anyone other than close family members.

Nick glanced down at her. "Do you want me to keep reading?"

Birdie smiled and pointed at the book.

Cassie exhaled, her pulse racing as she reveled in the glimpse of the child her daughter had once been. Strong willed. Outspoken. A force of nature.

Nick looked at Cassie, his eyes seeking her permission, and she nodded.

"Okay. Well then, where was I?" Nick thumbed through the book, then resumed his silly, high-pitched voice.

Cassie could barely contain her joy as she watched Birdie giggle and squeal at his antics. Nick finished the book, then picked up a second book from the pile on the couch and started reading. Birdie crept closer and closer to him, until finally, she was leaning against his leg, smiling up at him. When he finished, she placed a third book in his hands. Without missing a beat, Nick read.

Enchanted at this change in her daughter, Cassie let it continue for two more books, but when Nick raised a sixth, she glanced at the clock and realized he'd been reading for thirty-five minutes. She jumped up.

"No, Bird, I'm sure Mr., uh... well, I'm sure Mr. Nick has places to go and things to do."

Nick laughed. "It's Koval. Nick Koval. And you sound a lot like Dr. Seuss yourself."

Birdie giggled again, and Cassie shook her head, still in disbelief. She hadn't seen her daughter act like this since before the accident.

First, her happiness and determination that morning while making blintzes and now, her exuberance while listening to stories with Nick. They seemed like such simple, normal things for a little girl to enjoy, but Cassie hadn't been providing them. Her throat constricted with guilt.

"I should probably get going, but maybe we could do one more short one?" He grinned hopefully at Cassie, and a small, frozen part of herself that she kept tucked away where no one could see it melted. Birdie jumped up and down in her seat and clasped her hands under her chin, her eyes begging despite her still silent mouth.

"Fine," Cassie said, suddenly anxious to get away from Nick and the odd fluttering in her chest caused by his easy smile. "I can see I'm outnumbered. I'll go get some lemonade for everyone."

Cassie's hand quaked as she poured the drinks. She set glasses and a plate of cookies on a tray, then gripped the counter and took a deep breath. Mumbled words poured out of her mouth like a soothing mantra. "There's nothing special about him. This is Birdie getting excited over the attention. It's not him. It's the attention."

What did that mean, though? Another pang of guilt torpedoed her. If attention was all Birdie really needed, why hadn't Cassie given it to her? Was she so wrapped up in her grief that she'd been ignoring how much her daughter needed her to reach out and interact?

Obviously. Birdie needed someone to focus on her, and Cassie had to fix that. She couldn't keep using Henry's death as an excuse to shut everyone out, including her daughter. She took another deep breath, steeled herself, and went back in the living room.

Cassie set the tray down on the coffee table. "Please, have some refreshments. It's the least we can do to pay you back for your rescuing and entertaining services."

"It's my pleasure." Nick smiled, and two large dimples creased his cheeks.

Her guard back up, Cassie appraised him critically, but still, she had to admit, he was pretty attractive. With short, light brown hair, bright blue eyes, and tanned skin, he looked like he belonged in an outdoorsman commercial.

"I haven't had such a captive audience since my sister and her boys were in town. They had me reading Dr. Seuss for hours," he said.

Cassie realized she'd been staring. She shook her head and latched on to the most recent thing he'd said. "You've got nephews?"

"Yep, twin six-year-old boys. They're a handful but a lot of fun. They live on the East Coast, though, so I don't get to see them often."

"That's too bad." She took a long drink of lemonade, and the book he'd just read caught her eye.

"Oh, I forgot all about this book!" She picked up the old Ukrainian picture book Bobby used to read to her as a child, her fingertips grazing the battered scene of a boy and a dog. She looked at him in disbelief. "You can read Ukrainian?"

Nick cocked his head in surprise. "Sure, can't you?"

Cassie shook her head. "I never learned. And my mom was just telling me they didn't have a Ukrainian school close to her, so she never learned."

"It was really important to my Baba that I go," Nick said. "Every Saturday morning, rain or shine. I hated it for a while, but it wasn't so bad, really. I learned a lot about where she came from and my family history."

Cassie frowned. "Bobby never really talks about Ukraine. Or her family. It's always been a big mystery to us."

"Well, there were some hard times in the old country, according to my Baba. It wasn't an easy life. Maybe it's painful for her to think about it."

"Yeah, maybe," Cassie said, already distracted by a new idea that had popped into her mind. "Do you have a second to read something for me?"

"Sure," Nick said.

Cassie ran to her room and opened her dresser drawer. She grabbed the notes and picture, walked back down the hall, and returned to the living room, setting them on the table in front of Nick. "I'd love to know what these say."

Nick furrowed his brow as he read the notes aloud. "Two cans of peas, side table. Three cans of sardines, south flower bed. One box of crackers, behind blue couch."

He flipped the paper over and continued. "Dried cherries, small desk. Pickled beets, guest bedroom closet." He looked up at her, his eyes wide, then paged through a few more of the notes. "They're all like this. Food items and locations. What is it?"

Cassie shook her head. "I'm not sure."

Nick's smile quirked the corner of his lips, but he didn't push. He then looked at the old picture and flipped it over. "Nothing on the back here but the date: September 1929. Pretty neat photo. Who is it?"

"I don't know that, either." Cassie tried to hide her disappointment.

"I like a good mystery," Nick said. "If you need me to read anything else, let me know. I'm glad to help."

She wanted to say: *Can you wait here while I go steal my grandmother's journal? You can read it to me so I can pry into her past to figure out what's going on with her now.*

Instead, she gave him a generic, "Thanks," and struggled to pull something polite from her distracted mind. "So, um, you live down the street? How's that going?"

"Yeah, in my Baba's old house. It needs some updating, but it's got a lot of potential."

"That was nice of her to leave it to you."

Nick looked down at his hands. "She was always looking out for me."

"It's what they do best," Cassie agreed.

"Definitely. Well, thanks for the lemonade and cookies." He stood and glanced around, then picked up the notepad Bobby kept by the phone. "I should get going, but before I forget, let me give you my number in case you need anything."

"Oh, I wouldn't want to bother you," Cassie protested, but Nick had already started writing.

"It's no trouble." His blue eyes met hers, and the corners crinkled as he smiled. "We're neighbors, right? That's what neighbors do."

He held out the paper, and Cassie's fingers brushed his as she took it. She jerked her hand back, her skin burning from the contact. "Thank you."

Nick left his hand suspended for a moment, as if he'd felt it, too. A perplexed look flashed across his face so fast that Cassie couldn't be sure she saw it before his signature grin reappeared. He offered his hand up to Birdie for a high five, and surprisingly, or maybe not so surprisingly, given her sudden affection for him, she responded with a resounding smack and a wide smile.

He paused, then bent over and picked something up off the floor. "Oh, I missed this one."

Cassie stepped closer and peered down at the short note. "I've never seen this. Maybe Bobby dropped it when she was sitting here. Looks like someone spilled coffee on it." A dark brown stain leeched across the yellowed paper, nearly marring the words.

Nick read the note aloud:

"You're so beautiful when you sleep that I couldn't bear to wake you. I love you. I'll see you soon. P."

"Wow." Cassie's hand fluttered to her chest in a vain attempt to quell the sudden ache piercing her heart. Henry had been romantic like that, always leaving little messages around the house for her to find throughout the day. "I wonder who 'P' is."

Nick held the paper up to his face and squinted. "I don't know, but this isn't a coffee stain. I think it's blood."

12

KATYA

Ukraine, March 1931

Normally, a bride moved in with the groom's family after a wedding, but with their extenuating circumstances and no further information on Tato's fate, the family had decided that Alina and Kolya would move to his parents' farm and Pavlo and Katya would stay with Mama.

They went on, existing in a state of borrowed happiness mixed with grief and fear. Katya never stopped thinking about Tato, worrying if he was safe, if he was alive, but she reveled in her new role as wife to Pavlo. To be free to touch and talk to him anytime she pleased fulfilled her in ways she'd never anticipated. Marriage to him was everything she'd dreamed. She tried her best to focus on that and forget that, in every other sense, their lives had changed drastically for the worse.

"Katya, we need to talk." Pavlo touched her arm as she walked by with an armful of hay for the evening feeding of the livestock.

"About what?" Katya unloaded the hay into the cow's manger and gave her a scratch on her head.

"I'm leaving."

Katya's hand jerked back from the cow, who blinked up at her, then continued chewing.

"What do you mean you're leaving? For where?" She whirled and glared up at him.

"I talked to my cousin from the next village over. They're trying to put together a resistance, and I want to be a part of it."

"But you're not even completely healed." She touched his wounded shoulder tenderly, and then punched his healthy one. "What are you thinking? You'll be no help to them when you're injured."

"I'm nearly well, and you know it. I've been working like I used to. I'm plenty strong enough to wield a weapon and fight."

"And what about me?" She hated the pleading tone that had taken root in her voice, but she could no more control it than she could the tears that had sprung to her eyes. "You can walk away from me just like that?"

"No, Katya, it will never be easy to walk away from you." He took her face in his hands. "You are my life, my love. But, if we don't fight, then what will become of us? You said yourself that we should fight back. Don't you remember that? If this works, then I can try to rally the people here to do the same."

She threw her hands up in defeat. "That was before they took everything from us."

"Not everything, my love." He kissed her then, salty tears flavoring their lips until she wrenched away. He took her hand. "Please understand, Katya. I have to fight, or what kind of life can we look forward to?"

"Take me with you," she begged. "I can fight, too. You know I can!"

"We need you here to work on the farm. Alina and Kolya can't manage both places on their own, and your mother needs you more than ever."

Katya gripped his arms. "I almost lost you once. What if this time I really do lose you? How will I go on? Have you thought about that? What will happen to me then?"

He stroked her cheek, infuriating her and soothing her all at the same time. "Katya, you are the strongest woman I know. No matter what happens to me, you'll be fine. I know that, deep in my soul. Here, I got you something."

"I don't want a gift. I want to be with you." She bit her lip and stared down at the ground.

He pushed a brown leather book into her hands. "It's a journal. For as long as I've known you, you've been writing down your stories on old newspapers and scraps of paper. Now, you'll have a real book so you can record what's happening to us, what they are doing to us, so someday our children and their children will know our story. Include the sad parts and the joyous parts. Write of our childhood friendship turning into the greatest love story of all time. Tell them how you dumped a bucket of water on my head when I pulled your hair in the school yard and of our first kiss under the moon and stars. Then, no matter what happens, I will always be with you."

She ran a hand down the smooth cover and cracked the spine open. The thick, creamy pages begged for words to be scrawled on them. She'd never seen a nicer book.

"Pavlo, this is beautiful."

"Promise me you'll use it however you want. I'd love for you to write our story, but if stretching your imagination and writing your dreams is what you need to do to get through this, then do that."

"I like your idea of documenting what is happening. And what has happened. With us, too. I've already started doing that on my scraps of paper. A fine book to keep it all together and in order would be nice."

"You'd need to keep it well hidden, of course."

She nodded, her mind already flipping through the possible places.

"Don't think this journal makes up for you leaving me," she said, her eyes glittering with tears. "I'm still angry with you."

"I would never try to buy your forgiveness. It's a gift."

"Is Kolya going? Does Alina know about this?"

"No, Kolya is staying here. We talked about it and decided one of us should be here with you three. He's not too happy about me leaving either."

"So, you've discussed this with Kolya, but this is the first I'm hearing about it?" She slammed the journal back into his chest as anger heated her face. "I am your wife, Pavlo!"

"And that's why it was so hard to tell you. I hate disappointing you." He took her hands. "You have nothing to worry about, and if anything does happen to me, Kolya promised he will take care of you."

"I don't want Kolya to have to take care of me. I want you!" The memory of finding Pavlo bleeding and unconscious materialized in her mind, and she scrunched her eyes tight, willing it away.

"Katya, look at me. Please, don't be angry. I only have tonight with you. I'm leaving at first light." He gripped her shoulders and stared at her.

Panic set in and her voice broke. "Tomorrow? When will you be back?"

"I don't know."

She turned away, then stiffened as he pulled her back into his arms. "Please, I have to do this. Don't you see?"

Katya looked into his handsome face and read the pain in his eyes, the loss. She understood his need for revenge. She wanted it, too, but he was right about her staying. She couldn't leave her mother now, right after losing her father. It would kill her. She ignored the hard knot of foreboding taking root in her gut and opened her arms to him.

She led him to the barn loft, their secret place, and opened the upper-level door so the moonlight shone down on them. They sank onto the old quilt she kept up here for such occasions and she kissed him until all the fear and worry faded to the back of her mind. She blocked out the fact that he was leaving and that this could be the last time she saw him. They spent the night tangled together, looking out at the stars.

"You must wake me before you leave." Katya nuzzled into Pavlo's neck and breathed in his scent.

He kissed her cheek and pressed his body against hers. "Hush. Don't talk of tomorrow. Let me enjoy tonight with you in my arms."

"My mother will wonder where we are."

"No, she won't. She was a young woman once too, you know. And I told her I'm leaving. She'll expect we wanted some privacy."

"You told my mother before me?" Katya propped herself up on one elbow and glared at him. "First Kolya, and then my mother? Do you want me to hate you before you leave, Pavlo?"

"Only a few minutes before, I promise! She overheard Kolya and me talking about it and asked me. I couldn't lie to her."

"Fine," she grumbled. "But I want to help. More than writing. You were right before; I do want to fight back. I've heard about the women in other villages rising up against the activists and taking back their grain and livestock. I could do that here. I could start a *Bab'i Bunty* revolt."

"No!" Fear twisted his face. "The situation has escalated since last year. They may have gone easier on a women's revolt before, but it's far too dangerous for that now. You'd be deported or killed for sure. If there is anything you can do here when the time comes, I'll tell you."

Katya grasped his chin and looked him in the eye. "You'd better. I mean it!"

"I know you do." He stroked her hair. "Just as much as I mean not to put you in harm's way."

"Good luck. I'm in harm's way every day merely existing here."

He gave a short laugh. "My Katya, always such a way with words."

"I only speak the truth." She lay back down and snuggled into his safe, strong arms.

"I know, that's what worries me so."

When she woke up the next morning, he was gone.

* * *

Time dragged on. Each minute felt like an hour and each hour stretched on as if it were a full, miserable day. Katya didn't have the evenings with Pavlo to look forward to, and the long walks to retrieve or forage for food were lonely. All of the solitude gave her too much time to think of all the people she'd lost. Sasha and her family, Tato, and now, in a way, Pavlo.

She tried to quiet the doubt and worry that paralyzed her with fear each night as she crawled into her bed alone to write in her journal, but her concerns only grew stronger with each passing day.

"Don't worry, Katya," Mama said as they prepared dinner one night. "He will come home to you."

"I know, Mama," Katya said, though she didn't really know anything. Three weeks had passed, and the longer he was gone, the more she became convinced he'd been hurt.

A knock on the door interrupted her thoughts. Before they could answer it, Prokyp, along with another activist, pushed into their home.

"We're here to collect your taxes," he announced. "The quota has been raised for our village, and everyone must contribute."

"We have nothing left to give," Mama said as she pulled herself up to her full height. Katya wanted to collapse in a chair from the exhaustion of this never-ending battle, but she straightened her back and emulated her mother instead.

"You still have a cow in your barnyard," Prokyp said. "We'll take that. It will cover your quota."

Mama blanched, then steeled herself. "Fine. If you must, then take her. But we have nothing left for any further taxes."

"Foolish woman! Your taxes are higher since you are not a member of the collective. If you would only join, your life would be so much easier."

Mama's jaw flexed. Katya reached out and put a hand on her arm.

"Take the cow, then," Mama choked out, her face red with anger.

"Oh, we will," he sneered. "If you decide to smarten up, you can join the collective at the town meeting tomorrow night."

"Would we get our cow back?" Katya didn't bother hiding the sarcastic edge in her voice.

Prokyp laughed as he slammed the door, and Mama slumped into her chair.

"I fear we no longer have a choice about the collective. What else can they take from us for taxes now? And what will we do for milk?"

"We still have the chickens and the goats. Honey should be pregnant by now, so hopefully we can share the milk with the kid when it comes. We'll find a way, Mama. We'll be fine. Don't worry."

"Maybe you're right." Mama gave an unconvincing nod.

"I'm going to go check on the other animals," Katya said.

She made her way across the yard, watching as Prokyp and his accomplice pushed and pulled the poor cow down the lane. She lowed mournfully and looked back at the farm until Prokyp gave her a kick in the hindquarters, and she finally plodded on.

Anger blurred Katya's eyes as she pushed open the barn door. She would miss that sweet cow, and she would especially miss the milk.

* * *

On Wednesday, the monotony of the week was broken up when they made their way into the village for another meeting put on by the activists. After their supper of black bread and the last bit of farmer's cheese left in the house, Katya and her mother cleaned up and walked to the village. The closer they got, the more people they met along the road. Nowadays, if you didn't attend the meetings, the activists would come to your house to find out why you hadn't, and nobody wanted any attention drawn to them and their home. Late, they took seats in the back of the church next to Lena and Ruslan. Lena, a sweet woman and Mama's cousin, reached out and patted Mama's hand as they sat. She could see Kolya and Alina in front of them, along with other villagers she'd known her whole life, but many were missing. The activists' zealous approach to dekulakization had led to nearly a quarter of the population being deported or killed.

Comrade Ivanov was already speaking, his voice booming over the crowd. "No longer will we tolerate blatant disobedience! No longer will we coddle the *kulaks* who refuse to help our great leader unite us and better our lives! From this point onward, anyone who does not join the collective farm will be considered an enemy of the state! A *kulak*! And we all know what happens to *kulaks*."

He paused, scanning the room with narrowed eyes, and a wave of worried whispers rippled through the crowd. He smiled, pleased with the response, and went on. "It is for the betterment of all that we unite. So come, join us now. Pledge your life, your land, and your livestock to Comrade Stalin! You will be rewarded richly for it later! After the meeting, any who have not joined will have one last chance to do so with Comrade Popov. If you choose not to, your fate is sealed!"

Katya and her mother exchanged a glance as nervous chatter rose up around them. The decision had been made for them. They could not escape the collective any longer. They had struggled to pay the taxes and avoid being noticed, but they could not be labeled *kulaks*. That would be like signing their own death warrants.

Mama reached out and squeezed her hand in a gesture of partnership. Katya turned to her in surprise, and Mama smiled. Warmth coursed through Katya as she realized that her mother didn't see her as a child anymore. They were in this fight together.

As they approached his table after the meeting, Comrade Popov spread his arms wide. "Ah, my comrades. I knew you'd come around. You'll see. Collectivism is the way of the future." His self-important smile made Katya want to smack him across the face, but she gritted her teeth instead.

Mama, eyes hard and hand trembling, wrote her name on their forms. A surprising rush of shame curdled Katya's stomach as she watched Mama sign away all they had worked for, all Tato had worked for, with the fading hope that doing so would keep them all safe.

The next day, four men came to take the horse, goats, plow, and tools to the collective headquarters. Katya had woken long before first light and walked Honey, the pregnant nanny goat, out to the barn at her cousin Sasha's abandoned farm. If they found her and traced her back to Katya, she would likely be shot or sent away to a labor camp, but she didn't care. They would need that goat's milk this winter.

* * *

The weeks that followed dragged by in a blur of labor as the spring planting began. Their collective was broken into brigades that worked the different areas of land around the village. Bohdan Vovk, Katya's collective brigade leader and a native villager, did the best he could for his people, but the constant scrutiny from state leaders didn't give him many options.

As farm laborers, Katya and her mother moved from field to field, wherever Bohdan told them to, and worked. She planted potatoes, millet, and oats, and took care of the livestock—all things she had done before, on her farm, but back then, they had given her joy and the satisfaction of self-sufficiency. She'd planted their wheat with her father, then harvested it and ground it into flour to make bread; she'd carefully cut potatoes and plant them in mounds so they could multiply and feed the family all winter; she'd lovingly tended the animals that put their trust in her family. These things made her and her family farmers.

Now, at the collective, she resented the drudgery of working for someone else's gain. She could no longer call herself a farmer; she was only a cog in the wheel of the state.

13

CASSIE

Illinois, May 2004

After Nick left, Cassie turned on Birdie's favorite cartoon and promised her she'd be right back to snuggle. She wanted to investigate.

The side table held two cans of peas, and the small desk contained a bag of dried cherries. She found a box of crackers behind the couch. The pickled beets turned up in the guest bedroom. She didn't bother to go digging in the south flower bed for sardines because there seemed to be enough evidence already. These notes documented hiding spots for food. But why?

As Cassie pondered Bobby's food issue and the mysterious note from "P," another disturbing thought buzzed around her head like a mosquito. Nick. His touch. The heat. What had happened there?

It couldn't be attraction. She still loved Henry. She would always love Henry.

Then why wouldn't Nick's face leave her mind? Why couldn't she stop thinking about his kind, easy manner with Birdie, or the way his cheeks creased into those deep dimples when he smiled?

Her conversation with Bobby about asking Henry to come to her flashed through her mind. She shook her head at the idea of it at the same time words started slipping out of her mouth.

"Henry, I miss you so much. I don't know what I'm supposed to do here without you." Her voice dropped to a whisper. "Please, come tell me."

She glanced around her bedroom, feeling silly about the whole thing, then tucked the notes and picture away in a dresser drawer. But, as she went back to cuddle on the couch with Birdie, it was Nick's face, not Henry's, that flashed into her mind, and a tiny seed of doubt over her loyalty to Henry festered in her unsettled heart.

* * *

A loud crash in the kitchen woke Cassie at 4 a.m. the next morning. Worried that Birdie had tried to get a glass of water and knocked over something or fallen, she pulled herself out of bed and rushed down the hall. As she rounded the corner, her eyes landed on Bobby. Muddy footprints tracked a path over the floor. The patio door stood open, and Bobby, holding a tray filled with fruit and packages of crackers, was making her way toward it.

"Bobby? What are you doing?"

Her grandmother spun around. Hair stuck out all over her head and her bare feet were covered in dirt and grass. A housecoat hung crooked and open over her long nightgown. Her eyes, wide and frightened, darted around the room.

"Alina! Did they follow you? Who knows you are here?"

"What are you talking about? Who would follow me?" Panic rose up in Cassie's chest, and she tried to tamp it down. *Alina again. Who is she?*

"The activists," Bobby scoffed. "You know that. We have to hide the food, or they'll take it."

Cassie held out her hand and walked slowly towards Bobby. "There are no activists here. It's only us." She took the tray from Bobby and set it on the counter. "Nobody is coming to take the food, okay?"

A deep sob tore from Bobby's lips, and she shouted, "They did take it! They took everything from us!"

"I know they did." Even though she had no idea what Bobby was talking about, Cassie played along, in hopes of calming her down. "But we're safe now. Nobody is coming tonight."

Bobby rubbed at her tear-stained face with muddy fingers, leaving streaks of dirt across her cheeks. "You're sure?"

"I promise." Cassie took Bobby by the shoulders and guided her out of the kitchen. "Come on, let's get you cleaned up and back in bed. You'll feel better in the morning."

Bobby shuffled along with Cassie, mumbling in Ukrainian. Cassie helped her get out of her housecoat and wetted a washcloth to wipe her face, hands, and feet before tucking her back in bed.

"Thank you, Alina," she said as she closed her eyes. Cassie waited for a few moments to make sure Bobby was really asleep, then crept out of the room and went back to the kitchen.

Slipping on a pair of sandals, she flipped on the back-porch light and walked out into the yard, looking for where Bobby had dug. In the perennial flower bed, under the old white mulberry tree, she found freshly turned dirt and a small trowel. Poking around a bit, she discovered two cans of peas, a plastic bag full of what looked like flour, and three tins of sardines in a shallow hole.

She glanced at her watch—4:30 a.m. Too early to wake up her mom. There was no way she could go back to sleep, though, so she carried the food back inside and put it all away, mopped the muddy floor, and put a pot of coffee on to brew.

* * *

Cassie picked at the protein muffin her mother had brought for breakfast. After she'd called her mother at 6:30, Anna had come right over.

"I thought maybe it was Birdie up for a drink of water, but it was Bobby, carrying food out of the kitchen to bury it."

"Bury it?" Anna's eyebrows raised.

"Yeah. She probably has a slip of paper somewhere with the foods and their location written down. That's what those notes were. I had Nick translate a couple for me."

"Nick was here? You didn't mention that."

"It's no big deal. Bobby tried to take a walk while I was in the shower, and he helped me get her home." Cassie downplayed the whole thing. She did not need her mother getting ideas about Nick.

Anna sighed. "You didn't mention a lot of things. So, she's still trying to go off on her own?"

"I was going to tell you all of it when you came over for dinner tonight, but then this hidden food thing threw me off," Cassie said.

"All right. One problem at a time, then." Anna poured herself a cup of coffee and sat at the table. "Did she say why she was burying the food?"

Cassie shook her head. "She said the activists would come and take it, so she had to hide it. And she called me Alina."

"Who's Alina?"

"I don't know. What are activists? And who are these two girls?" She showed her mother the tattered picture of the two girls in front of the sunflower field. "It looks like the drawing Birdie drew. The one that upset Bobby so much."

"A little bit. Bobby must have shown it to her." Anna squinted at the photo. "I think this one on the left is Bobby. It looks like her eyes and nose."

"Who's the other girl?"

"I have no idea." Anna pinched the bridge of her nose, her lifelong tell that she was fighting off a headache.

Cassie sipped her coffee. "I think we need to get her to talk about it. Maybe if we can understand why she's flashing back and wandering off, we can help her cope with it better."

"Good morning." Bobby shuffled into the kitchen, Birdie on her heels.

Cassie and Anna straightened in their chairs and shared a guilty look as Bobby opened the refrigerator. "Who would like blintzes for breakfast?"

Birdie waved her hands in the air and jumped up and down.

"Didn't you just make blintzes the other day?" Anna asked.

"You can never have too many blintzes," Bobby said. "Besides, they are Birdie's favorite. What other reason do I need to make them?"

Cassie eyed her grandmother warily. She seemed normal and completely in control—no signs of last night's escapade. "How did you sleep, Bobby?"

"Fine, fine." Bobby leaned into the fridge and took out some strawberries and cream cheese. "Cassie, get me a bowl, please."

Cassie glanced at her mom. "What do you think?"

Anna said in a low voice, "Let's give it a couple of days, but I'll still call the doctor and update him. Keep an eye on her, and if it happens again, let me know right away."

Anna stood and smiled at Bobby and Birdie. "I have to go get ready for work. You girls have a great day, and don't forget, tomorrow is pancake Saturday! I'll be by early to make breakfast, and I'll need your help, Birdie."

Cassie waved her mother off and watched as Bobby mixed up the batter and reminded Birdie how to fold the blintz. She seemed completely fine. What had happened last night? Who was Alina?

* * *

Cassie jolted upright in bed. Her dream came flashing back to her in a rush—the salty sea air, the waves crashing onto her bare feet.

Henry.

Cassie lay back down and closed her eyes, trying to cling to every beautiful detail.

Walking hand in hand with her on the beach where they'd honeymooned. Henry. Letting go of her hand. Pushing her ahead.

Be happy. Live your life.

The words echoed in her ears, and she clenched her fists, trying desperately to retain the feel of his hands in hers.

A leaf blower roared outside her window.

The spell broke. Her eyes flew open. She sat up again, and with an angry yank, ripped open her curtains, ready to yell at whatever poor lawn service sop her mother had hired. Instead, she saw Nick, dressed in his work uniform, blowing old leaves out of the flowerbeds. He whistled, not that she could hear him, and moved to the beat of whatever song was playing on his headphones.

His eyes, attracted to the movement of the curtains, looked up and connected with hers. A wide grin spread across his face, and he waved. Horrified, she snapped the curtains closed and sank back into her pillow. She rubbed her face and tried not to read too much into the fact that right after she'd finally dreamed of Henry, she'd woken up to Nick.

She groaned and rolled out of bed. After she'd brushed her hair and teeth and got dressed, she went into the kitchen. Once again, her eyes locked onto Nick, who sat at the table with Bobby and Birdie and a plate of pancakes in front of him.

"Well, you're everywhere this morning, aren't you?" She didn't try to hide the annoyance in her tone, though it was more with herself than him, and kissed Birdie on top of her head.

"Good morning." Her mother handed her a large mug of coffee, then went back to the stove and resumed flipping pancakes. "Nick brought Bobby's paper up on his way home from work and offered to blow the leaves out of the landscaping."

"I stopped as soon as I saw I'd woken you." His eyes glinted with merriment.

"It's fine," Cassie said, holding up a hand. "I was up."

Bobby, sitting across from Nick, snorted. "You were not."

Her face reddened, and Nick smiled. "Your bed head gave you away."

She touched her hair, now contained in a messy bun. "Well, it was a bit early for yard work, if you ask me. Why were you doing that, anyway?"

Nick shrugged. "I saw some perennials sprouting, so thought it would be nice to get things ready here so you guys can plant annuals whenever you want."

"Nick is such a helpful boy," Bobby said.

"Yes, wasn't that nice?" Anna beamed at them as she slid another pancake onto Birdie's plate. "Here, sweetie, have some more. Oh, I forgot. I left some groceries in the car." She undid the apron she had tied around her waist. "I'll be right back."

Nick stood. "Let me get them for you."

Anna waved him away. "You eat while your pancakes are still warm. It's not much."

"It's all right. I'll help her," Cassie said.

Nick sat down reluctantly, then laughed when Birdie made a silly face at him.

Cassie narrowed her eyes at the scene, then slipped on her shoes and followed her mother outside. "You're sure about him?"

Anna shot her an apologetic look. "I know you weren't convinced by my bulb planting encounter with him, so I asked around, and I've heard nothing but nice things. I think Bobby is right. He's just a nice guy who doesn't have any family nearby."

Cassie leaned into the trunk and grabbed the paper bags. "If you say so. It's like Bobby adopted him as her surrogate grandson or something."

"Bobby's always felt motherly toward young people without family. When I was a kid, we had people who had nowhere else to go coming over for dinner or staying for the holidays all the time." She paused and met Cassie's eye. "He hasn't done anything untoward to you or Birdie, has he?"

"No." Cassie ground the toe of her shoe into the pavement. Even she could tell that her animosity toward Nick was excessive, but the alternative was way too scary to contemplate. "I mean, he read to Birdie the other day. For over a half hour. Actually, she really loved it. I haven't seen her act that happy in a long time."

"I thought she seemed a lot more comfortable around him today than she normally is around new people," Anna said. "I think we jumped to the wrong conclusions. So far, all the poor guy has done is help an old lady without being asked or paid, planted bulbs for his dead grandma, and read to a little girl. Really, he seems pretty amazing. And that's not even mentioning his killer smile."

"Mom! Being good looking doesn't disqualify him from being a serial killer."

Anna scoffed as the sound of Birdie's laughter filtered out the half open door. "Oh, come on. Would you let someone you suspected of being a serial killer read to your kid? You're awfully defensive about Nick. Maybe you like him more than you realize, and it scares you."

The grain of truth in her mother's glib observation momentarily stunned Cassie, and it took a few seconds for her to choke out a response. "Oh, please, that's not it at all."

"Uh huh, that's what I thought," Anna laughed.

"Moving on from that wildly inaccurate accusation"—Cassie slammed the trunk with more force than necessary—"I didn't get the chance to tell you that I dreamt about Henry last night."

Anna cocked her head and appraised Cassie.

"Don't look at me like that. I know you think it's all a bunch of crap." Cassie grew indignant. "But it meant a lot to me that he might have visited."

"Visited?" Anna stopped and rested her bags against the car hood. "Really, Cass?"

"Bobby said I should ask him to come to me, so I tried it. I didn't think it would work, but maybe it did."

Anna rolled her eyes. "You don't really believe in all that, do you?"

Cassie tried to shrug away her mother's cynicism, but it stung. She wanted to believe in this. "I don't know."

"Okay, fine. I'll bite. What did he say?"

"Be happy. Live your life."

Anna pressed her lips together. "I'm glad if that brought you some comfort, but my theory is that it's your subconscious telling you that it's okay for you to have feelings for Nick."

"Well, I don't have feelings for Nick, so your theory is junk," Cassie said with more venom than necessary.

She flinched at the wounded look on her mother's face and tried a different track. "Didn't you ever dream about Dad?" Cassie's father had passed away from cancer ten years earlier, and for all of Anna's talk about moving on and finding closure, she rarely opened up about that loss.

Anna stiffened. "Of course I have dreams about your father now and then, but that doesn't mean anything. Dreams are merely a manifestation of your subconscious."

Cassie quirked an eyebrow. "Really, Mom?"

"I only want you to come to terms with Henry's death in a healthy way. If stuff like this makes you feel better, fine. But it might also help if you put yourself out there. Socialize. Try to connect with people."

"Like dating?" Cassie blew out an exasperated breath and hefted the grocery bag onto her hip. "And we've come full circle. I'm going inside."

* * *

Three days later, Cassie set Birdie up at the table with paper and crayons next to Bobby and her solitaire game while she talked to the internet guy Anna had sent over.

"You guys should have internet here. It's important to stay connected, and one day soon, you'll want to start writing again. You'll need to connect with your old contacts at the magazine. I'll even pay for it," Anna had said the other night at dinner. Cassie's protests had fallen on deaf ears, and she'd finally given in.

"When you're ready, you plug this into your computer." The technician held up a cable that came out of the wall near the kitchen table. "And you're all set. With broadband internet, you don't have to use the phone line anymore."

"Thank you," Cassie said, though she couldn't have cared less about the whole process. Her mind kept sneaking away to the box in Bobby's closet and the note Bobby had shoved into it when she was crying. Was it another note about hiding food? Or was it something different? She didn't want to pry, but it was time to be more aggressive in figuring out what was going on with her.

She ushered the man out, then checked on Bobby and Birdie. Both had abandoned their independent pursuits, and Bobby was teaching Birdie how to play a simple version of solitaire.

Satisfied that they were well occupied, Cassie tiptoed down the hall and into Bobby's bedroom. "I'm doing this to help her," she said to herself, in a vain attempt to alleviate the guilt she felt at snooping.

She slid the mirrored closet door open. Pushing aside the clothes on the shelf, she dug around until her hand hit a cardboard box. She scooted it forward and flipped through the contents: the old leather-bound journal wrapped in a long, embroidered *rushnyk*, a bundle of old black and white photographs in an envelope, a dozen or so loose notebook pages with Ukrainian writing on them, and the old candle and candleholder she'd first seen next to the journal.

So much information, and Cassie could decipher none of it.

The doorbell rang, and Cassie hesitated, trying to weigh the need to help Bobby against invading her grandmother's privacy. She grabbed a handful of notebook pages she assumed wouldn't be missed and pushed the box back behind the clothes.

"I'll get it!" Cassie folded the papers and shoved them into her jeans pocket, then ran down the hall. Safe in the living room, she let out the breath she didn't realize she'd been holding and, hoping her face didn't look too guilty, pulled open the front door.

"Hey, Cassie," Nick said. Dressed in his navy fire department pants and shirt, he held a stack of plastic food containers. "I wanted to stop by and return these."

"That's a lot of dishes." Cassie took them and set them on the side table.

His face reddened. "Your grandmother likes to send food home with me, and I never say no."

"Heading into work?" Cassie nodded towards his uniform.

"Yeah, for a couple of hours so a guy can take off to see his kid's t-ball game." He eyed her quizzically as she stepped toward him, blocking the doorway.

"That's nice." She tucked her hair behind her ears and glanced over her shoulder.

"Are you going to invite him in?" Bobby called from the kitchen.

"He can't stay!" she yelled back. She put her hand on Nick's arm, guiding him onto the front porch, all while resisting the sudden and startling urge to squeeze his thickly muscled bicep. *Focus, Cassie.* "Uh, can I ask you something?"

"Sure, what's up?"

She pulled the door closed. His proximity made her feel quivery inside, but, to her surprise, she didn't step back, and neither did he. She dug into her jeans pocket and pulled out the wad of papers.

"Another translation?"

"If you don't mind?" She could smell his cologne and a trace of smoke. "Did you go to a fire?"

He cocked his head as he pondered her question, then blushed. "Yeah, last night. Sorry. Do I smell like smoke? I feel like it oozes out of my pores sometimes, no matter how much I shower."

"I don't mind. It's kind of nice. I mean, it's not offensive." She cleared her throat and held out the papers.

His eyes stayed locked on hers for a few beats before he unfolded the sheets and started reading.

"Forgive me, Alina. Forgive me, Alina." He scanned the page, then turned it over and read the back. "That's all it says. Over and over." He flipped through a few more. "I think they all say that."

Cassie wrapped her arms around her middle. "Oh, man. This is getting weirder and weirder."

"Who's Alina?" Nick asked, concern etched on his face.

"I don't know," Cassie said. "And I have no idea why Bobby wants her forgiveness so much."

14

KATYA

Ukraine, May 1931

Four more excruciating weeks of hard work passed without any news of Pavlo. Katya ached to feel his long body pressed against her, to have him tease her out of her bad moods, to talk with him when the world seemed so bleak. Some days, she thought her time as his wife had been imagined. A beautiful dream she'd created as a welcome alternative to the bone–weary drudgery of her days.

Today, she'd worked in the collective stables, mucking stalls and hauling manure. It was back-breaking work, but she appreciated the mindlessness of it. As dusk fell, she walked over to Sasha's old home. Luckily, their place was far enough out from the village that the activists hadn't seized it for their own quarters. Every night, she made this trip to put Honey out to graze, and every morning, she woke before dark and hid the goat back in the barn, always wondering if the goat would be waiting for her, or if someone would have found and stolen her.

Eerie silence clouded the abandoned homestead. Dried out remains of Aunt Oksana's flowers from last season spiraled in unruly tangles out of their beds. Young weeds choked out the wooden fence, giving the yard a dark and forlorn ambience. Even the cold, empty house seemed sad with its broken windows and front door hanging crookedly from the hinges.

"I'm sorry, Aunt Oksana," Katya said. "I'd tidy it up for you, but I need it to look deserted so no one suspects our goat is here."

She turned her back on the bleak sight and pushed open the barn door. Honey bleated out a greeting, bringing a relieved smile to Katya's face as she scooped up an armful of hay. The goat's belly, thankfully growing fat with a kid, served as a reminder that soon, they would have goat's milk to supplement their food again.

"What would we do without you, Honey?" Katya gave the animal a scratch between her horns as she kicked the door shut behind her. "I know you're lonely out here, but at least you're safe. Hopefully."

Her words tapered off as the door swung open. The dusky evening glow highlighted a large frame, and her fear turned to joy as she recognized her husband.

"Katya, I've missed you." His voice came out in a low groan as he pressed his lips to hers. "Your mother said you were out here."

She melted into his embrace, pulled back to look him over, and then kissed him again, while trying to speak. "I've missed you, too."

"I'm sorry," he murmured, his mouth moving to her neck.

Their words faded away as they came together in a frenzy of fear, longing, and love. Katya's body sang under Pavlo's attentiveness and all thoughts of their time apart faded away.

Afterward, he cradled her against his chest and ran his fingers through her hair as he talked.

"The surrounding villages are fighting more than our village ever did. They've been more secretive about their plans, not as open and foolish as Tomas was."

"What are they doing?" She gripped his hip, afraid to let go lest he disappear like he had so many weeks ago.

"A larger revolt is being planned, but for now, small bands of us have attacked wagons taking food out of the villages and returned the food to the villagers."

"How? Did you kill the activists taking the food?"

He nodded and dropped his eyes. "Do you think less of me for killing?"

"No!" The anger in her voice surprised her. "They've taken from us for far too long. And the food? Do the villagers get it back?"

"We try. We've only done it twice. The first time, we drove the wagon back to town and everyone crowded around it and took what they wanted. Fighting broke out. Hunger makes people ugly toward each other. When the Party officials still in the village realized what happened, they began shooting at the people as they left the wagon. It didn't work as we had hoped. One villager was killed. So, the second time, we hid the grain out in the woods and the villagers came and took back what had been taken from them."

"And that worked better?"

He nodded and held up a small bag of wheat for her to take. "Some people shared as a thanks. But none of these are long term solutions. We need to get rid of the activists completely. We need to unite all the local villages and rise up together."

"But how?"

"We're still working on that. We need more weapons so we can hold our own against their numbers, and we'd have to cut communication so they couldn't ask for outside help."

Katya shook her head. "This is foolishness. They will always be able to call for help. They have trained soldiers and all the Twenty-Five Thousanders to fight for them. You may take out one village activist group, but they'll just replace it."

"Then you think it is hopeless?" Pavlo asked.

"I don't know what to think. All I know is that I want you here. With me. I have a bad feeling about where this is going."

"Katya, I want to be with you too, but we have to try to fight. You used to believe that."

She sighed. "You're right. I still believe it."

"What's wrong, then?"

"They took our cow. And we had to join the collective. They said anyone who didn't join would be labeled a *kulak*. We didn't have much choice after that."

He scowled and swore under his breath. This anger, so unlike him, disconcerted her. Her hands trembled as she smoothed her hair and changed the subject.

"Did I tell you that Alina is expecting?"

That earned her a smile, and the old Pavlo reappeared. "Is she now? Good for them!"

"Dinner should be done. Let's go and eat." She took his hand and squeezed, squelching down the impending sense of doom she felt whenever she looked at him.

* * *

Katya woke up the next morning alone with a note next to her pillow.

> *You're so beautiful when you sleep that I couldn't bear to wake you. I love you. I'll see you soon. - P*

She cursed at him under her breath, then tucked the note into her shirt so his words would be close to her as she worked.

* * *

Katya sighed as she stepped out into the yard to gather vegetables from the garden. The July sun shone down on her, but it didn't fix her dour mood. It had been over six weeks since Pavlo had left again, and her melancholy had returned in full force.

A few early red tomatoes hung heavy and fragrant on their vines, and Mama wanted some for supper since Kolya and Alina were visiting. Luckily, they were still allowed to keep their gardens, though rumors had been floating around for some time that this would be changing in the future and their personal gardens would become property of the state. Katya wanted to harvest, preserve, and hide as much as she could before that happened.

Katya picked two of the ripest tomatoes as her eyes strayed over to the sunflower patch. Separate from their regular sunflower field, Tato had always planted a small area just for Katya and Alina and left a bare spot in the middle of the towering pillars that created a secret room. The green stems served as walls, the bobbing yellow flowers and blue sky the ceiling. She and Alina had spent many hours lying on their backs, heads cushioned by dandelions and periwinkles, dreaming and talking. Tato called it their "sunflower palace."

"It's a magical place," he'd say with a wink. "Any wishes you make in there will come true."

With her father gone, no one had thought to plant the sunflowers. But fallen seeds and Mother Nature continued the tradition and rebuilt the palace now, even when the girls no longer used it. Abandon and forlorn, it called to Katya, waving in the wind and caressing her with memories of childhood.

With a quick glance back at the house, she set the tomatoes down and dashed over to the sunflower palace. Crouching low, she pushed aside wayward stems and made her way to the center of the patch. Without her father cultivating it, the middle no longer remained clear. Weeds and rogue sunflowers made it difficult to find an open spot, but nostalgia still coursed through her as she ran her hands over the soft tufts of dandelion fluff. She sat down and rolled onto her back, staring up through petals as she had when she was a girl. Katya closed her eyes and inhaled the smells of her youth. Fragrant flowers, rich earth, baking bread wafting out from the house. She could almost pretend she was ten years old again, carefree and happy.

Her sister broke the reverie. "Katya! Where are you? Mama wants those tomatoes!"

Katya crawled to the opening and waved her in. "Alina! Come here, the sunflower palace has missed us!"

Alina glanced back at the house. "Our mother misses us, and I fear her wrath more than the sunflowers."

But she scrambled in beside Katya and grabbed her hand, just like when they were young, and they lay back and stared up at the sky.

"Well, your dreams did come true," Katya said.

Alina rubbed her belly. "Yes, I married Kolya, and I'm soon to be a mother. In the midst of everything else, at least I have that." She took Katya's hand and pressed her hand against her stomach. "Sometimes I think I can feel her moving, but Mama said it's too soon."

"I still can't believe you're having a baby. Mama's so excited."

Alina sighed. "It's good she has this to focus on."

Instead of Tato.

The unspoken words hung in the air, and Katya stilled as a rush of emotion washed over her. "Do you feel him here? Tato?"

Alina closed her eyes and nodded. "I miss him so much."

"Me, too," Katya said. "But it's odd. I'm not sad here. I feel safe. Happy, almost. Like Tato is here with us."

"That's because these sunflowers connect us to our fondest family memories. And as long as we have those, we will always have each other."

Katya squeezed her sister's hand. "Sisters forever."

"Girls! Where are my tomatoes?" Mama called from the house.

"Coming, Mama!" Alina called out.

"It's like when we were children." Katya smiled.

Alina gave her a quick hug, then they giggled as they clambered over each other in an attempt to get out fast.

"You still go in there?" Mama smiled as they ran toward her. "I thought you were far too old for such daydreams."

"It's a happy place, Mama. It feels good to be in there." Katya kissed her on the cheek and handed her the tomatoes.

She snorted. "Perhaps I should spend more time in there then. Come, this *varenyky* will not make itself."

Mama had the dough mixed and two bowls of filling ready on the table.

"Both meat and potatoes?" Katya asked. "What's the occasion?"

"Kolya brought home some pork that we need to use up before it's confiscated. And we have potatoes and onions from the garden. With those things on hand, how could we not make them?"

"Do we have any butter?" Alina asked.

Mama pulled a small jar out from under her bed. "Just enough to fry the onions."

Katya whooped with excitement. After the skimpy meals of late, *varenyky* with onions fried in butter would be a special treat.

They sat around the table and made *varenyky* the way Mama had taught them, and the way her mother had taught her. Katya rolled the dough flat, then cut circles from it using a tin cutter. She held up her left hand as if she were holding a cup, then rested a circle of flattened dough on top of it. She took a spoonful of the potato mixture, because it was her favorite, and pushed it into the space where the dough sagged in between her thumb and fingers. With a flick of her wrist, she moved the *varenyky* on its side and, after dabbing her fingers in a cup of water, pinched the ends together to form a perfect crescent of stuffed dough.

She set her handiwork down next to the others. Katya's, nearly as perfect as Mama's, made Alina's look like a mangled mess.

Alina sighed. "I will never be a good *varenyky* maker."

"You overstuff them," Mama said. "And your dough isn't rolled out thin enough. Watch Katya. She reminds me of my mother. Her *varenyky* are all uniform. That's when you know you've got it."

Katya flushed with pride at her mother's praise. "Don't worry, Alina. I think *varenyky* making might be the only thing I surpass you at. In everything else, you always win."

Alina chuckled and leaned over to rest her head on Katya's shoulder. "That's not true, and you know it, but for today, I'll take it, little sister."

* * *

That night, Katya dreamed of her father. They walked through their wheat field together. She ran her hands over the stalks of wheat as they shimmered and waved, a moving creature rolling across the hills behind the house. It was a perfect crop.

"Try some." Tato held out a handful of kernels.

She poured some in her mouth and bit down. Still chewy. No telltale crunch between her teeth signaling ripeness.

"Not yet," she said.

Her father smiled sadly. "You see, Katya. A farmer plants and nurtures today, so he can harvest a good crop in the future. You must always look to the future."

"I miss you, Tato."

"I miss you, too." Her father cradled her face in his hands. "I wish I were there to help you. Things will get worse before they get better, but you are strong. Just make it through today and hope that tomorrow will be better. Can you do that?"

Gunshots broke through the peaceful scene.

Tato's eyes widened, and he pushed at her. "Go, Katya. Go to him. There isn't much time."

Katya sat straight up and gasped. The silent night echoed around her, but something felt wrong. She jumped out of bed as Alina burst in the house.

Alina faltered, surprised to see Katya already standing. "How did you know?"

"Know what?" Katya asked, though a hard knot of fear in her gut told her the answer.

Alina's voice broke. "Pavlo's hurt."

"What happened?" Katya wrenched on her boots and grabbed her coat as Mama rose from the other bed.

"He's been shot," Alina said. "Kolya found him in the yard. It's bad, Katya."

A thousand questions raced through her mind as Katya sprinted across the field. She pushed open the door and ran into the room.

"Where is he?"

Kolya stood up from where he'd been leaning over the bed and strode toward her. Grief rippled across his face as he grabbed her shoulders

"You need to know, Katya, that his wounds are severe. I don't know how he survived long enough to drag himself here."

"Let me see him!" She pushed past Kolya and dropped to her knees next to Pavlo.

His pale face, streaked with dirt and dried blood, felt cold against her hand.

"He has two bullet wounds, one in his stomach and one in his arm." Kolya kneeled beside her.

"Pavlo, can you hear me?" Katya stroked his face, kissed his lips. "I'm here now, Pavlo. I'm here to take care of you, just like last time. Let's see where you're hurt."

Her mother, who must have followed, began barking directions about boiling water and clean rags as Katya inspected Pavlo's body.

His eyes cracked open, and he turned toward the sound of her voice. "Katya? I made it home to you. I promised you I'd see you again, and I couldn't bear to break that promise."

"Of course you did." His right arm hung twisted and blood oozed out from under the rag Kolya pressed on his gut.

"We need to see if the one in his stomach went clean through," Kolya said. He moved the rag to the side to check the wound and uncovered a red mass of mangled flesh. A wave of nausea washed over Katya.

Together, they rolled him, and Pavlo moaned.

"No exit wound," Kolya said. "It's still in there."

"We need a doctor!" Katya said, her voice frantic. "Someone needs to get a doctor!"

"And tell them what?" Kolya scowled at her. "Tell them my brother was shot while fighting against the OGPU? Who would risk their life to help him?"

"The doctor was deported last month," Mama said. "We'll have to help him ourselves."

"Mama, there's too much blood!" Alina's hands held a fresh rag on Pavlo's stomach, but blood continued to ooze out.

"Keep applying pressure." Mama's voice wavered.

"Katya? Where are you?" Pavlo thrashed weakly and opened his eyes. "I need to see you!"

Katya dropped her head close to his. "I'm right here, Pavlo. Shh, now, don't fuss. We're trying to help you."

"No, it's too late." His glossy eyes locked on hers and he pressed his good hand to her lips when she started to protest. "You need to be strong for me, Katya. Kolya will care for you. He's promised me. We have to say goodbye now, but you will always be my love, my Katya."

Tears ran down her face. The room and everyone in it faded away until it was only Pavlo whispering to her.

"I have loved you all my life." His voice hitched as he struggled to take a breath. "Even when I pestered you and teased you, I loved you. Always you, only you." He coughed and his body shuddered. "You must survive this and tell the people of the world what has happened here, so it doesn't happen again. Use your pencil and paper and weave your beautiful words to keep our memories alive. Don't let me die in vain, Katya."

She nodded and choked back her sobs. "I won't. I promise."

"I will always love you." His eyes widened and she felt the shift in his body, the flight of his soul like a knife to her heart.

"Pavlo? Pavlo!" Katya screamed his name, but he didn't respond. Arms pulled her off him, but she pushed them away and fell back onto him and looked down into the face of the man she loved. His open, lifeless eyes stared back at her. They held none of the sparkle and life that Pavlo possessed. They were hollow and empty, like her now. A sob slipped out before she could stifle it. She needed to close his eyes, but she couldn't bear the thought of never looking into them again. Instead, she crawled onto the bed next to him and wept.

When she finally pulled herself up, her unsteady legs buckled, and she pitched forward. In an instant, Kolya was next to her, his strong arms holding her up. She leaned into his solid bulk while he stared down at his brother. His chest shuddered under her cheek as he bit back his grief.

"My brother. My baby brother." His ragged words ripped through the silence of the house and now he leaned into her. "I've lost him, Katya."

"I know." She reached out and closed Pavlo's eyes with trembling fingers. "We've all lost him."

* * *

Numbness settled over Katya, heavy and cold, like a damp wool cloak, slowly choking the life out of her. And she was glad for it, because what kind of life could she have without Pavlo?

Bleary eyed, Katya read the last note he'd given her over and over.

You're so beautiful when you sleep that I couldn't bear to wake you. I love you. I'll see you soon. – P.

The words both soothed her and enraged her. Now bloodstained from her time spent pressed against his wounded body, she no longer tucked the note in her shirt. Instead, she pressed it into her journal so she wouldn't risk losing it while she worked. It was the last piece of him she had.

Every night, she tossed and turned, the sweet oblivion of sleep unattainable for her tortured soul. And, every morning, she started off the day with a violent bout of vomiting, which, in her more delusional moments, she imagined was her body rejecting Mama's attempts to sustain her through the food she forced down her throat. Katya's body simply wanted to die along with Pavlo.

Three weeks after his death, Mama grabbed Katya by the arm and asked how long she'd been sick in the morning.

"It started right after..." Katya trailed off, unable to finish the sentence.

"And how long since your last monthly?"

The question confused her for a moment, then a flash of under-standing dawned. Alina had had morning sickness in the beginning of her pregnancy. Now, midway through, she finally had shaken the unwelcome morning ritual.

"Oh, no," Katya moaned and sank into a chair. "It's been well over a month. Probably two. I've lost track. Mama, how can I do this without him?"

"Hush, now." Mama pulled her daughter toward her. "I'll be here to help you through. It's a blessing, Katya, for a little piece of Pavlo lives on inside you."

That idea soothed her. Katya rested a hand on her still flat belly and gave a small smile. "He would have been so excited."

But the smile melted away as the realization that Pavlo would never know or hold this child washed over her.

She collapsed into sobs against her mother's chest. Mama stroked her hair and told her that everything would be fine, but Katya knew it was a lie.

15

CASSIE

Illinois, May 2004

Cassie set her pencil down on the notebook and glanced at the clock. Her mother and Bobby should be back from the doctor anytime now. She ran a hand across the word–filled page and smiled. That afternoon, the sudden urge to write about her favorite memories of Henry had made her fingers twitch. She almost didn't recognize the feeling. While she hadn't been able to bring herself to use her old laptop to write articles or stories yet, journaling by hand had proven to be cathartic.

Bobby had been right.

Some pages bore the tear stains of her grief, and other entries made her laugh out loud as she recalled his antics. When she was done, if she could ever really be done writing about him, she would keep the book for Birdie so she would always have a way to remember her father.

Cassie stood and stretched the kinks out of her neck and upper back, then went to check on Birdie. She smoothed the damp hair off her daughter's forehead. Birdie always got so hot when she napped. Her breath, slow and even, fell from parted lips still sticky from the chocolates Bobby had given her. Without a doubt, Bobby enjoyed having the little girl here to spoil. Just last night, they'd spent hours working together as Bobby taught Birdie how to embroider flowers on a white cloth.

"That's how you taught me," Cassie had said.

"And it's how my mother taught me," Bobby replied. "She was an artist with her needle and thread. I could never create pieces as beautiful as hers, but she made sure I learned the craft."

Cassie eyed the framed, embroidered picture hanging over Birdie's bed and made a mental note to ask Bobby who had made it. Golden stalks of wheat wove up between scarlet and blue flowers. Green vines and leaves framed the bouquet. It truly was a piece of art.

Her mother's voice echoed from the kitchen and Cassie slipped out of the room, closing the door behind her so Birdie could keep sleeping.

"So, how was the appointment?" Cassie helped Bobby into her chair at the kitchen table, then sat next to her.

"Bah! Ridiculous!" Bobby said. "They asked me so many questions it made my head spin. And I had to draw a clock. Waste of time."

Anna, her face strained, fell into the chair next to Cassie's. "I told you, it's a standard test to assess your mental faculties."

"I'm fine." Bobby slammed her fist on the table. "I don't need doctors to tell me that."

Anna massaged her forehead. "Cassie, will you get me some aspirin? I think there's some in the medicine cabinet. If not, then check the nightstand in Bobby's room."

"Sure, Mom." Cassie left the two of them still bickering and opened up the mirrored doors above the bathroom sink. No aspirin, but since the last time she'd checked, three cans of beets had taken up residence there.

She walked down the hall to Bobby's bedroom and pushed open

the door. The room smelled like old lady perfume and incense. Family pictures and colorful embroidered pictures filled the walls.

Cassie resisted the urge to pilfer through the box in the closet again and instead sat on the bed and rifled through the various bottles on top of the nightstand. When she didn't find what she was looking for, she opened the top drawer. There, next to a loaf of bread and five cans of sardines, she found the small bottle of aspirin.

Curious, she opened the next two drawers and found them packed to the brim with bags of prunes and raisins, cans of diced pears, and boxes of macaroni and cheese. Cassie cursed and grabbed a can of pears.

"Here you go." She set the pill bottle on the table. "So, what did they say at the appointment?"

Anna gave a tight smile. "Her doctor wants to do further testing."

Bobby glared at Anna. "I'm fine!"

"Bobby, we aren't doing this to be mean." Cassie held up the can of pears she'd tucked under her arm. "We're worried about you. Why are you hiding food all over the house? Why are you wandering around the yard at night burying it?"

Bobby paled. "Where did you find that?"

"In your nightstand. Along with a bunch of other stuff."

"Who put it there?" Bobby demanded.

Cassie cocked her head. Did she really think someone else had done this? "You did. Don't you remember when I found you the other night out in the yard? You were burying food. Barefoot. At four in the morning."

"No. I didn't do that." She pushed away from the table, her eyes clouded, as if she'd disappeared into some distant part of her mind and couldn't be reached. "I haven't had to do that in a long time," she said as she walked into the living room.

Cassie frowned. "There's got to be something else going on that we're missing. Some kind of trauma she went through long ago that's exacerbating this whole thing. Maybe it's related to those notes I told you about? The ones asking for forgiveness from Alina?"

"I wouldn't know since she won't talk about it. My whole life, I've had no idea who my grandparents were or if I had any cousins, or aunts and uncles. It was just us." Anna crossed her arms. "Let's give her some time. Today took a lot out of her."

"And you, too, by the looks of it," Cassie said. "Why don't you go home and get some rest? I'll keep an eye on her."

Anna scrubbed her face with her hands. "Thanks, I will. I'll check back in later."

After her mother left, a strangled cry rang out from the living room. She ran in and found Bobby kneeling on the ground next to her holy icon corner.

"It fell! Do you know what that means?" Bobby said.

Cassie dropped to her knees and gathered up the fallen picture and *rushnyk*. "I'm sure it's nothing. The nail probably slipped out. I can rehang it for you."

"No." Bobby shook her head and fixed her glassy stare on Cassie. "When an icon falls, death is coming. I'm running out of time."

"Bobby, stop talking like that. I can't think about losing you." Cassie's stomach knotted as she pulled Bobby to her feet. "Now, come on. Let's get you into bed so you can rest."

Cassie tucked Bobby in, then sat on the edge of the bed and held her grandmother's hands. "I'll sit here with you until you fall asleep."

Arthritis had long ago deformed Bobby's joints, but her left hand was far more swollen than her right. Cassie ran her fingers over the crooked fingers and bulbous knuckles that required ice on bad days.

Bobby's voice startled her. "Do you know death is not the end? It's just another reality. In the old world, we knew that. We welcomed the dead into our homes. We set places for them at the table at Christmas. Held feasts in their honor. But here, I've forgotten those ways. I need to prepare, so I'm ready for my death."

"Stop, Bobby."

"I'm not afraid of death," she went on. "Only of disappointing her. I never got the chance to tell her what I needed to. I never got the chance."

"Who are you talking about?" Cassie gripped Bobby's gnarled hand tighter.

"You must do something for me," Bobby demanded, her voice suddenly strong and decisive. "Go to my closet. Behind my clothes on the middle shelf, there's a box. Take it."

Cassie retrieved the box without mentioning that she'd already looked through it. She set it on the bed, and Bobby turned her head away. "I can't look at it anymore. I tried, but it hurts too much. You and your mother have always wanted to know about my past. Everything is in this box."

Both excitement and guilt coursed through Cassie as she flipped through the contents. Maybe Bobby would finally explain all of it so she could actually understand. Bobby stilled her hand.

"Not with me here. You'll need Nick to help you. It's all in Ukrainian, but he's a good boy. He'll help. He likes you, you know."

"He does not," Cassie said automatically, but she was only half listening. Her mind was already focused on the treasure trove of information sitting in front of her—her key to helping Bobby.

* * *

The next few days passed by smoothly without any more incidents. Birdie seemed to be settling into their new life, and Cassie had to admit her mom had been right. She felt happier here than she had at her old house, as if she'd shed the hard outer shell of her grief. Cassie found herself smiling and laughing more, like she was slowly waking up from a long hibernation.

The box was her one source of frustration. She'd spent hours staring at the journal, running her hands down its worn leather cover, and trying in vain to decipher the words within. She'd even tried looking online, but it was impossible to type the Cyrillic letters into the search engine. When she got tired of that, she'd pored through the black and white photos and looked for glimpses of Bobby in the young women.

"You must ask Nick to help you," Bobby had said again over breakfast.

"Why can't you read it to me? Or tell me about it?" Cassie begged. She wanted to hear the story from Bobby in her own words.

Bobby shook her head. "No. Surviving through it once was hard enough. It's important that you know, but I will not relive it."

"Just call Nick," Anna had said. She, too, was dying to know what was in the journal, and, as she'd let Cassie know on more than one occasion, she was more than a little miffed that Bobby had skipped her over and given the materials to Cassie.

"I will," Cassie said. And she intended to—as soon as she had a better grip on her reaction to him.

* * *

That afternoon, she, Birdie, and Bobby walked to the park down the street. There, Bobby sat on a bench in the sunshine while Birdie played on the jungle gym. Cassie moved back and forth between the two as necessary.

"She reminds me of you when you were little," Bobby said, as they watched Birdie sliding down the tallest slide, then racing back up to do it again. "She's fearless."

"She used to be, before the accident," Cassie said. "But, for a long time afterward, I couldn't get her to leave my side. Since we've been here, I've seen something in her shifting."

The warm breeze rustled the budding tree branches canopied overhead, bringing the spring scents of damp earth and newly awakening plants with it. Bobby scrutinized the young girl.

"I still see it in her," Bobby finally said. "She's like you. She'll get back to her fearless self."

Cassie drew in a wavering breath. "How do you see that when I've been such a mess?"

Bobby patted Cassie's knee. "It doesn't matter what I see. It's what you see."

As Cassie thought about that, Birdie ran off the playground toward the street, waving her arms.

Cassie jumped up. "Hey, where are you going? Don't go in the street!"

Birdie stopped on the sidewalk and waved again.

"Who are you waving at?" Cassie asked as she jogged over.

"Hey, Cassie," Nick called out. Dressed in running shorts and a sleeveless shirt, and dripping with sweat, he looked like he'd just run a 5k.

"Oh, hi, Nick." Cassie tried not to stare at his thick, muscled arms and ended up staring at the sky. "What are you doing here?"

Nick looked up too. "Just out for a run. What are you looking at?"

"Nothing." Cassie's face flushed. "I thought I saw a bird."

"Me, too!" Nick gave Birdie's arm a gentle squeeze. "My favorite bird."

Birdie giggled in delight.

"Nick!" Bobby slowly made her way over to them. "I'm glad we ran into you. I wanted to invite you to dinner tonight. We're making borscht."

"We are?" Cassie said at the same time Nick said: "I'd love to! Borscht is my favorite."

"Good, come by around six."

"I wouldn't miss it! I'll see you guys then." He threw out a wave and jogged off.

"Why did you do that?" Cassie asked as they walked home, Birdie skipping ahead in front of them.

"Do what?" Bobby asked.

"You know what! Ask him to dinner. And since when are we making borscht?"

"I always make borscht. It's good," Bobby said.

"I know it's good. But do we even have what we need for it?"

"Of course. I may be old, but I'm not crazy." She wagged a crooked finger at Cassie. "You can tell your mother that, too. I put beef shanks on the stove to simmer this morning. Didn't you see? And Anna bought the beets and cabbage when she went to the store for me yesterday. She's coming, too."

Cassie sighed. "Fine, but next time you decide to throw a dinner party, a little warning would be appreciated."

"I didn't know your mother and a neighbor coming over would bother you so much."

"It doesn't bother me." Cassie hesitated. "It's just different."

"Different because it makes you feel happy? And you haven't been happy in so long?"

Birdie stopped to smell a forsythia bush in their neighbors' front yard.

Cassie ignored Bobby. "Birdie, you can't run into people's yards."

Birdie shot Cassie a pouty look and ran ahead to Bobby's yard to investigate her flowers.

"So?" Bobby asked.

"So what?"

"So, you didn't answer my question. Does he make you feel happy?"

"Who?" Cassie feigned innocence. "Nick? I hardly know him."

"Mm hmm. But even though you try to hide it, I see how you are whenever he's around. I haven't seen you like that since…"

"Don't!" Cassie held up her hand. "Don't even compare. I don't feel anything for him, and there is no way he's remotely like Henry."

"Nobody is comparing," Bobby said gently. "All I said is you seem happy. Henry doesn't have to be the last man to make you happy. And you have a favor to ask of Nick, yes? Here's your chance."

Cassie shook her head as they went in the front door. How could

Bobby bring up Henry's name so easily in comparison to Nick? Even if she did find him attractive, he was no Henry.

The admission gave her pause. She found him attractive. That was the plain truth. She found him attractive, and it scared the hell out of her. But noticing someone was good looking wasn't a crime, right? It was perfectly normal. Human nature. He was a neighbor, and she'd have to deal with him a lot more if he was going to translate, but she could handle it.

Live your life. Be happy. Henry's words echoed in her mind. She rubbed her hands over her face. She had only been a widow for fifteen months. How could she be attracted to someone already? What kind of unfaithful monster was she?"

As they entered the house, Bobby walked over to her holy icons corner and carefully lowered herself to her knees.

"Do you do that every day?" Cassie refrained from commenting on how impressed she was that Bobby could still maneuver her body like that, as she didn't think the older woman would appreciate it.

"I've come back to it," Bobby said. "I had a long dry spell, but now, it gives me comfort."

Cassie plucked at a loose string on the back of the couch as Bobby lit a votive candle in a red glass holder. "You know, I tried it. I asked Henry to come to me, and he did. Kind of. In a dream. Mom thinks I'm being ridiculous."

Bobby looked sharply at her. "Did it help you?"

Cassie nodded. "I think so."

"That's all that matters." She turned back to her icon corner. "When I'm done here, we'll make the borscht."

16

KATYA

Ukraine, December 1931

"Fetch your sister and bring her back here to live," Mama said.

Katya looked up from the coat she was mending. "You want Kolya and Alina to move in here?"

"Of course. It makes sense that we all stay together now that Alina's time is so close. What if the baby comes and only Kolya is there to help? He doesn't know the first thing about helping a woman in labor. She needs to be here. They can have my bed. It will give them the most privacy. I'll sleep with you."

"Yes, Mama." Katya wondered what Kolya would think of having his privacy in the first year of his marriage consist of a sheet hanging across the length of his bed. It did make sense, though. It would be easier to have them all in one household. "I'll go talk to them this afternoon."

"Don't just talk, Katya," she replied. "You tell them. You tell them I said it would be what's best for the family. Don't let Kolya's pride stand in your way."

Katya kept her eyes down on the mending, her response monotone. "Yes, Mama, I won't let him stand in my way."

"He's a good boy," she went on. "He takes good care of her, provides well. But he has no idea of what taking care of an infant would be like, or, God forbid, having to deliver a baby if we're snowed in. No, they should come here as soon as possible, and probably stay for a long time. Maybe for good. That makes the most sense."

Katya continued sewing as her mother prattled on. Lately, she'd found the mindless, repetitive movements of mending clothing soothed her. It wasn't until Katya could feel her mother's stare boring into her that she realized Mama had stopped talking. She jerked her head up and said dutifully, "Yes, Mama."

"Well, what are you waiting for, then? Go now! Some exercise and fresh air will be good for you and your baby."

"Oh, of course," Katya mumbled. "I can do this later." She pulled herself awkwardly to her feet. She still had a few months left before she was due, but Alina's time could be any day now. She pulled on the unfinished coat. No matter. The rip in the sleeve was small and wouldn't bother her too much. It was better to go now and appease her mother.

She tromped through the snow to Alina and Kolya's house. Since they had joined the collective, life had only become harder for all of them. They worked tirelessly, but still never seemed to have much food at home. Their small vegetable garden had helped, but for the first time in their lives, they had issues with people stealing the vegetables right from the yard.

Before the Soviets overtook them, Mama had run a strict household. The house sparkled, food filled the home, and the only time she sat was in the evenings when she did her needlework. Her hands created the most beautiful designs with a needle and thread, and her work was well known throughout the area. *Rushnyky* and pictures with birds, flowers, and trees detailed in tiny stitches still adorned the walls of their home, but Katya hadn't seen her mother create anything new since her father had been arrested.

Now, she wanted Katya to tell Kolya to abandon his family home and come move in with his mother-in-law and sister-in-law. Katya almost smiled as she imagined his reaction, and the upward movement of her lips felt unfamiliar and stiff on her pinched face. Her mother had always been presumptive, but this was going to be interesting.

"Alina?" Katya called, knocking gently on the door of the small home. Months had passed, but she could still feel the sadness that hung in the air like a blanket over the house. She closed her eyes as she stood there. A thousand memories rushed back, pulling her in different directions. Pavlo was everywhere here, but she couldn't touch him or bring herself to reach out to him in any way. It still hurt too much. A dull ache throbbed at the back of her throat.

"Katya!" Alina opened the door and welcomed Katya with a hug. Even though neither of them had gained as much weight as they should while carrying a child, Alina still looked awkward with her round belly protruding in front of her. Mama was right; her time would be soon. That was the only thing that might make presenting this idea to them easier.

"Hello, Alina," Katya croaked, pulling back the reins on her emotions. She glanced around. "Is Kolya home, too?"

"He's out in the barn. Why? Is something wrong?"

Alina waddled rather ungracefully to the *pich* where she was cooking a pot of borscht. Katya's eyes flickered involuntarily to the spot where Pavlo had died, and the vision she'd been hoping to avoid returned. Pavlo, battered and limp, his beautiful eyes, open and staring at the ceiling. The coppery smell of blood flooded her senses, and she broke out in a cold sweat. Suddenly, she was there, watching Pavlo die all over again.

Katya shuddered and squeezed her eyes shut, willing the memory away.

"Are you well, Katya?" Alina asked, her kind face creased with worry. She put her hand on Katya's arm. "I'm here to talk if you want."

"I'm fine," Katya said. How could she tell Alina that she could barely make herself get out of bed every morning? If she opened the floodgates of her grief, she would drown them both, so she locked them tight and went right into the reason for her visit. "Mama thinks it's best if you and Kolya move back home with us."

"Oh." Alina furrowed her brow in contemplation. "I'm not sure. I'll have to talk to Kolya."

Katya had the sudden urge to press her finger into Alina's forehead to smooth it, like Alina had done for her at Olha and Boryslav's wedding. A lifetime ago, back when they'd worried about silly things like falling in love and getting married. Now, Katya spent her time wondering what she would eat each day and if the activists would tire of taking their food and finally arrest them.

Katya balled her fists. "Mama wants me to bring you home today. You know how she is."

"Oh," Alina repeated as she carefully lowered herself down into a chair at the table.

"She thinks you should be around women, because your time is near."

"That makes some sense," Alina said. "Maybe until the baby is born, but I'll have to talk to Kolya first."

As if on cue, Kolya entered the house. His eyes instantly went to Alina, oblivious to the fact that a visitor sat at his table. Katya could see the love emanating from him toward his pregnant wife. It made her happy that her sister had someone who cared for her so, but it also sharpened the knife that perpetually twisted in her gut. Kolya looked so much like Pavlo, and to see the way he doted on Alina... for a moment, Katya wondered how miserable it would feel for her to see their obvious love for each other every day, all day: a constant reminder of all that she'd lost. Ashamed, she quickly pushed the selfish thought from her head.

"Kolya." Alina welcomed him with a warm smile. "Katya is here to make us an offer."

Kolya regarded her, and she could sense him assessing her wellbeing. "Hello, Katya. How are you feeling?"

Ever since Kolya had found out she was pregnant with Pavlo's baby, he'd become very protective of her. He made sure she and Mama always had plenty of firewood chopped so she wouldn't have to do it and came by after work at the collective as often as he could to help with chores around the house.

"I don't need special treatment," she'd told him again and again. "I worked every day through the harvest, I still scour the woods for firewood for the collective, and I help milk the cows there every day. I'm not delicate."

"I know that, but I must look out for you and the baby. Pavlo would do the same for me if things had turned out differently," he'd said.

Katya nodded. "I'm fine, thank you, Kolya. But it's not my offer, it's Mama's. She wants you both to come live with us, since Alina's time is so close." Katya left off the part about Mama wanting it to be permanent. She'd let her address that when she had them stuck under her roof.

Kolya ran his hand wearily over his face. Dark bags cradled his eyes. They'd all joined the collective at the same time, and he was working hard to maintain this home and help with Mama and Katya's on top of everything else the collective required. Katya could tell the idea of moving didn't appeal to him, but for his pregnant wife, he was giving it much consideration.

"Is this what you want, Alina?" he asked.

"It might make it easier for when I go into labor," Alina said.

Kolya glanced back at Katya. "I suppose your mother wants an answer from you today."

She nodded. "See, Kolya, you already know her so well. Living with her will be easy."

He chuckled softly. "Go tell your mother we will be by this evening. If it will help Alina, then we will make it work."

* * *

As usual, Mama was right. Three days later, when Katya came home after checking on the nanny goat and her kid, she found Alina in bed and her mother putting water on to boil.

"Grab some sheets," she barked. "Do you know where Kolya is? It's time!"

"He should be coming home from the collective any minute now." Katya pulled off her coat and hurried to do as commanded. Alina tensed and groaned as another contraction tore through her.

"This baby is coming fast," Mama spoke over her shoulder. "I need you to go fetch Lena."

"I want Kolya!" Alina yelled. The tendons in her neck popped out against her pale skin as she bore down with another contraction. "Go get him, Katya! Now!"

"I will." Katya yanked on her coat and went back into the cold. Walking through the snow took a lot more effort during late pregnancy, but she was glad to have something to do that would help Alina. She made it halfway back to the collective farm headquarters and almost to Lena and Ruslan's house when she saw Kolya walking home.

She cupped her hands around her mouth and yelled, "The baby is coming!"

He froze, then sprinted toward her.

"I'm going to fetch Lena," Katya said. "Alina needs you now, though!"

He skidded to a stop and grabbed her by the shoulders. "How bad is it? Is she all right?"

"She is in pain, but she's doing well. Don't worry, she'll be fine."

"Don't worry?" He dropped his arms and glared at her. "She's all I have left in this world. How could I not worry? Now hurry and go get Lena!"

He ran toward home and left Katya staring after him. Anger heated her face, and she bit the inside of her cheek until she tasted blood. *At least you still have her!* she wanted to yell after him. To scream. But she didn't. How could she judge his grief? He'd lost so much, too. His mother. His father. Pavlo. She shuddered under the weight of that anguish, and as quickly as it had flared, her rage dissipated. She gripped her swollen belly and took a deep breath. She and Kolya might have shared Pavlo's loss, but it didn't make it any easier to bear.

Emotions in check, Katya trudged on toward Lena's house as fast as she could go. Lena ushered her in to warm by the *pich* while she prepared her things and peppered Katya with questions. "How far apart are her contractions? Did her bag of waters break? When did the labor start?"

"I'm not sure," Katya repeated several times. "I got home from work and came right back out to get you."

"You poor dear." Lena patted her cheek. "This must be a bit frightening for you. Well, don't be afraid. What you see for Alina today may not be the same for you. Every woman labors and handles pain differently."

Katya nodded. Right now, she didn't feel like she was handling her pain very well. Her feet ached, her back throbbed, and she only wanted to get back home and sit down.

Lena wrapped a heavy shawl around her shoulders and head. "Ruslan, I'll be back later," she called into the back room. "I'm going to help Alina have her baby."

Lena helped with many of the births in the village, even though she'd never had children of her own. She moved fast for an older woman, and in no time, they were looking upon a scene very similar to what Katya had left earlier, only this time Kolya kneeled next to the bed, holding Alina's hand.

Upon further inspection, Katya could see that Alina had calmed significantly. Mama must have brushed her hair back for her, and her clear eyes were focused on Kolya.

She gave a low moan. "Lena! This baby is coming soon!"

"Well, let me see if you are right." Lena paused to make the sign of the cross in front of the wall where the holy icons usually hung before bending low over Alina. After a few minutes of silent assessment, she shook her head. "No, it will be some time yet. Try to rest when the pain wanes."

Time marched on as Alina struggled, and the household waited. It wasn't until the sun rose the next morning that Lena finally declared Alina ready to push and the house filled with the sounds of Alina's efforts. Groans and screams of pain tore from her lips.

The look on Katya's face drew her mother's attention. "Don't judge her too harshly," she admonished. "You wait. When your time comes, you will be the same. Birthing a child is not an easy task."

Katya pursed her lips and bit back a retort. She would not scream; she would welcome the agony of birth. To feel something besides grief, besides despair, would be a joy, no matter how much physical pain it brought. And with that pain would come a small piece of Pavlo. For that, she would endure all the pain in the world.

Pallid and weak, Alina pushed for hours with no result. Finally, when Katya had grown alarmed that the child would never come, a tiny baby slipped into Lena's hands. Katya watched as Alina's cries of pain changed into cries of joy. She cradled the baby against her chest, and Kolya wrapped his arms around both of them. A family unit, all together and ensconced in their love. The beauty of it was not lost on her, though she could not help but feel a pang of jealousy. Pavlo would never hold her as she cradled their baby.

Katya watched Alina stare down at her new baby and share secret smiles with her husband. With steely resolve, she swore that she would never let her pain and jealousy come between her and Alina. Katya loved her sister and wanted her to have the life she always dreamed of. She'd lost too much already, and she couldn't bear to lose Alina as well.

* * *

"Open up!" The loud voice startled everyone. Mama's spoon froze over the pot of food she was cooking on the stove. It was ground up millet, goat's milk, and some potato peelings Kolya had stolen from the pigs at the collective farm in a vain attempt to supplement the one piece of bread he, Katya, and Mama each brought home from work every day.

Katya stood up from where she'd been sitting next to her sister, fear knocking her knees together. Alina closed her eyes and rubbed a hand down her tiny baby's back. Born only a few weeks ago, Halyna—or Halya, as they'd all taken to calling her—was somehow thriving through this ordeal that had become normal life. Alina, however, had remained very weak after birth, and Mama insisted she rest as often as possible to try to increase her milk supply.

"Open up! I know you're in there! I see the smoke!" the voice at the door shouted again. Katya recognized it now. Prokyp.

"I'm coming," she called, trying to buy some time and thinking frantically. If he caught them with the stolen potato peels and goat's milk, he could arrest them all. Her eyes darted around the room, searching for a hiding spot. She ran over to the chest full of linens and opened the top, then waved at her mother.

Mama pulled the pot off the stove, quietly placed the lid on it, and tucked the pot under some sheets. Closing the chest, she nodded toward Katya, who'd already walked to the door.

Katya smoothed her skirt and tried to put on a calm face as she opened the door. Prokyp pushed past her, and a young man she'd never seen before followed. Prokyp looked the same as he always did, with mean eyes, dirty hair, and rotten teeth. The activist with him was more of a boy. Most likely, he was a member of the *Komsomol*, Stalin's youth group.

Katya thought about the flyers the activists had thrust into her hands when they first arrived, trying to lure her and other young people like this boy into the *Komsomol*. She was glad Pavlo had crumpled that paper—glad she hadn't succumbed to the brainwashing that allowed these people to enforce unspeakable punishments, sometimes even against their own flesh and blood.

"It smells good in here," Prokyp leered, baring his filthy teeth toward Mama. "You've been cooking something."

"You're mistaken," Mama said in a firm voice. "My son-in-law brought home some food he earned from working at the collective yesterday. That must be what you are smelling."

Prokyp glanced around, his eyes finally falling on Alina. "Where is that strapping young son-in-law of yours? Working today, eh? Too bad he'll miss this."

"We have nothing," Mama said. "We work hard for the collective. Please, leave us be."

"You know it's not that easy. We need grain for the spring planting, and we know you people are hiding it from the collective." Prokyp waved his hand at his companion. "Check the room!"

The young man pulled a long, thin metal rod out of his bag, raised it high, and plunged it into the empty bed. His rod ripped through sheets, pillows, and blankets and fury burned in Katya at the needless destruction of their possessions.

"This is ridiculous!" she shouted. "You're ruining our things! And we have nothing!"

He ignored her protests and moved on to the next bed. "Move!" he ordered Alina.

Katya and her mother rushed over to help Alina up. Mama grabbed the baby and Katya put an arm around Alina's back and pulled her to a sitting position, but he hardly waited until she was gone to thrust the metal rod into her bedding. Katya yanked her sister to her feet before he rammed his metal rod through her while systematically poking holes down the length of the bed.

"Nothing inside!" he finally announced. Katya closed her eyes and thought of Pavlo and how she had continued the trips into the woods to hide whatever food they obtained. Once again, it had saved them.

"Did you check that?" Prokyp pointed at the linen chest.

"No, sir," the young man replied as he strode across the room. He flung open the lid and shoved the rod inside. Metal clinked on metal.

Katya sucked in air through her teeth as cold sweat sprang up on her back. Mama crossed herself and closed her eyes in defeat. Prokyp stormed over to the trunk and began ripping linens out. He squealed like a stuck pig when his bare hand hit the hot pot.

"No food, eh? You've lied to me and the state!" Gripping the pot with a sheet, he pulled it out and set it on the table. He pushed the lid off, grabbed a spoon, and began poking around in the contents.

"Potato peels? I wonder where you could have found potato peels," he mused. He brought the spoon to his lips. "Ah, you make this garbage taste rather good."

Food splattered from his lips as he began shoveling their only meal of the day into his rotten mouth. When there was almost nothing left, which didn't take long because there was hardly anything to begin with, he turned the pot upside down and began banging it out onto the floor.

"No!" Katya and her mother gasped simultaneously.

"This is stolen from the state! I should arrest you all!" He shook the pot, flinging precious bits of potato peels all over their house.

He set it down and walked over to Alina. She turned her head, refusing to look at him as he ran his filthy hand down her cheek "Even after childbirth, still so beautiful. It's a shame you didn't choose me. You wouldn't be starving here. You would be the wife of someone important. I could have taken care of you, unlike the idiot you wanted."

"You animal!" Katya pointed her finger and stepped toward him, the words snapping off her tongue like bullets. "You speak your lies of love to her, but you may have killed her! She's weak, and she needs food! The baby is taking everything from her, and you just ate her only meal of the day!"

Prokyp's eyes flickered to Katya with a look that froze her blood.

"You're jealous of the attention I give your sister, eh?" He sauntered over to her and touched her hair. "You may not be as pretty as her, but you're not so bad. You'd do in a pinch, even if you are with child. And there's no one here to save you now, is there? Your man is dead, isn't that right?"

Anger rolled through Katya, but it was quickly replaced by fear as Prokyp grabbed her and dragged her over to the door.

"Put your hand on the frame!" He pushed her against the wood.

Katya pressed her lips together and shook her head. *You must stay strong.* Pavlo's instructions echoed in her mind. "No!"

"Now!" Prokyp yelled. He backhanded her across the face, and her vision clouded. She fell forward into the doorway and caught herself, her hand splayed across the frame just as he'd requested.

Prokyp gripped the door and sneered. "No stealing food, thief!"

He slammed the door shut on her hand, and Katya screamed. Pain shot up her arm and doubled her over. The room faded around her as she straightened, cradling her throbbing left hand. Tears welled in her eyes, but she forced them back and stuck her chin in the air. *You must stay strong.* She would not give Prokyp the satisfaction of seeing her cry. Her mother wrapped an arm around her and guided her to a chair.

"It's lucky for you that I have bigger worries today than stolen potato peels. I must collect the grain from other thieving households, but we will be back, and we won't be so nice next time." He lumbered out the door, yelling at his companion. "Check the yard with your pole!"

The young man gave them a dirty look and spat on the floor before following Prokyp out. Mama rushed over to Katya and picked up her injured hand.

"Can you move it?" She pressed on the inflamed knuckles of Katya's left hand. "I don't feel any broken bones, but it's hard to tell. It's so swollen already. I'll get a cloth to wrap it."

"I'll be fine, Mama." Katya spoke through teeth clenched against the pain. She pulled her hand away and dropped to her knees. With her good hand, she picked up wayward potato peels and chunks of millet and put them in a bowl, desperately trying to salvage every drop of the precious food Prokyp had flung on the ground.

17

CASSIE

Illinois, June 2004

"Hurry," Bobby urged Cassie as soon as she came in the kitchen. "It's two o'clock already. The afternoon is nearly gone."

Bobby laid a bag of potatoes and a knife on the table next to a large pile of beets. "Here, grate these beets. I'll cut cabbage. The beef shanks have been boiling since seven this morning, and the bread is already baking in the oven."

Cassie chopped off the tops of the beets and commenced the tedious process of rubbing the root across a metal grater. The bright pink juice seeped out and stained her hands. In a few minutes, it looked like she'd just finished finger painting. She stared at her hands in disdain. "This is a lot harder than I remember."

"It's worth it in the end," Bobby said with a nod. "And makes your hands stronger."

"And pink," Cassie quipped. She tried not to stare at Bobby's twisted hands as she pulled the outer leaves off the cabbage head. She favored her left hand and adjusted her movements to allow her right hand to do most of the work.

"How's your arthritis?" Cassie asked. "It looks like your hand is bothering you today."

"It's fine," Bobby said. She paused and massaged the bulbous knuckles. "Maybe a little more stiffness in this one."

Birdie, not quite strong enough to grate the beets, enjoyed running her hands through the shreds. She waved pink fingers in her mother's face and giggled.

When the last beet was finally shredded, Bobby instructed Cassie to add them, the cabbage, and a chopped onion to the beef and water boiling on the stove. The rich, earthy smell of beets hitting the boiling liquid did not seem reminiscent of her childhood borscht memories.

She wrinkled her nose. "It doesn't smell like borscht."

"Of course not," Bobby scoffed. "It must cook down until the beets are dissolved. Takes a few hours. While we wait, you can get the potatoes cut."

Cassie went to work peeling potatoes. When the pile size satisfied Bobby, she stopped.

"We wait to add them," she instructed. "But go stir the pot and add a bay leaf."

They spent an hour in near silence while Bobby played cards with Birdie and Cassie tidied up. Then, she added the potatoes, and twenty minutes later, the sour cream. The deep reddish color morphed to a pretty pink, mottled with small white flecks.

"Mmm, it smells amazing in here!" Anna breezed in through the back door. "I haven't had borscht in forever!"

"That's because you never make good Ukrainian food anymore," Bobby said.

Anna ignored Bobby and kept talking. "So, I hear we're having company?" She cast a sidelong glance at Cassie.

"Don't look at me," Cassie said. "I didn't invite him."

"Of course, you wouldn't. You have the social skills of a hermit crab lately." Anna stirred the pot and inhaled. "Ooh, I can't wait!"

"For the record, hermit crabs are very sociable, so your analogy is terrible," Cassie said. "And I value my alone time. What's wrong with that?"

"Nothing," Bobby interjected before the conversation got too heated. "I invited Nick to say thank you for helping me. That's all."

The doorbell rang, and Birdie jumped out of her chair.

"Wait, Birdie." Bobby pointed to the loaf of round bread she'd baked. A shallow hollow in the center held a small bowl of salt. "You must present Nick with the bread and salt to show our hospitality."

Bobby took a *rushnyk* embroidered with red flowers out of a drawer and instructed Birdie to hold her hands out. She draped the cloth over Birdie's outstretched hands so that the identically decorated ends of the oblong white cloth hung down toward the ground.

Then, Cassie helped steady Birdie's hands as Bobby set the bread on top of the *rushnyk*.

"This was always my favorite part of hosting parties when I was a kid. It's a very important job," Cassie said.

Birdie nodded solemnly and tiptoed toward the door, where Anna was waiting to open it.

"Hey, everyone," Nick grinned as he stepped in. He'd changed from his running shorts and T-shirt to khakis and a button-down shirt with the sleeves rolled up his forearms. He was no longer sweaty, but still quite arresting. Cassie found herself staring again.

Birdie held up the bread and Nick kneeled down. "Bread and salt! Just like my Baba used to make." He ripped off a piece of the bread, dipped it in the salt, bowed his head in thanks, then popped it in his mouth. "Delicious. Thank you, Birdie."

He offered a bouquet of sunflowers to her, and Anna took the bread so Birdie could accept them. "I wanted to bring something for the dinner table, and I thought flowers might be more appealing than anything I could cook."

Birdie took them and squealed. "Sunflowers are Alina's favorite!"

The bread tipped precariously, and salt spilled onto the floor as Anna whirled around. Cassie's breath hitched. She'd waited for this moment for fifteen months. Heart pounding in her ears, she took two wobbly steps toward her daughter, then fell to her knees and grabbed Birdie's shoulders.

"Birdie, you talked!" Cassie wrapped her arms around the little girl and began to cry. Over Birdie's head, she saw Bobby stagger and fall onto the couch, then drop her head into her hands.

Cassie shot to her feet, hesitant to leave this amazing moment with Birdie. "Bobby, are you okay?"

"I'm fine." Bobby waved a hand, dismissing the question. "Don't worry about me. I'm just happy for Birdie."

Anna put an arm around Bobby and asked Birdie, "Who's Alina? Is she a friend from the park?"

"No," Birdie said, her voice a touch rusty from disuse, but sweet. "She's my new friend but not from the park."

"Where did you meet her, then?" Cassie kept one nervous eye on Bobby.

"Here," Birdie said. "Right here on this couch."

Bobby made a choking sound, and Cassie frowned. "Bobby, are you sure you're okay? Do you need some water?"

She caught Nick's eye as he moved toward Bobby, and he nodded. "I'll get her a drink."

He returned with a glass of water and sat on the other side of her. "Are you sure you're fine? You do look pale."

"It's the shock of hearing her talk," Bobby replied, refusing to meet anyone's eyes.

"Well, you were right, Bobby. She just needed time," Cassie said. She gave her daughter another hug. "Oh, I've missed your little voice."

Birdie giggled. "Alina said I had to talk, so I did."

"Well, whoever this Alina is, I like her." Cassie's smile fell away as the name clicked into place. Alina. The same name Bobby had written letters to begging for forgiveness. The same name she'd called Cassie when she was having one of her episodes.

"Alina?" Bobby repeated, then muttered a few Ukrainian words. Cassie's brows furrowed as she stared at her grandmother.

"Mom, Nick, do you guys think she needs to be checked out?"

Before anyone could answer, Bobby snapped, "I'm fine. I told you."

An awkward silence fell over the room as Bobby closed her eyes again. Birdie looked up at Cassie. "Is Bobby mad at me?"

"No, darling, I think she's just having a rough day." Cassie spoke low so as to not upset her grandmother again. "Maybe she needs some dinner."

"Good idea," Anna agreed. "Come on, everyone, let's eat while it's still warm."

Cassie watched in surprise as Bobby let Nick help her up and walk her to the kitchen. Normally, Bobby scoffed at offers of assistance, but today, she leaned on his strong arm and let him guide her. She saw Nick covertly checking Bobby's pulse as he guided her and when he gave her a calm smile, she relaxed.

Cassie approached Anna, busy at the stove dishing up bowls, and leaned close. "Do you think Birdie heard us talking? She must have, right? It's not like Alina is a common name."

"Of course that's what happened." Anna rolled her eyes. "Although if she's been listening to you and Bobby, who knows what kind of absurd things she thinks? Here." She thrust two bowls into Cassie's hands. "Bring those over. And the salad, too."

"Right," Cassie said, letting the jab slide off her back. It was a very logical explanation, and it was the one she wanted to hear. Birdie heard the name and created an imaginary friend to go along with it. And if it helped her talk again, who cared about the technicalities? After more than fifteen months of silence, Cassie had her daughter back, and that's what was important.

"This looks amazing," Nick said. "My take-out dinners can't compare to home cooking."

Bobby remained quiet as she ate. Birdie receded back into her silence, and Cassie felt so overwhelmed with relief that Birdie had finally spoken that she could hardly think, so it fell on Anna to keep the conversation flowing with their guest.

"How are you liking the house, Nick?"

"It's great. I was in an apartment previously, so it's nice to have a yard now. I'm thinking of getting a dog." He gave Harvey an affectionate scratch behind the ears.

He told them of his plans to renovate the small house, and Cassie listened but kept her attention focused on her grandmother and daughter.

Bobby seemed to have returned to her old self for the most part, but she kept glancing at Birdie as if waiting for her to say more. Cassie realized she was doing the same thing.

It wasn't until Nick rose to leave that Birdie spoke again.

"Nick, will you read me a story?"

"How could I say no to that? That is, if your mom is okay with it." He glanced at Cassie.

"I don't think I'd say no to anything she wanted tonight."

Nick smiled, then turned to Bobby. "Thank you for dinner. Your borscht reminds me so much of my Baba's."

"Good," Bobby said, sounding more like her normal self. "You can come by for food anytime. Soon, I will teach Birdie how to make *varenyky*."

"*Varenyky* are my favorite! Name the date, and I'll be there," he said. "You know, sometimes my Baba called them pierogi. Do you?"

Bobby nodded. "Same thing. People used different names depending on where they lived. Pierogi is Polish."

Birdie ran back in the kitchen, book in hand, and tugged Nick from the table. "Come on, Nick!"

As Nick laughed and let himself be dragged along, Anna pulled Cassie aside. "Are you going to talk to him tonight?"

"Yeah," Cassie said. She couldn't put it off any longer. "I think whatever is wrong with Bobby is getting worse. We need some answers, and he seems to be the only who can help us get them."

* * *

After dinner was cleaned up and two books read, Nick rose to leave.

"Cassie, I'll get Birdie ready for bed," Anna suggested. She gave Cassie a knowing look and nodded her head toward Nick as she took the little girl's hand. "Will you see Nick out?"

"Yes, please do," Bobby agreed as she pulled herself up and began shuffling down the hall. "I'm going to bed, too. Thank you for coming over, Nick."

Cassie raised her eyebrows at their transparency but complied. "Sure."

"You don't have to get up." Nick waved a hand at her as he made his way to the door. "I'm capable of opening and closing a door myself."

"It's no problem." She stood and walked with him. Here was her chance to ask about the journal. "Thanks for coming over. Bobby enjoys cooking for people."

"Well, that works. I enjoy eating food people cook for me." Nick grinned at her. His blue eyes locked on hers, those two dimples popped up on his cheeks, and all thoughts of the journal fled from her mind.

She smiled back involuntarily. She didn't want to like him. Didn't want to feel that draw toward him. But she did. No matter how much she denied it, it was there, and it terrified her.

Cassie took a deep breath and tried to focus. What was she supposed to ask him?

"Birdie's a great kid." Nick spoke first.

Cassie ran her hand through her hair and sighed. "Thanks. It's been a rough year for her. For all of us. But ever since we came back home, she's been improving." She gave a small laugh. "Don't tell her I said it, but my mom was right about moving here."

"I'm glad she was able to convince you." His face reddened, as if he'd said too much, and he cleared his throat. "So, anyway, there's a carnival in town this weekend. I was wondering if you and Birdie wanted to go see it? With me?"

Cassie's mind raced. Was this a date? Did he like her? Did she like him? Her mouth opened and closed enough times to make her feel like a goldfish, but she couldn't form any words in reply.

He looked down at the floor and flipped his keys in his hand nervously. "You don't have to," he said, when her silence stretched on for too long. "It's no big deal. I thought Birdie might like it. And I thought it would be fun to spend some time with you."

"I'm a widow," she blurted. Her hand flew to her mouth, horrified at her response to a question he hadn't asked.

"I know," he said softly.

"Right. Of course." Cassie had no idea what to say or what she wanted. Confusion made her head ache, and sweat prickled the back of her neck.

He glanced at her left hand. "I'm sorry. I don't want to pressure you at all if you're not ready. And if you're still wearing your ring, then maybe you're not."

Cassie clutched her hands to her chest and squeezed them together. The band pressed into her finger. She forced her lips to move. "I don't know."

"Why don't you think about it? If it's something you want to do, give me a call. If not, no hard feelings." He grinned. "I'm in no rush."

Cassie exhaled, not realizing she'd been holding her breath, and nodded. "Thank you for understanding."

Nick reached out and ran his hand down her upper arm, his fingers cool against her bare skin. "Good night, Cassie."

She wavered as he turned and walked out the door. She wanted to go. She wanted to have fun again. To live again. Her eyes flashed toward the family picture on the mantle. Taken right after Birdie had been born, it depicted a very exhausted Cassie and an exuberant Henry. "I'm a dad! You made me a dad!" he'd said over and over to her.

"Henry would want you to be happy again," her mom said gently from across the room.

Cassie whirled. "How long have you been eavesdropping?"

"Long enough to know you're missing a chance to spend time with a great guy. You don't need to punish yourself. Henry died, but you didn't."

Cassie twisted the plain band on her left ring finger and bit her lip.

"It's one night at a carnival. Birdie would have a lot of fun. And you might, too," Anna prodded.

Before she could change her mind, Cassie flung open the front door. Stepping onto the porch, she called out, "Nick!"

He paused and looked back at her.

"I'd like to go. To the carnival, I mean."

He broke into a wide smile, his cheeks dimpling either side of it. "Great! I'll pick you and Birdie up around six on Friday, if that works?"

Cassie nodded, anxiety already swirling in her stomach. This would be the first one-on-one time she'd spent with any man besides Henry in over a decade. What had she done?

"What did he say about the journal?" Anna asked as she stepped back inside.

Cassie covered her face with her hands. "Ugh, I completely spaced. We started talking about Birdie and then he brought up the carnival. I can't believe I forgot."

Anna chuckled. "He really flusters you, doesn't he?"

"No!" Cassie glared out at her through her splayed fingers. "I got sidetracked. That's all."

"Then just call him tomorrow morning and ask." Anna smirked. "No big deal, right?"

"Yeah." Cassie grimaced, her pulse already increasing at the idea of "just" calling him. "No big deal."

18

KATYA

Ukraine, February 1932

Katya pulled herself out of bed, and a gush of water spilled down her legs.

"Mama?" Her voice wavered, and fear made her mouth dry. "Are you awake?"

Mama sat up, looked down at the wet ground, and sprang up as if she'd been coiled and waiting for Katya's word to release her. "Lie back down," she instructed.

"But it's not time yet!" Katya cried. Her legs shook as she fell back into the bed. "It's too early!"

Mama shushed Katya, but worry clouded her face. She barked out orders for Kolya to go fetch Lena, then ran a cool hand over Katya's brow. "Lay back and try to relax. These things usually take some time."

Katya nodded as a wave of pain rolled through her stomach. She clutched at her mother's hand. "It hurts!"

"I know, Katya, but you must be strong. At the end of this pain, you will have your sweet baby."

Alina approached the bed on unsteady feet. "How are you feeling?"

"It's getting better," Katya said, as the vice squeezing her abdomen waned.

"I don't want to lie to you." Alina's worried eyes looked large in her peaked face. "It will get much worse."

"I know," Katya said. "I saw you go through it, remember?"

Alina gave a weak laugh. "You're much tougher than me. Always have been. You'll be fine, Katya, and I promise, it's all worth it in the end." She took Katya's hand. "I am here with you, sister. I won't leave your side."

Katya shot her a grateful smile. "Thank you."

Unlike Alina, Katya's labor progressed fast. By the time Kolya returned with Lena, and then slipped back out the door, the contractions were coming every few minutes. They ripped through Katya like nothing she'd ever experienced, tightening her abdomen into a hard knot, but she didn't scream. This suffering would lead to her baby and to that piece of Pavlo she'd been dreaming about.

"It's good to shout." Lena looked up at Katya from between her legs. "It will help you push."

Katya shook her head no, but a groan slipped past her lips as Mama wiped her forehead. Doing this alone, without Pavlo, meant she had to be strong enough on her own. So Katya shoved a pillow in her mouth and bit down with each push.

"We are here with you, Katya," Alina said, as if reading her mind. "You are not alone."

Katya clenched Alina's hand and gritted her teeth so she wouldn't scream. "Yes, I am alone. I am all alone!"

"The baby's head is very small." Lena frowned. "How far along are you?"

"About eight months." Fear lodged like a hard lump in Katya's throat. "But the baby will be all right, won't it?"

"Hush now, everything will be fine. I've seen babies born younger live," Lena said, but Katya saw the look Lena gave her mother, and her heart sank. "You're only a few pushes away now. Get ready!"

Tears seeped out of her eyes. How could she do this? The baby was too early, Pavlo was dead, and no matter how hard she tried, she wasn't strong enough.

"Katya!" Mama shook her. "Don't you dare give up. You have to fight! This child needs you."

"I don't think I can anymore, Mama. I'm so tired of fighting." Despair choked out any hope Katya had once possessed, and she fell back on the bed, her head dropping down on the pillow.

"What do you think being a mother is? It's a constant battle. It's endless fear. It's continuous worry. And it's always work! But it's worth it, Katya; I swear to you, it's worth it."

Mama smoothed back Katya's hair and kissed her brow. "Now push!"

Katya propped herself up, huffed in a lungful of air, and bore down. She let out a low moan and swore her body split into two as the baby slipped out. She decided later that it wasn't only her body splitting, but a piece of her heart breaking off. That's what being a mother was—ripping out a piece of your heart and giving it to your child.

"It's a boy!" Lena placed the warm, wet body on the bed next to Katya.

"He's so small." Katya touched his face. His lips were blue, and his eyes stayed closed. "Why isn't he crying?"

Lena took him away and vigorously patted and rubbed his back until he began to splutter, then she toweled him off. Mama handed her the *rushnyk* she had embroidered for the baby's birth, and Lena wrapped it around him. "Some start on their own, others need a little help."

Lena gave him back to her then, and, as his gray-blue eyes stared into hers, Katya fell in love. The warmth of that love spread through her, enveloped her, until nothing else mattered. She felt no pain as

Lena helped her deliver the afterbirth and took no notice of Lena and Mama cleaning her up and putting fresh bedding under her. Her whole world lay tucked into her arms, a tiny version of Pavlo snuggled into her.

"Feed the child," Lena said. "He won't get much until your milk comes in, but his suckling will encourage that."

Katya put him to her breast and watched as he latched on and began to rhythmically suck. She flinched at the pain, and Lena reassured her that it wouldn't hurt always; she would toughen up.

"He's a natural," Lena smiled. "That's good. He's early but eating well will help him thrive."

"I'd like to name him for Tato." Katya smiled up at her mother. "Viktor. My little Viktor Pavlovich."

Mama, for once at a loss for words, nodded her approval.

Alina sat on the edge of the bed, her frame so slight Katya couldn't feel her there, and introduced Halya to her double cousin. Alina smiled, her gaunt cheekbones poking out on her beautiful face. "See, I told you it was not so bad."

Katya snorted. "You screamed so loud birthing Halya that the next village over could hear you!"

"Bah!" She waved her hand. "You always exaggerate. But I'm not surprised you barely made a sound. You may be younger, but you were always the tougher one."

For that brief moment in time, happiness enveloped Katya as Viktor filled a hole she didn't think could ever be filled.

Katya had two blissful weeks with Viktor before she woke one morning, and he didn't. His cold little body lay next to hers, his fingers splayed on her breast, his mouth still open from nursing.

Then, she could not hold back her screams.

* * *

"He was not meant for this world," Mama said to Lena.

She nodded in reply. "I could see it the day he was born, but who am I to make such prophecies?"

Katya ignored them and continued staring at the wall. Her breasts, aching with their fullness, were a cruel reminder of Viktor's death two days ago. They leaked steadily, soaking her shirt, and chilling her body, but she didn't care. She hadn't left her bed except to urinate, but even that had tapered off as she'd stopped eating and drinking. There wasn't much food to go around anyway, so she figured she might as well give her share to those who cared to live. Mama had finally called Lena in for help in her efforts to get Katya to rejoin the world again.

From her bed, she could see Alina nursing her baby. She could see Alina's husband come home from working at the collective and kiss her cheek. Katya could see all Alina had and remember all she'd lost.

She tried not to hate her sister, but a tiny part of her couldn't help it. Why did Alina have both a husband and a child when she had nothing? Why must she suffer all the loss while Alina's life went on as she'd always wanted?

Of course, the rational part of her knew this wasn't completely true. They'd all lost their way of life as the collective and activists changed everything, and Alina had lost her father, just as Katya had. Even though they all held out hope that he would return to them, they still hadn't heard a word from anyone about him.

Katya hated herself for these thoughts, but she didn't know how to stop them.

Now, she had to listen to Mama and Lena discuss her as if she couldn't hear. As if she wasn't there.

"She needs to nurse Halya before her milk dries up," Mama said. "Alina's milk production is low, and I'm afraid she will run dry and Halya will have nothing to eat. The baby already cries for more now."

"It's not a bad idea." Lena nodded in agreement. "Katya's milk is plentiful. It would be a shame to waste it."

My milk was meant for Viktor! Katya wanted to scream at them. To shout and break things. To tell them all to leave her alone and let her waste away and die so she could be with Pavlo and Viktor.

But she didn't. And when Alina approached timidly, tears in her eyes, holding sweet, hungry Halya in her arms, Katya held her hands out and took the baby. Alina was her sister. Halya, her niece. How could she not help them?

Halya's tiny mouth latched on to Katya, quickly instigating the familiar pinpricks, the heaviness, as the milk let down. The life force of Katya's body, the milk that hadn't been enough for Viktor, flowed from her to Halya. Katya studied Halya's face as she nursed greedily, uttering little grunts of satisfaction. The excess ran down the corner of the baby's mouth and wet her blanket while Katya's tears flowed down her cheeks and wet hers.

19

CASSIE

Illinois, June 2004

Cassie stared at the box. Now, more than ever, she needed to figure out what was going on with Bobby. She touched the worn leather journal and let her fingers follow the grooves, imagining a much younger Bobby secreted away, writing her innermost thoughts. What had Bobby seen to scar her so much that she felt the need to hide food in her backyard and pen repetitive apologies to a woman named Alina?

Nick was the only option if she wanted to finally get answers, but she was afraid to connect any further with the man who made her question her loyalties to Henry.

"How can that be a good excuse when you said yes to going out with him?" she said to herself. "Anyway, helping Bobby is what's most important."

Before she could talk herself out of it, she snatched up the phone and punched in the number he'd left with her.

He answered on the first ring. "Hello?"

His smooth, deep voice sent shivers down Cassie's spine, and, once again, her thoughts scattered like dandelion fluff in the wind.

"Hi," she breathed.

"Cassie? Is that you?"

She nodded, though he couldn't see her. "Uh, yes. I have a favor to ask you." Nice. Skip all the pleasantries and just ask him to do something for you. Real classy.

"Whatever you need," he replied instantly.

His eagerness made her stomach somersault. "I have something written in Ukrainian, and I'd be grateful if you could translate it for me. Again. But this is a lot more than a note. It's a whole journal. And some more notes. If you could. Please." She bit her lip. Why was this so hard? And why did she suddenly have trouble speaking in complete sentences?

"Sure. I can swing by and take a look now if you'd like." He laughed. "I'm just relieved you're not canceling our date for this weekend."

"No, of course not." *A date. I still can't believe I have a date.* Cassie glanced at the clock. "That would be great. Birdie and Bobby should both be napping for a while yet, so we could be alone." She slapped her palm to her forehead. What kind of message was she trying to send him? *Help, I'm widowed and lonely and need an afternoon visit from my single neighbor?*

She could practically hear his grin through the phone, but to her eternal relief, he didn't comment on her newfound brazenness. "I'll be there in five minutes."

"Great. Meet me on the back patio. Don't ring the doorbell." Cassie set the phone down and ran to get her laptop. She paused in front of the mirror and smoothed her hair, then scowled at her reflection. "You're being ridiculous on so many levels."

She stacked the box on her laptop and stepped out onto the patio right as he came in the gate.

"Thanks for coming over at such short notice." She set everything on the patio table and sat down.

"What's all this?" Nick pulled a chair up next to her, so close she could smell the shampoo on his damp hair.

Her heart fluttered, and she took a deep breath. "It's Bobby's. A journal, letters, pictures. She never talks about her life before she came to America, but lately she's been sleepwalking and having these odd flashbacks. She's talking about getting ready to die and how she wants me to know everything, but she can't bear to tell me herself."

Nick frowned. "That's pretty heavy. She's okay with me going through all of this?"

Cassie nodded. "She suggested it."

"This is all in Ukrainian?" Nick thumbed through some loose notebook pages, pausing to read a few lines here and there.

"Yes, and I'd like to transcribe it as you translate so I have a record I can read."

His arm brushed against hers as he scooted his chair closer, and goosebumps popped up all over her body. She unwrapped the embroidered cloth, revealing the brown leather journal. Inside the scuffed cover was her grandmother's life—a story Cassie had been waiting her whole life to discover. What had she seen? What had she survived? She opened the journal and more loose papers that had been tucked inside spilled out. Writing filled every available inch of blank space on all of them, front and back.

"Where do we even begin?" Cassie asked, amazed at the number of words.

Nick scanned through them. "At least she dated every entry."

Cassie let out a sigh of relief as Nick laid out the pages and checked the dates in the front and back of the book.

"Some of these papers pre-date the journal," he said, "and it looks like a few of them came after she finished it. Let me sort them quickly to make sure we're going in order."

As Nick organized the notes, Cassie flipped open her laptop. She'd plugged it in last night so it would have a full charge, but it had been fifteen months since she'd used it. Hopefully, it still worked. As it whirred to life, she ran her hands over the keys, reacquainting herself with the old friends. She didn't realize how much she missed them. How much writing was a part of her life.

She smiled. "I'm ready when you are."

Nick read for two hours as Cassie's fingers flew across her keyboard. He was faster than he let on, and a few times she had to stop him so she could catch up.

"So, the P in the note was for Pavlo. Her first love. That explains a lot. And Alina was her sister." Cassie pressed a hand against her chest and took a shaky breath. "I can't believe she had a sister we never knew about. What if she had kids? Cousins we never knew? I can't wait to tell my mom."

"But we still don't know what happened to them and why she feels so guilty," Nick said.

"No, but we know Stalin's men were taking their food." A thrill of satisfaction ran through Cassie at the connection. "That's probably why Bobby is hiding it now. Her memory is slipping back to when she had to."

* * *

Cassie threw the purple sundress onto the pile of old clothes littering her bed and sighed. What did people wear on dates these days? Sure, she'd spent the night before sitting out on the patio with Nick for a second round of journal translating, but this felt totally different. Last night, they'd had a focus, a common goal. Tonight was a date.

She dug through her clothes one more time and pulled out jeans and a black V-neck shirt that hadn't seen the light of day since her decision to live solely in yoga pants and T-shirts. Finally dressed, she took out the make-up she hadn't worn in a year, and, with an out-of-practice hand, tried to apply it. Birdie, confused by the process, kept touching Cassie's face and trying to feel her eyelashes.

"It's been so long since I wore this that you don't even remember what it is, do you?"

Birdie shook her head and pointed to her cheeks. "Can I try?"

Cassie tipped her head back and sighed with joy. Birdie hadn't stopped talking, and every word felt like a gift.

"You're so pretty you don't need it, but we can use a little this one time." Cassie swiped the brush down Birdie's nose and cheeks. "Maybe we can get you some fun make-up to play dress up with."

The little girl nodded, then giggled and preened in front of the mirror while Cassie experienced a last-minute panic attack when she thought she'd have to wear flip flops or gym shoes. Luckily, Anna swooped to the rescue with a pair of strappy black sandals for her to borrow and the ensemble was complete. Simple, but complete.

"I can't believe I'm so stressed about this." Cassie ran her fingers through her hair one more time. "I shouldn't have said yes."

"You'll be fine," Anna said. She'd arrived an hour earlier to stay with Bobby while Birdie and Cassie went out and had already talked Cassie back from canceling three times. "And I'll be here waiting up so you can update me on what you've read in the journal so far."

"I can skip this and tell you now," Cassie said.

Anna shook her head. "I don't want a rushed report. That's why I didn't want you to tell me anything yet. I want to sit down with you and hear the details in person. Besides, think about Birdie. She's so excited to go. You can't cancel now."

Cassie's eyes fell on her daughter. Dressed in a bright pink and orange striped sundress, she whirled in a patch of sunlight coming through the window. Her dress spun out in a rolling wave around her knees.

"Look, Mama!" She giggled as she fell over. "My dress makes me dizzy!"

"I'll never get tired of hearing her talk," Cassie said.

Anna snorted. "Wait till she's a teenager. Now quit stressing. This will be fun. For both of you."

"Then why don't you go instead?" Cassie said.

"Stop it." Anna glanced out the window. "Nick's here. I'm going to check on Bobby and see if she's up from her nap. You get the door."

Cassie's stomach plummeted. Hands shaking, she pulled open the door before Nick had a chance to ring the bell. He'd dressed casually in khaki shorts and a blue slim fit T-shirt that hugged his muscular frame. His tanned face was freshly shaved, and he held two bouquets in his hand: a small, child-sized mixture of miniature sunflowers and daisies, and a large, brightly colored assortment of wildflowers. She squeezed the door to still her quaking hands.

"You look beautiful," he said. His trademark dimples punctuated his easy smile as he held out the flowers.

Her self–preservation instincts screamed for her to run away, but she found she couldn't break the inexplicable connection sparking between them. Her heart rate slowed. Her breathing evened out. The trembling in her hands and belly settled and she realized something: he soothed her. His presence alone made her feel better. Feel safe.

"Come on in." She took one step back to let him in, but it felt like she'd jumped off a bridge into an icy river.

"I figured a shorter bouquet would be easier for Birdie to enjoy," he said. "Where is she?"

"Nick!" Birdie ran down the hall and jumped into his arms. "I missed you!"

"Hey there! I missed you too!" He caught her easily and swung her around, the tiny, forgotten bouquet crushed between his hand and her side. Birdie's squeals of delight filled the room.

"Are those pretty flowers for me?" Birdie asked as he set her down.

Nick kneeled next to her and straightened the squished flowers, then presented them with a flourish. "Pretty flowers for a pretty girl."

Cassie smiled at their easy banter while Birdie led Nick into the kitchen to put her flowers in water.

"She's crazy about him, isn't she?" Anna said as she came back in the living room.

Cassie nodded, trying to sort through the myriad of confusing feelings coursing through her. Excitement, fear, hope, happiness. It was all too much. She started to hyperventilate.

"You okay?" Anna asked. "I know you think I pushed you to do this, but you need it."

"What are you, a shrink now?" Cassie's voice shook as she drew in a shaky breath.

"No, I'm just your mom. I know you." Anna tucked a lock of Cassie's hair back behind her ear as Nick and Birdie came back into the room.

"Are you ladies ready?" Nick held out an arm for Birdie to take.

"Yeah!" she squealed. "Let's go to the carnival!"

* * *

Muggy summer air suffocated them as they wandered through the rides and games set up in the grade school parking lot. Cassie, never one to pick style over comfort, now had her hair tied in a loose ponytail. Still, she fanned herself with the flyer she'd grabbed on the way in and regretted not wearing shorts.

"We can try the Ferris wheel," Nick said. "Maybe if we get up, away from the crowd, we'll catch a breeze."

Cassie agreed as Birdie began to chant, "Ferris wheel! Ferris wheel!"

So far, Nick had bought her a corn dog, a lemon shake-up, and a funnel cake. Cassie had suggested a food and spinning ride break after the funnel cake, as she didn't want to see it all come back up.

'Sorry." Nick smiled sheepishly. "It's fun to see how excited she gets. I love seeing this place through her eyes."

"I know." Cassie softened and grinned. "It's great to see her so happy. But, if she pukes everywhere, she won't be happy anymore. And trust me, we won't be either."

"Hey, Nick!" a woman called out to him as they passed the Fun House. She waved and made a kissy face with her bright pink lips. "Haven't seen you around lately!"

Nick blushed and waved back without stopping. "Hey, Denise. Just keeping busy, you know."

Denise gave Cassie the once over and, after a little smirk, turned back to Nick. "Well, don't be a stranger. You know where I live."

She shot Nick another kissy face that made Cassie want to vomit more than any spinning rides or funnel cakes ever could.

"She seems friendly." Surprised at the punch of jealousy to her gut, Cassie fought to keep her voice steady.

"Sorry about that. She's an old friend." Nick gave a pained grimace but didn't explain further.

Cassie bit her lip and tamped down her retort. Why should she care if Nick was close with another woman? She had no right.

"Can we do the Ferris wheel now?" Birdie asked.

Cassie pasted a smile on her face. "That's a good idea, little bird. Let's do that."

* * *

That night, after Birdie had had her fill of all things carnival, and two more women had approached Nick to tell them they missed seeing him around, Nick walked them to their door.

"Thank you for a lovely evening, ladies," he said as he bowed toward Birdie. "It's been my pleasure."

Birdie giggled and threw her arms around him. "Thank you, Nick!"

Cassie opened the door, and Birdie ran inside, calling out for Anna. Cassie sighed, then turned and faced Nick. "Thanks. I had a nice time."

"I did, too." He hesitated. "I'm sorry about Denise. She was a long time ago, but she seems to keep popping up when I least expect it."

"Jan and Tiffany, too?" Cassie's eyebrows raised.

He blushed and started to stammer another apology.

Cassie held up a hand to stop him. "It's all right. We all have a past, don't we?" She dropped her hand and twirled the ring on her left ring finger.

"We do. But I like to look toward the future." Nick's voice came out low and husky. He ran the back of his knuckles down the side of her face. She instinctively tensed, then softened at the feel of his rough hand gently touching her cheek. "Good night, Cassie."

* * *

"Well, how was it?" Anna pounced on Cassie as soon as Birdie was all cleaned up and tucked in. "Did you have fun? Come have some tea with us."

"It was nice." Cassie sat down and inhaled the sweet herbal scent of the bedtime tea her mother set in front of her.

"Just nice?" Bobby's eyes twinkled over her teacup.

"Nick was fine. Very much a gentleman. And I enjoyed being with him," Cassie admitted. "He was so sweet to Birdie."

"Grandma!" Birdie shouted from her bedroom. "You forgot to sing me a song!"

"You don't have to, Mom." Cassie pushed away from the table. "I'll get her."

"No, she called for me. I'm thrilled you guys live here now, and I can do this all the time," Anna said over her shoulder as she jogged out of the room.

Cassie dropped her head under Bobby's probing eyes. She stared at the cup of tea and tried to think of something mundane to say.

Bobby beat her to it, but it was hardly mundane. "It feels wrong, doesn't it? Enjoying yourself with another man."

Cassie's head snapped up, surprised at Bobby's perception.

Bobby sat back and folded her hands. "I've told you, your grandfather was not my first love."

Cassie sipped her tea too fast and burned her tongue. "Ouch! Yes, we read about Pavlo. I'm sorry. That had to be so hard to lose him."

"You'd know that better than anyone else," Bobby said.

"It's hard to imagine you loving someone else. You and Dido were so happy."

Bobby smiled sadly. "Yes. I loved your grandfather, but first, I loved Pavlo. I thought we'd be together forever."

Burned tongue forgotten, Cassie leaned forward to listen.

"When he died, I thought I would die, too. That I could not live without him. But I could. And I did. With all that was going on, I still wonder how I survived. Every day, I got up and made it through until night, then I woke up and did it again." She closed her eyes, remembering.

"Did Dido know you loved someone before him?"

"He loved another before me, as well. We both understood that loss, and it bonded us."

Cassie sat back, thinking. Nick didn't have a connection like that. Or did he? From what she could tell, he seemed to be quite the ladies' man. She'd be the one bringing all the baggage along. And who would want that?

Bobby spoke, as if reading her mind. "You don't know his story. And even if it's very different from yours, it doesn't matter. My point is, people can move on from loss. You can still have a life, even when you think there's nothing left, because there is always something to live for. You'll see. It's all in that box."

Cassie mulled over Bobby's words as Anna breezed back into the room. "Birdie's all tucked in and almost asleep. So what did I miss? Did he kiss you?"

"Mom! No, he did not kiss me! He was a perfect gentleman." Cassie blew on the tea in her cup and tried not to wonder what it would have felt like if he had kissed her.

20

KATYA

Ukraine, September 1932

"Bring me my baby!" Alina wailed from her bed.

Mama shook her head. Katya moved away and turned her back on her sister so Alina wouldn't see Halya in her arms, fast asleep. Her eyes met Kolya's anguished face before he dropped his head into his hands.

"She's sleeping, my darling." Mama spoke softly, trying to soothe Alina. In the past week, as her fever raged, she'd become delusional, speaking of events that happened years ago as if they occurred yesterday and mumbling nonsensical things. Starvation and her weakened body had allowed a vicious illness to take hold. She could only keep down the tiniest bits of food, and her belly swelled up from her emaciated body so that she almost looked pregnant again.

Her desire to feed Halya distressed her more than anything else, though. She cried to feed her baby, but her milk had completely dried up when the collective cut back the food allotments even more. At the moment, Katya was Halya's sole source of food, and thankfully, she was still producing enough. For now.

"I need to feed Halya," she cried. "She's so hungry. I hear her cries all day long."

"You can't feed her anymore, Alina," Mama said firmly. "You have nothing left to give her; you have nothing left for yourself. You're ill, and your milk is gone."

"No, no, it's not. I can feel it flowing from me," she sobbed, her hands scrabbling at her hollowed chest. "Please, let me feed my baby."

Mama took Alina's hands and raised them to her lips. "You can try, but do not be disappointed if it doesn't work."

Mama signaled Katya to bring Halya over. Katya's throat burned as she fought to hold back her tears at the sight of Alina's devastating descent into oblivion. This had been going on for days, and it was only making things harder on Halya. She, too, wanted to nurse from her mother, but when Alina encouraged her to suckle a breast that had nothing to give, it infuriated the baby. She'd scream and flail against Alina with her little fists, and Alina would sink even deeper into her own world, receding from the pain of not being able to provide what her daughter needed most to survive.

"Do you want to put them through this again?" Katya said to her mother as she placed Halya into Alina's arms. "It doesn't end well for either of them."

Mama ignored her and spoke to Alina. "Daughter, if this does not work today, we will not try it again, do you understand?"

Alina nodded, her eyes fixed zealously on Halya. Katya doubted a word Mama had said registered with her. Despite her misgivings, Katya helped Alina situate the baby with pillows, because her weak arms could no longer support her daughter. Halya roused, eagerly searching for her mother's breast and the life-giving milk she so desperately needed.

Alina laid her head back, exhausted from the effort of holding it up, and everything was silent for a few moments as Halya's little mouth worked. Alina could not have produced any milk because she wasn't eating, but with each second, Katya held her breath, desperately hoping that some miracle would occur, and Alina would suddenly be able to nurture the baby she wanted so desperately to take care of.

Kolya came over and smoothed Alina's hair back, then kissed her forehead. "There's my beautiful girls."

Katya dragged her eyes away. After all this time, it still hurt to watch them and see what she didn't have. She'd tried to harden herself and pretend she didn't care, but she did.

Halya suckled voraciously, and when she didn't receive milk for her efforts, she screamed. Alina grimaced in frustration, and Mama reached in to pull the crying baby from her chest.

Alina grabbed her wrists. "No, please. I need to try a bit longer. Maybe the other side." Her ragged voice tugged at Katya's core "I have to feed her. I can't leave her like this. What kind of mother am I to let my baby starve?"

Mama's lips pressed into a tight line as she shook off Alina's grasping hands and pulled Halya away. Alina's head fell back on the pillow, and she closed her eyes.

"Here." Mama thrust the furious baby out at Katya. "Feed her."

Halya's cries instigated a primal response in Katya, and the familiar pinpricks signaled her milk letting down. She felt the precious drops wetting her shirt and hurried to pull it open and put Halya to her breast.

Mama took a deep breath, then turned back to Alina. "Halya is fine. Katya will take care of her. She won't be hungry. I swear, we will make sure she is always fed."

Alina's eyes flew open in alarm and began the cycle again. "My baby is hungry? Where is she? Bring her to me, I'll nurse her. At least I can do that for her."

Mama dropped down onto the bed in defeat. After a few minutes, Alina closed her eyes again and began humming an old song Tato had sung to them as children. A low wail burst out of Mama, and she clamped her hand over her mouth and shuddered with the force of her sorrow. After a few minutes, when she'd contained herself, she pulled back the covers and curled up next to Alina. Humming the song along with her, Mama cradled her oldest daughter's slight, fevered body in her arms and rocked gently.

Kolya stepped toward Katya and Halya. He stared down at his baby, cradled in Katya's arms, and his voice cracked. "I don't know what to do anymore, Katya." He reached out and stroked Halya's small head with his rough hand. "I'm afraid she's slipping away from me."

She put her hand on his arm and squeezed. "Don't lose hope. She's strong. She'll survive this."

Katya's eyes welled up as she watched her sister's child nurse greedily. She didn't quite believe the words she spoke, but she willed them to be true for all of their sakes.

* * *

Walking through the woods with Kolya reminded Katya of the long ago trips she took with Pavlo to hide their grain. Two years later, none of that food remained, but she hoped to replenish some of those stores during these harvest months. Fear of the upcoming winter weighed on her, and she wondered dully if she'd ever not be hungry again.

Katya glanced over at Kolya. His frame, normally larger and broader than Pavlo's had been, was now slender. His hunched shoulders bore the weight of the sleepless nights he'd spent holding Alina as she moaned and writhed through her delirium. Exhaustion underscored his eyes with black circles.

"I can't bear to see her like that." Kolya stooped low to check their first snare right inside the woods. "It's empty." He reset the snare and they moved on.

"If we can get more food for her, I think she'll be fine," Katya said.

Kolya gave a bitter laugh. "Yes, just get her more food and all will be well. If only it were that easy."

"Well, we can't stop trying," she snapped. "There's still things to be found in the woods. Mushrooms, nettles, acorns. And we're still getting milk from the goat, at least. I'll give her my share to help build her strength back up."

"No, you won't." Kolya's voice softened. "You need to keep your strength up, too. For Halya. I worry that food won't help Alina, though —that she's too far gone to come back from this."

Deep down, Katya agreed with him. Alina barely got out of bed each day. Her weakened body couldn't fight off the simplest of infections, and often, fevers and coughs ravaged her body. Every time it seemed as if she couldn't go on, Katya or Kolya would bring home just enough food to sustain her for a little bit longer. Sometimes it felt like a cruelty, to keep her lingering on the fine line between life and death, but Katya said none of this. Giving in to those fears, voicing them, would only make them more real, and she needed to cling to every bit of hope she could muster. She needed to be strong for all of them.

"She's not dead yet," Katya said firmly. "And if I have anything to say about it, she won't be for a very long time."

She glimpsed a patch of brown fur at the next snare, and with a cry of joy, removed a large rabbit. Stewed into a broth with the goosefoot greens she'd found, it would be just the thing to help Alina.

"See!" She held up the rabbit. "Tonight, we'll have a real meal."

Kolya's face creased into a smile that didn't quite reach his eyes and he clapped her on the shoulder. "You're a fighter, Katya. I've always admired that about you."

She gave a determined grin. "We can save her. I know it. If we get enough food for her consistently, she'll be able to heal."

When they arrived home, Alina sat propped up on her pillows, her eyes lucid. A small smile curved on her lips, and she waved her sister over. Katya shot Kolya a look that said, *See, I told you she'll be fine.*

Katya sat on the bed next to her and Alina took her hand. "I need you to promise me you will take care of Halya, no matter what."

Katya straightened. "What's this about? I'll always be here for her.

You know that. But there is no need to talk of such things."

"There is, and it makes me feel better to hear you say it. She's getting nothing from me anymore; you're the one keeping her alive. Please promise you will continue to nurse her, as long as you can, and that you'll love her like your own. I need you to promise me that."

"I promise." Katya patted her sister's leg and quelled her alarm at the conversation. She could feel Kolya's haunted eyes watching them, so she forced a bright smile. "And you will be here to see it happen."

Alina shook her head and smiled sadly. "I just need to know she will be loved."

"Don't be silly. Of course she's loved." Katya leaned over and gave Alina a hug, trying not to flinch at the feel of Alina's frail body in her arms. "By all of us, and her mother. Now let me fix up this rabbit for your dinner so you can get your strength up."

Before the food was done, Alina's fever had returned, and she was wailing to feed Halya again.

* * *

As October's cooler weather set in, Kolya butchered the kid goat. For almost a week, their daily meal felt like a feast, but it was gone now—every bit of marrow sucked dry, every organ cleaned and eaten, and the broth from the bones and scraps cooked down and diluted so many times it eventually became water.

Since then, they'd made do with ground oak bark and grass pancakes and cooked dandelions greens. Katya and Kolya were able to eat a watery soup and a piece of black bread every day they worked at the collective during harvest, but they always brought the bread home to share with Alina and Mama.

Aside from that, they had nothing. Because the collective hadn't reached Stalin's ridiculously high grain quota, activists raided every village home, emptying it of food, goods, and tools as repayment. They'd even lost control of their kitchen garden, the very vegetables growing outside their door now considered state property. They'd still "stolen" what they could from it earlier in the season, before the vegetables were even ripe, eating green tomatoes and small, bitter cucumbers before anyone else could take them.

Katya sat up as Kolya came in the house, hoping he'd had luck foraging. He gave a slight shake of his head, and she sagged back into her chair, her stomach aching for sustenance.

"I'll go check our hidden stores," Katya said. She couldn't bear to sit there and do nothing while Alina faded away.

"Maybe it's time to butcher the nanny goat, too," Mama said.

"Not yet." Katya pulled on her coat. "We're still getting some milk from her. I'll find something else."

"Then hurry, Katya. Your sister needs to eat." Mama leaned over and wiped Alina's fevered head with a damp cloth.

"I will." Katya met Kolya's worried eyes and forced a smile that she hoped looked more encouraging than she felt.

Katya climbed into the barn loft and dug through the loft, but only one note remained.

Rye, buried in hollow half-dead tree north of house five hundred paces.

The leaves crunched under her feet as she crept through the woods behind the house, their noise echoing like gunshots. Her nerves sparked with awareness and her eyes never stopped scanning the far corners of the land. With activist guards patrolling the countryside and neighbors desperate to take any food they could find, she couldn't afford to relax for one second.

Tall and thick, the pale, barkless tree stood in sharp relief against the inky sky. Before the last raid on their house, she'd hidden a jar filled with rye flour in the hollow of the crack and covered it with rocks. Disappointment made her shoulders slump as she sank to the ground and saw the rocks were gone. The knobby roots of the ancient oak stabbed into her knees as she pawed through the dead leaves and pebbles until her fingers bled, but it was useless. Someone or some-thing had taken the flour. She wiped her hands on her skirt and stared down at the trails of mud and blood her hands left behind. *Think, Katya.* She had to fix this. She had to bring food home tonight.

The moon peeked through the clouds, barely visible in the black, starless night and an idea flitted into her head, unbidden. *Maybe I could sneak onto a collective field and take a bit of food.*

She knew it was a terrible idea as soon as it occurred to her. Stalin had issued a decree in August, stating that anyone caught taking any produce from a collective field could be shot on sight or imprisoned for stealing socialist property. There were only a few fields still left to be harvested, and armed guards patrolled them on foot and horseback or from watchtowers. But what other choice did she have? She couldn't let her family starve. She couldn't let her sister die. Katya brushed herself off and stiffened her backbone. Her feet dragged as she took those first steps, but she'd made her decision.

She walked through the woods and approached the back end of the field at a snail's pace, slinking from tree to tree until she could almost reach out and touch the rustling corn stalks. So much food grew right in front of her, sowed by her and her family and neighbors. They would reap it soon, but taste none of it.

She glanced around, assessing her options. The long, flat field held only one guard tower off in the distance. She couldn't be sure, but she didn't think the guard could see anyone lurking behind the trees this far away. Katya edged forward on her belly, sweat prickling the back of her neck. Fear, thick and oily, choked her until she was panting as she crawled, inch by inch, toward the rustling corn. This field was feed corn, typically used for livestock, but it would fill her family's bellies all the same. She pictured Halya's hungry face, then swallowed down the apprehension so that it settled into a hard knot in her gut. She shot to her feet, hidden under the tall, brown stalks. As noiselessly as she could, she ripped off ears of the corn and stuffed them into her shirt.

Her belt caught them at her waist, and they filled out her clothing in sharp contrast to her narrowed, empty abdomen.

When she'd gotten as much as she could reasonably carry, she emerged from the field and slunk back along the ground toward the forest, not breathing until she reached the cover of the trees. As she melted into the woods, she sucked in a lungful of the night air and closed her eyes, relief making her sweat–soaked body tremble. She'd no sooner congratulated herself on the partial victory than a high-pitched voice rang out in the quiet night.

"Stop! Thief!"

Shock froze her for a moment, but common sense prevailed, and she bolted. No shots rang out, and she wondered at the identity of her assailant. The voice sounded young. Perhaps not a guard, but one of the Young Pioneers?

Katya still couldn't believe how thorough the Communist Party was in its indoctrination efforts. Even the school children were drafted into the Young Pioneers program, and encouraged to report anyone with illegal goods, including family members. And they did. Katya had been appalled when the neighbors down the road had been turned in by their ten-year-old son for hiding grain.

When the voice rang out again, this time much closer to her, Katya halted, certain now that she was hearing a young child. If she didn't stop the ruckus he was making, he would surely draw the attention of an armed and less easily manipulated assailant before she could escape. She clenched her fists and turned around.

The boy ran toward her and puffed up his chest. "I command you to come with me and turn yourself in!" he ordered, his voice deepening in his best imitation of a man.

Katya recognized the boy—she used to watch him during harvest season. He must be only eleven or twelve by now. Anger coursed through her, straightening her back and raising her chin. This child thought he could stop her from saving her starving niece. Katya's emotions exploded, taking over her common sense as they had when she was younger, and she marched up to him and slapped him across the face.

He gasped and raised a hand to his cheek incredulously. "You can't do that."

"Ivan Yarkop!" Katya whispered as fiercely as she could. "You should be ashamed of yourself!"

"You can't speak to me like that either," he replied, his voice now shaky with uncertainty at her lack of fear and respect. "I could have you shot."

"I changed your pants when you were small and chased you in the yard while you waddled around. I'm like family to you, yet you choose the state over me?"

He looked around, unsure what to make of her tirade, but Katya didn't give him time to think.

"My niece is dying because she has no food. I work in fields like this every day. Every day! Do I get to have any of that grain for myself? Do I?"

"No," he said. "But the state gives you food! That's how it works. You work for the state and the state takes care of everyone. And as a Young Pioneer, it is my job to help the state take care of everyone." He brightened a bit as he rationalized his actions to himself, but his gaunt cheeks told another story. His precious state didn't give him enough food either.

"Ivan, you're telling me that the state giving me one piece of bread a day for my labor should be enough for my sick sister, my mother, my baby niece, and me?" Katya asked. "No! It is ridiculous, it is cruel, and I will not stand to hear it from a child. And you're one to talk. You look terrible. Are they taking such good care of you?"

He shrunk a bit in his boots. "I'm only doing—"

"I said *no!*" Katya spoke as loudly as she dared, her voice quaking with fury. "You listen to me, Ivan. This village is dying because of the damn state, and you're helping. Shame on you as a Ukrainian for abandoning your people when they need you most."

Poor Ivan had no idea what to say to that. His eyes grew wide, and his lower lip quivered as it fell open.

"I'm going to walk away now, and you should go home," Katya said. "If you have any brains in that thick head, or an ounce of compassion in your heart, you'll forget you saw me."

His mouth clicked shut. He nodded slightly, and as Katya turned to walk away, she looked back over her shoulder. "Forget you saw me, Ivan, but do not forget what I said. You are helping to kill your people. Someday, it will come back to haunt you."

Katya didn't look back again to see his response. She meant everything she'd said, but despite the exhilaration she felt at speaking her mind, it wasn't a wise thing to do. Ivan could still report her, and they would take his word over hers.

Even when she made it home, her nerves wouldn't settle. Her hands shook as she helped Mama scrape off the corn and cook it down into a mush, saving the cobs to soak and eat later. Mama fed Halya and Alina as much as they would eat before splitting the remainder between herself, Katya, and Kolya.

"Why do you keep looking out the window?" Kolya asked as she put away the dishes. His shrewd eyes appraised her—as if he could see all of her secrets—and her face reddened.

"I like looking out at the night sky."

Later, when Mama went to bed, he tried again. "What happened tonight? You can tell me, you know. We're in this together." His mournful gaze fell on Alina's pale, sweat-soaked face, lying in bed.

"We are," she agreed. But the fewer people who knew about her illegal acts, the better. At the very least, it would protect him from having to cover for her if asked by the state. "Nothing happened." She rocked back and forth to lull Halya to sleep. "I fetched some corn. We fed Halya and Alina." This wasn't a lie, but it wasn't the full truth either, and somehow she knew he realized that.

"If you say so." His voice lacked conviction, but he didn't press her. "Be safe out there."

"Of course. I'm always safe."

For days, Katya looked over her shoulder, waiting to be arrested. Ivan could turn her in at any time, and that weighed heavily on her, but she was happy to bear that burden if it bought Alina and Halya a few more days of life.

* * *

For a week, they sorted through thousands of potatoes from a late harvest. Good ones went into one pile for the state, rotten ones into another for the livestock. There was no pile for the villagers, and each time Katya left work for the night, she was checked to make sure she hadn't hidden any in her clothes to bring home.

A young activist member had taken great pleasure in running his hands up and down her legs and torso, "searching" for stolen potatoes. Katya's face still blazed from the violation.

She wasn't stupid enough to hide any on herself, but she'd left four potatoes buried in the corner of each field she'd helped harvest. She planned to sneak back later and take the hidden potatoes home.

The wind whipped past her, pushing her hair out from the kerchief she'd tied around her head. Her arms ached, her back screamed with fatigue, and it took everything she had to move one foot in front of the other along the dirt path toward home.

Katya's discomfort disappeared as the house came into sight and she heard Halya's cries ringing out through the open front door. Cold fear gripped her as she charged down the path.

Mama sat curled up in a ball on her bed. Halya lay next to her, screaming, as Mama absently patted her back. Alina's bedding formed a path toward the door. Her bed was empty.

"What happened? Where's Alina?" Katya grabbed her mother's shoulders with shaking hands.

Mama looked up with glassy eyes. "They took her. They came and took her."

"Who took her? Why?" Katya picked up Halya and put a finger in her mouth to settle her.

"Prokyp and another man." Mama spoke so low Katya could hardly hear her. "They said she stole grain from the state."

As the realization of what had happened struck her fully, Katya clutched Halya close and dropped onto the bed next to Mama. Her stomach threatened to heave, though there was nothing in it to give up.

"Dear God," Katya whispered, even though she had long ago given up asking anything from God. Panic seized her, and she gave an anguished cry. "Mama, it was me. Me, not Alina. They wanted me!"

Mama's gaze sharpened as she looked at Katya. "What do you mean?"

"The corn I brought home last week; I stole it from a cooperative field. Ivan Yarkop saw me, but I didn't think he would tell."

Mama slapped Katya then. Hard. It seemed to surprise Mama more than her. Katya raised a hand to touch her stinging cheek.

"I'm sorry, Katya." Mama's trembling hands covered her mouth. "I don't know what came over me. It's not your fault."

"It is. I stole the corn, not her. It's me they want."

"You were only doing what you had to do to feed us," Mama said, but her eyes told Katya a different story.

"How long ago did they take her?" Katya pushed Halya into Mama's arms and stood. "I have to go talk to them."

Mama clutched frantically at Katya's hand. "No! They'll take you, too! Don't go! Kolya can go when he gets home."

This scared woman barely resembled her once strong mother, and bitterness welled in Katya. Bit by bit, the state had taken Mama from her, just as much as they had taken everyone else.

"Mama, I must go. I can't sit here while Alina is punished for my crime. Tell Kolya I went after her." Katya didn't wait for her response, but she could hear Mama crying out behind the slammed door.

She ran as fast as she could, all thoughts of sore muscles and her empty stomach long forgotten, while memories of her sweet sister flooded her mind. Alina, holding her through the night when she was small and scared. Alina, teaching her how to braid her hair. Alina, handing over her child and trusting Katya to care for her. A sob escaped Katya's lips and broke her stride.

If she could tell them it was her who had stolen the corn, not Alina, then maybe they would let Katya go in her place. Katya could handle being deported better than her sister. Alina was so frail; she'd never even survive the train ride.

Katya's whirling thoughts crashed to a halt when she saw the bodies propped up against the prison house. A keening wail ripped from her mouth, and she fell to her knees. There, lined up with three other "enemies of the people," was her sister. A bullet hole pierced the perfect skin on her forehead. Bright red blood trickled down her beautiful, still face. Her clear blue eyes stared out accusingly at Katya.

The sign above their heads read:

THIEVES WILL BE SHOT!

"It wasn't her!" Katya screamed as she slapped at her chest. "It was me! It was me!"

A large hand clamped over her mouth, and an arm wrapped around her middle, wrenching her to her feet. Grief and anger made her wild, and she fought with all she had, but the arms were much stronger.

A voice hissed in her ear, "Hush, Katya! They'll kill you too if you don't stop, and then what will become of Halya?"

Katya stilled at the familiar voice. Kolya. Her breath came in ragged gasps, and she collapsed against him. His body trembled, the emotion he held in check thrumming under his tense muscles.

The door to the prison house opened, and a burly activist with a pencil-thin mustache walked out. "What's this? Do we have another thief? A confession, perhaps?"

Kolya strengthened his grip on her. "No. She's crazy with grief. I'll take her home."

Without waiting for a response, he dragged Katya alongside him and marched away from the prison house. From the activist. From his dead wife.

Anguish clouded Katya's vision so that she didn't even recognize when they were back in their yard until Kolya finally released her. She fell to the ground, sobs racking her body. Kolya glared at her with red, puffy eyes.

"What did you mean back there when you said it was you? You stole and let Alina take the blame?"

His accusation stung, and Katya welcomed the pain. She deserved it. "I stole the corn I brought home the other day. The food hidden in the woods was gone, and I needed to bring something home for Halya and Alina. So, I went to the collective fields and took some."

He balled his fists and spoke through gritted teeth. "You told me nothing happened! If you were seen, why were you not taken then?"

"It was a Young Pioneer boy. I talked him into letting me go."

"But why Alina? Why did they not take you?" He paced in front of her as he yelled. The front door opened, and Mama peered out.

"I don't know!" Katya shouted as she stood up. "I wasn't home yet. Maybe the boy was confused when he said which sister it was."

"Alina confessed." Mama stepped out into the yard. "She told them it was her, not you."

"What?" Katya whipped around to face her mother. "I never wanted her to do that! Was she delirious?"

"No. It was the most clear-headed I've seen her in months. Maybe she was afraid they would take you from Halya and then she would have nothing to eat." Mama wrung her hands, her eyes darting between Kolya and Katya. "Are they deporting her? Or keeping her for a few days? I'm hoping they go light on her since she's a woman and so ill."

"No." Kolya's eyes bore into Katya's, though he spoke to his mother-in-law. His agony hit her in the stomach so hard she doubled over. "She is dead."

* * *

Two days later, the OGPU allowed the family to bring Alina home. Kolya carried her in his arms the whole way, refusing to let anyone help or to bring a wagon.

"I would gladly give my life for hers. I loved her." Katya's voice stayed strong as he set Alina on the bed, but her insides quaked. Mama threw herself on Alina's legs and wailed.

Kolya's face crumpled as he dropped it into his hands. "I know that, Katya." He leaned on to Alina's frail chest and cried. His body shook with silent sobs, his grief palpable in the air.

Alina had not been far from death before she'd been murdered. Starvation had drained her until she was a shell of her former self. Once upon a time, she'd been one of the prettiest girls in the village, with her thick dark hair and flashing blue eyes. Now, her thin, lackluster hair revealed bare patches of scalp where it had started to fall out in clumps. Her eyes, closed for the last time, were sunken deep into her head, like her cheeks. But admitting how long she'd been fading away didn't make her death any easier.

Katya swallowed her anger and screams, keeping them bottled because she had to. Someone had to stay strong. Someone had to be there for her mother, Kolya, and Halya to lean on. If not Katya, then who else?

Kolya wiped the back of his hands across his eyes and stood shakily. Katya wrapped her arms around him, steadying him as he had steadied her when Pavlo died.

"She's gone," he said, his voice raw as he buried his head in her shoulder and sobbed.

Tears scorched a path down Katya's face, each drop branding her a failure. She'd let Alina down. She'd let everyone down.

21

CASSIE

Illinois, June 2004

Cassie regarded the tidy backyard and gave a contented sigh. The sun was shining, and the scent of flowers perfumed the warm spring air. Her date with Nick at the carnival a few days ago had gone well—aside from the excessive number of women who'd approached him—and they had plans for him to come over today and dive back into the translations. She couldn't remember the last time she'd felt so eager to take on the day.

She swelled with joy as she watched Birdie helping Bobby in the garden, just like she had when she was a child. Bobby handed the small begonia plant to Birdie, who patiently waited for instructions.

"Put it in the hole, then gently push dirt in around it. Fill it in and pat it down," Bobby said.

Birdie complied, her brows knit in concentration as her chubby hands followed the directions exactly. "I want to do another one!"

Bobby smiled. "We have two flats full of flowers. You'll get to do plenty!"

Birdie whooped and ran to do cartwheels down the length of the yard. Cassie laughed as she sat back on her heels. Sunlight bounced off her wedding ring, catching her eye. Henry had placed it there on their wedding day, and she'd worn it ever since. It had become a part of her, a symbol of the beautiful relationship she'd shared with her husband. But she would always have those memories, wouldn't she? Whether she wore the ring every day or not, Henry would always be a part of her.

After a long, slow exhale, she twisted off the ring and stared at her bare hand, testing out the sensation. The pale circle of skin normally hidden under the ring stood out like a brand, but the overwhelming grief she usually experienced when thinking about what the ring symbolized, about life without Henry, didn't strike her. She flexed her fingers and realized her free hand felt okay. Maybe not completely normal, but okay.

"I should set this aside for Birdie to have one day."

Bobby nodded. "If you're ready. You're the only person who can know that."

Nick's face flashed through her mind, but this wasn't just about him. This was about her and her readiness to move on with her own life.

"I think it's time."

She slipped the ring into her pocket. She'd put it in her jewelry box when she went back inside, and someday, she'd give it to her daughter.

"Who planted all those flowers?" Birdie ran up to them, ready to plant again, and pointed to the perennial beds along the fence and below the white mulberry tree.

"They're perennials. I planted them a long time ago, and they come back every year," Bobby said.

Birdie reached out and took another begonia from Bobby. "Why don't you plant sunflowers?"

Bobby stilled at the question, her hand suspended over the flat of begonias resting on her lap.

Cassie pushed herself to her feet, brushed the dirt off her knees, and kept her voice casual. "Maybe they won't do as well here. Or maybe Bobby doesn't like them."

Bobby folded her hands in her lap. "No, that's not why. Sunflowers are pretty, but sometimes they make me sad."

Birdie wrapped her dimpled hand around Bobby's knobby one and leaned over to whisper, "Is that because they were Alina's favorite?"

A chill ran down Cassie's spine.

Bobby's breath caught, and her clear green eyes focused on the girl. "Yes, and my father's, too."

Cassie bit back the questions poised on her tongue. Bobby wouldn't answer them, but hopefully, after talking with Nick this afternoon, she'd know more.

* * *

Cassie found Nick on the couch as she emerged from Birdie's bedroom. "Hi. I just got her down. Thanks for coming over."

"My pleasure. Your grandmother let me in, then she went to take a nap herself." He stood up and took a few steps toward her. "It's nice to have an excuse to see you again so soon." His cheeks reddened, and he shoved his hands in his pockets. "Sorry, I didn't mean to say that last part out loud."

"It's okay." Cassie blushed furiously. "I know you didn't mean it."

"Oh, I meant every word of it." He looked down, then peered up at her through thick eyelashes. "I just probably shouldn't have said it."

"Oh." Cassie's mind went blank. "I'll, uh, I'll go grab everything and meet you in the kitchen." Grateful for the reprieve, she went to her room and grabbed the box. After taking a few calming breaths to slow down her racing heart, she made her way to the kitchen.

"That's a lot of sunflowers." Nick looked up from Birdie's latest pile of drawings, then moved to take the box from her.

"Yeah, Birdie has developed quite the obsession with them."

"They're the national flower of Ukraine, you know." He set the box down. "Did she always like them?"

"No, it's a recent development." She sat down and felt a rush of excitement when he scooted his chair closer to hers before sitting. *This is ridiculous. I'm like a lovesick teenager.*

Without thinking, Cassie put a hand on his forearm. "I'm grateful for your help."

Nick covered her hand with his own. "I'm honored to be a part of this. Are you ready?"

Cassie left her hand there, sandwiched between his arm and his calloused hand, for several seconds. It felt so natural to touch him. To be near him. His eyes locked on hers and her breath hitched.

This was happening too fast.

She snatched her hand away and cleared her throat. "Let's start."

* * *

An hour later, Cassie couldn't breathe.

"Stop. Please, I need a break."

She could smell the coppery scent of blood and hear Pavlo's last shuddering breaths as Katya held him. The terror was palpable. And familiar.

Except she hadn't gotten to hold Henry as he died.

Nick reached out as if to touch her arm, then pulled back, his brow furrowed with uncertainty. "I'm sorry, Cassie."

Guilt over her earlier reaction to his touch mingled with her grief. "No, I'm sorry. This is harder to hear than I anticipated."

"Hi, Mommy. Hi, Nick." Birdie blinked as she meandered into the kitchen. Her tousled hair stood out from her head in a tangle of knots. "Who's Katya?"

Cassie swallowed hard and pasted on a smile. "You didn't nap long. Where did you hear that name, sweetie?"

Birdie scratched her elbow. "I think Alina told me."

Nick pointed to the name written in clear Cyrillic script inside the cover of the journal. "Kateryna Viktorivna," he translated. "Katya is a diminutive of Kateryna. It's your grandmother's name. Or, at least, it's the name she went by in Ukraine. And Viktorivna is her patronymic name, meaning daughter of Viktor. She'd have a family name too, but she didn't write it here."

Cassie stared at him, stunned. "I didn't know any of that."

"So is Katya Bobby?" Birdie tugged at Cassie's sleeve.

"Yes, I guess so," Cassie murmured. Her mind raced.

After a few beats of silence, Nick stood. "Birdie, how about we take a walk with Harvey and get some fresh air?"

"Yes! Can we, Mommy?"

Grateful for the distraction, Cassie nodded. "All right, but just up and down the block in case Bobby wakes up from her nap."

Nick grabbed the dog's leash and the three of them set off, Harvey trotting happily alongside them.

"You looked a little pale back there. You've really never heard the name Katya until now?" Nick asked as Birdie skipped ahead.

"No. I know her as Katherine. Birdie said Alina was talking about a Katya, but I don't know how she could know that name if I didn't."

"Your Bobby probably told her," Nick said. "Maybe she and Birdie have talked about Alina more than you realize."

"I'm sure. She and Birdie do spend a lot of time together," Cassie agreed, but a niggling feeling in the back of her head made her question the veracity of the statement.

"You know, I'm not saying this is what's happening, but in the old world, it was very common to "speak" to the dead," said Nick. "I remember when my aunt died, my Baba set out a glass of water every day until the funeral for her to drink. She didn't consider her sister gone, just in another place where she could still be reached. There are a lot of Ukrainian customs around death that we might think are strange, but for them, it's part of the culture."

"Bobby mentioned speaking to Henry. She said I should ask him to come to me." Cassie forced a laugh at the absurdity of it. "It sounds so bizarre to say it out loud."

Nick slowed his pace, and she could feel his eyes boring into her. "Not at all. Did it work?"

"I dreamed about him." She clenched her hand, remembering the feeling of his grip. Of him letting go. *Be happy. Live your life.*

"I hope it helped you, Cassie. I mean that. I can't imagine losing someone you loved that much."

They passed a neighbor's honeysuckle arbor, and Birdie paused to sniff the flowers. Nick's blue eyes crinkled into a smile when Birdie squealed with delight at the intoxicating aroma, and warmth flooded through Cassie.

"I think it did help." She bent close to Birdie. "They smell amazing, don't they? It's honeysuckle."

"Yes, but they're not as pretty as sunflowers," Birdie said.

Nick broke off a small branch and wound it into a circle. He plucked a few violets and dandelions growing up along the sidewalk and tucked them into the vine. Birdie giggled as he placed it on her head like a crown.

"Beautiful." Nick said. "Now you have a *vinok* like a proper young Ukrainian girl."

"Look, Mommy!" Birdie twirled around, holding the flower wreath to her head. "I have a *vinok*!"

"It's lovely, sweetie. Bobby used to make those for me when I was your age."

"My Baba used to make them for my sister, too. Hers were much nicer than mine, though." He leaned over to pet Harvey, then suddenly spoke in a rush, as if he were afraid he'd chicken out. "Cassie, how would you feel about going out to dinner tomorrow night? Just me and you? I know we've only recently started talking, and you're still grieving and—"

The endearing offer touched Cassie, and she shocked herself and Nick when she cut him off. "I'd like that."

Nick's expression registered surprise and joy in quick succession. "That's great!"

"Let me check with my mom first to see if she can watch Birdie," Cassie said. "You know she'll be devastated that she doesn't get to come."

Nick grinned. "I'll make it up to her."

22

KATYA

Ukraine, November 1932

Katya slipped inside the barn, hoping for a few minutes of solitude before going into the house, but instead, she walked right into Kolya.

He steadied her with one hand and held up a lantern with the other. "Where have you been? I was getting worried."

Katya shoved down the shame and fury twisting inside her and focused on what was important. "I have food for Halya." She set four potatoes on the ledge next to Kolya and let the shadow of a victorious smile stretch her bruised mouth.

Kolya stared at the potatoes for a moment, then let his gaze move up her body. Color flooded Katya's skin as he took in the blood on her legs, the torn skirt, and her swollen face.

The concern in his expression morphed into rage. "What happened to you?"

"I left potatoes hidden in the fields during harvest, so I went back for some. I'm fine." Katya's voice wavered despite her bravado.

"You're not fine!" Kolya scrubbed at his face with his hands. "And what if they come for you like they did for Alina?"

"They won't." She squeezed her eyes shut, trying to block out the activist's voice. *I'll let you go this time, but it will cost you. And if I catch you again, I won't bother arresting you. I'll shoot you on the spot.*

Kolya hung the lantern on a hook and gripped her chin. Tilting her face to the light, he traced a finger over her puffy cheek with such tenderness that the tears she'd fought to contain spilled over and ran down on his fingers.

"You'll have a black eye," he said.

A black eye was the least of her concerns. Food was the priority. Feeding Halya was the priority.

"At least tell me who did this to you," he demanded.

"It doesn't matter." She pushed his hand off. "There's nothing to be done now. Any retaliation would only get you killed, and I can't be responsible for another death."

He sagged and closed his eyes. "Nobody blames you for what happened to Alina."

"Then why can't you say that while looking at me?" Katya barely heard her own voice, it came out so low. "Why can't you ever look at me?"

He opened his eyes and stared at her. "Most days, I can't look at you because you remind me of my dead wife. Now, I can't look at you because I see my inadequacy in your bruised face and ripped skirts. I can't look at you because I see how close we came to losing you tonight, and I can't do a damn thing about it. That terrifies me. I don't know what any of us would do without you. Especially Halya."

Stars danced across Katya's vision and her knees gave away. Kolya caught her before she fell and held her against his firm chest. She took slow breaths in time with his heartbeat and let the heat and strength of his body seep into hers until he kneeled and placed her in the soft hay. When he let go of her, the cold and despair flooded back in, and she had to stop herself from reaching out to him.

"He hit you pretty hard. You should be in bed," he said, his voice deep and gruff. He backed away from her and wiped his hands on his pants, as if trying to remove any trace of her essence from him.

"I don't want my mother to know what happened." She hated how weak she sounded, how broken she felt.

"Fine. Maybe we can tell her we were hauling wood, and I accidentally turned and hit you with a piece I had on my shoulder." Kolya's expression hardened, and he turned and spat on the ground. "But you must swear to me you will never do anything to put yourself in this position again!"

A shrill laugh escaped her cracked lips. "Do you think I willingly bartered my body for potatoes? You have some nerve, Kolya. My choice was this or my life. I chose life. The potatoes were a bonus he let me keep. Lucky me." It was her turn to spit on the ground as she glared up at him.

He dropped his head. "I'm sorry. I shouldn't have said anything."

"No, you shouldn't have. You have no idea what it's like to be a woman. Men think they can take whatever they want, whenever they want from us. We never have a choice in that."

Katya stood and brushed herself off. "Let's go in and eat."

She didn't tell him that she'd search the fields again. She'd pay any cost to keep Halya alive, because her survival was Katya's sole purpose for existing.

"Not all men," he said, his voice so soft Katya could hardly hear him.

"No, maybe not all men." She pulled herself up to her feet. "Now let's go in the house. The baby needs to eat."

* * *

That night, as she lay in bed, Katya flipped through the tear-stained pages of her journal. She'd written about losing Pavlo and Viktor, and she would write about what that vicious man had done. She'd promised Pavlo she would record their story, even the unbearable.

She picked up her pencil and began. The words flowed in a monotone voice, documenting the horror of that night as if it had happened to someone else. In her recounting of the incident, she felt nothing. Absolutely nothing.

Maybe my heart has finally given up, she thought. After all, it can only take so much, and I think I have far surpassed what most hearts can endure. Perhaps it is only an empty shell now, incapable of feeling anything.

She finished the entry and looked over at the sleeping baby. Halya, her lashes thick against her pale cheeks and her dark curls framing her thin face, sighed and turned toward Katya in her sleep. A fierce and desperate love surged through Katya, and she reached out and pulled Halya close. As Halya's warm body snuggled into hers, Katya knew she was lying to herself. Her heart could never give up while this sweet child still needed her.

"She will survive this, Alina," Katya said into the cold night. "No matter what I have to do. I swear it."

She closed her eyes and imagined Halya, grown up and beautiful with dark hair and flashing blue eyes like Alina. Katya sighed as she tucked the pencil inside her journal, then she wrapped her arms around Halya and slept.

* * *

"I have good news," Kolya announced one evening when he came home from the village.

As always, he went straight to Halya and scooped her into his arms. She giggled as he nuzzled his face into her cheek and tickled her. A surprising surge of affection rose up in Katya as she saw the love shining on his face for his daughter.

He tucked Halya against his chest and went on. "They've opened a

Torgsin store in the next town over. We can bring any gold or jewelry we have there and trade it for food."

"How is this good?" Katya set a bowl of watery potato soup on the table and put her hands on her hips. She'd snuck back to another potato field early that morning, thankfully without running into any other angry activists. "We don't have any gold or jewelry to trade. They've already taken everything."

"That's not true. I still have my grandmother's ring." Mama went to her bed and dug into her pillow, searching for the hidden ring. She held it up, admiring the glittery red stone set on a thin band of gold. "It will do me no good if we're all dead. Our lives are more important than jewelry."

Katya frowned. "How can they offer food for the very things they have said we should not possess? What if it's a trap?"

Kolya shook his head. "This is their way of ensuring they own every last one of our precious items. They won't have to come searching for it. We'll deliver it to them."

Mama slipped the ring off and set it on the table. "I thought I'd seen everything, but apparently there is no end to their deception."

"I may have some more things to trade," Kolya said.

Katya looked at him in surprise. "What do you have?"

"There are some things hidden at my parents' house. Nobody's been living there for some time, so it hasn't been searched recently. My mother had some jewelry that she always kept tucked away. When the activists first started in with their raids, she had Pavlo..." He trailed off as he glanced at Katya.

She tried to keep her face blank so Kolya wouldn't see the pain that shot through her whenever she heard his name. After all this time, his death still hurt as if it had happened yesterday. Kolya stared at her as if he could read her mind, and she pushed her feelings back down where they lived in a tight knot in her gut.

"It's fine. You don't have to be afraid to say his name."

Kolya looked down, then went on. "We separated the pieces and hid them in different spots around the house and yard. I know they found a few things but not all of them."

"Why haven't you spoken of this before now?" Mama's eyebrows arched high in disbelief.

"What would it have mattered? If they hadn't found where it was hidden, it may as well stay there. Until now, I couldn't get anywhere to sell it without arousing more suspicion."

"Yes, of course," Mama said. "And now, how do you feel about seeing if any of it is still there? Could you part with it?"

Winter had shown its cold face, and already they barely ate anything each day. Without help, they wouldn't survive.

Kolya rubbed his rough knuckles against Halya's translucent cheek. "Of course. The baubles are nothing to me. I will gladly trade them all for food for us."

"We should parcel up the food we get and hide it back at your parents", Kolya." Katya spoke up as the idea occurred to her. "Like you said, they don't look there anymore, because it's abandoned. Everything will be safer there."

Kolya's parents' farm had fallen to ruin. People weren't allowed to chop down trees or gather wood from the forest anymore because the state owned the woods. If they picked up a stick or log or took anything from the forest, they were stealing from the state. With no other option for firewood, Kolya and Katya had already dismantled some of the outbuildings in the cover of night and hauled the wood back home to use. Weeds and overgrowth had taken over the yard that had once been filled with beautiful flowers. Considered abandoned, the state left it alone.

"That's a brilliant idea." He shot Katya a rare smile as he handed Halya to her grandmother. "We'll have to hide it well enough that thieves can't find it. I'll leave first thing tomorrow morning."

"I'm going, too," Katya said. "I know the best foods to get for our trade, and I want to see this store."

"Yes," Mama agreed. "Two of you going will be safer than one." She rested her hand gently on Katya's face. "But you must be careful, daughter." She didn't say any more, but Katya could read the hidden message in her eyes. *They've already taken one of my children. Don't let them take another.*

* * *

Katya walked silently through the snow over to Kolya's old farm, steeling herself for the task ahead. She'd been there recently to help dismantle the barn for firewood, but she hadn't made herself go inside since Kolya and Alina had moved back home. She would never overcome her aversion to that house.

Katya hesitated when they reached the door. The large wooden slab closed off the tiny house, a physical barrier between her and the memories inside. Now, as she stood there in front of it, her stomach rolled at the thought of entering. She took a step back.

"It's fine, Katya," Kolya said. "You can wait here. I'll be only a minute."

Grateful, she walked off to wait for him near the old barn site. She couldn't even bear getting a glimpse of the interior. Squeezing her eyes shut, she instead thought about one of her favorite memories with Pavlo.

"Pavlo, wait for me!" She laughed as she chased him through the hay field.

"Come on, you've got to keep up," he shouted back. His long legs carried him so far ahead that she lost sight of him, but she followed blindly anyway. She would follow Pavlo to the end of the earth if he asked.

When she finally reached him, he was sprawled under an old linden tree, his hands folded under his head, creating a pillow.

"Katya, come lie with me and watch the clouds pass us by."

She sat down next to him, gasping for air. "All right, but I can't stay long. I need to get back and help my father with the chores."

Pavlo leaned up on one elbow and stared at her with a grin playing on his lips. "Do you realize how much you need me in your life? You would toil away all day without any fun if it weren't for me. I balance you out to make you the well-rounded woman I've grown to love."

"If you had your way, we would run around all day and get nothing done," she laughed. That was far from the truth. Pavlo was one of the hardest working men she'd ever met.

"And if we lived your way," he countered as he reached out and twirled a lock of loose hair around his finger, "we would work the days away to an early death and never enjoy life along the way. Admit it, you need me."

"Maybe," Katya allowed. "But if that's the case, and I do need you so much, then tell me, Pavlo. What do I do for you?"

The smile dropped from his face. "Absolutely everything. You are my life, and I can't imagine living without you."

Katya took a shuddering breath.

But now, I am living without you. The words surged up from within her so hard and fast she almost screamed them out loud.

"Katya?" Kolya touched her arm. She jumped, and her eyes popped open. The first thing she saw was Kolya's concerned face, and for one brief, amazing moment, she thought it was Pavlo. Then she blinked, and the illusion shattered.

"Are you okay? I'm sorry, I know this is hard for you, but you seemed fine when we came to tear down the barn."

"I'm just resting my eyes." Katya searched his face for any sign of pain. She'd never understood how he and Alina could live in that house after he'd lost so much there. But his eyes were no more haunted than they were every day. Perhaps he carried his pain everywhere with him and no one place could make it any worse, whereas Katya shoved the hurt deep into her soul and only faced it when she was forced too. Like now.

"How do you do it?" She touched his arm, needing to feel a solid human presence here and now more than ever.

He stilled and stared at her hand on him. "Do what?"

"Come here. Where you've lost so much."

"I do it because I have to. For Halya. For your mother." He put his hand, warm and heavy, over hers and squeezed. "For you."

Her hand burned under his touch. She gasped at the startling sensation and jerked away. "Did you find what you came for?"

Kolya stepped back from her, his face red. "Yes."

He pulled a pair of gold earrings, a silver cross, and a gold ring from his pocket. Katya recognized the ring as the one his mother had worn for special occasions. It had been handed down through her family for generations, as Katya was sure the other pieces had been, and as her own family ring had. Before all of this, those items would have been passed down to Halya. Now, their loss to the family would help keep her alive.

"Let's go, then." Katya turned her back on the sad little house. "It's a long walk."

"I've never thanked you." His words stopped her.

"For what?"

"For taking care of Halya. Feeding her, after losing Viktor." His voice faltered. "It can't be easy for you."

At the mention of Viktor's name, her stomach twisted. Of course it wasn't easy. But Kolya didn't know that sometimes Katya closed her eyes and pretended Halya was Viktor. Or that other times, she'd imagine that Halya was the baby born to her, and she'd never experienced the losses of her child, sister, and husband. If she could pretend Halya was truly hers, Katya could forget how they'd really come together. How grief and death had forged a bond between them that couldn't be fully described. Katya didn't love Halya any less or resent her for surviving when Viktor didn't. Instead, she clung to the baby like a drowning person grips a raft. Halya gave her purpose and motivation to get up every morning. A reason to find food at any cost so Katya's body could keep making food for her. Halya's survival had become Katya's sole purpose in life.

Instead of saying any of those things, Katya replied, "I love her like my own. And Alina would have done the same for me if she could have."

Kolya reached out and tugged Katya's hair, like he had when he used to tease her as a boy. "I'm glad I have you with me," he said haltingly. "Not only now, I mean. But every day. Fighting to survive. Fighting for Halya. Together. It helps to know I'm not alone."

She glanced up at him, shocked to hear the rawness in his voice. Before she could respond, he cleared his throat, and the emotion his face had betrayed only seconds ago disappeared behind the familiar, hard planes of his grief.

"We should get going," he said, and he started walking down the road without waiting to see if she followed.

* * *

The frozen ground crunched under their feet as they walked through the still landscape. Gray skies loomed over the colorless, snowy scene. They headed toward the main road that went through their small village and wound around the countryside before connecting to the next nearest town.

"*Holubtsi*," Kolya blurted out.

"What?" Katya raised an eyebrow at him. "What about *holubtsi*?"

"It's something I miss," he said. "The soft cabbage leaves wrapped around the meat and millet. And the sauce. Oh, I miss that rich tomato sauce poured over it."

Katya's mouth watered. She could almost taste the flavors rolling over her tongue.

"I miss *nalysnyky*." Her stomach growled and she pushed a fist into it. "Sweet *nalysnyky* with cherries. My mother makes the best I've ever had."

"She does," Kolya agreed. "But no one can hold a candle to my mother's *varenyky*." He reddened and coughed. "Could hold a candle, I mean."

Katya put a hand on his shoulder. "Her potato ones were my favorite."

Kolya gave her a grateful smile. "I liked the meat ones better. With onions fried in butter."

"Lots of onions and butter," Katya said. She grinned up at him as a warm feeling spread through her. She'd missed the camaraderie of her sister and Pavlo. Talking with Kolya like this felt good.

Kolya stopped short and made a strangled sound.

"What's the matter?" Her eyes scanned the area, searching for hidden dangers.

"Don't you see them?" His voice cracked.

Katya's eyes followed his line of sight and she shuddered in horror at the scene: bulky mounds of frozen bodies littering the path to town. Apparently, many people had tried to make this trip, but their bodies didn't have the strength to succeed. So, they sat down where they were and never got back up. At least a dozen people who had given up their fight for life right here adorned the road.

The first one lay crumpled in their path twenty feet ahead. Katya's mouth went dry as they approached the dark mass of rough cloth that stood out starkly against the barren landscape, but she felt pulled toward the corpse, as if it called to her. Kolya pulled the fabric back from the white face to see who it was, and Katya gasped. "Ivan!"

She thought about her last words to him and his betrayal that had cost her sister's life. A strange mixture of compassion and rage twisted through her as she stared down at his small gray face, pinched into grimace. He looked so young. So lost.

"Wasn't he a member of the Young Pioneers?" Kolya asked.

"Yes. He thought he was one of them. He thought they would take care of him."

Kolya gave a harsh laugh and started walking again. "They only take from us; they don't take care of us. He learned his lesson for turning on his country."

"He was only a boy." Katya surprised herself. The defensive words came out of her mouth of their own volition.

"Yes, well, Alina was only my wife and only your sister, and she's dead now, too. We could say something like that for everyone, Katya."

She bit her tongue. She'd never told Kolya that Ivan had been the one who turned her in and put Alina's death in motion. Telling him now would serve no purpose.

The state had misled young Ivan, like they had so many others, children and adults. Too young and foolish to know they lied to him, he remained loyal until the end. Now, he lay dead and alone on the side of the road. Katya wondered if his mother knew. But then, she was probably dead, too. Maybe that was why he'd embarked on this trip to town. Maybe he had nowhere else to go.

They stopped once more and saw Lavro's ice-covered face staring back at them. He would never make his famous *horilka* again. After that, they didn't halt to look at any more of the frozen bodies they passed along the road. They didn't want to see their haunted faces or know who else they'd lost.

As they approached the town, they passed the railroad station where so many of their friends and relatives had been deported from. Beyond that lay the grain bins where food was stockpiled before being shipped out to the rest of the country. Normally, at this time of year, the bins would be empty. Now, they stood full. Armed guards stationed outside the grain bins patrolled their perimeter. Past the bins, three more armed guards surrounded a large pile of rotting potatoes.

"Kolya!" Katya stopped and gaped. "It's all of our food."

"They aren't even using it!" Spittle flew from his mouth as he barked. "Those bins are bursting they're so full, and it all sits there rotting while we starve!"

Despair pulled at Katya, tugging her down into its dark depths. She put a hand on his arm, both to quiet him and anchor herself to something solid. "Shh. Don't draw attention to us."

His jaw muscles twitched on his cheek. "This is not about getting us to produce more food," he said, as the impossibility of survival suddenly became so painfully clear to both of them. "They want us all dead."

* * *

They stopped in the small building next to the *Torgsin* to trade in their family heirlooms for a piece of paper stating their worth. Katya argued that their value was much more than they were given, but the clerk would not change his stingy appraisal. Kolya finally dragged Katya out of the store and to the end of the line to enter the *Torgsin*.

Kolya leaned toward the woman in front of them. "How long have you been waiting?"

"An hour or so," the woman rasped. Her bloated face encased eyes reduced to tiny slits. Liquid oozed from cracks along her lips. "The line was much longer yesterday."

As it was, the line wrapped around the building so far that the end was almost back at the entrance. They limited the number of people in the store so as to keep better control. The line moved forward, and the woman shuffled ahead, turning her back on them. Katya glanced down at the woman's feet and saw that she'd cut her boots so that her enlarged feet would fit inside them. The swelling must have pained her, for her gait was awkward and stilted. Swelling seemed like an odd symptom of starvation, but many people suffered with it. As Katya wondered how the woman would get to where she was going after she got her food, the woman's legs gave out, and she fell face down on the ground. Katya squatted and tried to turn the body, but it was heavy with fluid.

"Kolya, help me!"

Kolya kneeled next to her and flipped the woman onto her back. Narrow eyes stared vacantly at the sky. She had died right here in front of them, right here as she waited for her food.

The line shifted. Kolya pulled Katya to her feet and stepped over the dead body. "Come, Katya. We must move ahead with the line."

"And leave her here?" Katya's voice rose as she pushed him away.

Kolya shook his head in disgust "Look around you! There are dead bodies everywhere. What's one more woman to them?"

The people behind suddenly surged forward and surrounded the woman's body. Kolya grabbed Katya's arm and yanked her away from the commotion.

"What are you doing?" Katya asked, horrified, as a young man begin to rifle through the woman's clothes. "Stop that! It's wrong!"

"Everything is wrong, Katya," Kolya snapped as he pulled her along. "Our whole world is wrong."

"What's she going to do with it?" the young man yelled.

Understanding dawned on her as she realized they were searching for her ruble certificate. Her repulsion faded, and anger replaced it. Why hadn't she thought of grabbing it first? The man was right. What was the dead woman going to do with it now? It might as well help feed someone else, like Halya. She had to think faster if she wanted to keep Halya alive. It was good to have compassion, but the dead were beyond its reach.

Snowflakes fell from the sky, blanketing her shoulders and head. The cold had pervaded Katya so fully by this point that numbness dulled her feet. She stamped them, trying to force the blood back through her legs. Small prickles rewarded her efforts, so she stamped harder for a few more seconds before exhaustion overtook her. She glanced back at the dead woman lying on the ground, thankful that her feet didn't look like hers. Yet.

As they rounded the corner of the back of the building, Kolya cursed and stopped in his tracks. Katya stumbled into him.

"What are you doing?" The rising wind whipped the words from her mouth.

"You don't want to see this." He turned around and blocked her path fully.

"See what? What can be worse than what we've seen?"

"This. This is worse," he said, his voice so low she could barely hear him. "So much worse."

Frustration made her snap. "I'm not a child anymore, Kolya. I don't need you to censor the world for me."

"Fine." He dropped his hand from her arms. "You've always been headstrong. Do what you want, then."

He moved aside, opening her line of sight to a horse-drawn wagon. Its full load swayed unsteadily as it made its way across the frozen ground. Piled high on its open bed were bodies. Men, women, children, stacked haphazardly and tangled all together. They'd been picked up and tossed into the wagon like logs, without any regard for their value as human beings. Legs and arms stuck out every which way, some so swollen they were still oozing, and others so emaciated their bones nearly jutted out through their thin skin.

"I suppose they have to pick up at least some of the bodies and throw them in a pit somewhere or we wouldn't be able to walk through them all." Kolya's voice dripped with bitterness.

Katya ignored him and watched, transfixed, as the wagon hit a rut in the road and bounced, jarring loose a small body. It fell off the wagon and landed lightly in the snow on the side of the road, barely making a sound. It was a girl, a tiny girl of no more than two or three years old. Not much older than Halya.

Blonde braids crusted over with ice peeped out from under the tattered blue scarf that framed her pale face and tied under her chin. Her eyes had frozen open, and now she lay, alone on the cold ground, staring at them as the snow began to slowly cover her. The wagon moved on, unaware of such an insignificant loss.

Katya's hand flew to her mouth and she bit down on her knuckles so hard she drew blood. Kolya folded her into his chest and turned her face away from the dead girl.

"Hush, now," he murmured in her ear. "We can't help her, but we can help Halya. Come, the line is moving again."

Her legs, like tree stumps rooting her to the ground, slowed them, but Kolya pulled her along and they made their way around to the other side of the building. Katya didn't see the girl again; she couldn't make herself look back, but she didn't have to. That image was branded forever into her memory, but in her mind, the girl's face was Halya's.

Inside the *Torgsin*, Katya's stomach screamed out for the vast amounts of food on display. She pushed a fist into the hollow where her belly resided to quiet it. Bags of flour, packages of cheese, bins of vegetables, and cuts of meat lined the walls of the building. Katya salivated as the smell of food, of life, assaulted her.

The well-guarded *Torgsin* was filled to the brim with the foods they had been dreaming of for months. It held everything needed to survive, but their certificate would only allow them to buy a few things.

How could there be a whole store full of food right here, in the middle of this devastation? If it opened its doors and gave people food, it could save both this larger town and her small village of Sonyashnyky. But things didn't work that way. The food remained locked away, untouched and unattainable for so many, like the grain bins and potatoes they had seen on the way to town. There was no question now that there was food available to eat. The state had just decided the villagers weren't worthy of eating it.

Katya tried to be analytical and choose the best options, but her head swam with the possibilities. Kolya walked along with her, his eyes glittering as he licked his lips. His hands shook as Katya piled her choices into his arms: powdered milk for Halya, eight kilograms of wheat flour, one kilogram of sugar, four kilograms of rice, and ten of cans of sardines.

Outside, they stopped to tuck the food securely in bags hidden under their coats. When everything was situated, Kolya pulled out one of the tins of sardines. "We should eat this. We'll need the strength to get back home."

Katya nodded and stared, her lips twitching in anticipation of the salty fish. Her stomach growled and she pressed close to him, blocking anyone from seeing what they were doing.

Kolya thrust his knife into the tin and peeled back the top. The savory scent wafted up to them and saliva pooled in Katya's mouth. With trembling hands, Kolya offered the can to her first. He swallowed hard and his eyes followed her movements as she thrust her fingers in and scooped a handful of the slippery fish into her mouth. She tried to chew slowly and savor each briny bite, but her desperate body took over and she gulped down the mouthful, then watched as he did the same. They took turns until the tin was empty, then used their fingers to wipe the sides. When every morsel was licked clean from their fingers, and Katya's mind returned to her, she stepped back.

Kolya's eyes met hers, and guilt racked her. The animalistic intimacy of the act they'd just shared shocked her. In that moment, nothing had mattered but eating. Now, heat flushed her cheeks as she recalled how she'd lost control. She tried to gather her thoughts, to speak, but as if he could see inside her head, Kolya gave a grim smile.

"I'm sorry. I wasn't myself there. We should get moving."

"I'm sorry, too," she mumbled, and they started back across town toward the road that would lead to their village. The snow had tapered off, but the wind still whistled around them. In the middle of town, a man stumbled out of a building, directly into their path. His clothes hung off his withered frame, and a cap sat low over his bearded face, but neither of those things could disguise the sunken cheeks and half-crazed eyes of a starving man.

"Prokyp?" Katya gasped.

Kolya growled and immediately put his hand out in front of Katya, blocking her path so she couldn't walk any closer to the man who had first begun requisitioning their food. "Seem a little down on your luck, Prokyp," Kolya said. "Isn't the state taking care of you anymore? Or have they finally forsaken you, like they have the rest of us?"

Prokyp's face contorted into a menacing sneer. "I didn't need them to take care of me when I could take whatever I wanted from poor fools like you, Kolya."

"It doesn't look like you're getting much of anything from anywhere these days." Katya pushed Kolya's arm down and stuck her chin in the air.

Prokyp turned his crazy eyes on her, and then glanced back in the direction of the *Torgsin* from which they'd exited. The sneer on his face transformed into a sick smile. "Well, Katya, it's good to see you alive and well. Always such a sweet soul. I know a God-fearing woman like you wouldn't deny a dying man a crust of bread. Please, I beg of you, I have nothing."

"We have nothing to give because scum like you took it all from us. Now, you want help from me? You call me a God-fearing woman and hope to gain my sympathies?" Something in Katya snapped, and her voice became shrill. "Do you hear this, Kolya? This crazy man begs of me? He begs of me! Did he hear my mother's pleas to leave us with enough grain to feed Alina when she was ill? Did he hear me implore him to leave our potatoes to mash up for the baby to eat? No, he took everything we had, and he did it with a smile on his face!"

"It was my job," he said. "I had to do it, or they would have killed me."

"You relished every second of what you did to my family, and to all the others as well, I'm sure." Katya spoke through gritted teeth as fury coursed through her. Her left hand throbbed with pain, as if he had slammed it in the door only yesterday. "You are a monster!"

Kolya grabbed her arm. "He's not worth it. Look at him. He'll probably be dead before the day is done."

Kolya spoke the truth; Prokyp looked half-dead already. Katya's fists itched to strike out, but she allowed Kolya to lead her around Prokyp, who looked at them with undisguised hatred. As they drew past him, Katya mustered up every bit of saliva in her dry mouth and spat at his feet.

Enraged, he uttered a snarl and turned to come after them, but he moved slowly on weak legs. Kolya drew back and dealt Prokyp one swift punch in the face. Katya didn't know how much force Kolya could have put into it, for he too, lacked his normal strength, but Prokyp's emaciated body was no match for a man half his age, even a starving one.

He squealed as he crumpled to the ground, and Kolya scowled over him, his chest heaving, until Katya shook his shoulder.

He stared at her, dazed, as if surprised at what he'd just done.

"We need to go," she said.

He finally nodded, and they walked as fast as they could without drawing attention to themselves, not speaking until the town was far behind them and out of sight.

23

CASSIE

Illinois, June 2004

"Birdie's down for the night." Cassie slumped onto the couch next to Bobby. "What are you doing?"

"Looking at this *pysanka*." She rolled the egg between her arthritic fingers, then held it out toward Cassie. "Your mother made this one."

Cassie took the finely detailed egg, dyed in the traditional way using wax to create intricate designs in layers of different colors. *Pysanky* eggs were an integral part of Ukrainian Easter celebrations.

"We haven't made any in years," Cassie said. "I loved helping when I was a little girl."

"We could teach Birdie," Bobby said. The phone rang, and she reached over to answer it. "Hello?"

Cassie's curiosity piqued as Bobby's eyes grew wide.

"Yes, yes, I'll give money. Wait, I'll get my wallet." She tried to pull herself up from the couch, but Cassie put a hand on her arm.

"Who's on the phone? Who do you want to give money to?"

Bobby pushed at her. "Go get my wallet. It's the state police. They need money."

"Let me have the phone." Cassie held her hand out.

Bobby gave her a dirty look but acquiesced.

"Hello, can I help you?" Cassie said.

She listened for a few moments. "No, thank you. Please take us off your list."

As she set the phone back on the receiver, Bobby grabbed her hand. "When they call, you give them money! If you don't, they will come for you in the night. Take you away and no one will ever see you again!"

Cassie's mouth dropped open. "Bobby, they were asking for donations for the state troopers' scholarship fund. You don't have to give money to them. Nobody will come get you in the night. This isn't Ukraine."

"That's what they want you to think! They come when you aren't ready, but I was always ready. I had a bundle packed."

"Ready for what?" Cassie asked, even though she knew the answer from her time with Nick and the journal. *Siberia. Sasha. The deportations.* Bobby was flashing back to her time in Ukraine again.

Bobby wrung her hands and ignored the question as she scanned the room like a caged animal.

Cassie's mind raced for a distraction. In a light voice, she said, "Tell me what you would pack to be ready."

Bobby's terror-filled eyes locked on hers. "I packed warm clothes and blankets. They put you on cattle cars and send you to the gulags. It's very cold. They don't give you blankets."

"That was smart to pack blankets. Here, why don't you lie back and rest, and I'll go look for a bag." Cassie spoke in a calming tone as she dimmed the lights.

"I packed food, too," Bobby went on, but her voice had quieted. "When I could. But we didn't always have food to pack."

"That must have been very hard." Cassie leaned over and smoothed her hair. "How about I take care of all that? Why don't you close your eyes and rest, okay?"

"For a little bit," Bobby agreed. "I am tired. But don't forget to pack our things."

"I'll sit here with you until you fall asleep, then I'll pack."

"Thank you, Alina," Bobby mumbled.

Cassie startled. Alina. Her sister. What had happened to Alina and why did she still haunt Bobby?

After a few minutes, Cassie crept down the hall to peek in on Birdie. She slept peacefully, one arm slung over her head, legs dangling off the bed. Cassie planted a soft kiss on her forehead, then straightened at the sound of Bobby talking.

On tiptoe, as to not startle her grandmother, she crept back down the hall and stopped when she saw Bobby sitting up on the couch.

"Alina?" Bobby said quietly. "Are you here?"

The silence echoed around them.

"So much has happened since I lost you." She paused, waiting for a response. "I have a great-granddaughter now. Would you believe I lived long enough to see such a thing? I've been telling her stories about when we were girls."

She gave a low sob, then went on, the raw grief in her voice so tangible Cassie winced. "I'm sorry, Alina. I'm so sorry for everything that happened. I never meant to hurt you. I hope you know that. I light the candle so you can come back to me, but I think I've failed you too much."

The clock chimed, announcing the hour. Bobby closed her eyes, and Cassie could feel her grandmother willing something to happen, someone to speak. Her pulse raced as she watched the tragic scene. As crazy as it was, she almost expected Alina to manifest in front of her.

But there was only silence.

Gingerly, Bobby lay down next to the spot Birdie talked to and reached her hand out toward the nothingness. Tears ran in crooked courses down her grooved cheeks. "I'll keep waiting, Alina."

She closed her eyes, and her breathing evened out. Cassie inched closer and watched her shoulders rise and fall in a steady rhythm. When she was convinced Bobby was asleep, she ran to the kitchen. If she couldn't read the journal on her own, maybe researching what life was like in Ukraine back then would give her some insight.

She plugged the internet cable into her laptop and—for once grateful for her mom's pushiness—punched in the login information stuck on the refrigerator, then opened up the search bar and typed "Ukraine, 1930s".

The first entries shocked her.

Holodomor, death by hunger, terror-famine, Stalin, death toll estimates from 4–10 million. The horrific words screamed out at her from the screen. Pictures of bloated bellies and emaciated bodies both drew her in and repulsed her at the same time. Children with large heads perched on spindly bodies stared out at her with haunted eyes.

Cassie blanched as she clicked on picture after picture. "Oh, my God," she whispered. "How did I not know about this? If she lived through a forced famine, it's no wonder she hoards food."

"What's a famine?" Birdie's little voice piped.

"I thought you were in bed!" Cassie slammed the computer screen down so her daughter wouldn't see the pictures. "A famine is when people don't have enough food. They get very hungry."

"Oh, yeah." Birdie nodded in an understanding way that belied her young age. "Alina and Katya were really hungry all the time. I heard all about it."

From who? Cassie wondered. But before she could press for more answers, her mom came in the back door.

"Hello!" Anna bent and kissed Birdie on the cheek. "Why don't you go pick out a few books for me to read to you. Wait in your room and I'll be right there."

Never one to turn down a story, Birdie ran back to her room. As soon as she was out of earshot, Cassie opened the computer again and spun it towards her mom. "Look at this. Have you heard of the Holodomor?"

"No, why?" Anna scrolled through the page for a few minutes and went pale. "This is terrible!"

"I know," Cassie said. "I'm pretty sure Bobby lived through it."

Anna shook her head. "No way. I would have known. My parents would have talked about it."

"Maybe it was too hard."

"I had a good childhood," Anna went on, ignoring Cassie. "A comfortable house, home-cooked meals every day, parents who loved me. We were happy."

"But what about before they came to America? We've never heard anything about that."

"I don't know. They didn't talk about it. But life here was normal. My mother and father were so in love. He used to bring her flowers every Friday night after work, and she'd light up when she saw them." Anna chuckled. "Every time, like it was a big surprise, even though he never missed a week. They'd sit in the garden snuggled up together while I caught fireflies in the summer and hold hands when we went ice-skating in the winter. The three of us were happy, and their love formed the foundation for it all." Her smile faded. "We struggled so much after we lost him, but it helped me knowing he'd had a good seventy-nine years on this earth. Or I thought he did."

Cassie touched her mom's shoulder. "It sounds like he had a wonderful life, but that doesn't mean there weren't harder parts."

Anna rubbed the back of her neck. "I guess there were little signs. Mama never let me waste food, no matter what. She used to say, "Bread is life. You always eat it." And there were those few times my father was sad, like that day in the garden. But that's normal. This..." Anna nodded towards the computer. "This is anything but normal."

"Experiencing a forced famine would explain both those things, and the recent food hoarding," Cassie said gently.

"It's hard to believe, though. How could she bear so much grief and still be such a wonderful mother to me?" Anna stood. "Maybe we should talk to her."

"No." Cassie folded her arms. "She shuts down. That's the whole reason she wants Nick to read it to me. We need to finish the journal first to see what it says, then we can decide how to approach her."

"Grammy, are you coming?" Birdie walked back in the kitchen, a stack of books in her hands.

"I'm sorry, sweetie. I'll be right there." Anna started after Birdie, then turned back to Cassie. "Fine, we can wait, but please move it along. If this is what really happened to her, I can't stand thinking of her reliving it."

* * *

The next morning, Cassie peered out the front window, watching as Nick dug through the bushes and found the newspaper. He'd continued the practice after she'd moved in, even though she was quite capable of getting the paper out of the bushes herself, but she didn't complain.

She yanked open the door right as he got to the front porch. "You know, I can do that."

Nick jumped and grinned sheepishly. "You startled me! I know you can. It just got to be part of my routine to stop by and bring it up. The paperboy always throws it over in the bushes, and your grandmother had a hard time getting it."

Cassie grabbed the coffee cups she'd set on the front table and held one out to him. "Coffee?"

"Sure. Thanks." He took the cup and followed her as she sat on the low bench hugging the front of the house. He glanced down at the cup, and his lips curled into a smile. "Were you waiting for me?"

Cassie bit back her own smile and played coy. She shrugged. "Maybe. I have a couple of questions for you."

Nick raised the mug to his mouth and sipped. "Good coffee. All right. I can be bribed."

"How old was your grandmother when she came to America?"

Nick pursed his lips. "Not where I thought this was going, but I'll play along. I think about twenty-five. She came after World War II."

Cassie leaned forward. "Did she ever mention anything about a famine?"

"You mean the Holodomor? Of course. I thought you realized that's what we were dealing with in your Bobby's journal."

"No. You say Holodomor like it's common knowledge." Cassie plucked at the hem of her shorts, her cheeks burning. "But I'm mortified to say that until yesterday, I had no idea about it."

"It is common knowledge for Ukrainians. We learned about it in Ukrainian school, but my grandmother didn't live through it. Her family was in western Ukraine, which, during the time between the World Wars, was occupied by Poland. They didn't have to deal with Stalin till World War II."

"What did she say about it?"

"She said it was horrible. Some people managed to escape into her village, and they told stories about whole villages in eastern and central Ukraine being wiped out. People were deported by cattle cars to Siberia, like we read about in your Bobby's journal, or forced to starve in their own homes after Stalin exported all of the food. Children were left at train stations by their parents in hopes someone would take pity on them and bring them home and feed them, but they rarely did. People died in the streets waiting for a crust of bread." He lowered his voice. "The worst were the stories of cannibalism. People spoke of being so desperate they ate dead bodies, and in extreme cases, killed other people to eat them."

Cassie's jaw dropped. "That's unbelievable. I feel so dumb. I'm of Ukrainian descent. I should know what my family went through. How have I never heard of any of this?"

"Well, the famine was covered up pretty much until the Soviet

Union fell, and there are still people who insist it never happened," Nick said. "Stalin put on a good show, made collectivization sound great, and the press and his allies either bought it or ignored it. Some even lied. Walter Duranty, from the *New York Times*, completely refuted that a famine was happening. Hell, he won a Pulitzer for his articles on it. Nobody wanted to believe the 'breadbasket of Europe' was being starved to death."

An ache swelled in Cassie's throat as the pieces clicked into place. Bobby hiding food. The terror. The grief.

"This explains so much about Bobby."

"She may have some major survivor's guilt. It's not always easy to talk about traumatic things. That's probably why she gave you her journal instead of telling you herself. Speaking of, when should we read some more? Maybe it will tell us exactly what she went through."

"What about now?" Cassie turned to face him. "Please. My mom was going to go to the park with us this morning. I can probably get out of it and stay here with you."

"It's a date. Let me run home quick and clean up from work." Nick smiled at her. "Two dates in one day. Watch out. You might get sick of me."

"Oh, my gosh, I forgot about tonight. I'm sorry. I'm monopolizing all of your time." Cassie waved him away. "Go, get on with your day and forget I asked."

Nick chuckled. "There's nothing else I'd rather be doing, though I am a little disappointed that you forgot about tonight."

Cassie flushed and stared into her coffee. "I didn't forget, exactly. I got distracted, and I want to read more of the journal so much."

"Don't worry about it. I'm only teasing." Nick stood and handed her the empty coffee cup. "I'll be back in a half hour."

* * *

While Bobby, Birdie, and Anna walked to the park, Cassie and Nick worked. They'd found their rhythm, and Cassie typed as quickly as Nick translated, not pausing until Alina's death. Cassie could feel him watching her, but she kept her eyes on her screen, reading the last words over and over.

My sister was dead.

"She blames herself for Alina's death," Cassie finally said.

Nick grimaced. "And that guilt is on top of the pain of losing so many others. Really, I'm amazed she's as stable as she is."

Cassie shook her head. "I don't know what to say to her."

"I wouldn't say anything yet. We still have a lot to get through."

"We're back!" Anna called as she ushered Birdie through the back door. "Birdie is going to finish her cone outside with you guys."

"Grammy bought me a treat!" Birdie held up a mess of pink frozen yogurt hanging haphazardly off a cone and slurped a mouthful off the top.

Nick tried to hold back his laughter as Birdie moved closer, her cone dripping a trail behind her. She looked over his shoulder at the pictures on the table and pointed a sticky finger.

"Hey, that's Katya and Alina!" Birdie licked off another messy bite. "Can I see it?"

"Nick will hold it for you," Cassie said. "Don't touch anything with those hands. It's all very old and delicate."

Birdie nodded as Nick held up the picture of the two girls that Bobby had dropped a few weeks ago.

"Yep, that's them," Birdie said. "I wish I had a sister like that."

Goosebumps popped up on Cassie's arms as Nick's brows furrowed.

"Birdie, how do you know this is Katya and Alina?" Nick asked.

Birdie shrugged. "I just do."

* * *

"Bobby telling her stories about Katya and Alina is one thing, but how would she know what they looked like?" Cassie asked Anna as they cleaned up lunch.

"I'm sure Bobby showed her the picture," Anna said. "You said you saw Bobby carrying it around."

"Yeah, I guess so." Cassie gathered up the sandwich ingredients lying out on the table and began putting them away.

"What did Nick say?" Anna asked.

"He's told me some pretty interesting beliefs his grandma had about death and the afterlife, but he hasn't given me his own opinion on it."

"Bobby has some odd notions, too," Anna said, wiping the table as she talked. "And if she's telling Birdie about them, then it's not so far-fetched for Birdie to think she's talking to Alina."

"It makes sense when you put it that way," Cassie said. But deep inside, she wasn't so sure.

"Now, let's hear the latest on the journal." Anna set the dishrag on the sink and turned expectantly towards Cassie. "How far have you gotten?"

Cassie grimaced. "I think you should sit down for this, Mom."

By the time Cassie had finished updating her mom, tears were rolling down Anna's cheeks.

"My poor mother. How did she bear it? First her husband, then her child and sister? I'm so glad you stopped me from asking her about Alina when we first found out she had a sister."

"It's no wonder she doesn't want to talk about it," Cassie said. "I barely survived losing Henry. If it weren't for Birdie, I don't know that I could have gone on. And Bobby lost so much more."

"She had Halya to keep fighting for," Anna said.

"But what happened to her? She'd be your first cousin. You'd think you'd know of her, at least." Cassie rubbed her aching temples, hoping to stave off the headache that had been brewing ever since she'd learned of Alina's death.

"Maybe she died, too," said Anna. "Even if she didn't, she'd be almost twenty years older than me. She'd have been an adult when my parents finally emigrated in 1950. She could have stayed in Europe or got married and moved to her husband's home country. Are any of the letters in the box from her?"

"I don't think so, but that doesn't mean there aren't more letters somewhere in Bobby's closet. That woman saves everything. But even so, why wouldn't Bobby have mentioned her to you?"

"I don't know, Cass, and I don't know if I want to know anymore right now." Anna stood and grabbed her purse. "I have to run to the bank."

"What do you mean you don't want to know? You don't want me to update you on the journal anymore?" Cassie couldn't believe her ears.

Anna fidgeted with her purse strap as she moved towards the door. "I want to hear it. Eventually. But I also want to hear about her happy ending—how she fell in love with my father and rebuilt her life after all of this. I need that balance of joy if I'm going to hear about all this heartache for her, so I think I want to wait to hear the whole story after you finish."

"But it might not be the happy ending you're expecting, Mom."

Anna paused, her hand already on the doorknob. "I know that, Cass."

24

KATYA

Ukraine, December 1932

"Katya," Mama's voice rasped from her bed.

"I'm here," Katya said from her spot on the edge of the bed Mama hadn't left in days. Mama dwindled away slowly and steadily. She'd been giving all of her food to Halya for weeks before anyone noticed, having decided that Halya's life was more important than her own.

Her engorged feet, too painful to walk on, cracked and oozed like the woman Katya had met at the *Torgsin*. The great mound of her belly rose up under the layers of blankets piled on top of her. Katya guessed it was the large amount of water Mama drank to try to fill her stomach that made it distend. but she didn't understand why her legs and feet swelled.

"There are some things I must ask of you, daughter," Mama said.

"Anything, Mama," Katya replied. Her voice faltered as she pushed down her fears about her mother's imminent death. Halya whimpered in her arms, and she swayed her upper body to quiet the child.

"I ask this for her." Mama reached out and rubbed her hand along Halya's sunken cheek.

Katya nodded, her mind racing to try to figure out what her mother could possibly want that Katya hadn't already given. "You know I would do anything for her, Mama."

"I know, and that's why I can leave this world certain you'll do the right thing by marrying Kolya."

"Marry Kolya?" Katya choked out as she jumped off the bed. "Why would I do that? He's Alina's husband. He's like a brother!"

The sudden movement caused Halya to cry again. Gently shushing her, Katya paced the room.

"I'm sorry, Mama. I can't do it." Katya flushed as conflicting feelings bubbled up in her gut. "I'll do anything else for you, but not that."

Mama closed her eyes and pressed her lips. "Katya, you must! You must marry him! Soon, you will live here alone with him. It isn't right."

"Are you worried about village gossip? Because nobody cares anymore. They're all dead, deported, or too busy trying to stay alive to worry about whether or not I live with a man I'm not married to."

"What about Halya? You are the only mother she has now. It's right that you be with her father. You must do it for her! It's what family does!" Mama brought her fist down on the bed for emphasis, expending energy she didn't have to spare.

Katya sat back down next to her mother and leaned close. "Stop worrying, Mama. We'll be fine."

Mama stared at her. The blue eyes that had once snapped and sparkled with life now lay in shadows, sunk so deep into her head Katya could barely discern their color. Her heart ached to see this once vibrant woman reduced to such a sad state. Mama's breath came faster, and she kneaded her breastbone as she wheezed.

"Please, Katya, swear to me you'll do it. I can't rest until I know this is taken care of."

"Fine, Mama, I'll do it, but please, relax before you make yourself feel worse." Katya tried to control the panic in her voice. "You have to calm down."

The sour taste of the words lingered in Katya's mouth long after they left her lips, but she could no more refuse her mother's dying wish than she could turn her back on Halya.

With Katya's promise assured, Mama relaxed into the bed. "She comes to me, you know."

"Who?" Katya asked, relieved at the change of topic.

"Alina. I see her." Mama smiled peacefully and closed her eyes.

Katya shivered as she laid a cold cloth on her mother's burning forehead. She didn't want to think about what Alina would have to say to her right now.

After a few minutes, Mama fell asleep, and the steady rhythm of her breathing signaled a brief reprieve.

Katya sagged with relief, then opened her shirt and offered her breast to Halya. She was barely producing milk now, but the baby took it, eager for any bit of nourishment. She was nearly a year old now, and she weighed practically nothing, like a feather in Katya's arms. Her face, wrinkled and wizened, looked like an old woman's, and her distended belly stuck out grossly over her stick like limbs. Tears welled in Katya's eyes. She saw her failure in Halya's pinched countenance, just as she saw it in her mother's painful demise.

The door blew open, and Kolya came in, stomping his boots and brushing the snow off his coat. His face had thinned, but he could still turn heads. He had the same unruly, sandy blond hair that Pavlo once had, the same high cheekbones, and the same tall, sturdy frame, but his eyes differed. Pavlo's eyes had combined a beautiful mixture of many colors to make a unique hazel, and easily crinkled into laughter. Kolya's solid-colored eyes mirrored the deep blue sky. Maybe, in the past, they had crinkled in laughter, but Katya couldn't remember anymore. Now dull and hollow, they reflected the haunted pain of the losses he'd endured.

Could she love this man as a husband? Maybe she could love the parts of him that reminded her of Pavlo. So many similarities existed between the brothers. If she only focused on those, there might be a chance she could love him.

But the betrayal it would be to Alina and Pavlo made her sick. How could it be right that their deaths led to her and Kolya getting married? Confusion made her head hurt so that she couldn't think straight.

"I need to check on the goat," Katya announced. She couldn't stand being in the house another minute. Kolya had been able to escape, working on and off in the collective horse barn all winter, but Katya hadn't left the house to work for the collective since her mother fell ill. Now, in the dead of winter, they had no food or work for her, so what was the point?

"Fine," Kolya said. He pulled his coat off and hung it near the *pich* to dry. He stilled, his expression inscrutable as his eyes fell on his child at her breast.

Flustered, she pulled her shirt closed and set the sleeping child on the bed. "I'll bring back some goat's milk for supper."

Kolya nodded and angled his head toward her mother. "How is she?"

"Not well," Katya replied, her mind churning as she came back to the problem at hand and her struggle to find a way to tell him what Mama had requested.

"I wish we could do something to make this easier on her. It's hard for her to know she can't take care of us anymore," Kolya said.

Katya rubbed her hands together and squared her shoulders. Maybe it would be best to just say it, and then leave. Then he could think it over on his own. "Actually, she has asked something of us."

He looked up from the chair near the stove where he sat warming his hands.

"She wants us to marry. For Halya's sake," Katya blurted out in a rush, her face flaming with embarrassment. "I don't feel right about it, but she made me promise. I couldn't refuse her."

Katya lowered her head in shame, waiting for his condemnation.

She only hoped he understood it was something she'd promised to her dying mother out of obligation, and not something she wanted for herself.

He remained silent so long that she finally snuck a glance at him.

"Why not?" He shrugged as her eyes met his. "What harm can it be to tell her we will? There are no priests left to marry us, anyway. By the time someone comes along, we'll either all be dead, or this will be a distant memory and she will understand it wasn't necessary anymore."

His cold appraisal of the situation stung. Katya had no wish for him to embrace the idea, but the complete ambivalence of his attitude made the situation even harder to accept than the rejection she'd expected.

"Fine, then it's settled." She pulled on her coat and left the house without meeting his stark, haunted eyes again.

Outside, the cold air made her hot face burn. So, they would tell her mother they'd marry. That wasn't so bad, really. It would make Mama happy. And, like Kolya said, they didn't have to go through with it. There were no priests left to perform the ceremony.

She arrived at her aunt and uncle's abandoned farm without any memory of the actual walk there, and as soon as she entered the yard, she felt a difference in the air. Something was off. Something was missing.

Fear seized her gut, and she ran into the barn. No bleats of excitement greeted her. The barn, typically filled with the warm, musky scent of the goat, now felt cold and stale. Honey was gone.

Katya tried to control her panic, but it coursed through her like a swollen river, and a despondent sob choked her.

No more milk. No breeding Honey again to get another kid and milk next fall. No promise of fresh goat meat if they became desperate. All of it was for nothing. Someone had stolen her.

* * *

Christmas passed by with no celebration—not even the typical plate set out at the table for deceased family members. Mama would have set out a plate if she was well enough to get out of bed, but Katya couldn't bring herself to hope that Alina or Pavlo or anyone else would visit. She wasn't sure what she believed anymore, but if someone had the chance to escape this hell, dead or alive, she certainly didn't want to invite them back.

They didn't have a Christmas meal to speak of anyway. Instead of the traditional twelve dishes of food, Kolya flushed out field mice burrows with water to steal their tiny stashes of stored grains. Katya ground the kernels up with oak tree bark, combined the mixture with water, and made pancakes.

The cold days passed slowly, and a few weeks after Katya's promise to her mother to marry Kolya, a gentle knock sounded on the door. Mama barely moved at the noise; her life linked to this world by only a thread.

Katya glanced up in surprise. They didn't have many visitors these days, and the visitors they did have banged loudly before barging in and yelling to turn in their food for quotas.

Kolya cracked the door and queried into the dark, "Who's there?"

"Vasyl Petrovich Fediy," a quiet voice answered.

Kolya opened the door wide. "Come in," he ordered, scanning the night before he pulled the guest inside.

"Vasyl!" Katya threw her arms around her second cousin. His bones poked through his tattered clothes and dug into her as she hugged him. She flinched at the fragile feel of his body. "What are you doing here? I heard you were deported some time ago."

"Yes, I suppose I was one of the lucky ones." He tried to laugh but wheezed into a coughing fit instead. After he recovered, he continued. "They only deported me. Many members of the clergy were shot down where they stood."

Ordained as a priest right before the trouble began, Vasyl had planned on moving to a neighboring village church but was deported before he could leave. Katya and Alina's joint wedding was one the last acts he'd performed as their priest. They hadn't seen him since then.

"Yes, how could we forget?" Katya replied. "But not you! And here you are, alive! Tell us, how did you get here? Where did they send you after you left the village? Did you see my father? I have so many questions for you!"

He closed his eyes wearily. "Please, cousin. I know you have no food to spare, but I long for a good night's sleep, next to a warm *pich*. Can my story wait until tomorrow? Maybe my dear cousin will be awake to hear." He cast a questioning glance toward Mama, asleep in the bed. "I haven't the energy to even think of my trials tonight."

"Of course." Katya's face flushed with embarrassment. "Where are my manners? Sleep now, and we will talk tomorrow."

That night, as Katya lay in bed, apprehension kept her awake. A priest at their door so soon after her discussion of marriage with Mama? What had seemed like an empty promise to appease her mother suddenly felt quite real and made Katya sick.

Mama hadn't roused at Vasyl's arrival. She'd deteriorated so much in the last few days that it was possible she might not be cognizant at all while he was with them. And if Mama didn't bring up the marriage to Vasyl, Katya could ignore it.

Guilt choked Katya at the thought. How could she wish her mother ill for any reason? But then, how could she marry Kolya? The impossibility of the situation overwhelmed her until she finally fell into a fitful sleep.

The next morning, Kolya woke before daylight to go check a snare and returned with a small hare. Katya cooked it into a stew with some cattail roots she'd gathered from the creek. Close to rotting, they tasted a bit rancid but filled their stomachs. They ate silently, like they always did now, shoveling the little bits of food into their mouth as fast as they could.

At the end of the meal, cousin Vasyl paused, the cleanly picked hare leg still in his hand, and stared at the bone in awe. "This was the first real meal I have had in… well, I can't remember. Thank you." His voice broke with emotion.

"It's our pleasure to share with you," Katya said. "I only wish we had more."

When he finished eating, he began talking. "They came in the middle of the night for us. It was only a week or so after I officiated for your weddings, and your parents' funerals." He gave Kolya's arm a pat. "After the walk to the railroad station, we were loaded onto cattle cars."

"And I'm sure nobody had coats or blankets." Katya pulled a thick shawl around herself and Halya and shivered.

Vasyl closed his eyes and nodded. "That was only the beginning of our ordeals, dear cousin. We spent days in those cars, crushed together, which provided some warmth, but not enough for all. Soon, we began to lose the very young and the very old to the bitter cold."

"Did they feed you?" Kolya leaned forward in his seat, his arms resting on his legs.

"They gave each car one loaf of bread for every ten people inside, and a pail of a thin watery soup. That was all. As you can imagine, it was hard to divvy up the food into fair shares. People became crazed with hunger. A few stepped up and took charge, trying to make sure each person had their due amount."

"Where did they take you?" Katya asked.

"Siberia." His shoulders sagged, as if even saying the name of the place brought back misery.

Tato's face flitted through Katya's mind. And Sasha's. So, Siberia was likely their fate. Had they survived, like Vasyl? Their memories didn't cut through her like they once did. Even though each report of the dead and lost gave her a new shock, so much had happened in the two years since the state took them that the pain of those early losses felt like a lifetime ago.

"The train let us off in the middle of a snowy wasteland. No shelter. They pulled the dead bodies off the cars and tossed them to the side of the tracks. They didn't let us bury them, or even say a prayer for them."

Vasyl spoke so low Katya had to strain to hear him. She sat forward in her chair, like Kolya.

"Those still alive were forced to march for hours through the wind and snow. The weak fell down and died where they lay. Little children who had survived this far collapsed. Some mothers tried to carry them along so their tiny bodies wouldn't be abandoned, but they, too, soon fell with the extra weight as they floundered through the deep snow. So, they had to choose. Leave their babies to die alone in the snow or stay with them." He paused and wrung his hands. "The guards shot those who refused to give up their children and continue."

Vasyl brushed his cheek roughly, and they sat in silence as he swayed with the remembered emotion. "I've never seen such a lack of humanity in my life."

Katya listened, numb to his words. She wanted to cry along with him, to know she could still feel compassion and empathy, anything besides despair, but she couldn't. Grief had pulled her so low that she'd never fully climbed back up from its depths. Now, melancholy was her constant companion, and it left little room for other emotions. It enveloped her, inside and out, and sat bitter on her tongue, like the taste of the dandelion greens she'd grown so familiar with.

Vasyl continued, "We stopped at the edge of a forest with no buildings in sight, and they told us that we had to build our dwellings. Although we were exhausted, the men and women began gathering branches to construct some type of crude shelter until we could build something better. We worked through the night, trying to make sure all had some type of protection, but nobody had much.

"The next day, they told us the men would be logging the wood the state was harvesting and shipping out, and the women and children would now be responsible for building the permanent shelters. And so the days went on, bleeding into each other. The only constants were the cold and hunger. People continued to die every day, but that changed nothing."

"How did you get out?" Katya asked.

"One day, I was far out with two other men, felling a tree. A guard stationed near us came close to check on us and see what was taking so long. He screamed that we were lazy and useless. One of the men I was working with snapped. He'd lost his wife the previous day and his five children at various points throughout the train ride and march. I guess he figured he had nothing left to lose, so he jumped the guard and managed to kill him with his axe before any shots were fired. "Nobody saw the scuffle, but they would come looking for the guard eventually. We took his gun, his clothes, and his knife, and the three of us set off walking. We didn't know where we were going, but anyplace was better than there."

They sat silently, Vasyl's words hanging in the air around them. That Vasyl had survived and made it all the way back was a miracle.

Kolya ran a hand down his face. "Did the two men you left with survive as well?"

Vasyl shrugged. "The man who first attacked the guard walked with us for a while, but we woke one morning, and he was gone. Wandered off in the night, I suppose. The other man made it with me to Moscow. We worked there together for a time, and then parted ways."

Katya took Vasyl's skeletal hand in her own. "You have suffered so much! Why come back here now? They could do the same thing to you again."

"I came because you are my people. I came to warn you that they will not quit until we are all dead. *Kulaks*, peasants, everyone."

"And after you warn us, then what?" Kolya asked.

A small smile touched Vasyl's lips. "After I have done all I can here, I am going to try to sneak out of the country and go to America."

"America?" The idea of the continent on the other side of the world felt so surreal to Katya, she could hardly imagine it.

"It is a land of opportunity," Vasyl said. "With food and jobs for anyone willing to work for it."

America. Katya rolled the idea over in her mind as her father's voice echoed in her head. *Look to the future.*

Mama, lying on her bed asleep for most of the morning, spoke for the first time since Vasyl had come into their home and stopped Katya's musings in their tracks. "Dear Vasyl! I'm so pleased to see you. Have you come to marry Kolya and Katya? It is all I wish, and they promised me it would happen soon."

Katya froze. Kolya turned his back on everyone. His shoulders sagged as Katya shakily pulled herself to her feet, walked over to Mama, and rested a hand on her hot forehead.

Katya's voice cracked. "Hush now, Mama, you just need a bit of food. I set some of the meat aside for you; let me fetch it."

"No, Katya!" She sat up in her bed. A violent fit of coughing racked her body. When she finally stopped, she pointed her finger at Katya. "You promised me, daughter, that you would marry Kolya and give Halya a proper family before I go. It is God's will that this is so. Why else would Vasyl appear on our door right now, of all times?"

She turned to Vasyl. "Please, marry them. It is my dying wish." Another fit of coughing forced her back onto the pillow.

"Of course, cousin," Vasyl replied. His eyebrows curved into question marks as he looked at Katya and Kolya. "If that is what they want."

Katya sank onto the bed and buried her face in her hands. She didn't want to get married, but how could she refuse her mother's last wish? What kind of daughter would that make her?

But then, what kind of sister would it make her if she married her brother-in-law? Confusion made her head throb as Halya cried out from the bed. Katya scooped up the baby, and, slowly rocking, she walked the floor and avoided Kolya's probing stare. *Let him speak. Let him refuse Mama if he wishes, then at least it's not on my shoulders.*

Eventually, he did speak, although what he said surprised her.

"Let us get married tonight then, Katya. Neither of us have anything left in our hearts, anyway." The bitterness and disappointment he radiated hung thick in the air. "Really, what difference does it make? It's all for Halya, right? Everything we do is for Halya, so what is one more act?"

A lump lodged in Katya's throat. He made sense, but the betrayal of Alina, of Pavlo, still screamed inside of her. She closed her eyes and nodded.

A few minutes later, they were standing together in front of Vasyl. Katya couldn't tell what he said, or if Kolya spoke false words of promise and love to her. She couldn't even say if she returned those words. Katya supposed she must have, for Vasyl wrapped a *rushnyk* around their hands and pronounced them married. The whole time he spoke, she could only think of Alina and how it should have been Pavlo there with her, not Kolya. She cringed as she remembered watching Alina marry Kolya right here in this same room. How her face had shone with radiance and love.

Katya couldn't even bring herself to smile. The sick feeling in her stomach clouded her thoughts, and the event passed by in a blur. She supposed it was better that way.

25

CASSIE

Illinois, June 2004

Cassie stood in front of the mirror and, for the first time since Henry died, honestly appraised herself. Usually, she barely gave herself a glance. What was the point? She had no one to impress.

Her long brown hair hung in lanky waves around her shoulders. It desperately needed to be cut and shaped. Her pale face looked skinnier than it did in the pictures she had from before the accident, pushing her cheekbones into prominence and making her blue eyes appear huge. Clothes that used to fit hung loose on her willowy frame. She'd lost weight in the last year.

Her mom leaned into the bathroom. "I know a fabulous hairdresser. I can get you an appointment, maybe even before the date tonight. I'll stay with Bobby and Birdie."

"Mom! Jeez, how about some privacy?"

"Oh, come on, you didn't even have the door closed all the way. It's like you were crying out for help"—Anna waved her hands around her head as if she were a genie—"and poof, here I am!"

Cassie leaned closer to the mirror and pulled the skin on the side of her eyes up. "Fine, you can call, but only because my hair is getting too long, and it's annoying me. Nick's picking me up at seven, so I'll need to be back well before then."

"I'm on it!" Anna sprinted down the hall to the phone.

If her mom had her way, she'd make a manicure and pedicure appointment, too. Cassie sighed. Better to let her focus on this than the journal.

Cassie thought her mom would waver and ask for more information, but she'd stood firm on her commitment. Since then, they'd stuck to light topics, like Cassie's lack of effort into her appearance and her big date tonight.

"How about a facial?" Anna called out two minutes later, her hand over the mouthpiece of the phone. "Suzy has an opening in an hour. Maybe even a mani-pedi?"

* * *

After two hours in the salon, Cassie had to admit, she looked and felt like a new woman. She'd been polished, scrubbed, painted, trimmed, and blown out. To top it all off, when she got home, her mother magically produced three sundresses she'd happened to find on sale the day before that "didn't fit her".

"They're perfect for your build, Cassie, and it would be a big relief if I could pass them on to you and not worry about returning them to all the different stores. Humor me and try them on, will you?"

Cassie sighed and took the dresses back to her room. The first one was a bit small, but the next two fitted well. She left the last one, a light blue and green paisley print, on and rejoined her family in the living room.

"Oh!" Anna clapped her hands and squealed. "I hardly recognize you. You look amazing."

"Thanks, I guess," Cassie said, not sure if she should feel offended at the insinuation that she looked terrible before. "I was that bad, huh?"

"Not bad," Anna hastily corrected herself. "Just not living up to your full potential."

Cassie stuck her tongue out at her mom and Birdie giggled as the doorbell rang.

"I'll get it!" Anna jumped up. "Go in the kitchen, Cassie, and then make an entrance after I let him in."

"I'm not doing that, Mom." Cassie grabbed her purse and walked toward the door. "This isn't prom."

Anna scowled at Cassie, and then switched her face into a sunny smile as she opened the door. "Nick! It's so nice to see you! Come in, come in!"

Cassie smothered a laugh at her mother's shifting demeanor, and then locked eyes with Nick. His blue eyes sparkled as he beamed at her.

"Cassie, you look amazing."

"Thanks." Her face warmed at his compliment. "You clean up pretty well, too."

"Hi, Nick." Birdie pulled on Nick's hand.

"Hey, Birdie." He squatted down and gave her braid a tug. "How was your day?"

"I helped plant flowers and read my books and went for a walk." She rattled off her activities as she counted them on her fingers. "It was a long day."

Nick laughed. "Sounds like it. Well, next time, I promise to bring you along. But since you couldn't come tonight, I brought something special for you."

He reached into the bag he held and pulled out an old, tattered Dr.

Seuss book. "This one was my favorite when I was a kid. I didn't see it on your shelf, so I thought you might want to read mine."

Her face lit up. "I don't have this one! Oh, I love it. I'll take the best care of it!"

"I know you will. And I promise to read it to you the next time I come over, okay?"

She clutched the book tight. "Okay, Nick. Grammy, look! Will you read it to me before bed?"

Hearing her sweet voice still made Cassie giddy. She touched Nick's hand and met his gaze. "Thank you."

"My pleasure. Shall we?" He held out his arm.

* * *

"This place is lovely." Cassie glanced around the intimate restaurant. Small tables—spaced comfortably apart and covered with white table-cloths—filled the dim space. Fresh roses, showcased in the center of each table, gave the room a sweet fragrance. The waiter guided them to a table next to a large picture window that overlooked the sun setting in the park.

Nick pulled out her chair for her, then sat across the table. The waiter passed out the heavy menus and took their drink orders. Everything was going just as it should for a date. A date. She was on a date.

Cassie started to hyperventilate. She pinched the flesh between her thumb and finger hard under the table and looked down. *Pull it together. This is no different than sitting next to him while he translates the journal.*

"So, Cassie, in all this time, I've never found out what you actually do for a living." Nick leaned forward, curiosity written on his face.

Cassie locked in on his gaze, and warmth coursed through her. She could do this.

"I guess we don't talk much about ourselves when we're working on the journal, do we?" *Because my brain seems to shut down whenever you're around.* "I'm a writer. Well, I was a writer. Articles for magazines, mostly. I've always wanted to do a novel, but then, with everything last year, I kind of gave up."

"A writer. I can see that. Maybe inspiration will strike, and you'll be able to get back into it."

"That would be nice, but I'm not counting on it." Cassie sipped the wine the waiter had delivered.

They paused to place their orders—fettuccine Alfredo for Cassie, and lasagna for Nick.

"How about you? How did you get into firefighting?" Cassie asked, after handing their menus to the waiter.

"I've always wanted to be where the action was, and I've always wanted to help people when they needed it the most. This career put those two things together, and I couldn't dream of doing anything else now."

Nick leaned forward in his chair. "Look, I know we both have our histories. I don't expect you to talk to me about yours until you feel ready, but I want you to know that whenever you want to, I'd love to hear about your life. About your husband. About what happened."

"It doesn't scare you? I've got a lot of baggage. 'Widow with child' isn't exactly high on the desirable traits list when you're dating." She laughed, but it came out sounding hollow.

"No, it doesn't scare me off at all." He hesitated. "And I want to be upfront with you about my past."

"Your past?" Cassie's eyebrows rose, along with her curiosity. Still, she demurred. "Nick, you don't owe me any explanations."

"I want to be completely open with you. My parents died in a house fire when I was pretty young. Not much older than Birdie. That's probably the biggest reason I got into firefighting. The other stuff I mentioned earlier is all true too but losing them made me want to help other people avoid that same loss. After they died, my grandma raised me. She was old world, right off the boat—made me go to Ukrainian school every Saturday morning, as you've heard, and was super strict, but I loved her like crazy."

He paused and cleared his throat. "She died last year, and I was alone. I had no family, no one to answer to, no one to hold me accountable, and I kind of went off the deep end. I started going out all the time. Partying. Dating tons of women. Women I wouldn't have dared bring home to meet my Baba. Well, you met a few of them the other night. I'm sure you could see why."

Cassie tried not to cringe at the memory of the women flirting with Nick.

"The thing was, I didn't care about anything. I went to work and then did whatever the hell I wanted. I guess I should be thankful that I kept my head level enough to not lose my job."

Without thinking, Cassie reached for his warm, rough hand. He gripped hers back.

"Nick, you don't have to do this."

"I do, though. Because as crazy as it sounds, that's all changed. Meeting you and Birdie woke something up in me that's been asleep for so long I thought it was dead. You've made me feel again. You've made me want to be the best version of myself." He smiled sheepishly. "This is all probably pretty heavy for a first official date, but I feel so comfortable around you, and I wanted you to know you aren't the only one with baggage here."

Be happy. Live your life. Henry's words from her dream echoed in her head and her skin flushed as she stared into his blue eyes.

The waiter interrupted their moment to set down the dinner plates. As they dove into their food, Cassie found herself opening up.

"I didn't really date in high school. I met Henry in college. Love at first sight, it was like we were the only ones in the room, all the clichés you could imagine. We got married right out of school, traveled a bit, and then settled down. Birdie came along, and I thought I had everything I could ever want. Then, one day, it all fell apart."

She took another sip of wine. The alcohol, combined with the cozy interior of the Italian restaurant, made her brave. "He took her out for ice cream after dinner. She'd learned to ride her bike that day, and he wanted to celebrate. I had an article deadline to meet for work, so I stayed back."

Cassie closed her eyes, trying to hold back the barrage of feelings that assaulted her whenever she recalled that day.

"A semi-truck blew a red light. Henry died on impact, and Birdie barely survived. The doctors put her in a medically induced coma. I didn't leave her side for weeks."

"Is that why she didn't talk for so long?" Nick asked.

Cassie shook her head. "We don't know why she didn't talk. They ran all kinds of tests, but there was no permanent damage that they could see. They told me it was psychological, which made sense. She went out for ice cream one night, woke up a week later and found out her dad was dead. It would be a lot for anyone, let alone a four-year-old girl. We didn't have Henry's funeral until I knew she would be okay. I couldn't even grieve for him until she woke up. I had to take one tragedy at a time and thinking about him being gone while I didn't know if I'd get my baby back was too much. I still feel guilty about that." Her voice broke. "About putting my feelings for him on hold, like it didn't matter that he died."

"Of course it mattered," Nick said. "But you were in survival mode. You were doing whatever you needed for Birdie. No one would fault you for that."

"Thanks." She gave a grim smile. "You know, no one would fault you for going crazy for a bit after losing your whole family. I lost Henry, but I still have my mom, my daughter, my Bobby, and honestly, I don't know what I'd do without them."

With her history laid out bare for Nick to see, Cassie relaxed. The serious talk took a backseat to carefree stories about Birdie's younger years and Nick's crazy fire calls. They talked as if they'd known each other forever. Nick made her laugh over and over, and the doubts that had plagued Cassie through the day faded away.

* * *

When they pulled up to Bobby's house, Nick jogged around the front of the car to open her door, then escorted her to the front porch.

The porch light shadowed his features, but his wide smile still shone. "I know we got into some pretty heavy conversations, but I had a great time with you tonight, Cassie."

Butterflies fluttered in her stomach. "I did, too."

He leaned in and kissed her on the cheek. "I'd like to see you again, if that's okay. Outside the journal translations, I mean."

She nodded but couldn't speak. Her face tingled where his lips had lingered, and she raised her fingers to the spot as if she could capture that feeling and save it.

"Good night, Cassie." Nick backed away, his eyes still holding hers.

She found her voice, but it came out in a throaty whisper. "Good night, Nick."

Inside, both her mother and Bobby waited on the couch.

"So, how was it?" Anna pounced on her as soon as the door shut.

"Nice," Cassie breathed, her hand still on her cheek. Confusion clouded her thoughts. She'd written off this part of her as dead along with Henry, yet here she was, pulse racing while the sweet kiss Nick had placed on her cheek played on repeat in her mind.

"Just nice, eh?" Bobby chuckled. "Looks like more than just nice."

"We had a good time. I talked way more than I should have, probably. But he did, too. I haven't talked with someone like that in forever."

"I knew it." Anna clapped her hands. "He's special."

"Mom, it was one date. Let's not get carried away."

"You can't see the look on your face. I haven't seen you this happy since, well, in over a year. I was beginning to wonder if I'd ever see you come back to life like this. Let me enjoy it!"

Later that night, when the house was asleep, Cassie wrote in her Henry memory journal. She recounted their first date, ten years ago, and how he'd picked her up in his rickety old car and taken her to the fanciest restaurant in their small college town. The whole meal had to have cost him a full paycheck from the sports store he clerked at on the weekends, but, despite her best efforts to go Dutch, he insisted that it was his treat. When she was done documenting the story, she ran her hand down the finished page and closed the book. One small teardrop trailed down her cheek and splashed onto the cover.

Then she pulled out a new notebook and began to write about her date with Nick.

26

KATYA

Ukraine, January 1933

For weeks, Katya had fallen asleep to the sound of her mother's labored breathing. Wheezing and rattling, it punctuated the minutes like a clock marking the time as they fell further into the nightmarish reality of their lives.

Three days after her marriage to Kolya, Katya blinked awake, her thoughts fuzzy and tangled, as unexplained trepidation made her shiver. She pushed herself out of bed and glanced around the room, searching for the source of her unease. Early morning light filtered in the window, landing on her mother's pale, still face.

She crept over, the empty silence of the room echoing all around her and touched her mother's cold cheek. She'd expected to feel sad. To feel lost. Alone. And she did feel all those things, but in a detached way, as if her heart had grown so hardened that even sharp, intense feelings could no longer penetrate it.

What she didn't anticipate was the sudden surge of relief.

Relief that this shell of her mother no longer suffered. Relief that she no longer had to agonize over the futility of trying to keep her alive. Relief that they didn't have to go to sleep each night wondering if her mother would wake up the next day, because finally, she hadn't.

Now, Mama was just one more person she had failed to save.

Halya began to cry, and Katya took a shuddering breath. "I'm coming, Halya." She pushed herself up on shaky legs and picked up the red-faced baby.

Katya glanced around the empty house. Kolya must have already left for work at the collective farm. She had no one to help her, no one to tell her what she should do.

What would Mama do?

Katya gave a firm nod of resolve. Her mother would take care of the necessary things, even if they couldn't follow the typical funerary customs. She gave Halya the last chunk of stale bread, then propped the baby up on the bed. Halya gummed the food and watched while Katya washed her mother's emaciated body.

Katya pulled Mama's finest embroidered shirt over her head. A masterpiece of brightly colored threads that folded together in a dazzling design of vines and flowers all around the edges and up the sleeves, Mama had spent hours working on it when Katya was young. She still remembered the pride on her mother's face when she finally finished it. Before the state had locked down their village and banned peasants from traveling to the cities, Kolya had brought most of his mother's and Mama's handiwork to the market in Bila Tservka to be sold off for food money, but eventually, there was no one to sell to— everyone needed food more than pretty clothes.

She smoothed out the shirt, straightened the skirt, and stepped back. She'd need to fix her mother's hair. Halya whimpered, and Katya stopped working and scooped the baby up into her arms. Comforting Halya soothed her own fears and uncertainty. In Halya, once again, Katya found purpose, and she clung to that.

Halya touched her grandmother's face, then touched Katya's cheek.

Katya took the tiny hand and kissed it, then together, they brushed Mama's long hair as she had done for Katya so many times. Only then did Katya let herself cry, her tears falling on Mama's gray and brown strands.

Katya stood abruptly as she finished. This was all she could do now. She'd need Kolya for the rest, but for now, she had to get out of this silent house.

Snow fell lightly through the sharp, cold air as she walked out into the winter day and away from the house that held her dead mother. Halya cuddled under Katya's coat, her little body tucked into a cloth wrapped around Katya's shoulders. Before long, she fell asleep.

Katya walked south until Lena and Ruslan's house came into view. Though she didn't want to talk about Mama's death, Katya thought that Lena would want to know, and she would enjoy seeing Halya, too.

Smoke trickled out of their chimney as Katya knocked on the door. A good sign. Anyone strong enough to make a fire was doing well for the moment.

Ruslan answered the door right away.

"Katya! Come in! Lena, it's Katya," he called over his shoulder as he ushered her inside. As soon as Katya's eyes adjusted to the dim room, she could see that something was off about him. His eyes, she decided, were wider than normal and darted around wildly.

"Oh, Katya, it's good to see you." Lena embraced her in a warm hug. Her sallow face framed dull eyes, but they still brimmed with kindness. Katya relaxed as her cousin leaned in toward her. "Is this Alina's little one?" She peeked inside Katya's coat, and Halya opened her large, sleepy blue eyes as the cool air hit her face.

"Yes." Katya glanced again at Ruslan, who was standing off to the side, watching the exchange. "This is Halya. She's a year old now."

"Oh, how precious! She looks like her mother," she said, stroking Halya's head. "I always wanted a baby, you know. It wasn't meant to be, I suppose."

"You would have been an excellent mother, but how wonderful that you were able to help so many other women bring their children into this world as a midwife. "Katya took a deep breath, anxious to get the hard part of the visit over with. "There is a reason for my visit, though. I have some unfortunate news."

Lena raised her hand to her mouth. "Don't tell me this news is of your mother! She's such a strong woman. I thought she would outlast us all. Sit down, please."

Katya took a seat at the small table. "The pneumonia took a strong hold of her lungs. With the hunger, she was too weak to fight. She passed away in the night." Katya stumbled over the last sentence. Saying it out loud made it so much more real.

"Oh, you poor dear." Lena fussed over her as the maternal instinct she never got to utilize came pouring out. "This must have been a terrible morning for you. Is there anything we can do? Do you need help with her body?"

"Or we could watch the little one for you while you tend to your mother," Ruslan offered, his eyes glittering as they met hers.

Lena glared daggers at Ruslan. An uneasy feeling Katya couldn't identify swirled in her gut, and suddenly, she didn't want to be here anymore.

"No, I've done all there is to be done until Kolya gets home." Katya stood and tucked Halya back into her coat. "Thank you, though. I should be on my way."

"Yes, well, thank you so much for coming here to tell us about your dear mother. We're so sorry." Lena's eagerness as she pushed Katya toward the door was surprising.

As Katya left, she stumbled over something sticking out from beneath the woodpile near the door. Glancing down, she saw a small shoe.

Katya went cold.

A child's shoe.

Lena kicked it away.

"Lena..." Katya's voice was shaky. Her eyes slowly lifted, meeting Lena's guilt–stricken face for one brief, telling moment before Ruslan slammed the door in her face.

27

CASSIE

Illinois, June 2004

Cassie inhaled the sweet summer air and gave a contented sigh. The backyard hummed with bumblebees stopping to sip at each of Bobby's beautiful flowers. Nearly in full bloom, the yard sparkled with so many colors it almost hurt her eyes to take them all in. She couldn't imagine a more peaceful setting.

"Your flowers are always so amazing, Bobby." Cassie picked up the gardening tools and settled down next to the one bare spot in the bed along the back fence. She ran the trowel down the narrow flower bed, creating a neat row. "But isn't it a little late to be planting sunflower seeds?"

"It's never too late to try to add beauty to the world." Even though Bobby sat in a chair and wasn't actually working in the dirt, there was no question who was in charge. "Go a little longer with that row, Cassie."

Birdie hopped back and forth on one foot, her excitement infecting them all. "Sunflowers and hollyhocks, sunflowers and hollyhocks. I love planting flowers, Bobby!"

Bobby chuckled. "I know, little bird. Me too. Now, open your hands."

Birdie held still as Bobby poured a packet of seeds into Birdie's dimpled hands.

"Put them in the rows Mommy made?" Birdie asked.

When Bobby nodded, Birdie dropped to the ground and placed each seed carefully in its spot, evenly spaced from the last one.

"You're very good at that." Bobby beamed at her great-granddaughter.

Birdie nodded in agreement with the unpretentious confidence of the young, making both Cassie and Bobby laugh.

"Now cover them with dirt and pat down gently," Bobby said.

Birdie worked diligently until the last seed was patted in place, then she jumped up. "I'm going to get a drink of water. Don't plant any without me!"

"Yes, ma'am." Cassie grinned. "Come right back out when you're done."

Bobby fiddled with the empty seed packet in her lap. "You're right, Cassie. These seeds may not bloom this year, but it's worth a try. It's always worth a try, don't you think? With flowers and with life."

So many questions danced on Cassie's tongue, but she bit them back and finally replied. "I guess that's what you did, isn't it? Tried to move on?"

Bobby nodded slowly. "And it's what you will do too, eventually."

Damn, she was good at turning the tables. But Cassie wasn't willing to dive into her own issues now, so she changed the subject.

"What made you decide to plant sunflowers? I thought they made you sad?"

"I decided it was time I stopped disliking them for the bad memories and choose to enjoy them for the good memories. It's something

I'm still working on." Bobby stared off into the yard, as if actively trying to do what she'd just mentioned.

Birdie tumbled out of the back door and ran toward them, her face beaming. "Guess what? Alina told me she's happy you're planting the sunflowers!"

"What?" Bobby's gnarled knuckles whitened on the arm of her chair.

The hairs on the back of Cassie's neck stood up, but she ignored the uncomfortable sensation. "Birdie! You shouldn't make up things like that. It upsets Bobby!"

Birdie's face crumpled. "I didn't make up anything."

"I'm sorry, I didn't mean it like that," Cassie said. But what did she mean? She didn't really think her daughter was talking to her dead great–aunt in there, did she?

"Because it's almost my time. That's why she's here." Bobby jerked her gaze toward Cassie. "I need to know you'll finish reading my things before I go. I need to keep my promise."

Cassie brushed the dirt off her trembling hands and stood. "Nick should be here any minute. We're planning on getting through a lot today."

"Good." Bobby slowly pulled herself up from her chair. "I'll go put Birdie down for her nap. I told her I'd read her a story. Then I'll go rest, too."

Birdie, tired after her full day of planting flowers, ran to her room. Cassie waited until Bobby made her way inside and down the hall before following behind. No matter how fine Bobby insisted she was, Cassie worried. Staying out of sight, she peered in the door and listened as Bobby stumbled through *The Three Little Pigs* for Birdie's sake. Love welled up inside Cassie. The woman could speak and read Ukrainian, Polish, and Russian fluently, but she still struggled on occasion with the written English word.

When the story was done, she pulled the covers up to Birdie's chin and kissed her on her forehead. Cassie smiled at the sight. No doubt, her mother had been right in encouraging her to move here with Bobby. Birdie would never forget the time she got to spend with her great-grandmother.

"Can you tell me another story about you and Alina?" Birdie asked.

Cassie's mouth dropped open, and she leaned closer to the doorway.

"What about the one with the mud pies?" Birdie asked. "That's my favorite."

"Let's play a game," Bobby said. "This time, you tell it to me. What do you think?"

"Okay." Birdie pursed her lips and tapped her finger on her chin. "Let's see. Once upon a time, you and Alina made mud pies. Alina decorated hers with flowers and grass. It looked so pretty that you wanted to eat it!" Birdie grimaced. "Yuck! Alina said you couldn't eat mud, so you tried to feed them to the pigs, but they didn't eat them either. They rolled in them!"

She dissolved into a fit of giggles. "Was that good? Did I tell it right?"

Bobby nodded slowly. "It was perfect. Now, you get some rest. Maybe Alina will visit you again soon." Bobby tucked the covers in close one more time and stood. "If she does, you tell me, okay?"

Birdie gave a sleepy nod as she yawned.

Prickles of unease tickled Cassie's scalp as she backpedaled away from the room.

* * *

Cassie tried to lose herself in transcribing—shoving down her reactions, letting the words flow in her ears and out her fingers. With every loss Katya accumulated—Pavlo, Viktor, Alina, her mother—Cassie's hold on her emotions weakened, but as Nick described Katya's wedding to Kolya, Cassie couldn't keep up the charade any longer. A sob tore out of her, and she pushed herself back from the table.

Nick looked up at her, his mouth hanging open. "Are you okay?"

"I can't do this, Nick." Cassie's voice cracked. "Don't you see? She's going to lose him. She's lost everyone, and he's going to die, too. Kolya wasn't my grandfather!"

Hearing Bobby's story hadn't just brought up old feelings. It had ripped her out of this fantasy world she'd been living in. Henry's death was the hardest thing she'd ever endured, and Cassie wasn't as strong as Bobby. She couldn't go through it again, couldn't risk opening herself up, because losing another love would kill her. She was a fool to think taking off her wedding ring would magically make her ready for a new relationship.

She was broken. Damaged goods.

Cassie wrenched away from Nick's touch and stood on shaky legs. "I think you should go."

Confusion clouded Nick's face. "Did I do something wrong?"

You did everything right. "No. It's me. I can't do this with you."

"Do what? The journal?" He stood fast, his forehead knotted in confusion, and his chair skidded back across the floor.

"All of it." Cassie bit the inside of her cheek. "The dating. The journal. I'm not ready for this, and I'm not sure I'll ever be. You deserve better than some broken widow. I'm sorry, Nick. I'll see if my mom will type the rest of this up with you, but I can't hear it, and I can't be with you." She bolted out of the kitchen before he could change her mind.

"Cassie, wait!"

Nick's voice trailed after her as she ducked into her room and closed the door on him.

* * *

A loud thump from one of the bedrooms startled Cassie out of her fitful sleep. She jumped out of bed and looked at the alarm clock. Six in the morning. Way too early for someone who tossed and turned until three. She ran into Birdie's room. The little girl was sleeping peacefully, one arm thrown over her head and the other wrapped around a stuffed dog. Cassie pulled the door shut and knocked on Bobby's door. When she got no answer, she pushed open the door and found Bobby on the floor, her eyes staring up at the ceiling. Short, shallow breaths wheezed through her lips.

"Bobby!" Cassie's mind went blank. She fell to her knees and touched Bobby's cool, clammy face. Bobby grabbed at Cassie's hand, her eyes wide with fear.

"I'm here now, okay? I'll get you help! Stay with me!" Cassie snatched the phone off the nightstand and dialed 911 with fumbling fingers. After giving them the information, she called her mom.

"I'm on my way!" Anna snapped into the phone.

"You should go straight to the hospital. You'll get there quicker, and you can meet the ambulance." Cassie's hand rhythmically squeezed Bobby's as she talked. "They should be here in two minutes."

"I'll come get you first. I don't want you driving when you're upset like this."

"I'll be okay," Cassie lied. Her body shook uncontrollably, and she still hadn't decided how she would shield Birdie from seeing Bobby like this. She hoped the little girl didn't wake up now and walk in on them.

The doorbell sounded, and she jumped up.

"They're here. I've got to go!" Cassie dropped the phone and hurried to the front door.

Two paramedics barreled into the house. As Cassie directed them toward Bobby's room, Nick, hair mussed like he'd just rolled out of bed, ran in the door.

She threw her arms around him in a fierce hug, her need for comfort in this moment outweighing any of the things she'd told him the night before.

"I had my radio on my nightstand. When I heard the address, I came right over." He pressed his cheek against her hair as he held her close.

"Thank you." Her voice broke.

"Cassie"—he pulled back and gripped her shoulders—"where's Birdie?"

"She's still sleeping," Cassie replied, focusing on Nick's face. His calm eyes stared back into hers and the racing thoughts in her mind slowed. She wrung her hands. "I don't want her to see Bobby like this."

"Do you want to go to her room and stay with her? I'll help Bobby get in the ambulance, then drive you both to the hospital."

Cassie let his soothing voice roll over her, and she nodded mutely.

Nick glanced past her. "All right. They're coming out with her now. Go on into Birdie's room so she doesn't walk out."

Cassie, afraid to break contact with Nick's steady presence, faltered for a moment as he nudged her down the hall and went in to talk to the other medics. She pulled herself together and tiptoed into Birdie's room. Somehow, the girl slept on through all the commotion.

"Birdie." Cassie shook the small shoulder. "Birdie, it's time to wake up. Nick's here, and he's going to take us to the hospital. Maybe he'll take you to the park while I go talk with Bobby and her doctor."

At the sound of Nick's name, the little girl's eyes flew open. "Nick's here?" She jumped out of bed and ran to her toy table. "I'm going to bring a bag with crayons and books, okay, Mommy?"

"That's a great idea." Cassie moved to stand near the door. As the medics carried Bobby out the front door on a stretcher, she clamped a hand over her mouth to hold back her cry.

Nick closed the front door, then turned and locked eyes with her. "Just a few more minutes to get them going down the street," he said in a low voice.

Cassie nodded, pushed the door shut, and turned to her little girl. "Tell me what you're packing, Birdie." They were the same words she'd uttered to Bobby to soothe her. She mustered up a tremulous smile for her daughter as the ambulance sirens screeched outside the house.

28

KATYA

Ukraine, February 1933

Katya curled around Halya's body, trying her best to keep the baby warm under their stack of blankets. The cold, an ever-present force, couldn't be kept at bay by their small fire, and Katya missed the warmth of her sister or Pavlo curled behind her.

Katya talked to Halya as she held up the picture of her and Alina from Olha and Boryslav's wedding. "See, Halya, this is your mother. She was the prettiest girl in the village, and you look just like her."

The picture shook in Katya's hand. *Sisters forever.* When she closed her eyes, she could hear her sister's clear voice uttering those words.

"Sisters forever," Katya whispered.

Halya's big eyes stared at the photograph. She was almost fourteen months now, though she didn't look it. Katya sang songs, told stories, counted, and did everything she could to brighten Halya's world, but still she worried it wasn't enough. Halya couldn't crawl or walk, and she only babbled a few nonsensical words, but sometimes, when Halya smiled, tiny glimpses of Alina appeared in her face. Katya lived for the joy of those moments, and she knew Kolya felt the same. His love for Halya, evident in the way he rocked her to sleep and tickled her to make her laugh, was what kept him going. The state had taken so much from them, but their love survived, even in the darkest times.

Knocks on the door broke the silence, and Lena burst into the house, her red face wild with rivers of tears and a tiny baby nestled in her arms.

"Lena! What's this about?" Katya tucked the blankets around Halya, then wrapped a shawl around her shoulders. She pulled a chair up next to the *pich* and ushered her cousin toward it. Kolya put one of their precious pieces of dismantled barn wood in it and built the fire up.

"I had to come here. I couldn't go home." Instead of sitting, she paced erratically around the room.

"Where did you get this child?" Kolya asked. His hair, rumpled from sleep, reminded Katya so much of Pavlo that a pang of longing shot through her. She had to avert her gaze before she could gather her thoughts.

"I found him. I walked to town to try to trade for some food, and I heard him crying in a house I passed. The whole family had passed away. Mother. Father. Two other children. His dead mother held him in her arms on her bed. If I hadn't found him when I did, he would have died like them."

Katya peered down at the baby in Lena's arms. From its tiny stature, she guessed it couldn't have been more than a few months old. Blankets wound around it until only large eyes peeped out of the gaunt face. Ukraine did not produce rosy, chubby-cheeked babies anymore.

"So why did you come here?" Kolya asked.

Lena dropped her gaze. "I can't take care of a baby. And you already have Halya here. I thought it might be easier..." She looked at Katya and trailed off.

Katya closed her eyes and saw the tiny black shoe poking out of the woodpile. She shuddered and pulled her shawl closer. "We'll take the baby."

"What? Katya, I don't know how we'll care for another child." Kolya glanced over at Halya. "We are hardly providing well enough for this one."

"She is loved!" Lena cried. "That's the most important thing. Here, hold him."

Lena thrust the baby into Katya's arms, and an ache stabbed through her womb. This slight boy reminded her so much of Viktor. She touched his soft cheek, and he stared up at her with big blue eyes.

Lena wiped her nose and backed out the door before Kolya could protest or ask any further questions. "Thank you, Katya. You are your mother's daughter, no doubt. I have to go now, before Ruslan realizes I've been gone too long."

The baby gave a soft mewl and Katya gasped as raw emotion swelled in her throat. Her rational mind warned her that this was a terrible idea. She'd already lost one baby, and now she had Halya to care for as her own. But a long dead part of her came back to life as she looked down at the sweet child. How could she not try to save a baby so much like her own?

* * *

For three weeks, she fed both children. Her own milk long gone, she'd prepare a watery gruel consisting of ground cattail roots, acorns, and tree bark. Some days, Kolya would come home with something caught in the snares, and Katya would make a meat broth for the babies. But game became harder and harder to find. The days stretched on until a week passed since they'd had any broth or meat.

Kolya walked in the door empty handed. "Nothing again today."

"He won't eat anything." Katya set the baby she'd christened Denys, after her lost little cousin, down on the bed and picked up Halya. She eagerly lapped up the gruel Denys had turned his head away from. "I'm afraid his body cannot process it any longer."

Kolya didn't respond. Despite her best efforts, the baby boy was fading before their eyes. Katya winced as she watched his attempt to smile, his thin lips momentarily curving up to look more like a grimace than a grin. His large head wobbled with the valiant effort, his neck no longer strong enough to support it. Exhausted from the hard work, he lay back down on the pillow, too weak to even cry.

"Maybe you can ask one more time at the collective for some goat's milk?" Katya suggested.

"I tried this morning." He sat down at the table. "They laughed at me."

"We just need to make it through today. Tomorrow will be better," Katya murmured into Halya's hair.

"What did you say? Tomorrow will be better? Bah!" Kolya snorted in disgust. "What could possibly happen tomorrow? We're tossed a scrap of bread for a day's labor? Or maybe they don't come and steal the food from our table?" He dragged the back of his hand across his eyes as his voice dropped to a fractured whisper. "We get our spouses back?"

Katya recoiled as the truth of his words pierced her. "We must try to keep our hope alive."

"My hope is dead," Kolya said, his words flat and lifeless. "Tomorrow will not be better. It will probably be worse, if we even make it until then."

* * *

Katya set down Halya, now asleep, and picked up Denys. She couldn't bear leaving him to lie by himself in this condition. His rapid, gurgling breaths reverberated in her ears, and he looked up at her imploringly, as if begging her to save him somehow. Her eyes smarted, and she blinked.

"Katya, you have to realize that baby was already starving and ill when Lena brought him here." Kolya peered down at the baby over her shoulder. "He never had a chance."

"Maybe so." She rocked gently back and forth, trying to get him to sleep. If he slept, at least he'd not feel the pain he must be enduring, and then she could pretend everything was fine.

Kolya stared at her, concern evident on his face. "This is not healthy for you."

"It's not me I'm worried about!" Katya snapped back. "It's Viktor!"

"You mean Denys," Kolya said softly.

Pity rolled off him in waves, and Katya's cheeks flushed. "Of course, Denys. I'm tired. That's all."

"Yes, because you are running yourself ragged caring for this extra child who never had a chance at surviving. You should be putting all your efforts into Halya, not this boy. He was already half-dead when he came here. What makes you think you can resurrect him when we can barely keep ourselves alive?"

She glared at Kolya and continued rocking the baby. "Then who are we, Kolya? Who are we if we turn away a child, let him starve without even trying to save him? I won't do it. I won't be that person."

Kolya shook his head, but instead of responding, he turned his back on her. "I'm going out to look for game again. I can't stand sitting here, watching you pour yourself into him when he will only die!" He grabbed his coat and slammed the door behind him, waking Halya.

Anger flashed through her. Kolya might not be strong enough to deal with the tiny, suffering child, but she was, and she would do anything possible to give him comfort.

Katya sat next to Halya and caressed the girl's cheek with her free hand. She bit back her bitter words and forced out a wavering smile. "Tato will be right back. He went to look for some food. How about I tell you another story?" Katya cuddled herself around the two frail babies. If she couldn't give either of them food, she would give to them all the love that she had. That much she could do, even though, deep down, she knew it wouldn't be enough.

Halya made a small sound that Katya took as a yes. "Good, let's see." She arranged the blankets around them and made sure each child had enough to stay warm. "I know the perfect story. You like this one, Halya. Maybe Denys will, too." Katya felt the slightest of movements as Halya nodded. "It's about two little girls who loved to make mud pies."

* * *

Katya sang a song her mother used to sing to her and Alina when they were children. She couldn't think of any other songs, so she kept singing that same one over and over. She didn't remember when she started or how long she sang. She simply sang until her voice dwindled away to not much more than a whisper. The babies seemed to like it very much, so she couldn't stop.

Kolya came into the cabin, stomping snow from his feet. The sound registered somewhere in her brain, but she didn't acknowledge him. She continued to sing for Halya. For Denys. For Viktor.

"Katya, I have meat! Maybe the babies could get some broth down."

Katya continued to sing.

"Katya?"

She heard him walk over and felt him looking at them, yet she still sang. He reached down and peeled back the blankets.

"Oh, Katya, I'm sorry." His voice cracked.

She continued to sing.

"Katya." He grabbed her arm and shook her. "Katya!"

She could hear him, there next to her, calling her name over and over, but he seemed so far away and unimportant. What was important is that she sing her song for the babies. They needed her now and she was not going to let them down.

The bed sank down as Kolya sat next to her. He tried to pull them away, but Katya tightened her grip on each child, one cold and one warm, and sang even louder, her voice now a low, croaking sound she no longer recognized.

They struggled like that, him trying to take away what Katya was trying to fix, until finally, he walked away. She didn't know how long she lay there singing to Denys's dead body. Hours. Days. All meaning-less markers of her grief. When her voice finally gave out, she let the truth wash over her. He was gone, and she had let another child die.

"You've stopped," Kolya said, relief evident in his husky voice. "Katya?"

"He's gone, Kolya." Her words came out in a hoarse slur. Denys's body, stiff and cold, felt like a crushing weight on her chest. She ran a hand along his pale face.

"I know. Have some water." He held a cup to her lips as she sipped. The hot water soothed her ragged throat. He set the cup down and took the baby from her embrace. "I'm sorry I left you like that."

As he set Denys down on the other bed, Katya dragged her legs to the ground. "Where is Halya? Is she alive? Tell me!"

She tried to stand, but her legs wouldn't support her. Kolya caught her as she fell and pulled her back onto the bed alongside him.

"Halya is still alive. We've lost only the boy. Here, drink this." He reached over and picked up another cup, then wrapped his big hands around hers and guided it to her lips. Katya's eyes widened in surprise as the richness of a meat broth rolled over her tongue and filled her hollow belly.

"Where did you get meat?"

Kolya didn't hesitate. "It was a rat from the grain bins."

Saliva pooled in her mouth. "Maybe you can find more?"

"Even the mice and rats are scarce these days, but I'll try. I'm sorry I was too late to help the boy. You were right. That's not who we are." He bowed his head in shame.

She guzzled down the broth while Kolya held her. The warm, solid bulk of his body cradled hers as she fought her way back to the world. When she'd drunk it all, he laid her back down in her bed, tucked the covers up around her, and sat holding her hand. His rough fingers kneaded gentle circles on her misshapen left hand as she fell asleep, but not before she heard him say, "Please, Katya. Just make it through today. Tomorrow will be better."

* * *

They buried Denys near their house under a willow tree, too close for foragers to venture. The dogs that had escaped being eaten by villagers or shot by the state ran wild now and wouldn't come near a human for fear of becoming dinner. Most lived on the bodies of the dead that were scattered around the countryside.

Kolya, who had professed disdain and doubt over taking the baby in, worked like a crazy man for hours to dig through the frozen ground to make a hole deep enough to ensure he would remain undisturbed. It took every last bit of strength out of him, and eventually Katya had to make him stop and rest before he collapsed.

"You aren't strong enough to work like that," she said. "Why are you pushing yourself so hard for a child you didn't even want?"

He scowled up at her. "Just because I didn't think we could save him doesn't mean I'm a heartless bastard."

"I never said that!" Katya's eyes widened in shock. "I'm surprised, that's all."

He grunted and kept digging. "Working takes my mind off of things."

"Working like that will kill you." She stepped toward him and put a hand on his arm.

He stilled at her touch, chest heaving, eyes downcast.

"It wasn't your fault, Kolya."

"I don't grieve for the child." His eyes flashed up to meet hers. "I'm sorry we couldn't help him, but that's not why I'm upset."

She flinched at the raw pain on his face, and before she could stop it, her hand reached up and caught the tear rolling down his cheek.

He grabbed her hand and pressed it to his chest so hard that she could feel his heart racing through his shirt.

"When you wouldn't get out of bed. Like Alina. I thought..." His voice broke. "I can't do this alone, Katya."

Katya's breath hitched, and for one fleeting moment, she wondered what it would be like to love him like she'd loved Pavlo. To share a life with him as his wife in more than name. To touch him, to be touched by him, and feel the heat of longing rise up inside of her once again.

Then, his mask of stoic indifference dropped back into place, and he released her hand as if it singed him.

"I need to finish this," he said, his face already turned back to the grave.

Her mouth dropped open, and she stepped back, her trembling hand now clutched to her own pounding chest.

29

CASSIE

Illinois, June 2004

"It's possible that she'll recover, but the next few days are critical. I don't want to give you false hope. A heart attack at her age is very often fatal." The doctor, an older, balding man, spoke in a clipped, hurried fashion. "She's clearly a strong woman to have made it this far."

"You have no idea." Cassie glanced over at Bobby. Under the harsh hospital lights, every wrinkle and blemish stood out on her pale skin. Machines beeped all around her, and a nasal cannula forced air into her nose. She hadn't woken up since they'd put a stent in her heart that afternoon.

"Do you think she'll regain consciousness soon?" Anna asked.

"We're hoping so, but there's no way to know for sure."

Cassie glanced down at her hands, thankful that Nick was keeping Birdie busy at home. She hadn't seen Bobby yet, but she'd been asking.

"I'll update you if we find out anything more." The doctor gave them a sympathetic smile and left the room.

"Cassie, it's been a long day," said Anna. "Why don't you take my car and go home to Birdie? I'll sit here with her for now. If you want to come up tomorrow, we can trade out."

Cassie scrubbed her eyes with her hands, her arms moving stiffly. "Okay, that sounds good. But I'll definitely relieve you in the morning." She leaned over and kissed Bobby, and then her mother, on the cheek. "I'll call you in a few hours."

She made her way home on autopilot. There, she found Nick with a feather boa wrapped around his neck, what appeared to be blush slathered on his cheeks, and half of his nails painted. He sat patiently at the table while Birdie worked on the remaining fingers. Despite her last conversation with him, her heart swelled with affection for this man who would subject himself to a full make-up and nails treatment to keep her daughter happy.

"Don't you look lovely!" Cassie bit back a laugh.

"Do you think? Birdie thought Summer Rose was a good color on me." He waved his free hand to show off the nails.

"It's perfect. Brings out your eyes." Cassie couldn't stop giggling. "I'm sorry, I think the stress has gotten to me." When she was finally able to control herself, she wiped her eyes and sighed. "Thanks. I needed that."

Nick put on an indignant face. "Well, I'm glad you were able to laugh at my expense. Birdie, I don't think she appreciates the work you've put into me."

"Mommy, this is not easy," Birdie agreed solemnly as she finished Nick's pinky finger. "He wiggles around a lot."

Cassie laughed again. "Thank you," she mouthed over Birdie's head.

Nick winked at her. "How is she?"

"The same." Cassie rubbed her neck and sighed. "Birdie, why don't you go brush your teeth. I'll be in soon to tuck you in."

Birdie bounced out of the room, and Nick unrolled the feather boa from his neck. "Cassie, can we talk?"

Cassie dropped her weary body into a kitchen chair. "There's nothing to talk about. I'm so grateful to you for your help, but I meant what I said last night. You're a great guy, and you deserve more than some damaged mess of a woman. I can't do that to you."

"Don't worry about me. I know exactly what I'm getting with you, and I want it. All of it. You, your grief, Birdie, everything. Your loss is a part of who you are." Nick twisted the boa in his big hands. "Look, I know it's been only a couple of months, but they've been the best of my life. I feel so comfortable around you, like I've known you forever. It may sound crazy to say it already, but..." He hesitated, and the torment he struggled with clouded his eyes into a dark gray. "I think I'm falling in love with you, Cassie."

The floor dropped out from under her, and all of her carefully constructed walls shook with the force of his admission. She hugged her knees to her chest and rocked back in her seat.

"Oh, Nick, I don't..."

He held up his hands. "I'm sorry. I shouldn't have dropped that on you now, and don't feel like you have to say anything. But I need you to know that I will wait as long as it takes until you're ready, because you're worth waiting for. There's no one else for me."

Fresh tears sprang from Cassie's eyes, and she dropped her legs to the ground. "Don't say that, Nick. Hearing everything Bobby lost gutted me. Don't you understand? It brought me right back to my lowest point. I can't risk opening myself up to that pain again. I can't risk loving you and losing you!"

"Katya did," Nick said quietly. He pulled the journal out of the box still sitting on the counter and set it in front of her. "I know we haven't found out the full story yet, but you know she fell in love again. She opened herself up. She risked that pain. And in return, she had a wonderful marriage to your grandfather and a family who loves her." Nick moved closer and took her hands. "She may have lost everything, but she never stopped fighting. Let me help you fight, Cassie. Let me love you."

Cassie stared at Nick as a flurry of thoughts and emotions steam-rolled her. Her heart wanted this so much, but her mind warned her that it was a terrible mistake. His gaze bored into hers and he raised her hands to his lips. "Please, Cassie. Just give us a chance."

"Mommy!" Birdie's screech interrupted them.

"I better go check on her." She pulled her hands away from his warm embrace and stood on rubbery legs.

"Of course." Nick sat back on his heels. The raw emotion exposed on his face tore at her gut.

Cassie backed away from him, her heart pounding in her ears, then spun on her heels and flew to Birdie's room. She tried, and failed, to push aside her confused emotions as she sat on the edge of the bed and smoothed back Birdie's tangled hair. "What's the matter, sweetie?"

"Alina said we have to go soon. I have to tell Bobby what Alina wants me to tell her before she goes back to sleep." Birdie pulled on Cassie's arm. "Please, take me now!"

"Honey, the doctors aren't sure when she'll wake up. We can't go now."

"She's going to wake up. Alina told me!" Birdie's voice took on a frantic note.

Cassie gritted her teeth. She couldn't deal with this, on top of everything else, tonight. "Birdie, you've got to stop with this Alina business. I know Bobby told you stories about Alina, but she's not here. It's too late for visitors, but I promise, I'll bring you up first thing in the morning. Now try to get some rest."

"But, Mommy, I have to go! Alina needs me to!"

"No!" The unfamiliar sharp edge in Cassie's voice stilled Birdie's fussing. Cassie massaged her temples and sighed. "I'm sorry. I don't mean to yell at you. I'm very tired, and I'm sure you are, too. Let's get some sleep and talk tomorrow, all right?"

Cassie pulled the covers up around her daughter, but Birdie pulled away and faced the wall. "I love you, Birdie."

"I love you, too." The muffled response lacked its usual gusto.

Cassie closed the door and pressed her head against it—the cool wood a temporary relief from the heat of her many failures.

"Is she okay?"

She jumped and whirled around. Nick stood at the edge of the hallway, looking down at her.

"She's overtired. She thinks Bobby's awake, and she wants me to take her there right now. She said Alina has to tell Bobby something."

"Maybe she does," Nick said.

Cassie rubbed her hands over her face as she walked into the living room. "I don't know what to think about anything anymore."

"I shouldn't have said that, either. I'm really on a roll tonight." Nick ran his hands through his hair. "I'm sorry about earlier. You have enough on your plate now. I didn't mean to add to it by dumping my feelings on you."

Cassie collapsed onto the couch. "I'm so confused and exhausted right now I can barely function. I can't give you any answers, Nick."

Nick nodded. "I understand. I don't ever want to pressure you, Cassie. I'll leave."

"Wait." Cassie's voice trembled as the weight of everything that had happened pressed down on her. She didn't know what she wanted forever, but she knew she felt better when he was near. And right now, she needed all the help she could get. "I shouldn't ask this, but will you stay with me? Just for a little bit? I'm going to wait up to make sure Birdie settles down."

"Always." He sat down on the couch next to her and she curled into him. Guilt spliced through her as conflicted emotions flickered over his expressive face, but when he pulled her close, she sighed with relief. His heart, steady and strong, counted time against her ear, soothing her bruised soul.

"You make everything feel better," she murmured.

"I'm glad." His husky voice vibrated his chest and tickled her.

Cassie fought to keep her drooping eyelids open, but the weight of the day tugged at her. The last thing she remembered was Nick tucking a blanket around her.

30

KATYA

Ukraine, March 1933

Denys wasn't her child; she shouldn't have cared so much. Katya told herself that over and over, but it didn't help her get out of bed. Losing Denys ripped open all the scars from Viktor's death she'd buried and ignored in her struggle to survive.

Nothing but being close to Halya seemed to matter anymore. Without her, Katya would have given up and died. Halya was all she had left, and Katya couldn't fail her like she had everyone else.

"Why don't you come with me to get wood from my parents' house? We can dismantle what's left of the furniture for firewood." Kolya's voice broke through the shroud of her sadness. "It might be good to get out of the house."

She looked up at him, at the dark shadows smudged under his eyes and shoulders heavy with exhaustion, and forced herself to nod. Relief flashed across his weary face before he turned away.

She thought about the moment they'd shared while he'd dug

Denys's grave, and a strange feeling constricted her chest. A knot of uncertainty, twisting and pulling her mind in different directions. For one terrifying moment, she couldn't recall Pavlo's face. Only Kolya's. A strangled cry escaped her mouth before she choked down her grief, making it hard to breathe.

Stop this, Katya admonished herself. Just do what needs to be done.

She dragged herself out of bed and dressed, then fashioned a cloth into a sling around her shoulders and tucked Halya into the warm pocket where she could rest snug against Katya's body. She pulled her coat over the bundled baby and made sure Halya could breathe before going outside. The little girl, warm and secure, rested her tiny hand against Katya's chest and sighed.

Her legs ached as they moved. Thick and swollen, they stung like dozens of needles were stabbing into her with each step. Odd that they swelled while the rest of her dwindled away. They hadn't begun to crack or ooze with fluid like her mother's or the lady she'd met at the *Torgsin*, so she supposed she was lucky. Being lucky had taken on much lower standards of late.

The moonlit snow brightened the world, the stars twinkled, and for a moment, as she stood suspended in that beautiful night, a tiny glimmer of a feeling she barely recognized squeezed into a crack in her broken soul. Wonder. Under the illuminated sky, Katya could almost forget the horror they lived in. She could almost imagine life as it was before Stalin sent his men to break them.

Then, she looked down the road and saw the abandoned farm, and it all came back to her like a punch in the gut. How could she ever forget, even for one moment, what she had lost? She deserved to be carrying this pain, feeling it always. She survived. They didn't. The crack in her armor sealed over and she hardened.

She braced herself as they went inside the house, welcoming the barrage of loss that assaulted her. The house was in shambles. They weren't the only ones searching for goods and scavenging firewood.

"People have been here." Kolya shook his head. He pointed at the bed Pavlo had died on. "I'm going to pull apart the bedstead. Start collecting any loose wood you can. We'll need to take as much as we can before it's all gone."

Katya wandered aimlessly around, her eyes seeing, but not registering anything. Her mind felt fuzzy and thick. Was that another sign of starvation? How many days had it been since she'd eaten?

A glint of light reflected off the lantern they'd brought and caught her eye. A mirror lay tucked halfway under the pillow on the other bed. Katya picked up the heavy piece, amazed that it hadn't been taken by thieves. She peered into it, and a stranger stared back. She could look down and see the bones poking out all over her body, like a living skeleton, but she hadn't seen her face in a very long time. Her cheekbones jutted out over pallid skin, her lips cracked and dry. Dark purple smudges sat under her eyes, which now looked huge in her face. With a gasp, she dropped the mirror on the bed.

"What's wrong?" Kolya called.

"Nothing," she said quickly. "Nothing that matters anymore."

Katya smiled bitterly, and her bottom lip split open with the unnatural movement. What did her pride matter now? It should have vanished long ago. Maybe when she'd eaten the earthworms she dug up in the garden while searching for potatoes, or when she'd boiled an old piece of leather into a soup.

She gave a sigh of disgust and turned the mirror face down.

"You're still beautiful, you know."

Katya jumped at the sound of Kolya's voice so close to her, then gave a hoarse laugh.

"You're kind to say so, but none of us look our best now."

Kolya sat down on the bed next to her. "No, we don't, but you have an inner beauty and strength that will always shine through."

Her face warmed under his gentle regard and she opened her mouth to respond, but before she could think of something to say, he jerked upright and walked away from her. She stared after him, unsure if she'd imagined the whole conversation, and the tangled knot in her chest constricted once again.

* * *

The first signs of spring appeared only a few weeks after Denys's death, and it took Katya that long to be able to bring herself to write of his existence in her journal. She pressed her pencil, now so small she had to pinch it between only two fingers, lightly to preserve the lead.

Nearly full, the journal Pavlo had given her contained everything she'd witnessed, everything she'd lost. Writing soothed her in a way she couldn't explain, and she did it religiously, as if preserving her loved ones on the paper meant they weren't really dead.

Kolya walked up behind her and blocked the light coming in the window.

"We should go to the collective and check in." He glanced at her journal, then snapped his head away, as if afraid to relive what she'd documented there. When she didn't reply, he went on. "Maybe they'll have food for us so we can gain our strength before they have us do the spring planting."

"I don't think they care about our strength," Katya said. In a former life, back when everyone she loved was alive, the short walk took no time at all. In her current state, Katya doubted her ability to even make it out of the yard.

"I still think we should try. Either way, we need to get out of this house, or we will go crazy. All of the houses anywhere near us are empty. Sometimes, it seems as if we are the only people left in the world."

"Fine," Katya agreed. She put away her journal and pulled on her coat, tucking Halya close inside.

Katya concentrated so hard on moving one foot in front of the other as they sloshed through the muddy road that they were practically on top of Lena and Ruslan's house before she realized it.

"We should see if they are well." Kolya walked through their gate, but Katya couldn't bring herself to go any further.

"I'll wait here," she said, as Kolya walked to the door and knocked. The booming sound shattered the still emptiness of the day.

"Lena! Ruslan!"

When no one answered, Kolya pushed the door open, but instead of going inside, he took a step back. He stole a glance at Katya as he put his elbow over his nose and entered the house. As the scent of death wafted out, Katya understood they hadn't survived. Ruslan's desperate, evil deeds had not saved him. Perhaps they had condemned him.

It didn't take Kolya long to come back out, shaking his head. "They're dead. Both of them."

He stood a moment, waiting for her response, but Katya couldn't muster up any feeling other than relief that she wouldn't have to face Lena and Ruslan and their terrible secret.

"How bad was it?" Katya finally asked.

Kolya appraised her, as if judging whether to tell the whole truth or not.

"She hung herself, and it looks as if he was stabbed." Kolya looked back at the house. "I heard rumors about Ruslan. Did he—"

She held up her hand. "I don't want to talk about it. It's done."

He clenched his jaw, then nodded. "I'm sorry, Katya. I know you were close to Lena at one time."

"Yes. But it seems like a lifetime ago." She should have more compassion for Lena's death. But she didn't. She was numb to such an insignificant loss after so many great ones.

Kolya wanted to see if they could find anyone still alive, so he knocked on the doors of the houses they passed. A few contained survivors barely hanging on, like them, but more stood empty. Some homes were rotting and dilapidated, unwillingly abandoned by their owners in the early waves of dekulakization. Other homes, still standing, served as tombs filled with dead bodies: mothers and children, old people and young people. So many dead.

One house held a woman hanging from the rafters. Her four dead children were laid out on the big bed in their best clothing. Katya knew the family. Her husband had been deported last year after the horse he used to harrow a collective field went lame and the state accused him of sabotaging government property.

Most of the people they found frozen right where they had died, their once happy homes now their final resting place. Some, who had collapsed with exhaustion, lay on the floor. Others, perceptive enough to know the end loomed near, had put on their best clothes before taking their final breath. Children lay dead in their mothers' arms. Old couples embraced each other in their beds. Whole families lay in ruins, defeated by Stalin's forced hunger, just as he had planned.

"How did we survive this?" Katya asked. "So many didn't. Why us?"

"Sometimes, I think they are the lucky ones," Kolya said, his voice hollow.

She took his hand in her own. His touch, rough and hard, had become an anchor, tethering her to this ugly life. He gripped her hand in return. They did not stop at any other houses.

As they walked on, the sun rose higher in the sky, warming them even more. Katya inhaled the smell of spring. The smell of the damp earth coming to life used to fill her with joy. It smelled of hope. It smelled of life. This year, it also smelled of rotting flesh.

The bodies of those who had died in the fields, in the streets, in their homes, had been frozen all winter, hidden beneath the heavy cloak of snow that covered the land. Now, under the warm spring sun, the corpses had finally begun their return to dust. So many bodies decaying all at once released a sickly sweet, noxious odor that filled Katya's nose and wormed throughout her body until she thought she would never smell anything else again.

As they neared the collective headquarters, the smell worsened. Dead bodies lined the road and spotted the fields in various states of decomposition.

"Look." Kolya stared out over a collective field. "They died in the field while they were digging for old rotten potatoes. Just fell, right there, and nobody moved them."

Katya pulled the wraps closer around Halya to shield her from the smell and shuddered.

Like she suspected, no food waited for them at the collective headquarters, so they turned around and trudged back through the dead bodies scattered around the village. Their outing today had brought nothing but the devastating realization that most of their fellow villagers hadn't survived.

Stalin must be proud. The activists and his OGPU had done their jobs well.

* * *

The next day, Kolya burst into the house as if the whole village was after him.

"I have meat," he gasped, slamming the door behind him.

"Did they give out food at the collective?" Katya asked, a tremor of hope wavering in her voice. They hadn't eaten any meat since the rat he had caught right after Denys died. "The snares have been empty for some time. Or did you catch a fish?"

"No, I have horse meat."

"How?" Katya sat up, but Halya barely moved on the bed next to her. "They guard those horses so strictly on the farm."

"They do. And once they are dead, they're stacked in the pits, and covered in carbolic acid, so they are inedible." He pulled two cloth-wrapped parcels out of the top of each boot and set them on the table. "I got to the horse before that."

He unrolled the packages and inside, long strips of meat lay coiled in a mass, cut down and rolled narrow enough to wrap around Kolya's ankles inside his boot. Katya's stomach growled at the sight.

"I can't believe we'll be eating real meat." Katya pulled herself up and made her way to the frying pan, her legs stinging with pain, then glanced out of the window. "It's dark already, so the smoke won't be noticed much. I'll fry it up now."

Kolya seemed jubilant and, despite his deep affection for horses, showed no sign of despair at the idea of eating parts of the animal. With little grain or hay, they were starving like everyone else. And, just like everyone else, Kolya couldn't help them. The state thought the wave of the future lay with tractor farming, so they didn't give the horses the respect or care they deserved.

Katya lit a small fire in the *pich*, her movements clumsy and heavy. The last of the dry wood they had wouldn't create a lot of smoke, but she wanted the fire to be as short-lived as possible. The activists had taken to searching out any homes with smoke coming from their chimneys and raiding them. Nowadays, any sign of life from the villagers was a personal affront to them, and they took great care to eradicate it.

"How did you get this?" Katya asked.

He paused as he watched her throw the sliced meat into the frying pan. Licking his lips and averting his eyes, he continued. "I'm the only one at the stables now, so the guards rarely bother to check me. When the horse first died, I didn't report it. I let it sit a bit, so the blood would congeal. Later in the day, I went back and used a knife from the barn to cut out its tongue. It's quick and easy. Now that we have a tractor at the collective, I can haul the carcasses to the pit myself. No one else gets close enough to the horse to notice the missing tongue."

The smell of frying meat filled the air, and it took all of her self-control to not rip the meat from the pan and eat it half-cooked. For a few minutes, they sat in silence, savoring the scent. Finally, Katya looked back at Kolya. "Our salvation may lie with the death of these poor horses. Are there many left?"

He shook his head but smiled. "No, but I can try to do it again next time."

Katya's soul warmed as she smiled back at the man she now called husband, but had known her whole life as friend. Maybe they could weather this change in their relationship and move past the shame and awkwardness of their forced marriage.

In their youth, they had enjoyed each other's company. He took on the role of the older brother she'd never had, teaching her things and teasing her like a little sister. After he and Alina married, and even after she died, they remained close to each other, always working toward the same objective: stay alive and keep Halya alive. It united them.

But that camaraderie had disappeared the moment they'd uttered their marriage vows. It cast a light onto a facet of their relationship that neither of them wanted to explore. Their once solid brotherly, sisterly bond now dripped with doubts and guilt.

The guilt haunted Katya. What would Pavlo think? Would he understand that she had to marry Kolya? Would he hate her? And Alina! If her sister could see Katya in her place as the wife of Kolya, would she ever forgive her?

A few months ago, she would have sworn that she could never love another man. Now, as she watched Kolya tenderly feed Halya tiny pieces of the meat, she wasn't so certain.

* * *

The early spring thaw tricked them into thinking winter had passed. Then, a late winter storm moved in and dropped a foot of snow on the village. The temperature plunged and all of the early signs of spring they'd welcomed now lay buried in snow and ice.

"I daresay the activists would not even travel in this weather. It's frigid cold!" Katya shivered where she lay curled up on the bed with Halya.

Halya slept so much now that Katya had to check throughout the day to see if she was still breathing. Each time she reached out to touch the still child, her heart pounding in her ears, she prepared herself for Halya to be cold and stiff. Like Denys. Like Viktor. And each time the child responded to the touch and Katya felt the warm, sluggish, body move under her hand, relief made her knees weak.

Katya would then wake her and gently force a few bites of food or broth into her. She'd found that small amounts of food distributed more often were easier for the child to take in. As Halya ate, Katya would tell her about their future.

"When this is over, Halya, we'll leave this place of fear and death. We'll make a new life where you can eat as much as you like every day. I promise you, like I promised your mother. I will give you everything I can." Vasyl's words about America danced through her mind. "Maybe we'll even cross the ocean."

The little girl listened, her large eyes following Katya's mouth as she talked, but she didn't respond. All of her energy had to be channeled into the act of eating.

Foraging through the deep snow took more energy than either Kolya or Katya had. Luckily, they had two crows—lulled back by the false spring—and about forty grains of wheat she'd found hidden in the hem of an old skirt. They would fare well in the snowstorm for a few days.

"Do you think you can eat the crows?" Kolya asked.

"Of course I can. I've eaten far worse." Her stomach rolled in revolt when she thought of what the birds ate, but her mouth watered at the idea of food. "Though it does seem eerily close to cannibalism to eat a bird so recently feasting on a human body."

Kolya's eyes darkened. "You can't think about that part. Just think of it as a chicken."

"I'm glad you have such good aim with a slingshot," Katya said.

"It's hard to miss when they are gathered by the dozens on the bodies left out at the cemetery. If I had the strength, I'd dig holes for those poor people." He stared down at his ragged, chapped hands with disgust.

"It's a terrible thing to see them laying there like that, but there's nothing anyone can do. The ground is frozen." Katya rested her hand on his shoulder to comfort him, but he recoiled at her touch and jumped up from the chair.

"I'll go fill a pot with snow for the broth." The words tripped out of his mouth as he stumbled for the door.

"Fine." Her eyes stung, and she clenched her hands so tight that her nails dug into her palm. She'd only wanted to comfort him. Was she really so repugnant to him that he couldn't bear her touch?

* * *

That night, Katya couldn't stop shivering, and from the look of Kolya in the other bed, he had the same problem. Their bodies had no fat left to insulate them and they were nearly out of firewood. The scant fire in the *pich* put out very little heat.

His eyes met hers across the dim room and he threw off his blankets and stood. "This is ridiculous. Let's share our warmth, Katya." He always said her name when he spoke to her, as though to remind himself that she wasn't and would never be his Alina.

He stalked across the floor, carrying his blankets, and Katya trembled from more than just the cold. Only a few hours ago, he'd been repelled by her touch. Now he wanted to come to bed with her? Uncertainty coiled inside of her, constricting her lungs. "What are you doing?"

Kolya stood in front of her, wearing only his threadbare undergarments, and for the first time, she saw how much weight he had lost. All jutting bones, he reminded her of the stick men Tato used to draw in the dirt to make her laugh.

"Surviving. Take off your clothes, Katya, and we'll share our warmth. It's no different than how you keep Halya tucked against you, and it may be the only way we will live through the cold nights to come with so little firewood."

Katya remained motionless, uncertain what to do. Yes, he was her husband, but they had never lain together, had never seen each other unclothed. She thought he'd wanted it that way. Now, she wasn't so sure. Maybe he wanted a more traditional union and all that it entailed. And what did she want? Suddenly, Katya wasn't sure about that either.

He climbed in and set his blankets on the bed. "Come on, now," he said more sternly. "Do you want to freeze to death after all of the work we have put into staying alive?"

Deep down, the words made sense. They would be warmer this way. It might be the only way they could survive, but she couldn't deny how wrong it felt.

Katya drew quick, shallow gasps of air as she began to undress under her set of blankets, pushing her clothes out from under the covers with wobbly hands.

Kolya turned away, his chest heaving. When she finished and lay shivering in only her shift, he leaned forward to tuck both sets of blankets around them, then spread out their clothes over the top of that. Katya tensed, her skin tingling, when he settled in and spooned his sharp body around hers as she was curved around Halya.

"You're still shaking," he said, his voice close to her ear. She couldn't tell now if she shook from the cold or the overwhelming sensation of his body pressed so intimately against hers. His warm breath danced across her cheek and the tang of his musky sweat filled her nose. The sheer power of his touch, of the physical connection of another human who understood exactly what she was going through, unexpectedly moved her to tears. She thought of the loss of her husband, her sister, her mother, and her father. All of the people who loved her and would have held her up now, at her lowest point, were gone. The two people in the bed with her at this very moment were the only people left in her cold, dark world.

It didn't take long for the warmth of his body to overtake her, and she finally relaxed against him and fell asleep. A few hours later, she woke to the feel of his body shuddering against hers.

"What wrong? Is it Halya?" Katya placed her hand on Halya's back, waiting for the rise and fall to tell her the child still lived, and when she'd confirmed Halya was fine, she twisted around to face him. "Are you sick?"

Kolya shook his head. "I'm fine," he rasped.

"You don't look fine." Moonlight spilled in through the window and cast the room in shades of gray, and she could see his expression, drawn and weary.

"I'm just... I don't know."

Katya reached up and touched his tear-stained face. Her pulse quickened, and she flushed with shame at her body's involuntary response to him.

Kolya pressed her hand to his cheek. "Could you hold me? Please?"

Her lips parted in a small sigh as she pulled him close. The embrace came easily, and it surprised her how natural, how good, it felt to hold Kolya against her. Entwined together, his face nuzzled into her neck, she gently stroked his hair until his tears slowed and he fell asleep.

The words Pavlo had said to her before he left to join the rebellion played through her head. *You have nothing to worry about. If anything happens to me, Kolya promised he will take care of you.*

I don't want Kolya to take care of me! I want you! she'd replied.

What did she want now? Guilt-stricken and confused, she remained awake, her mind filled with traitorous thoughts about the man she held in her arms. Her brother-in-law. Her husband.

31

CASSIE

Illinois, June 2004

"Mommy?"

A little hand patted Cassie's cheek, and her eyes fluttered open. Darkness shrouded the room, and her neck ached from its awkward position on the couch. She reached over and flicked on the lamp. Nick was sprawled out on the loveseat, his lanky frame hanging halfway off the cushions.

Even though he had moved across the room, embarrassment colored Cassie's face as she sat up, her muscles stiff. "We must have fallen asleep. I'll have to wake Nick and tell him to go home."

"He can come, too," Birdie said.

Cassie swung her legs to the ground and rubbed her face. "What are you talking about? Come where?"

Birdie touched Cassie's cheek again, her chubby fingers soft and persistent. "Bobby's awake. Can we go? Please, Mommy."

A different type of weariness settled over Cassie and, tired of fighting, she gave in to it. "Fine. Go get dressed. We'll go now."

* * *

The phone rang as Cassie pressed the lid on to her to-go cup of coffee. Nick had popped up off the loveseat bright eyed and chipper—an occupational necessity, he claimed—but Cassie needed caffeine to face the day this early.

"Bobby just woke up a few minutes ago." Anna's voice was breathless. "The hospital called. I'm going up there now."

"Are you serious? She's awake?" Despite Birdie's insistence, Cassie hadn't really believed there'd be a change in Bobby's status.

"Of course I'm serious! Why would I joke about that? She hasn't spoken much, and I'm not sure she's understood everything I've told her, but she's awake."

Birdie tugged at Cassie's sleeve. "I told you, Mommy. Come on!"

Cassie stared at her little girl. "All right, Mom. We're on our way."

* * *

Cassie gripped Birdie's hand as she peered into the hospital room. An oxygen tube curled under Bobby's nose, and dripping lines pushed IV fluids into her arms. As Anna sat on the bed with her, Bobby's eyes fluttered open.

"What happened?"

"You had a heart attack." Anna reached over and straightened the covers. "You were alone in your bedroom, and you fell on the ground. Cassie heard the thump and found you. Luckily, they got you here in time."

"I hate that Cassie found me like that."

Cassie wanted to run in there and tell Bobby she was being ridiculous. She would live through that a hundred times over if it meant saving Bobby, but Anna had decided that it would be better if she went in alone first, so Cassie bit her tongue.

"I'm glad she found you! Thank goodness she's living with you now. If she hadn't called for help, you might not have made it."

Bobby shrugged. "Maybe I was supposed to go. It's my time, you know."

"Let's not start that kind of talk. Everyone's here to see you." Anna waved Cassie, Birdie, and Nick into the room.

Birdie hesitated, but when her eyes fell on Bobby, her face lit up.

"My little bird!" Bobby opened her arms. "Come fly to me."

"Careful," Cassie warned as Birdie climbed up onto the bed and snuggled into Bobby's arms.

"I've missed you, Bobby." Birdie's sweet little voice still thrilled Cassie.

"I've missed you too, Birdie. But now, we are together again."

Birdie sat up and looked into Bobby's eyes. "I have to tell you something. But only you."

Bobby nodded and turned her ear toward the girl.

Birdie held her dimpled fingers up in front of her mouth and leaned closer. She tried to talk quietly, but her voice echoed in the sterile room.

"Alina says she isn't mad at you. She never was. She's glad you made a good life. Okay?"

Bobby's face went white, and her heart monitor shrieked a warning. Anna moved to get a nurse, and Cassie reached out to pull Birdie off the bed.

"Wait," Bobby croaked. Her head fell back against the pillow. "I'm fine. Birdie, tell me again. Please."

Birdie put her hand on Bobby's cheek. "She's been wanting to tell you for a long time. She said she's not mad and she loves you. Doesn't that make you happy? It made Alina happy to tell me."

Cassie and Anna exchanged a look. So that was the "message" Birdie had to get to Bobby. Cassie still didn't know what to think about the whole thing, but there was no denying that Birdie's words, whatever inspired them, affected Bobby. A lump formed in Cassie's throat.

The heart monitor slowed. Bobby squeezed her eyes shut and a tear meandered down her wrinkled cheek, changing direction with each groove and crevice it caught. She hugged the girl close. "Yes, little bird. It makes me very happy."

Anna pursed her lips and shook her head.

Bobby directed her steely gaze toward her. "I know you don't believe in these things, Anna, but our relationship with the dead was very different in the old world."

"It just seems—" Anna started in, but Cassie covertly kicked her.

"You don't have to believe me. I know what I know," Bobby said. "And I want to apologize to you both. I was so good in burying the painful parts of my past that I buried the good memories, too. There was much more I could have shared but opening myself up to my old life hurt too much. So, I kept everything locked away and you lost out on all of it."

"That's not true, Mama. You passed on Ukrainian recipes. We made *pysanky*. You taught me how to embroider." Anna took Bobby's hand. "Mama, you gave me a wonderful life."

"Thank you for saying that, Anna, but I could have done more, and I can't change that. It's a regret I will carry to my grave." Bobby turned to Cassie. "Have you finished the journal?"

Cassie pulled the *rushnyk*, journal and pictures out of her bag and set them on the bed. "Almost, but not quite." She could feel Nick's eyes burning into the back of her head, but she couldn't bear to look at him.

Bobby ran her hand down the *rushnyk* and touched each symbol. "My mother made this for my wedding to Pavlo, and the priest bound our hands together with it. The open wreath symbolizes our open lives ahead of us. The larks are for joy and vigor. The sunflowers are for fertility and prosperity, and the poppies are for love."

She looked at Cassie. "Maybe this will be hard to believe, but once, long ago, like you, I loved to write. I promised Pavlo that I would write our story and tell the world what happened to us. What was done to us. I did what he asked. I wrote it here." She pointed at the journal. "But I could never tell the world. I was too scared. I don't just want you to know my story, Cassie. I want you to write it for me. Share my story, our story, with everyone, so what happened to us never happens again."

Cassie shot a guilty glance toward Nick. "Oh, Bobby, I don't know that I could do it justice. And actually, I think my mom is going to finish it up with Nick instead of me."

"I am?" Anna said at the same time Bobby scoffed. "Bah! You are the writer in our family. It has to be you. Please, do this for me. It will be the last thing I ever ask of you."

Way to drive that guilt home. Cassie met Nick's eyes, and heat flooded her face. Her feelings for him were so tangled and complicated. She didn't know how she could bear working so closely with him without hurting him or herself, but what choice did she have?

"All right, if Nick doesn't mind helping me, I'll do it for you."

"I'll do anything you need," Nick said.

Bobby exhaled and visibly relaxed. "Thank you. I don't think I could leave knowing I failed on that promise."

She glanced down at the top picture on the pile and picked it up. "Oh, I always loved this one of us."

"That's Alina and that's you!" Birdie pointed to each girl. "Alina looks almost the same, but you look different."

Bobby chuckled and touched her wrinkled cheek. "Yes, I look very different, don't I?"

32

KATYA

Ukraine, May 1933

That spring, when the earth came back to life, so did the collective, and word spread that work and food were available again. Katya supposed the state figured that anyone left alive was broken enough to do whatever they wanted, and they were right. Once, everyone had cursed the collective. Now, Kolya and Katya, with Halya on her hip, along with the other survivors, eagerly made their way to the collective farm to work every day. They planted that season's crops, hardly able to stay on their feet as they sowed the seeds. But for each day of work, they received a bowl of watery soup and a chunk of bread. Every day, more people came with their haunted, hollow eyes and blank faces, all of them half-dead and void of emotion. They barely spoke to each other. What was there to say?

Still, people continued to die. Some in the fields, right before the food was doled out, and others after they ate, their bodies unable to process the food they so desperately needed. Somehow, some way,

Katya, Kolya, and Halya survived this as well. Each meal they were given was small and weak, but it was the most food they'd had consistently in months.

To supplement that, Katya harvested flowers from the blossoming acacia trees, earthworms moving through the spring soil, tadpoles from the pond, and the dandelions sprouting in her yard, and bit by bit, their bodies began to recover.

As their strength gradually returned, life began to assume a rhythm again. They rose early and walked to the fields together. They worked with the remaining villagers and the newly imported Russians—sent in to replace all of the dead Ukrainians—living day to day with no promise of anything to look forward to. They ate the food the collective gave them, thankfully and carefully, never spilling a precious drop.

* * *

As the weather warmed and summer arrived, Katya moved Halya to a small trundle bed so the girl could sleep later each morning without Katya bothering her when she woke. Slowly, but surely, Halya was gaining strength and growing. When she scooted herself across the bed for the first time, Katya celebrated as if Halya had taken her first steps or read her first words. Every milestone, no matter how small, was a triumph.

She waited for Kolya to return to his bed, too, but he didn't. Each night, she stripped down to her underclothes and got into bed, and each night, he climbed in with her.

The old Katya would have said something to him, she wrote in her journal. *Asked him why he still lies with me, but now, I am afraid to say or do anything that might stop one of the few sources of joy I have every day. I find more and more that I want him pressed close against me, that I revel in the feel of his lean body touching mine.*

Shame filled her as she composed the disloyal words. Her feelings for Kolya weren't right or reciprocated, but she didn't know what to do about them.

One night, she woke to find herself splayed across him, arms and legs tangled, her head resting on his chest. His body vibrated under hers like the thrumming of a hummingbird's wings.

She sat up and found him, eyes wide open, watching her. She sucked in a breath. "I'm sorry. I'll move over."

His face was inches from hers, his voice husky. "No. Don't."

She froze, her heart hammering against her ribs. "Don't move?"

He reached out and ran his hand through her hair. "I like you close to me."

"You do?" Her voice wavered at the thrilling feel of his fingertips on her skin.

"I do. I'm sorry, Katya. I've tried to be strong. To fight this. But I don't think I want to fight it any longer."

Katya stared into his eyes, her grief mirrored there like twin pools of anguish. She felt the pain emanating from him in waves, but another, foreign feeling accompanied it. She cocked her head, appraising him and trying to control her racing pulse at the same time. Did he feel as she did?

Kolya took her chin in his hand and tilted her face toward his mouth. He paused, waiting to see if she would resist or participate, and when she softened, pliable in his embrace, he gave a strangled groan of defeat. Their lips met and Katya tasted the salty tears of their shared losses, and something more. Something promising. Feelings she'd thought long dead unfurled in her cold heart like a flower opening its petals to the sun on the first day of spring. Whispers of the possibilities of a new life, a new love, filled her soul, and the sudden yearning for him made her dizzy.

He pulled back. "Are you sure this is what you want?"

Katya slowly exhaled, then reached up and touched his lips. He kissed her fingers, then leaned his face into her palm. She didn't understand why or how this could have happened, but she knew it to be the truth with every fiber of her being. She wanted him. She loved him.

"Yes," she said. Then, she pressed her lips to his.

They clung to each other, two lost souls in a broken world, seeking solace in the most unlikely of partners.

They continued spending their nights together, physically connecting as much as they could with their frail, broken bodies, their hearts slowly coming back to life. But in the light of day, Kolya barely spoke to her, and when he did, it was never of what happened in the dark. So, she suppressed her confusion and went on as if nothing had changed, counting the hours until nightfall, when she could come alive again in his arms.

* * *

"Are you ready to go to the collective?" Kolya called from the door.

"Go ahead without me. I have some things to do here." Katya stared at him, waiting for him to say more. To ask her to come along. To tell her he wanted to spend time with her.

But he said nothing. Just like every day. They'd still never spoken of their physical relationship. During the day, it was as if the love they shared at night didn't exist and maintaining the charade of indifference during the day was wearing on her. She wanted to talk about it. She wanted to know how he felt. To tell him how she felt. But her battle-weary heart didn't have the strength to fight for its desires anymore.

She waited twenty minutes, then made her way to her assigned potato field and sat Halya on the side of it with the other children. There was none of the typical running and playing, but every now and then, the soft chortle of a child's laughter reached her ears and gave Katya hope. It did little to take her mind off Kolya, but the cadence of the work suited her, and she tried to focus on the motion of her body instead of the thoughts running rampant in her head.

When the field was done and they were dismissed to go home for the day, she could no longer silence her worries. How could she ever explain that she'd taken her sister's life? She'd married her husband, raised her child, and now had the audacity to fall in love? To try to start a new life with the shattered remains of what they'd once been.

How could anyone forgive that?

Kolya broke through the fog of her mind as he shook her arm, concern on his face. "Katya, did you hear me? I'm heading to the horse barn. I promised Halya I'd bring her there to see the new horses they brought in. We'll be home later." He leaned close and peered into her face. "Are you well?"

Katya nodded fast, perhaps too fast. His hand scorched her, made her want to press against him, tell him of her love, her secrets. "I'll be fine. I'll see you at the house."

But she couldn't bear going inside yet, where Kolya's presence lingered on every surface—the cup he drank from, the chair he sat in, the bed they shared. Instead, she climbed into the barn loft, where she'd spent so many hours dreaming and talking with Pavlo, tucked away in their little nest of safety, and retrieved her journal from its hiding place in the wall.

The smell of sun-dried hay and memories of Pavlo enveloped her like a warm hug. She filled her lungs with the sweet scent as an ache rose in her throat. She could almost hear his voice echoing as she walked toward the big door that looked out over the barnyard.

Katya, stay here with me always. We don't need to think about what's going on out there. Here, we are safe, and we have each other. Maybe we'll never come down.

Someday I'd like a house, though, she'd teased back. It would be a hard thing to raise our children in a barn loft.

She pushed the door open, and sunlight flooded into the room. From her high vantage point, Katya could see Pavlo and Kolya's old farm.

Pavlo's voice whispered in her ear.

Then you shall have the grandest house. There, see that open spot over there? My father told me he will give it to me as a wedding present. We will build our home there. A strong, solid house filled with our babies. Our children will run through these fields like we did. Can you see it?

Tears filled her eyes. Katya couldn't see it anymore. She used to see it as clear as day. Now, Pavlo's face blurred with Kolya's and confused her.

I want flowers all around the house. Poppies and sunflowers.

Then we shall plant them.

She pressed her lips against the journal cover and let the words inside soak into her soul. Her memories. Her love story. Her Pavlo.

As she lowered the journal, Kolya walked through the yard down below with Halya perched on his shoulders. Katya watched him move towards the house, long-limbed and lanky, with a rugged grace that made her heart ache. Her past clutched in her hands and her future laid out in front of her, painted against each other in stark relief, but how could she bridge this divide? Life had set her down a path she'd never imagined traveling, and now she was stuck with one foot in each world—the before and after.

She stared out across the land, the ground shimmering before her as the tears she'd held back finally spilled over. The forgotten patch of sunflowers, buried in the weeds of the overgrown yard, smiled up at her. The sunflower palace. Her and Alina's secret place. Despite everything, they fought to grow, to live, to rise up amidst the ruin of their land, somehow still blooming right here, for her.

Like her.

Deep down, beneath the sharp edges of her guilt and memories, she wanted this marriage to work. Kolya might not love her now, but maybe someday, he would let her into his heart, just as she had found room for him in hers. Their union represented all they had lost, all they had struggled to live through. Why had she fought to survive if it wasn't to live her life and find hope again?

Katya's lips quivered as her sister's name came out in a sigh. "Alina. Forgive me, sister, but I love him. I just don't know if he'll ever love me."

"Katya."

Katya spun around at the sound of Kolya's voice. He stood at the far end of the hayloft, his hands clenched at his sides.

"Halya is in bed. She was asking for you."

Katya wiped the back of her hand across her eyes and set the journal back in its hiding spot. "I'm sorry. I come up here to think sometimes. I'll go sing to her now."

Kolya walked towards her slowly, the look on his face indiscernible. "Who were you talking to?"

Katya stiffened as color flooded her face. "No one."

He stopped inches from her. His hand moved up to cup her cheek, his words piercing. "Who do you love?"

Katya's mouth wouldn't move to answer the simple question he'd asked. She drew in a ragged breath and tried to tear her gaze away from his, but his other hand came up and cradled her face.

"Is it me?"

"Why?" She exhaled the question out into the space between them —one word encapsulating so many questions. It unlocked something inside of her, freeing the frustration she'd been choking on for months, and she found her voice. "Why do you care? You may love me like a wife at night, but you barely look at me in the day."

Kolya dropped his hands and his gaze. "I'm sorry. I know I've pushed you away, but I've been so confused about my feelings. About Alina and Pavlo. Can you forgive me?"

"There's nothing to forgive. I've had the same confusion." She grasped at the shattered pieces of herself, pulling them together, finding strength, then took his chin and pulled it up so she could look in his eyes. "But I need to know now. How do you feel about me, Kolya?"

Kolya stared at her, his brilliant blue eyes shimmering like the summer sky. "I'm hopelessly in love with you, Katya. I can't deny my true feelings any longer. And I don't think Alina and Pavlo would want us to. After everything we've lived through, they would want us to be happy."

His hand slid around to the back of her head as he kissed her. His firm lips pressing against hers reinforced all the feelings he'd put into his speech. Katya kissed him back, the broken shards inside her smoothing out into a beautiful path towards her future.

33

CASSIE

Illinois, June 2004

Cassie set the plate of *varenyky* on the table in front of Nick. Birdie was down for the night, and Nick had come over after work to help Cassie finish the journal. Luckily, Bobby had a good store of frozen *varenyky* that Cassie could boil up quick and serve with fried butter and onions. The crescent-shaped dough pockets of potatoes and meat were by far one of Cassie's favorite foods, but she'd never mastered the uniform shape and pinch technique that Bobby made look so easy. There was no way she was tackling making those on her own while Bobby or Anna couldn't help, and she knew Bobby wouldn't mind her using her stash to feed Nick.

"Thanks for the late dinner." Nick scooped three of the meat *varenyky* onto his plate, then topped them with the sour cream Cassie had grabbed from the fridge. "What's the latest from the hospital?"

"She hasn't woken up again since we all talked to her yesterday."

Cassie got up to turn off the stove before the tea kettle could whistle. She poured hot water into her cup and sat next to Nick.

Nick paused with the fork halfway to his mouth. "What does Birdie say? Does she mention Alina anymore?"

"No. Not a word about her since she gave Bobby her 'message'." Cassie air quoted the word message.

"Well, whatever happened, it seemed to give Bobby some peace. That's probably all that matters in the end."

"You're right. I should let it go." Cassie pulled the box across the table and took out the journal. "You know, it's been brutal waiting for you to come over so we could read this."

A mischievous glint shimmered in Nick's eyes. "What was brutal? Waiting for me or waiting to hear what's inside?"

"Both, I guess." The response slipped out before she could stop it, and she flushed. She was supposed to be holding herself back, but the banter came so easily with him. Everything did.

She straightened in her chair and opened the laptop, then redirected the conversation to where it needed to be. "So, now we know why Bobby feels so guilty about Alina."

Nick went to the sink to wash his hands. "And we know that eventually your grandmother ends up happy with your grandfather." He spoke casually, but she could feel the intensity beneath his words, and her mind raced.

How had Bobby opened her heart after such tragic losses? Will I ever be able do the same?

Cassie cleared her throat. "Right, but there's been no mention of him yet, and now she's married to Kolya."

Nick stilled. "Wait, what was your grandfather's name?"

"His name was Nicholas, actually."

Nick's eyes widened. "Oh man. That's a whole other level of guilt. No wonder she's been so upset."

"What are you talking about?"

Nick gave a wry grin. "He's been mentioned. Cassie, your grandmother didn't lose two husbands. In Ukrainian, Nicholas is Mykola, often shortened to Kolya."

34

KATYA

Ukraine, July 1934

The first year after the famine, life went on. The OGPU disbanded and became the NKVD. They continued to purge enemies of the state at an alarming rate, but they loosened the starvation noose that had once choked the villagers and allowed more food to trickle back into the countryside. Everyone moved slowly and carefully, always afraid to offend an activist or be caught with too much food, but a small harvest was sown and reaped. Their hollow stomachs ached for adequate amounts of food, but they reveled in the meager quantities they had available in comparison to the winter. People still died and were taken from their homes in the middle of the night, but nothing like before.

Halya thrived because of Katya and Kolya's foraging skills. That, compounded with the food the collective now gave out, meant her small body finally had a chance to grow. She no longer spent her days in bed, sleeping, but explored the house and yard at Katya's side.

"Eat?" Her tiny voice sounded so sweet to Katya's ears.

"Yes, Halya?" Katya bent low so she could hear. "You want some food?"

Halya nodded. Her head, still too large for her small frame, wobbled far less than it had last year.

Katya scooped some *kasha* into a bowl and placed it at the table. "Come, sit with me and I'll help you eat."

Halya scrambled up into her lap, and Katya helped her grasp the spoon in her small hand. At two and a half, Halya was still far behind where a child her age should be, but they made progress every day, and her bright smiles as she learned gave Katya all the hope she needed to keep trying.

"Is breakfast ready?" Kolya came in from the barn. Now that they were subdued and considered good citizens of the state, they were allowed to keep chickens and a cow again. Small improvements, but they made all the difference in their daily life.

He tickled Halya under the chin until she giggled, then filled a bowl for himself and took a seat across from Katya.

With his lanky frame slowly filling back out, his cheeks appeared less gaunt. His smile at Halya's laughter brightened his serious face. A swell of emotion rose up inside Katya. She'd never wanted to fall in love with Kolya. She didn't plan it. But when she watched him swing Halya around until she shook with laughter or prop her up on a horse so she could "ride," she saw a man she wanted. The hard exterior he'd put up to survive cracked, the grief and pain fell away from his face, and in response, something warm and bright blossomed in her. Love.

It wasn't like the love that consumed her for Halya. Halya's survival was Katya's reason for existence. Halya's smiles, coming more frequently now, kept Katya going. Her words showered Katya's ears with joy. She didn't think anything ever could compare with her love for the small child, because tangled up in that love were all of her feelings of grief, loss, and guilt. That wasn't fair to Halya, but Katya could no more change it than she could bring back the ones she'd lost.

Nor was it like the pure first love she'd shared with Pavlo, either.

Her love for Kolya grew from the bond of survival they shared. What they'd endured, what they'd seen, left an indelible mark on the two of them and created a connection that she couldn't explain if she tried. He had become her safe haven in a terrifying world. They had united to keep Halya alive, and to keep each other alive. The feelings that followed occurred without any suggestion from either of them, but they couldn't be denied or ignored.

After breakfast, they made their way to the wheat field near their house. There, Katya settled Halya with a girl who tended the children off to the side and went to work.

Kolya walked in front of her, the lean muscles in his back flexing and bending in rhythm with the other men in the field. He moved slowly, methodically, swooping his scythe through the large swatches of wheat. The stalks fell in loose piles, and Katya followed behind with the other women, gathering them into sheaves she tied with loose straw. When they had enough sheaves, they stacked them into a shock to dry. It was the way they used to harvest, before the collective leaders brought in the new machinery. With those machines being rotated amongst a few fields, they had to work here the old-fashioned way. Although the wheat wasn't solely theirs, the familiarity of the work soothed Katya and the hours passed by swiftly.

Katya sighed as she bent to gather the wheat and resume her work. Nothing had turned out like she expected. Her dreams of Pavlo had begun fading away. Sometimes, she would think about what their lives could have been like together, but it hurt too much to do that often. He was gone from her life now, his memories a sweet haunting melody that thrummed in her heart, but no longer pained her so constantly. She'd moved on in her own way, because she had to in order to survive, but she would never, could never, forget him.

Kolya paused, wiping his brow with his forearm, and turned to face her. "How are you feeling?" He reached out and cupped her cheek.

She placed her hand on top of his and smiled. "I feel wonderful."

He leaned forward and kissed her—his lips soft and salty with sweat—then pulled back, a grin playing on his mouth. "Then so do I, Katya. So do I."

Katya curled her bare toes in the warm dirt and turned her face up to the gentle sun. Her father's voice echoed in her ears. *Look to the future.* Life would move on with or without her, so she chose to fight.

She chose to live.

35

CASSIE

Illinois, June 2004

"That's it. Her entries end there." Nick closed the book and set it on the table in front of Cassie.

"You were right. She fell in love with Kolya. Alina's husband and Pavlo's brother. My grandfather. She lost so much, but she found happiness again."

Cassie pressed her palm into the worn cover of the journal. The theme of love after loss wasn't lost on her, and though she still wasn't ready to face her own issues head on, she wondered if Bobby had pushed her to read the journal for more than one reason.

"It's pretty amazing," Nick said. "But that guilt must have been over-whelming."

Cassie took a deep breath. "I can't imagine. It's hard enough to move on from the death of a husband, but then to fall in love with your double brother-in-law?"

"But she didn't lose two husbands," Nick pointed out. "Well, not till much later, at least. She found her happy ending."

"In love, yes. But what happened to Halya? Why have we never heard of her?" Cassie stood, questions racing through her mind. "I have to go see her."

"Of course. I'll stay with Birdie, if you want," Nick offered.

"Are you sure you don't mind? I hate to take advantage of you again, but I don't know if this conversation is going to be kid friendly."

"Don't be silly. That's what friends are for." Nick inspected his fingers. "Maybe she can do my nails for me again. They're looking a little rough."

Cassie laughed and grabbed her purse. "Thank you, Nick. I owe you!"

"I take payments in *varenyky*," he called as she walked out the door.

An hour later, after Cassie had picked up Anna and filled her in, she pulled a chair up next to the hospital bed. Bobby's eyes were closed, and she looked frail and small, as if the life were slowly draining out of her.

Anna sat on the end of the bed, wide-eyed, and nodded towards Cassie. "You start. I'm still processing."

Cassie picked up the wrinkled hand in her own. "Bobby, we finished the journal."

Bobby's eyelids fluttered open, and she squeezed Cassie's hand. "Finally."

Cassie chuckled. "It's not an easy read."

"It wasn't an easy life." Bobby looked over at Anna and smiled. "So you know too?"

Anna nodded tightly. "What happened to her? To Halya?"

Bobby closed her eyes again. "I lost her."

"Please! No more vague answers, Mama. I deserve to know. She was my sister!"

Bobby met Anna's angry stare, her face grim. "You're right."

"Take your time." Cassie shot her mom a warning look, and Anna ducked her head. Coming in hot wouldn't help anyone.

Bobby struggled to sit up a bit. "After the famine, things never went back to normal. Collective farming changed village life forever, and the Soviets continued to purge us, deporting people to gulags for the slightest reason. Outside of our walls, the world was terrifying, but in our home, with the three of us, I could pretend none of that was going on." Bobby squeezed Cassie's hand. "Halya loved to plant flowers, like you, Cassie. She went to school, fell in love with poetry, and grew to look more like her mother every day. Your grandfather and I doted on her, and we were grateful for every moment we had together.

'When the Germans invaded during the war, we thought things might finally get better, but they were as bad as the Soviets. They destroyed our villages, killed people, and they took Ukrainians to use in their factories and on their farms in Germany. Lots of Ukrainians." She sank back into her pillow, her voice soft. "They took Halya."

Her breath hitched, the pain etched on her face as fresh as if it had happened yesterday, not decades ago. "She was so beautiful and good. All the best parts of Alina lived in her."

A lump formed in Cassie's throat. "And she never came back?"

Bobby shook her head. "The factory she worked at was bombed by the Allies."

"After all that, she died in a bombing?" Anna asked.

"That's what they told us." Bobby plucked at the end of the blanket on her bed. "We'd fled our village as the eastern front grew near. We couldn't live under the Soviets again, and the fighting was so close we could hear the mortars exploding. So, we loaded up our wagon and left. We were going to find Halya and start over fresh somewhere new."

She took a deep breath and met Cassie's eyes. "We traveled through Poland and ended up in the Allied occupied zone of Germany when the war ended. After that, we spent a few years in the Displaced Persons camps. We kept looking for her, just in case, but there were so many refugees. Millions of displaced people with no home, no country, no family. It was like searching for a needle in a haystack. As the years passed, we realized we had to accept that we'd been told the truth— she'd died in the bombing. She was lost to us, like my father, and like my father, we never found any more answers."

Bobby choked down a strangled sob. "I kept her safe through the Holodomor, but I couldn't save her from the war."

"Oh, Mama." Tears glistened in Anna's eyes as she leaned closer to Bobby. "Why didn't you ever tell us?"

Bobby stroked Anna's cheek. "I found out I was pregnant with you the same day we were approved to go to America from our DP camp. I'd never forgotten the way my cousin Vasyl had talked about it, and I knew we could begin our new life there. Your father and I decided that if we wanted to truly move on and be happy, we couldn't speak of the painful things in our past; we would keep those memories buried and only look to the future. And our future was you, Anna. Our miracle baby."

Anna took a shaky breath. "What about what Stalin did to you? People should have been told about the famine."

Bobby sighed. "You must understand, no one spoke of those things. Stalin denied the famine, and the world believed him because they needed his force to beat the Nazis. Speaking of it or sharing my journal would have only drawn attention to us, and people were arrested for such things and sent away to labor camps for decades. I couldn't risk that."

"But what about when you left? You could have told people then," Cassie said.

"The Soviet reach was far. In the camps after the war, they were repatriating people like us back to the USSR every day, telling them they were going home but really sending them to gulags and labor camps for 'collaborating with the enemy'. Even here, in America, we were afraid to say anything."

Cassie thought about the phone call from the police charity and the money Bobby had tried to give them to ensure she wasn't arrested in the night. Guilt needled her. The scars of living under an oppressive regime ran deep, and she hadn't realized the extent of her grandmother's wounds.

Bobby gave a sad smile. "The longer I said nothing, the easier it became to leave that part of my life sealed off. We were so happy. We had each other, our beautiful little girl and a chance at a new life. We vowed to make the most of every day, to live in the moment."

"But it wasn't ever fully sealed off, was it?" Cassie said. "It was always there, in the back of your mind."

"Yes." Bobby nodded slowly. "You can never forget love, Cassie, but you know that. Now, at the end of my life, it's all I can think about."

Cassie gently picked up Bobby's twisted hand, and the image of it being slammed in a door flashed through her head. "Bobby, you were put in unthinkable situations. You did everything you could."

"I'll never really know that, though, will I?" Bobby said. "Life is a series of choices, each one pushing you towards the next. Maybe if I'd chosen differently in the very beginning, things would have been better."

"Or maybe they would have been worse," Cassie said.

Bobby shrugged one bony shoulder. "Maybe. But what's done is done, and I can't change it now. I can only say this: I made a mistake in thinking I could bury it all. Looking to the future doesn't mean you have to forget the past. You can have both, Cassie, and be all the richer for it."

* * *

"Do you think you'll write the whole thing, like your Bobby wants?" Nick asked later that night when Cassie got home. "Or change any of it?"

"I wouldn't change it. It's an important story." Cassie sat next to him, her imagination already running with ideas on how to execute the project.

"It is," Nick said.

"I hope I can do it justice. You know, up until she started writing those short letters to Alina, if you could call them that, I'd never seen Bobby write. Maybe when she couldn't fulfill that promise to Pavlo, she gave up. I'd love to help her rectify that." As she spoke, Cassie fidgeted with the finger that used to hold her wedding ring. Ever since she'd taken it off, she found herself constantly touching the spot where it used to sit.

"And her request is helping you to fix the fact that you don't write anymore. It's like a full circle of healing," Nick said.

Then why do I still feel broken?

She cleared the unsaid words out of her throat and forced out a smile. "Well, lucky you, I suppose. Now you won't have to spend your free time over here deciphering old Ukrainian handwriting anymore."

She meant to be flippant, but a hollow feeling settled in her stomach at the thought of not seeing him regularly.

"You're right," Nick agreed. He stared down at his hands. "I'm sure you'll be glad to have me out of your hair."

Cassie sagged in her chair. She shouldn't have expected a different response. She'd told him she didn't want a relationship, and, being the gentleman he was, he'd backed off.

Be happy. Live your life. Henry's words pounded in her head. She closed her eyes and heard Bobby's voice. *Looking to the future doesn't mean you have to forget the past. You can have both.*

But what did she want? What choice did she want to set in motion?

Nick looked up. His deep blue eyes locked on hers, and warmth pulsed in her veins.

This. Choose to live.

The empty feeling in her stomach morphed into resolve. She stared at Nick so long and so intensely that he touched his mouth. "What? Do I have something on my face?"

Awareness surged within Cassie and pushed her to her feet. "I'm only thirty-one!"

Nick folded his hands behind his head and grinned. "I would have guessed late twenties."

She blushed. "That's not the point. But thanks. The point is, I'm still young. Bobby lost so much more than me, but she found a way to go on. Maybe I can, too. I think... I think Henry would want me to live my life."

A hopeful expression grew on Nick's face, and his voice quieted. "Then you should."

Before she could think or over-analyze the situation, she leaned over and kissed him. His soft lips moved against hers differently than Henry's had, but their touch sent ripples of excitement surging through her and her heart soared above the ache of the loss she'd been trapped in for so long.

His arms wrapped around her, enveloping her in his warmth and strength. "Are you sure, Cassie?"

She nodded and spoke against his lips. "Yes."

When they finally broke apart, a smile stretched across her face. "I'm sorry. I don't know what came over me."

"Whatever it was, I hope it's a permanent condition," Nick said, and he kissed her again.

36

KATYA

Sunflower Palace, July 2004

The legs running beneath her weren't her own. Or, if they were, they were a much younger version. Far too nimble for her old body, they held her up, sure and strong, each step a leaping bound into the next. She looked down at her hands. Smooth and supple. The gnarled knuckles had disappeared. No pain or twisted fingers. She touched her face. Firm, young skin bounced back against her fingers. Around her, wheat stretched out in a golden, rippling blanket. She inhaled and the smell of rich earth and wheat kernels baking in the sun filled her soul. This was Ukraine. Home.

Sunflowers waved in the distance. Their tall stems bobbed and swayed over the wheat. She moved toward them, and heard her name being called. The voices sent shivers through her. Alina. Pavlo. Kolya.

They were waiting for her.

If this was a dream, she didn't want to wake up.

She sprinted toward the sunflowers.

EPILOGUE

CASSIE

Illinois, May 2007

"There, Mama! I found Bobby!" Birdie's voice rang out over the birds singing in the cemetery. Full of excitement, she ran ahead of Cassie and Nick to the grave tucked under a blossoming crabapple tree.

"Can I put the flowers in the vase?" The bouquet of miniature sunflowers waggled in her hand, and a smile stretched between her rosy cheeks as her dark wavy hair danced in the breeze.

Cassie gave her a thumbs up, then returned her hand to Nick's and watched as Birdie divided the bouquet and placed half in the vase on Bobby's stone and half in the vase on the stone next to it.

"Alina would like some, too," she explained to Cassie and Nick as they got close. "Remember? They're her favorite." She reached out and traced her finger along the etched words of the memorial stone they'd had placed next to the headstone Bobby shared with Dido.

IN MEMORY OF ALINA BILYK, PAVLO BILYK,

& ALL THE OTHERS LOST IN THE HOLODOMOR

"Of course Alina should get some." Nick said as he squatted down to help Birdie.

Cassie clutched her swollen belly as their baby kicked, her fingers brushing against the ring Nick had given her two years ago in a quiet garden ceremony where they'd bound their hands together with Bobby's wedding *rushnyk*. This man, and Bobby's example, had given her a second chance at happiness. Love for all of them welled up in her and made her misty-eyed.

She touched Nick's shoulder. "Could I have a moment alone? I want to tell her."

He kissed Cassie's cheek. "Of course. Come on, Birdie, let's take a little walk."

As they stepped away, hand in hand, Cassie opened her purse and pulled out the envelope her editor had forwarded on to her. She'd already read it a dozen times, but it still didn't seem real.

"Hi Bobby, Dido." Cassie waved her hand towards her grandparents" headstone and the memorial to Alina and Pavlo. "I guess this news is for all of you, really, so I hope you can hear me. I got something in the mail yesterday that you're going to want to know about. Something that I wish had come when you were still alive. It changes everything."

She unfolded the thin piece of paper.

Dear Cassie,

Please forgive this intrusion, but I recently read your book about the Holodomor. Your story was very familiar to me, but when I read your author's note, I knew I had to write. You see, I used to know a Kateryna Viktorivna Bilyk in another life, but we were separated in the war, and I thought her dead. I thought everyone from my family was dead. But it seems I may have been wrong. Please call me at the number below when you can.

Sincerely,
Halyna Mykolayovych Bilyk

Cassie pulled out a tissue and dabbed at her eyes. "You didn't fail, Bobby. She lived. Halya lived. You kept her alive, and your story helped her finally find us. I called her right away, and she's flying out next week to meet everyone. She wants to come here to see you, too. All of you."

A wave of emotion hit, so strong it nearly knocked Cassie over, and she gripped the headstone, grounding herself against the cool granite.

"Mommy! Look!" Birdie cried. A gust of wind swirled through the cemetery, and the crabapple tree released a flurry of petals in a shower of pink snow around the little girl.

Arms outstretched, Birdie spun in a circle, giggling as they fell around her. "Look! They're happy, Mommy! Bobby and Alina are happy!"

AUTHOR'S NOTE

I hope you enjoyed *The Memory Keeper of Kyiv*. This story is very important to me.

Cassie's Bobby is, in many ways, my Bobby. My Ukrainian great–grandmother was a strong woman who survived Polish, Soviet, and German occupations, never wasted food, loved her flower beds, and, until my mom intervened, really did think she should give money to any type of police officer or state trooper fundraising telemarketer to avoid them coming to arrest her in the night. She also, at the behest of her dying sister, married her widowed brother–in–law to raise their child. Whether it was a love story or not has been lost to history; it was something she never talked about.

My journey into Ukraine's history began with the intent to under–stand the stories she told me when I was a girl—how she, my great–grandfather, and their three children fled their western Ukrainian village during World War II—but the more I found out about the Holodomor, the more I knew this novel had to come first and that their history would inspire my second novel. My great uncle was both instrumental and endlessly patient in helping me with Ukrainian cultural and language details. He, along with my and my mother's memories of my grandfather and great-grandmother, helped bring the Ukrainian heritage aspect of Cassie's story to life. I am eternally grateful to them, and any errors that occur are mine.

My great–grandparents may have borne witness to Holodomor survivors' testimonies, but this isn't my family's story—thankfully they didn't suffer that horror. Inspired by the snippets of tales my great–grandmother passed on, I did extensive research into written and oral interviews of survivors, scholarly journals, books, and museums. While artistic license is always a factor in a work of fiction—such as placing Pavlo's rebellion in 1931 instead of 1930, when most rebellions occurred, or using *Slava Ukrayini* as a toast instead of a greeting—the facts of this atrocity were horrific enough without me having to embellish them. I wish I could say the historical details surrounding this novel were exaggerated, but the truth is, the Holodomor—or death by hunger—was devastatingly brutal and only one part of Joseph Stalin's larger assault against the Ukrainian people.

Between 1932 and 1933, one in every eight Ukrainians died in this manmade famine. And it was absolutely manmade. During this time, the USSR exported tons of apples and tomato paste, barrels of pickles, honey, milk, and almost two million tons of grain in 1932 alone. Stores of crops, rotting sometimes as they awaited exportation, sat at railway stations and on the sides of roads under guard while the people starved within sight of them. Grain procurement quotas were kept unreasonably high, even though the spring seed grain had already been seized and the farmers of Ukraine had nothing left to give.

Across the Soviet Union, food shortages resulting from the chaos of collectivization and dekulakization, and Stalin's refusal to lower grain quotas in the wake of these issues, led to an estimated 8.7 million deaths. This included people in Soviet Ukraine, Kazakhstan, and certain provinces of Russia. In August 1932, Stalin issued a statewide decree known as "The Law of Five Stalks of Grain," calling for ten years' imprisonment or death for anyone caught taking any state-owned property—which, to be clear, was *everything*—even a handful of grain, rotten potatoes from a field, or fish from a stream. Armed activists patrolled the countryside and sat in watchtowers, shooting, beating, and arresting men, woman, and children as they tried to avoid starvation by eating the very crops they'd sown or gathering food from the land they'd lived on their whole lives.

Stalin's measures affected the entire region, but he targeted Ukraine with further brutal decrees in an attempt to subjugate the Ukrainian nationalism and culture he saw as a threat to Soviet ideology. Guards closed Ukraine's borders and a new internal passport system effectively prohibited travel between villages and cities, locking Ukraine into one giant death camp. The state began "blacklisting" communities that didn't meet their grain quotas, leading to punishments such as the banning of trading or receiving any food or manufactured goods—including kerosene, salt, and matches—and new higher food requisition quotas. To fill these quotas, activists visited homes and ripped apart ovens and walls, then plunged metal rods into hay, yards, and bedding to find every last bit of hidden food and remove it from the already starving peasants. All of this followed an ongoing assault on cherished Ukrainian cultural traditions—holidays and events such as Christmas, Easter, weddings, and Sunday services were banned, churches were desecrated and their bells melted down for their metal, and priests were arrested and deported en masse.

Due to a lack of adequate records, death toll numbers have varied widely through the years. While we'll never be able to fully calculate the losses, studies in 2018 estimate 3.9 million Ukrainians died in the Holodomor.

In a stark reminder of the effectiveness of Stalin's anti-Ukrainian policies, Ukraine lost 12.9 percent of its population. Over 1 million people died in the Kyiv oblast alone. While Katya's village of Sonyashnyky is fictional, the raion of Tetivv, where I placed her village, is real. This district of the Kyiv oblast had a death rate of 50 percent. At the height of the famine, roughly 28,000 Ukrainians were dying each day, and 30 percent of those were children. Desperate people resorted to eating tree bark, leaves, grass, weeds, grains flushed out from vermin burrows, worms, tadpoles, baby birds, rotting livestock carcasses, crows, cats, dogs, and corn cobs.

Despite these horrifying numbers—which do not reflect the hundreds of thousands deported during dekulakization or the decimation of Ukrainian religious, cultural, and political leaders—the existence of the famine was simply refuted. Walter Duranty, a *New York Times* journalist, won the Pulitzer Prize for his articles downplaying the rising hunger and lauding the success of collectivization. When the 1937 census showed a significant decrease in the population, Stalin arrested and executed many of the census bureau workers, then ordered a new census with falsified numbers showing a population surplus. Collectivization was declared a success and, in need of Stalin's support against the threat of Hitler, world leaders ignored the truth of the Holodomor. Any Ukrainians who dared to speak out were arrested, and the realities of the famine were left to be carried on in oral histories and hidden away in journals buried in walls or yards.

I can barely touch on the full scope of the Holodomor in this author's note, but I encourage you to look further into it because, as you know, history repeats itself. Two books I highly recommend to start with are Anne Applebaum's *Red Famine* and Miron Dolot's *Execution by Hunger*. For a list of the books and resources I used in my research, including virtual museum visits, survivor accounts, recent research on the statistics of this terror–famine, and links to organizations dedicated to keeping the memory of the Holodomor victims alive, please visit erinlitteken.com.

ACKNOWLEDGMENTS

I'm so thankful to everyone who has helped and encouraged me on this journey. My agent, Lindsay Guzzardo of Martin Literary Management, whose guidance and excitement for this book helped this dream come true. My editor, Tara Loder, whose keen insight and passion made this novel so much stronger. The Boldwood Books team, the support you've shown me has been phenomenal. Jeni Chappelle, when I was about to give up, your editorial advice and kind words gave me hope. Early readers Lisa Herron, C.H. Williams, Susannah Wiley, and Jen Johnson gave me encouragement and suggestions. Andrea Green, our constant messaging kept me sane through the publication process. The online writing community–in particular the #HFChitChat group and the #MomsWritersClub–has made all the difference for me in what is often a solitary career. The scholars and historians working to untangle the web of buried facts about the Holodomor–your work is so important.

My great uncle, who taught me so much about our history and Ukraine, I'm beyond grateful for our connection. My grandpa and family story teller, who I lost the day before I signed this book deal. My dad, who shares my love of all things history. My grandma and partner in genealogy research. My mom, who walked every step of this process with me, never once doubted I'd get here, and reminded me of that whenever I needed to hear it. Kurt, my calm in the storm and staunchest advocate. Calla and Owen, my inspiration and hope. I couldn't have done this without you. I love you all.

And, to my Bobby, who taught me how to speak my first Ukrainian words and made the best nalysnyky (or blintzes, as she sometimes called them). The bond I shared with you shaped me in so many ways, and I miss you every day. When I need to be strong in my life, I look to your example.

READING GROUP QUESTIONS

1. The propaganda and division sowed by the activists when they arrive is powerful and pits neighbors and family members against each other. How did that contribute to breaking down the fabric of village life? Are there parallels in today's society?

2. Cassie is shocked to find out her grandmother survived a forced famine. How does such an atrocity disappear from history? Had you heard of the Holodomor?

3. After escaping to America Katya and Koyla never speak of the Holodomor. How do you think that affected Anna and Cassie's lives?

4. Katya faced an unthinkable choice when her mother asked her to marry Kolya. Do you think Katya made the right choice?

5. Katya falls in love twice. Was her love for Kolya different to her love for Pavlo?

6. How does Cassie's journey through Bobby's life inspire her to rise above her grief of losing her husband?

7. Katya clung to her humanity by trying to save children after she lost her own child. Do you think she would have survived without Halya to care for?

8. Katya broke the law again and again to get food for her family, even after Alina's death. Did she make the right choice? Why do you think Alina sacrificed herself and took the blame for Katya's theft?

9. Katya's guilt is a major theme of the book. What do you think she felt the most guilty for–causing Alina's death, marrying Alina's husband, or losing Halya?

10. At the end of the book, Katya chooses to fight and live her life as best she can, even though the Soviets still occupy her village and her life has changed irrevocably. Was there a better option for her? Would you have continued fighting?

11. Bobby and Anna disagree on whether their loved ones visit after their death. Do you think Birdie spoke to Alina or did Bobby's stories cause Birdie to create an imaginary friend?

12. Putin's invasion of Ukraine bears parallels to Stalin's oppression of Ukrainians during his rule, including a desire to eliminate Ukrainians and their culture and history. In what ways can we, as a society, work to ensure such things don't happen again?

MORE FROM ERIN LITTEKEN

We hope you enjoyed reading *The Memory Keeper of Kyiv*. If you did, please leave a review.

If you'd like to gift a copy, this book is also available as an ebook, digital audio download and audiobook CD.

Sign up to Erin Litteken's mailing list for news, competitions and updates on future books.

https://bit.ly/ErinLittekenNews

ABOUT THE AUTHOR

Erin Litteken is a debut novelist with a degree in history and a passion for research. At a young age, she was enthralled by stories of her family's harrowing experiences in Ukraine before, during and after World War II. Her first historical fiction title, *The Memory Keeper of Kyiv*, draws on those experiences. She lives in Illinois, USA with her husband and children.

Visit Erins's website: https://www.erinlitteken.com

Follow Erin on social media:

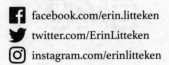

facebook.com/erin.litteken
twitter.com/ErinLitteken
instagram.com/erinlitteken

Boldwood

Boldwood Books is an award-winning fiction publishing company seeking out the best stories from around the world.

Find out more at www.boldwoodbooks.com

Join our reader community for brilliant books, competitions and offers!

Follow us
@BoldwoodBooks
@BookandTonic

Sign up to our weekly deals newsletter

https://bit.ly/BoldwoodBNewsletter